RED WITCH

THE TALES OF INGRID REDSTONE

RED WITCH

THE TALES OF INGRID REDSTONE

A NOVEL BY

SEAN PATRICK TRAVER

RSB

LOS ANGELES

Magic (maj'ik), *n.* **1.** The art and science of causing change to occur in conformity with will (Aleister Crowley). **2.** The manipulation of symbols, words or images to achieve changes in consciousness (Alan Moore). **3.** A basic imagination technology (Grant Morrison). See **WITCHCRAFT**.

THE HOLE IN THE SKY

Chapter One

—West of Los Angeles, 1910

INGRID Redstone approached the Tree that grew below the Hole in the
Sky.

She was alone, on horseback, and clad in the sort of blue canvas
dungarees the old gold-miner-'49ers wore. The tight 'blue-jeans' sure
needed those patented copper rivets that figured into their advertising, as
the garment hadn't been cut with hips like hers in mind. Ingrid was
twenty-seven years old and conspicuously statuesque. The pants did hug
her posterior in a way she rather liked, and she smiled to recall the
shocked, open-mouthed stares she'd drawn from a number of field hands
during the long ride out here. Proper ladies might glare and cluck and
flutter when confronted with a woman in male attire, but Ingrid had
every reason to believe that the men who saw her riding by found the
way the coarse blue pants clung to her exaggerated curves every bit as
fetching and feminine as she did.

She took off her broad-brimmed hat and squinted up into the old oak
tree's proliferation of gnarled branches. Late-summer sun filtered down
through the canopy, as slow and golden as dripping honey. The light
seemed to ignite the wisps of dark red hair that fell across her face. The
heavy braid hanging down the midline of her back could have been a
cable of copper filaments fashioned in the workshop of an electrical
engineer.

Ingrid dismounted and stood in the shade of the ancient tree. The
encino, as the locals called them, was at least three times taller than any
other oak she'd ever seen. Its limbs were black, contorted like corpse-
fingers, and its foliage was a drab, dusty green. The October afternoon

was warm and windless, lacking breeze enough to stir a single leaf. There were no buildings or other signs of civilization anywhere in sight. Ingrid felt like she might've stepped back in time a thousand years. The natural field the encino stood in was several acres wide, dominated this late in the year by tall yellow grasses. The sky contained not a single cloud. All of creation felt becalmed here, as frozen as a photographic still. The scene reminded her of one of those quiet yet kinetic paintings by a dead Dutch madman (who'd signed himself only as 'Vincent') that Ingrid had occasionally run across and fallen in love with in the obscure galleries and private collections of Europe.

This had to be the place.

Ingrid removed two waterskins from her saddlebags and slung them over her shoulder. She had other items in there as well—a pistol in a leather holster, which she clipped to her belt, and a dagger she sometimes strapped to her thigh when she was wearing a skirt. She didn't know what to do with it now. After a moment's consideration she went and tucked the knife into her belt, too. A coil of hemp rope with a small boat anchor tied to one end went over her other shoulder, with one of the anchor's hooks tucked into her back pocket so it wouldn't swing or catch on anything while she climbed.

Lastly, at the bottom of the bag, wrapped in waxed paper, were half a dozen small-to-medium sized mushrooms Ingrid had plucked earlier that morning, in the hills to the northwest of downtown Los Angeles.

She closed the saddlebag and slapped her horse on the hind end to send him on his way, hopefully toward home. She wouldn't be getting her deposit back on the rented animal this way, but realworld concerns like that hardly seemed to matter anymore, now that she'd finally found the legendary Tree. After months of searching she was bound for territories unknown, and she knew she might never see this world again.

She meditatively chewed the fungi, cap by cap, grimacing at the bitter, fibrous quality of the stalks. Her pupils expanded while she planned out a route up to the top of the ancient encino, and they began to pulse in a slow rhythm as her empty stomach went to work on the less-than-palatable offering. The canopy of foliage above soon seemed to be vaguely breathing as a result.

Ingrid hadn't climbed a tree since she was ten years old. She'd have to scale the trunk itself for the first thirty feet or so; beyond that, many of the branches looked thin, or brittle. She had to wonder if they'd support her weight. She was close to six feet tall, and hardly a waif. Plus, according to the map she'd seen, the sacred Tree, while enormous, probably a hundred and fifty feet high, only barely reached the Hole in the Sky. Hence the rope and the makeshift grappling hook, in case those uppermost limbs couldn't hold her.

If she fell, that was it. There was no help to be had for miles.

The instructions on the back of the hand-drawn map in the archive of the Ordo Aurea Catena stipulated that only a supplicant with a mind as dilated as Ingrid's eyes could hope to find the sacred Tree. To that end, Ingrid had eaten nothing since riding out before dawn other than a cold biscuit, an orange poached from a grove, and as many of the mushrooms within which dwelt the spirit Teonanactl as she'd been able to find. The landscape had indeed seemed to fall into accord with her hastily-made copy of the secret map, when on previous outings it had borne no apparent relationship to the territory at all.

By the time Ingrid finished her mushrooms and addressed her task, the Tree no longer seemed menacing or apt to betray her in any way. It had become yielding according to her perceptions, a conscious thing that wanted to help, to embrace her and experience her, and she felt just the same toward it. The massive trunk was burled and crevassed, providing niches that invited the insertion of fingertips and rounded bits that were impossible not to cup. Ingrid pressed against the Tree, feeling close to it, running her palms over it in order to find the optimal places to grip. She ascended, inching along like molasses that dripped up rather than down, propelling herself skyward with her moccasin-clad toes by the tiniest increments at a time. She'd assumed the soft slippers would be more practical than riding boots when it came to climbing, and she'd been right. She found herself nestled in the crux of the oak's first major fork before she knew it, and barely felt winded for the effort.

The sun had drifted a long way toward the western edge of the sky in the meantime, though. It glared from the horizon like a great red eye. Ingrid felt a touch of vertigo when she looked back down. She was already high enough for a fall to kill her, yet only about a third of the way up to the top of the Tree. It was still astonishing to her that such a monstrous specimen could have been so hard to find. There was no sign of a mythical SkyHole above (not yet), and Ingrid would soon be climbing in the dark.

She returned to it.

The going was easier now that she had branches to stand on, even if they were so densely and irregularly placed that Ingrid had to contort in some rather acrobatic ways in order to squeeze through the tangles of grasping limbs. The Tree still seemed to be enjoying her presence, and she suspected it might be trying more to prolong the contact than to actually impede her progress. Still, she lost her hat to gravity and clutching twigs undid her braid, freeing her dark red hair to spill out over her shoulders like a flow of cooling lava.

It was well after dark before she found she could go no higher. She wedged herself into the last V of branches that would hold her, ones that approximated the circumference of her thighs. Their bark was similar in texture to her jeans. A few green shoots reached higher than her perch, but they didn't do Ingrid any good. Her supporting limb already swayed when she moved around, so attempting to stand up in the last available bifurcation when there was nothing to hold onto above didn't seem like a great idea.

Nor did there seem to be any point in it.

There *was* no Hole in the Sky, as far as she could see. There was nothing. She was trapped at the top of an oak the height of a modest Manhattan skyscraper, and she didn't know if she'd be able to get back down without breaking her neck. She was sore, hungry, and had sap in her hair.

The view, though, was almost enough to render those concerns incidental. The stars overhead looked close enough to stir with her fingers, and there were enough of them out to gild the landscape with silver light, all the way from the northeastern mountains down to the Pacific, which Ingrid could just see from where she sat. Kerosene lamps winked from distant farmhouse windows, and Los Angeles proper looked studded with bright new electric jewels. She caught a few notes of raucous music from a distant, fire-lit migrants' camp that was closer than downtown's cluster of east-coast style towers by many miles.

Only eagles were meant to survey the world from a vantage like this. It took Ingrid's breath away.

Since she had nothing better to do, she fished a silver cigarette case and matchbox from the breast pocket of the loose cotton workshirt she was wearing. She'd rolled the herbal cigarettes inside it herself, and filled them with ground hemp flowers purchased from the same Chinese apothecary from whom she'd been buying her favorite green tea these last few months. They were intended for special occasions, or for times when she really needed to think, and this particular instant seemed to qualify as both.

Ingrid lit up and drew aromatic smoke deep into her lungs, savoring the way it brought Teonanactl's sensual influence back to its full intensity. She enjoyed the sensation of being malleable, half-melted into the embrace of the branches that cradled her body. She kissed rings of blue smoke loose into the night, and they seemed to light up faintly as they rolled away.

Minutes passed before she thought about the oddity of that.

She frowned, took a drag, and blew a deliberate plume of smoke straight up into the still air. It again seemed to glow just a bit as it rose beyond a certain height, as if it were passing out of a shadow, or through a beam of weak light.

She saw no light source overhead, however; nor was there anything apparent that might cast a shadow.

So what was lighting that smoke?

Ingrid pinched out the resinous cigarette and returned the remainder of it to her flat silver case.

She shimmied up the half of the branchfork in front of her, just enough that she was able to get a foot into the treecrotch that supported her. She stood, carefully, as none of the shoots she could reach would hold her weight if she needed them to. She reached up, but there was nothing to feel except empty air. She stretched further, up onto the ball of one foot, and the branch she was clutching began to bend forward. Still Ingrid reached, until she heard a sharp wooden *crack!* and her heart nearly stopped in her chest.

She dropped into a crouch, desperate to reduce the leverage on the fracturing branch—but right before she did, she could've sworn her fingertips brushed against something solid yet invisible up there in the sky.

Ingrid's head swam as her only support continued to bend ominously forward, then swayed back in the other direction without breaking off and sending her tumbling down to the pulverizing death she could all too vividly imagine.

She settled into a sitting position, barely able to hold on with her rubbery arms. She could feel the sharp edge of the break biting into her thigh, but at least the fork wasn't too badly cracked to hold together.

Ingrid looked back up. There was still nothing to see overhead besides the stars, and yet she knew she'd felt something up there, just the same.

The legends were true. There *was* a Hole in the Sky, and she had found it. That had been the pale light of another world she'd seen filtering through her exhaled smoke—an otherworld that was almost within her reach.

'Almost' being the important word here. As in, 'almost but not quite.'

Well, that was why she'd come prepared.

Ingrid unhooked the small anchor she'd brought along and un-looped its long coil of rope from her shoulder. There wasn't a lot of room to swing it without tangling it in the branches, nor did she dare to make any broad movements. The compromised limb beneath her might give way at any time, so she didn't want to risk standing up to reach for the SkyHole again.

Finally Ingrid threw the anchor overhand, a weak and timid effort. Not because she *couldn't* throw, if she had a mind to, but because she didn't dare to put that much force behind it from her precarious position.

The anchor tumbled away through empty space, as Isaac Newton had long ago predicted that it should.

Ingrid hauled the anchor back up, ripping it past snarls before it was in her hands again. She was starting to feel exceedingly silly. She had a promising career in the flicker shows ahead of her, if she wanted it (her first moving picture had premiered just two months ago), and now here she was, hurling anchors at the sky. She'd need her pretty face if she meant to act again, and even a non-fatal fall was apt to alter it without regard for aesthetic concerns.

That was her nerves talking, though. She figured it was only natural to feel jumpy and uncertain when you were standing at the very threshold of the unknown.

She wound up and threw the anchor again, and this time, instead of falling away as natural law demands... it disappeared.

Ingrid heard it clatter as it might against a hard floor, and she was left holding a vertically-suspended line that seemed to vanish into thin air some five or six feet above her head.

Now that was just shockingly real.

Ingrid tugged on the line and felt the anchor at the far end move. She even heard it scrape as it might over rough stone or tile. She grinned to think of how most of the dilettantes she'd known in the Hermetic Order of the Golden Chain would've soiled their union suits by now, despite their wizardly pretensions. She, a lone woman with a stolen map, was making more progress toward this particular initiation than any of that order's ascended masters ever had, and she was almost as high on her own sense of accomplishment as she was on the Cantonese cannabis and Mexican mushrooms racing around in her bloodstream.

The anchor tumbled back down out of the Hole in the Sky. Ingrid shied away to keep from being clocked on the head by it.

She threw it again, a little bit harder this time. More wood fibers crackled somewhere deep within her supporting branch, but she barely registered the sound.

She pulled on the line and this time, she felt resistance. Her anchor was stuck. Ingrid tugged and it popped loose from its unseen mooring with startling ease. She drew it slowly across whatever surface was up there, until it slid into view and dangled off the invisible lip by one of its prongs. Ingrid put as much weight on the line as she dared, which in truth was not a lot. It looked so insecure. A rowboat anchor was not a grappling hook by design, but it was the best she'd been able to do. And it had caught on something up there for a minute. So maybe this was just a matter of another try.

Ingrid reared back and threw again, holding nothing back this time. She couldn't ignore the groan emitted by her branch as the fork in it widened by worrisome inches. Her midsection turned to liquid, but the oak was strong, and its fractured branch held true. She hastily pulled the slack out of her rope, only barely hearing the anchor scrape the floor now, as it had penetrated much more deeply into the unseen space with this throw.

Then, it stopped. And held. Ingrid pulled, but the line seemed firm. She put weight on it, her biceps flexing as she lifted herself up out of the branchfork by an inch before settling back.

So far so good.

Ingrid drew her foot up and stood in the fork again, using both a green branch and the taut rope for balance. The point where the line disappeared was barely two feet out of her reach.

As she was thinking of jumping for it, her perch gave way with a dry snap.

Ingrid screamed as the branch in her right hand bent and splintered. She released it, letting it whip away from her in favor of the rope, which she clutched in a two-fisted deathgrip. The half of the fork she'd been standing on crashed away through the foliage below. Ingrid hauled herself up the anchored line, heart thundering like a timpani, completely unmindful of the strain she was giving her shoulders. They could scream about it later, if she survived. When she had hold of the lip of the Hole in the Sky she chinned herself up, seized the rope where it was stretched across the floor, and dragged herself in to the waist.

When she looked up, she almost forgot that her ass was dangling a hundred feet above the earth. Anyone below would've seen half a girl floating above the Tree, like a weirdly-staged version of one of the illusions Ingrid had made her living assisting with in London for the past few years.

She was looking into a room fashioned from rough mud bricks, perhaps a dozen feet to a side. There was a doorway in the far wall, through which flickered a wan sort of firelight, cast by guttering torches that hung on either wall of the inner sanctum. She saw yet *another* doorway beyond that, in the second room's far wall, opening onto what looked like an overcast day.

Between Ingrid and the far exit was what appeared to be a round slab of bloodcaked stone, elaborately carved with glyphs and figures. It was an ancient sacrificial altar, one that dominated the second chamber.

And her anchor was hooked on it.

Now that was going to be a poor way to curry favor. The body language of the robed and hooded figure that was looking down at her makeshift climbing tool seemed to indicate as much. He stood so still that Ingrid hadn't noticed him right away.

He turned his head, following the line of her taut rope out the door and across the floor, until his eyes lighted on her.

Or so Ingrid assumed. The man's heavy cowl obscured the upper half of his face, including any eyes he may or may not have possessed, but the lower, visible half was stripped of flesh all the way down to the bone. His bare teeth made for a humorless rictus of a grin. He straightened up and came to the door between the rooms, and Ingrid almost dropped backwards out of the Hole in the Sky, in spite of herself.

"You are female," he said, after a long moment of bemused consideration.

"Men usually do pick up on that," Ingrid agreed.

The figure of Death nodded. He grasped her rope, coiled it around the exposed bones of his hand, and used it to haul Ingrid up into the empty room between them without effort, as easily as she might jerk a minnow out of a pond.

She stood and brushed off her shirt and jeans. She felt dizzy, unsure of the impossible stone floor beneath her feet, although it seemed perfectly solid and as real as anything. Logic told her it couldn't be there, but her senses delivered a contradictory report. She was standing, not falling, and she decided to trust in that, for the moment. The floor felt a lot sturdier than her trembling legs.

Ingrid Redstone crossed the room in the sky, stood before the doorway that separated the twin chambers, and looked right up into the face of Death itself.

"Are... are you *Mictlantecuhtli?*" she asked. "*El Rey de los Muertos?*"

"I am," the skeletal figure answered. His voice echoed like he was at the bottom of a well. Ingrid wasn't even sure she was hearing him with her ears, or if his words simply occurred in her head as he intended them. He had no lips, after all, and his jawbone didn't seem to move when he spoke. "The King of the Dead."

She noticed he wore a garland of eyeballs looped around his neck and shoulders. She didn't have to ask if they were human to know the answer.

"I'm called Ingrid," Ingrid said before she could falter, aware that the King would need to know her true, heartfelt, and original name in order to accept her. "Ingrid Redstone, daughter of Alfred and Astrid Redstone of San Francisco, and I have come to seek your patronage, Mictlantecuhtli."

"You are female," said the King.

"So?"

"My priests are men."

"Do they have to be?"

The skinned skeleton under the heavy cowl considered this for a long while.

"Perhaps not," he said.

"Hasn't there *ever* been another woman up here?" Ingrid asked, unable to quite believe that she was the first female ever to make her way to the Hole in the Sky in all of history. The legends about it were of ancient provenance.

Mictlantecuhtli thought about the question, peering into Ingrid's room and concentrating as one might while looking something up in a book. She looked around self-consciously, but she seemed to be alone. She couldn't see whatever it was he saw.

"There *is* another woman who comes before me," Death told her, with a nod. "In another now. One with the Pyramid instead of the Tree."

"Well, that's a relief," Ingrid said, though she didn't know if it was, or what he was talking about with regard to pyramids and trees. She didn't know how much clarification it was safe to ask for, either. Casual questions could have unforeseeable consequences in situations like these, or so her previous training had led her to believe.

Ingrid considered herself well versed in the theories surrounding such occurrences—the ones generally deemed 'impossible' by the populace at large. She was a fourth-degree Philosophus in London's Order of the Golden Dawn, and she had (past tense) held an equivalent rank within Los Angeles' Aurea Catena, the Golden Chain, before copying their secret map and disappearing on them. In the past seven years she'd studied metaphysics, mastered meditation, and learned to operate several complex systems of practical magic all on her own. She'd communicated with a wide cross-section of the assorted entities the imagination had to offer, and learned the hex techniques that kept them in their place... yet none of it had prepared her for this.

Her audience with the King.

She felt like she ought to ask him something, so as not to waste this moment, but thinking of something not entirely stupid was suddenly not the easiest of tasks.

Mictlantecuhtli, for his part, seemed content to eye her up and down, from his side of the doorway between the chambers. Ingrid felt exposed, and she was nothing if not used to being looked at. Unnerving her was no small trick. Her silly blue pants left the shape of her hips so clearly delineated she might as well have been naked, and she could feel hot blood rising to her cheeks. She'd never imagined that Death would radiate such an obvious sexual hunger in her direction. It was like he wanted to eat her alive.

"Is this... is this where the dead cross over?" she asked. She'd performed before audiences ranging from roughnecks to royalty, and never had her voice quavered the way it did now.

"Yes," was Mictlantecuhtli's only answer.

"So when do they get here?"

Death cocked his skull in apparent confusion. "'When?'" he repeated.

"Yeah, where are they?" Ingrid said. "I'd think there'd be a line."

"Ah," the shrouded figure of Death replied. "I believe I take your meaning."

He stepped away from the doorway, back into the sacrificial chamber, and gestured for Ingrid to join him. "Cross," he said, "if you would see."

The grin beneath the cowl was fixed, unchangeable, and yet Ingrid could swear it widened.

"Let me see your face," she said. "Before I come in."

"Why, Lady?"

"So I can look into your eyes and know that I can trust you."

Ingrid was, in truth, only stalling. She didn't expect he had any eyes, judging by the condition the lower half of his face was in. When he pushed back his hood, however, she was proved quite wrong.

The heavy robe fell to the floor, revealing Mictlantecuhtli as a muscular, handsome, and apparently living man. His face was angular, with a prominent nose and intense black eyes. His oiled hair was brushed back into needles that resembled porcupine quills. He'd kept his necklace of eyeballs, but now he also wore hammered gold bands around his bare upper arms, and his back seemed as broad as the trunk of a normal-sized oak tree. He stood at least half a foot taller than Ingrid (which she noticed approvingly, in spite of herself).

"Please, join me," the new and improved version of the King said, extending a hand.

Responding with a smile, Ingrid did. She stepped across the threshold between the rooms.

Mictlantecuhtli reared back, jerking his hand away before Ingrid could take it.

"What?" she said, feeling self-conscious once again. The King was aghast, looking at her like she was crawling with bugs or something.

"How did you do that?" he demanded.

"Do *what*? I didn't *do* anything!"

"*Exactly my point!*" Mictlantecuhtli bellowed, causing Ingrid to cringe, though she'd be damned if she'd scurry away because he wanted to yell. If he wanted to hit her he'd get hit right back, although she didn't imagine things were apt to go so well after that.

He didn't hit her, though, and he even seemed rather impressed that she'd stood her ground, if no less astonished by her presence.

"Can you go back over?" he asked. "Do it now, show me."

Ingrid took a step back across the threshold. She still couldn't see what all the fuss was about. But Mickey (as she was already starting to think of him, for the sake of expediency) seemed like some of the theatrical directors she'd known, and that gave her some sense of how best to deal with him.

The King shook his head and let out his breath in a rush as he considered her remarkable ability to step through a doorway.

"This is… most unprecedented," he said.

"*What* is, for fuck's sake?" Ingrid snapped, her refinement expiring along with her patience. "You gonna fill me in, or leave me to twist?"

"You have crossed the unbreachable barrier," Mickey said. "Yet your flesh and your freedom remain your own."

"You thought they wouldn't?" Ingrid asked, her anger kindling. "When you invited me in?"

"I thought you would become my companion and my concubine, at the cost of your living skin. Such is the way it works."

"Yeah, well, not today," Ingrid said.

"Cross back over and join me. Let us ponder the meaning of this occurrence together."

"I don't think I want to now."

"Do it," commanded the King.

"Make me," countered Ingrid.

Mickey seemed taken aback. Flummoxed, even. He was plainly unaccustomed to defiance in any form.

"*You* can't do it, can you?" Ingrid asked, grinning as the King's fundamental limitation became clear to her. He was as bound to his realm as his subjects were. "You can't walk through this doorway yourself!"

"Perhaps not," Mictlantecuhtli said. "But that hardly means I am powerless."

He stepped back, raised his arms, and screamed "*Tzitzimime!*"

Ingrid winced as he continued:

"Stop the interloper, and fetch her to me!"

Ingrid turned on her heel, making a break for it, meaning to jump out of the Hole and into the Tree blindly, if she had to, but a wall of tiny insects that boiled up out of the cracks in the floor drove her back. Ingrid shrieked and danced out of their way. More bugs scrambled out of the walls and tumbled from the ceiling, cutting off her exit and pushing her back toward the King.

"All right, already!" Ingrid yelled. "I'll come back over! Just call off your bugs! *Please!*"

The King made a gesture and the rising tide of insects abated, leaving Ingrid cringing just before the door between the rooms. Creatures with more than four legs could arouse a visceral, irrational loathing she had trouble talking herself out of, especially when confronted with large numbers of them at once.

The rustling swarm kept its distance from her, but it didn't disperse.

"Cross over," said the King.

Ingrid did so. It still didn't seem like anything special, and yet Mickey stared with the avidity of a pervert at a peepshow.

"So, I'm supposed to be dead now, or what?"

"Yes," Mickey said flatly. "Your flesh should have crumbled like powdered clay, leaving only bare bone behind."

"That's what happens when the dead cross over?"

"That is what happens when the *living* cross over," the King said. "If you would know of the dead, look behind you."

Ingrid whirled and realized first that the insects had vanished, to her immense relief. The Hole in the Sky looked, from this side, like it had been rudely smashed through the wall of the empty chamber. She could see the starry sky of her own world through it. It looked terribly far away.

A young woman with blonde hair sat up from the stone floor. Ingrid hadn't even noticed her lying there. She was naked and rather thin, as well as confused and frightened.

The blonde girl got to her feet and looked around.

"Hello?" she called, and the King stilled Ingrid with a hand on her shoulder.

"She is already dead to her world," he murmured in Ingrid's ear. "You cannot help her now."

"But... she looks all right to me."

"Hello?" the young woman said again, uncertainly. She peered through the doorway, into the sacrificial room, but seemed to notice neither Ingrid nor the King. "Is anyone there?"

"Her discarded flesh lies moldering in the earth of your world," Mictlantecuhtli whispered. "What you see before you is merely a figment borne of memory and habit, of which she must be divested before she can move on."

Ingrid didn't think she liked the sound of that, but she held her tongue.

"Hello?" the frightened girl called. She stood mere feet away from Ingrid, but seemed to look right through her. "I don't know where I am, or how I got here. Can somebody help me? Please?"

"Wait for her," whispered the King.

Eventually, the woman entered the sacrificial room.

Mickey pushed Ingrid away from the door and out of sight. He stepped in behind the girl as she crossed the threshold and approached the grisly altar. Ingrid intuited that they would now both be visible, should the blonde happen to turn around.

Mickey's flesh fell away from his bones and reshaped itself into a new robe and cowl.

The girl turned, and found herself staring up into the face of Death.

He seized her by the throat before she could scream and threw her down onto the round altar like a ragdoll. His insect army, the things he'd called *Tzitzimime*, came roiling back up from the floor and clumped together into four shapes that solidified into half-human beings right before Ingrid's eyes. There was a black spider, a fat-bottomed wasp, a lithe red ant, and a green praying mantis, each of them segmented, armored, womanly—and taller than she was. They each pinned one of the thrashing blonde girl's hands or feet to the floor, stretching her out over the altar stone. Drawing her thin body taut.

Mictlantecuhtli, the unfleshed skeleton, stood over her and held up a hand-chipped obsidian blade. The torches' firelight pooled in its dark facets.

When the girl on the altar saw it she began to pray, tripping over the words of her Hail Marys in her haste to spit them out.

"I don't want to see this," Ingrid said.

"Then you should not have come," Mictlantecuhtli told her, and she stood back, chastened.

He was right about that, after all.

Ingrid watched without comment as Mictlantecuhtli placed the glass blade in the center of the girl's forehead and slit her open, down to the pubic bone, in a single smooth motion. As if he'd done this countless times before. She never stopped chanting, not until the blade punctured her airways and drowned her invocations in a froth of blood.

The King reached into the woman's opened throat, gripped her spinal column, and yanked her skeleton loose from its moorings, all in one piece. Organs tumbled from their wet red cavities and splatted on the floor as Mickey stood the girl's bones upright before the altar, where the hideous bugwomen had already begun to eat her deflated, unsupported skin.

Clothing appeared around the fresh skeleton. Strange, utilitarian-looking garments of a sort Ingrid had never seen before, especially on a woman. Both her pants and her many-pocketed coat were printed with a pattern of tiny squares that clumped together in earthy-looking patches. The pants tucked themselves into thick-soled boots, and a helmet appeared on her skull. She was suddenly holding a mechanism that Ingrid assumed to be a rifle, because of its shoulder stock, although it was more complex and menacing than any gun she'd seen before.

Even the dead girl's blonde hair sprouted back beneath her khaki helmet and grew down to her bony shoulders.

She looked around with her empty sockets, at silent Mictlantecuhtli, at the insect women nibbling on her discarded skin… and finally at Ingrid.

"What's your name, honey?" Ingrid asked softly.

"Private First Class Cynthia Jane Iverson, United States Army," the strange skeletal soldier girl told her automatically. Then she held up and stared at her own bony hand in grim amazement.

"Do you remember what happened?" Ingrid asked.

The bones of Cynthia Iverson nodded. "Guess it's sorta obvious, isn't it?" she said ironically, in reference to her ossified condition. She'd died. What else? "But… yes, I remember. I think I remember. I was in a Humvee, one without armor, and my unit was shepherding medical supplies down through the Khyber Pass. There was… an explosion, I guess. A flash, a noise. Too fast to hurt. An IED buried in the road, I remember thinking, and I was afraid… and then I was here. Just… here."

Ingrid nodded. She'd only understood about a third of what the corpse had said, and yet she thought the point came through. She wondered what sort of people would sacrifice their daughters to Mars, along with the standard ration of sons he has always demanded. The dead girl claimed to be a private in the US Army, but Ingrid didn't see how that could possibly be true.

It troubled her. If she didn't know better, she would've guessed the girl hailed from a point far in her own future. (Although Cynthia's vocabulary didn't sound as different from her own as hers did from Shakespeare's, for example, with less than four hundred years separating the two of *them*, so maybe the soldier girl's strange future wasn't as distant as Ingrid wanted to think.)

"What happens now?" asked the remains of Cynthia Iverson.

"You move on," said Mictlantecuhtli. He pointed toward the far door, the one that opened out onto an overcast day.

Cynthia looked to Ingrid. "What's out there?" she asked.

Ingrid shook her head. "I don't know. I'm sorry. I just got here myself."

The skeleton looked her up and down, jealous of her flesh. "Looks like you got a warmer welcome."

"I came a different way," Ingrid said. "Makes the rules different, for some reason."

At least she hoped it did, but Cynthia was already losing interest in the privileged redheaded tourist, in light of her own situation.

"Will I see my family out there? My grandma, or my aunt Jane?"

"Perhaps," Mictlantecuhtli said. "If you can find them."

He led Cynthia out the door with one flayed hand on her back and Ingrid accompanied them, like she had every right in the world.

She didn't need to shield her eyes when they stepped out onto the top of a monumental pre-Columbian pyramid. It dominated the rolling chaparral landscape it stood in for miles in every direction, under a flat gray sky. Smoke blew in wisps and billows that had the disconcerting habit of looking, for an instant or two, like skeletons wandering along the endless plain, in varying degrees of torment or confusion.

"Holy shit," Private Iverson said, and Ingrid thought she could second that emotion.

"Begone, now," Mictlantecuhtli told the girl. "Join your fellows on the ground below. Seek whom you will amongst them. It matters naught to me."

"Is this what happens every time?" Ingrid asked, of the King of the Dead. "You dress 'em out and turn 'em loose?"

"And then we feed," the King said. "Myself and the denizens of my realm. Many of the dead fight to retain the habits of their flesh. They struggle to keep their skins, as if they were made of something more than dream and memory. As if they were good for something beyond our nourishment." He nodded toward Cynthia Iverson. "This one gave hers up readily, though not as readily as some."

Iverson shrugged. "Well, like I said, there was that flash, and that noise... I guess I sorta knew, on some level. Not like somebody who dies totally out of nowhere, right? I bet they're the ones that really lose it."

"It is as you say," Mictlantecuhtli said. "The confused take more convincing. The prepared suffer less from the blade."

"You could explain it to them," Ingrid said. "Instead of your little 'chop now, pray later' routine. Not that it isn't just dramatic as hell. Really affecting."

"I think I'm glad he got it out of the way," Iverson's bones said. "The fear was worse than the pain. Now... I don't know what I feel. I don't know if I feel anything."

Mictlantecuhtli nodded. "See?" he said to Ingrid. "We leave them their bones, and some memory of themselves. They need nothing more."

"You're the embodiment of compassion," she replied.

The King tipped his cowled skull in acknowledgement of what he perceived as a compliment. Apparently they didn't have irony in the otherworld.

"Begone," Mictlantecuhtli repeated, for the benefit of Cynthia Iverson.

The dead soldier from the future looked one last time to Ingrid, and wistfully eyed her vibrant red hair. "Guess I'm glad you're beautiful," she said, "if you're the last living person I'm ever gonna see."

Ingrid didn't quite know what to say to that. "Good luck, Cynthia," was the best she could manage.

Private Iverson turned away and started down the long flight of stone stairs that led down the side of the mountainous step Pyramid.

She faded into the mists long before she reached ground level.

"So, is that it, then?" Ingrid asked. "Is she still out there somewhere, or what?"

"She is a part of my realm, and therefore a part of me," said the King. "'I am large. I contain multitudes.'"

"You've read Whitman?" Ingrid was quick when it came to identifying quotations. It was her father's influence. Alfred Redstone was an habitual spouter of verse. "*Leaves of Grass?*"

"I consumed him."

She nodded, bemused. "Good book, I guess?"

"No, Lady. You mistake my meaning. I ate his heart, and I wear his eyes. Their color is exquisite, enriched and deepened by all they viewed in life."

"You... you're wearing Walt Whitman's eyes?" Ingrid said, her own eyes dropping down to the double-looped garland of ocular orbs the King always wore, in any form, like it was some sort of badge of his office. "You're wearing them right now?"

"Not this now," Mictlantecuhtli said, "but yes, I wear them in many another."

"What does that mean? Now is now, isn't it?"

"I am in any moment or every moment or in none of them at all, according to my choosing. Nows are to me as sands on a beach or stars in a sky are in the memories of the newly dead—an endless, jumbled mass of points, each similar to all others and yet utterly unique. Would you see your Wit Man, Lady?"

"What?" Ingrid was still distracted by the implications of everything the King had said.

"The one you call Wit Man. Would you see him?"

"You mean I can meet Walt Whitman? His ghost or what have you? His soul?"

"If that be your desire."

"Yeah, why not?" Ingrid said. "Let's do it."

Her head was spinning a bit.

The sensation wasn't helped when Mictlantecuhtli made a gesture and they both vanished to reappear in another place. Or maybe it was that everything changed around them. Ingrid couldn't tell, but the experience left her reeling, and the King had to steady her for long moments while her orientation restored itself. His hands on her shoulders were large and strong, and she only belatedly realized that he'd reassumed his lifelike flesh during the transition. He'd adorned it with a loincloth, his Aztec ornaments, and little more.

When Ingrid looked up she saw they were indoors, in a hospital ward with rows of beds on either side of a center aisle. Everything around them had a grayish cast to it, but otherwise seemed perfectly real. Ingrid could hear bedsprings creaking as the occupants of the cots shifted, as well as the rustlings of sheets or shuffling feet.

There were also distant screams. Bloodcurdling ones, though the wounded skeletons languishing here seemed to accept them as background noise, the way people who lived near rail lines ignored the regular thunder of passing trains.

"What is this?" Ingrid asked.

"Your Wit Man," the King said, as he nodded toward a bearded, be-hatted skeleton that was reading aloud to one bed's occupying bones. "This is his world, as he recalls it."

"Yeah, but what *is* it?"

"The remains of a feast," said the King, and Ingrid decided to start taking his explanations with a grain of salt. If not the entire shaker.

"Can he see us? Can I talk to him?"

"If that be your desire."

Ingrid nodded like she was sure about it, and approached the dead poet. "Mr. Whitman?" she said.

The middle-aged man who looked up at her had a face, not a bare skull. Ingrid glanced around. Other men, the broken ones in the beds, had also been re-sheathed in torn, suppurating flesh. Mictlantecuhtli had made it happen in less time than it took to turn one's head. Colors looked richer as well, and textures had more detail. A subtle gangrene smell insinuated its way into her sinuses. The King—Mickey—was an incongruous Aztec chieftain standing amidst the prostrate ranks of Civil War casualties.

"Yes?" Walt Whitman said, looking up at Ingrid with weary eyes that were just as blue as her own.

Ingrid didn't know what else to say. The poet's eye contact was unusually direct, lacking the up-and-down appraisal that most men semiconsciously greeted her with.

"You're doing more to rouse these boys back to health than I ever could just by standing there, aren't you?" he said. The kid he'd been reading to—and he *was* just a kid, even from the superannuated perspective of Ingrid's twenty-seven years—nodded his grinning agreement. Ingrid had to smile for him. It wasn't easy, though. War appalled her, precisely because of scenes like these. The suffering reiterated bed by bed was too harrowing for her to contemplate for long, and yet she felt cowardly and ungrateful for wanting to turn away. Her paternal grandfather had died in the War Between the States, at an age not too much more advanced than hers. He might've been one of the shattered men lying here, wondering what the next world held in store and never guessing that it was little more than a pitiless vivisection by *el Rey de Los Muertos*. These young men were all dying alone together, and there seemed to be no one to offer them comfort beyond this one tired writer, who was here because he felt he had to be.

Ingrid had to remind herself that none of this was 'real.' At least not from where she stood. The dead seemed to be taking it literally, though, and that upset her.

"You don't have to be here, you know," she said to Whitman. "I don't think you do." She turned to her out-of-context Aztec King. "Does he?"

"This place is the construction of his own memory. He is equally free to enact another recollection."

"I don't think he is," Ingrid said. Whitman blinked, snapping out of his reverie, and went back to the article he'd been reading to the injured boy. Neither of them saw her anymore, or seemed to remember that they ever had.

"I have not decided this fate, Lady. He remembers as he chooses. They all do. I pay their choices little mind."

"I think he remembers as he has to," Ingrid opined. "I think he's stuck where he feels like he couldn't do enough good."

Mickey frowned. "Does that displease you?"

"Yes, it displeases me! Of course it displeases me! How could it not?"

The King seemed genuinely surprised. "Well... what would you have me do?"

"*I* don't know!" Ingrid said. "*I'm* not the goddamn King of Death, though, am I?"

Mickey frowned and rubbed his block of a chin as he considered. "Poet!" he said, making himself visible as he stepped forward to address Whitman's ghost. "Desist with this illusion. It distresses my guest."

"Mickey! No! That's not... no. That's not going to help."

The bear of a man sitting beside the bed looked up, slowly, taking in both the tribal King and his fox-haired consort with a surprising lack of dismay. Ingrid had the feeling they were flitting through the ghost's consciousness like daydreams might flit through her own. Barely-considered figments that vanished as randomly as they appeared.

"I... I can't go home, just yet," Whitman told the King. "Not just yet. There are still so many... so much they need, so many little things the nurses are just too busy for. There's nobody else, no family, not for most of them. They're far away from home, these boys, and there's only me…"

The sad man's eyes drifted away from his odd visitors and out across the rows of identical beds that stretched away to nowhere, like some sort of funhouse mirror effect.

"He deserves better than this," Ingrid said to Mickey.

The King ignored Whitman, but continued to study her with undisguised fascination. "And what will you do for me if I grant this dead man a boon?" Mickey asked.

Ingrid shifted her weight to the other hip. "Impress me and we'll negotiate," she said.

He grinned in a way that made Ingrid wish she'd been a lot more specific.

Then he reached into the back of the poet's head. It rippled, showing bone under the illusion of flesh as he rooted around, feeling for something Ingrid couldn't even imagine. Whitman continued reading to the man in the bed, unmindful of the fact that Mickey had his forearm buried to the elbow in his memories. It looked like a stage magician's feat. The procedure seemed to cause no pain, however, so Ingrid watched without objection while the King did his intercranial thing.

He concentrated, sticking the corner of his tongue out the side of his mouth, looking for all the world like a plumber feeling down a drain for a stubborn clog.

"Ah!" he said at last. "There. This will better suit your ideals, I think."

Mickey turned something within the poet's head, and the world changed around them again. It was as disconcerting to Ingrid as being brought down from the top of the Pyramid had been. Gone were the beds filled with damaged men, replaced in an instant by a city street that looked somewhat antiquated, from her point of view. Ingrid guessed that the revised illusion represented New York as it had been some seventy years before her own time, before the War Between the States and the aftermath that haunted the older man's later recollections. Decades of age and experience fell away from Whitman himself as Mickey pulled his hand out of the poet's mind and stood away from him.

Walt's back straightened, his arms plumped with young muscle, and the gray drained out of his hair. He stood up from his chair, which turned to smoke as his need for it vanished. The bed before him turned into a horsedrawn cart, while the boy in it became the driver. They clopped away, down a street that had moments ago been a narrow recovery-ward aisle.

All the other injured men similarly re-grew their missing parts and took up occupations, becoming the good people of old New York. Tradesmen, cops and shopkeepers, captains of industry, criminals and derelicts—everyone needed to populate the thriving city Whitman remembered from his salad days. They may still have been in thrall to

Walt's powerful imagination, but Ingrid had to imagine that the dead men involved were happier taking part in this dream, relative to the poet's last one.

So many of the dead seemed confused to her, perhaps traumatized by the circumstances of their deaths. Too damaged to do much more than stagger through tortured recreations of their own fractured memories. It seemed that a few of them, certain forceful personalities, retained a little more coherence and were able to conscript others into their private dreams, like extras and supporting cast members.

She supposed things were often not that much different amongst the living.

Whitman broke into a grin, vitalized by the kinetic activity all around him. A city that throbbed and sprawled like a living thing, with him at the center of it. Without a look back he swung up onto a horsedrawn trolley as it rattled past, and he was borne away, up the street and into happier memories.

Ingrid turned back to Mickey. He looked completely out of place in the middle of gaslit Brooklyn, dressed as he was in feathers, gold, and a woven loincloth. Ingrid herself would've looked only marginally less strange in her dungarees and man's shirt, had anyone been able to see them. Mickey could change the rules about that sort of thing on a whim, and the dead all went along with it.

"Thank you," Ingrid said. She was comforted by the alteration to his kingdom that he'd made at her request.

"I am gratified to have pleased you," he replied, and flashed that predator's grin again. "Now—what shall be my reward?"

Ingrid looked him up and down, wondering for the first time if he'd selected this form especially for her. He didn't seem to have a lot of limitations here in his own realm, and he could hardly have chosen better if he'd intended to entice her. His skin was a dark coppery bronze, and he would've been a giant amongst ordinary men—which made him a good six or seven inches taller than Ingrid herself. She liked that. His back was as broad as a beam. She'd have to reach if she wanted to put her arms around him.

Which she did, she realized, even as she stepped up close to him to do it. The possibilities offered by his world were starting to make her incautious, as though she were a little drunk.

Ingrid kissed the King of the Dead passionately, crushing her whole body against his, plunging her tongue right into his mouth with no regard for modesty or manners.

Then she pulled away and stood back. She tucked a stray strand of hair behind her ear.

"How was that?" she asked.

Mickey, for his part, seemed utterly flabbergasted, as Ingrid might've expected had she laid the same treatment on a shy fifteen-year-old boy, rather than a timeless embodiment with regal pretensions. He stared at her, astounded, reaching up to touch his own lips.

"Do it again," he commanded... then relented. "Please."

"All right," Ingrid said. "Since you asked nice."

She kissed him again, less hungrily this time, though it generated a similar degree of slow heat between them. The King pulled her close with arms that were strong like a pair of pythons. Ingrid gasped. Mickey could have easily lifted her off her feet. His kisses were eager and insistent.

Ingrid suddenly wished she was clad in something other than her stupid tree-climbing attire, and as the thought entered her head, she realized her wish had already been granted. She was wrapped in silks, and her feet were bare.

She pulled back, startled, and looked down at her new costume: a full Japanese *kimono*, embroidered with images of mountains and flames, earth and fire, the elements that defined her being.

So now she had to wonder how far into her head Mickey's reach extended. Enough to pick up on a clear desire... and maybe more.

She was going to have to take more care around him. She began to mentally run through the steps of a banishing (the Golden Dawn's tried-and-true Lesser Pentagram Ritual) that would screen off the core of her mind from nosy interlopers. It was something she could do in her sleep, if she needed to, as readily as a monk could chant his mantra.

The new robe closed high across her breasts, leaving the back of her neck bare down to the tops of her shoulderblades, the way a proper *geisha* would have worn it. The exposed nape was said to be unutterably erotic to the Japanese taste, and, as Mickey kissed her there, just below the line of her newly-upswept hair, causing her to shudder with delight, Ingrid thought she understood why.

When he dropped his hands to her waist, over the broad silk *obi* that was cinched around her middle, she could feel that both the gun and the knife she'd tucked into her belt a reality ago were still there, under the folds of fabric and pressed flush against her skin. They hadn't disappeared with her clothes (maybe because she didn't think of them as part of her outfit).

"Does this please you, Lady?" the King asked, gently pulling her back against him by her hips.

"I think you know it does," Ingrid said.

"May I please you further?"

His voice was rich with insinuation. Ingrid couldn't help but grin.

"You can sure as hell try," she said.

Mickey moved to kiss again, but Ingrid stopped him.

"Not here," she said. Whitman's simulacrum of old New York was still going on around them. "Somewhere... comfortable, if we could. And private."

The King nodded, and the street they were on became the bedroom of a lush hotel suite, just like that. The noises and smells of the city were instantly muted.

They were all alone within the room's luxurious hush.

Mickey had abandoned his feathers, his ornaments, and even his loincloth during the last shift, though he'd kept his caramel skin.

Ingrid shrugged out of her robe to join him in nudity, loosening the obi just enough to wiggle it off her hips before stepping free of it. Her intention was to keep from losing her gun and her knife should Mickey choose to make the new kimono vanish into the same ether that had absorbed his loincloth, but he seemed to appreciate the dramatic unveiling, and so the weapons stayed on the floor, draped under mounds of discarded silk.

The King's first sight of her naked body stunned him speechless.

He stepped closer, rolling his eyes over every inch of her flesh, and quite familiarly laid his hand right on her bare breast, over her heart.

"Is it not uncomfortable to have that muscle beating within you?" he asked.

"You get used to it," Ingrid said. "Don't you have one?" She placed her pale hand on his dark pectoral, mirroring his gesture. "You don't, do you?"

"No."

"Can't you, though? If you want? If you can make skin…"

Ingrid slid her finger down his torso, and the hide he'd created responded by breaking into very credible goosebumps.

"Why don't you try?" she whispered.

Mickey nodded, and closed his small, clever eyes. He concentrated, furrowing his brow. Ingrid moved closer to him, until their thighs were touching. She let the hand that wasn't feeling for a heartbeat fall to his hip. He must have felt the humidity of her breath against his neck.

After a pause just long enough for Ingrid to start to think it wasn't going to happen, something jumped deep within his chest, startling her.

"Oh!"

Whatever he'd generated under his sternum seemed to rustle, then thump, then smooth out into a steady rhythm that fell into sync with her own hurried heart rate.

Ingrid pressed her body against his, trembling and enjoying the feeling of being soft against his solidity. She stretched to kiss his throat, just below the corner of his jaw.

"Here too," she murmured, and felt a subtle carotid pulse start up against her lips. "And in your wrists."

"It moves fluid, does it not? Red life's blood, pushed through tubes beneath your skin."

"Yes," Ingrid said. "That's what a heart's for, unless you're some sort of poet."

Saying that made her think of Whitman, whom she'd saved from his own memories, after a fashion. She felt like she'd done a good thing, or at least gotten Mickey to do a good thing in her stead, and he seemed happy to have pleased her.

She let her body take the reins again before her mind could start to imagine what else he might be willing to do, if properly motivated. She hated to be seen as opportunistic about such things, and that could be difficult, as rich and powerful men had routinely been compelled to make her insane promises since she was about sixteen. She'd never been tempted by their offers, though. Talent, intellect, or physical appeal might seduce her, but attempts to buy her, no matter how lavish, had always left her cold.

It was easy to put aside thoughts of gain or power or anything else with Mickey, as the intimate act of teaching him to imitate cardiac function had left her quite desperately aroused.

She couldn't say why, exactly, but the sensation was undeniable.

"Lay with me," Ingrid coaxed, taking the King by the hand and leading him to the room's massive four-poster bed. He came along willingly enough.

As soon as she had him on the mattress, she pounced. Ingrid was never shy once she'd made up her mind about doing a thing like this.

She couldn't see the harm in it, either. If the illusion of circulation was a new and startling innovation, it would be *years* before he figured out the intricacies of a reproductive system, and even then an approximation might be the best he'd ever achieve. He was a symbol, ultimately, a figment, no matter how self-aware, and Ingrid couldn't imagine that human complications would ever ensue due to a dalliance with an entity like Mickey. He didn't even have real blood, or the veins to carry it, in spite of his fancy new pulse.

He certainly felt real enough, though, as he thrust his hips up against hers. She was sure by now that he'd designed this body to appeal to her desires, and she hated to be a discourteous guest. It would've been rude not to enjoy him.

Convinced, Ingrid let her cognition unravel as she gave herself over to the moment, automatically chanting the steps of her mental banishing ritual all the while.

Chapter Two

WHEN she awoke, the light seeping in from behind the heavy curtains seemed exactly the same as she remembered. She might've dozed for minutes or through an entire day, and she couldn't tell which.

As she yawned and re-gathered herself, she remembered where she was. It was always the same gray moment in the King's realm, though they could pretend time was passing, if they wanted to. Or rather he could if *he* wanted to, as Ingrid supposed was more truly the case.

Mickey was someone she could lead by example, though. She knew that already.

"You lost consciousness," he said, from a chair in the corner, behind her.

Ingrid sat up, not bothering to pull the sheet up for modesty. "I fell asleep," she said. "I get tired after that much… exertion."

"I do not."

"I noticed that."

Ingrid slid off the bed and crossed to the pitcher and basin stationed on a dry sink in the far corner. She could feel Mickey's eyes ticking like a metronome as she walked across the room, swinging in time with the undulation of her ass.

His relentless fascination with her was, in truth, a little frightening.

That's why she had to keep this situation well in hand, she thought as she looked into the mirror. Her hair resembled an ongoing wildfire.

Ingrid poured cool water into the basin on the counter and washed off expediently.

She required less cleansing than she might've expected after a comparable night of passion spent with a human lover, and she found that comforting. Mickey was still insubstantial, not truly physical, no matter how sore and wrung out she felt on this lovely… pseudomorning.

A chamber pot sat under the dry sink. Ingrid nudged it out with her toe, and looked to Mickey.

"Do you mind?" she asked nicely. "A moment of privacy?"

"I prefer not. I would understand the mechanism and purpose of bodily elimination. These things are unknown to me."

Ingrid sighed. "What if I tell you all about it later?"

The King frowned, and Ingrid interjected before he could make a decree:

"Please, Mickey? People like me are shy about this sort of thing."

Mickey nodded at that, pausing again to stroke his chin. "If the denizens of your realworld approach this act with shame, then your rituals and wishes will be respected. I would learn and know more of you, above all things."

Then he was gone. Just gone, without even a pop or a wisp of smoke to suggest he'd ever been there.

Ingrid darted over to her dropped kimono. She didn't know how long her 'moment' was apt to last.

Her knife was there, buried in silk, as well as the small pistol. The gun only held a single round, but she could also hurl that blade with near-surgical precision, if the need arose. She'd once assisted in a knife-throwing act, and the theatrical skills she was exposed to always came into her possession as readily as the steps to a dance.

Of course, no amount of skill in wielding them guaranteed that realworld weapons would be of any use, over here.

Still, they were something she had, and something was more than nothing. She strapped the knife to the side of her thigh. The gun was more problematic, heavy and bulky as it was, apt to fall out of a loose robe. She resolved the issue by unfurling the complex obi and snipping off a few yards of ragged-edged silk with a pair of crane-shaped sewing scissors she found on the dry sink, then twisting the fabric into a fat cable that she knotted around her waist. It hid the pistol well and held it snugly in place, and she thought it would continue to do so as long as she didn't engage in a lot of acrobatics. She also situated the robe to emphasize cleavage at the expense of nape, to better conform with the westernized tastes she best understood.

Then she hurried to put the chamber pot to its intended use. Her bladder, at least, was operating under the assumption that a number of hours had passed.

She stood up, straightened her robe... and waited.

Then waited a little more.

She sat down on the bed for a moment, sighed, then went to the window and peeled back one of the velvet drapes. Mr. Whitman's urban sprawl was still repeating itself down on the street. Ingrid let the curtain fall back into place.

"Mickey?" she said aloud.

Receiving no answer, she went to the suite's door and opened it, expecting to find a hallway lined with similarly numbered doors. Instead, she was greeted by the sight of that gray, endless plain, with its black oaks and pair of fixed winter suns swimming in the mists at either horizon. There were also moons overhead, Ingrid noticed for the first time—a whole waxing and waning line of them, spread out like a chart of lunar phases across the silver sky. She was right at ground level, too, when the window had showed her a second-story view of an old-fashioned city street.

She left the door open and crossed back to the window, where she threw the drapes open wide, rattling the curtain rods. Flat light flooded into the room.

Old New York was still out there. Ingrid could hear the clop of hooves and the clatter of wheels through the slightly distorted glass.

She pushed up the window and the view went with it. Outside was the gray plain: Mickey's world. She could still see Brooklyn happening in the upper half of the window, like it was some kind of cinematic projection on the panes and not a proper view of anything at all.

The effect was dizzying. Ingrid blinked and stepped back.

New York faded from the upper portion of the window even as she watched. There was nothing left out there but Mictlan—the unchanging realm of the dead.

Ingrid turned away from the duplicitous glass and exited the suite. It disappeared before she could even turn around.

When she did, Mickey was waiting for her, again adorned as befitted an Aztec King. The gray plain stretched away behind him.

"Have you completed your ablutions?" he asked.

Ingrid nodded.

Mickey licked his lips. He liked the way she'd chosen to wear her robe. It was easy to tell—he was in no way self-conscious about his interests.

"Your headdress," Ingrid ventured. "And your gold. They're Aztec?"

"They are emblematic of the people who call this realm Mictlan," he said. "Those who know me, respect me, and treat me right, and therefore enjoy my favor."

"Knew you, you mean. Right?"

"I am neither new nor old. I am as I am."

"No, Mickey, you don't understand. I mean they knew you in the past, right? They *used to* enjoy your favor. They don't anymore."

"You are correct, Lady, in that I cannot grasp your meaning. They do as they do in their now, as you do in your now and others do elsewhere. What troubles you in this?"

"You do see how the 'nows' are strung together, though, right?" Ingrid asked, frowning in response to his confusion. "You see the order they go in?"

Mickey just stared at her.

Ingrid was realizing that he actually did not perceive chronological order—at least not in the same way she did. All those moments that made up the flow of time were distinct and unrelated particles, as far as the King was concerned.

"There is *order*," he said wonderingly, "and structure, and not just similarity between the nows?"

"The 'nows' that look alike are probably close together in time," Ingrid offered.

"Yes, yes, I have often heard the dead use this term," he said, looking philosophical. (Ingrid didn't know if 'mortosophical' would qualify as a word.)

"'Time,'" the King continued. "It is rumored amongst my subjects to be both too long and too short. How is this feat accomplished?"

"That's mostly a matter of perspective," Ingrid said, almost dismissively. The wheels in her head were starting to whirl. "Mickey, are you really serious about this? Are you saying you can be in any moment you want?"

"I can look out onto every human moment I desire, yes. They all are as one, however, on this side."

"Can you show me a moment other than the one I came from?"

"Certainly."

"Just like that?" Ingrid asked, and Mickey raised his hand.

In the next instant they were atop the Pyramid again, inside the sacrificial chamber. Ingrid wrinkled her nose at the charnel smell that rose from the bloodglazed altar stone. She turned away from it to suck down a draught of the clean, cool air that wafted in from the hole in the back wall of the first room. The black sky beyond it was full of stars.

"There is the now next to the one in which you arrived," Mickey said, pointing across the antechamber.

"That's the moment in my world right after the one I left?"

Mickey nodded.

"I could go back and it would be like I was never even gone?"

"You and you alone could do this," he said. "I can find no other who has entered my realm and left it again alive."

"No other?"

"None, though few amongst my living servants dare to make the attempt."

"Hmm," Ingrid said, unable to keep from feeling a touch of contempt for those who knew and never tried. She had to remind herself that she might not have gambled her life either, had she not been tricked into it and gotten miraculously lucky.

No power on high had chosen her for this. Ingrid nominated herself, because revelation had to come to somebody, so why not her? Being a 'witch' was, in her mind, about shaping her experience according to her own design, in defiance of anybody else's dogma or strictures. Her commonness had become a point of stubborn pride as she approached these mysteries. But now that it seemed like she might be something of a special case after all, she wasn't sure how to feel.

Other than more curious.

"Can I see a different now?" she asked. "One that's very far away from this one?"

Mickey made a gesture, and it was day out beyond the Hole in the Sky. Ingrid could see the peaks of the Santa Monica Mountains in the distance. The sky was so blue it stung her eyes.

"When is that?" she asked, squinting against the light.

"A now in which a living woman knows my favor, even though she is pledged to my opposite, to the Fire of Life, before me," Mickey said. "I think you would consider it quite distant from your own."

Presently, Ingrid heard voices speaking in a tongue she didn't recognize, as well as the slow shuffling of more than a few pairs of feet, as if men she couldn't see were trudging up a flight of stairs, outside. Feathered heads bobbed into view through the far doorway, a whole coterie of them, marching as if up steps. The bronze-skinned faces below the elaborate headdresses were old, wrinkled, sunken—Ingrid's first thought was that these were priests, not warriors, laden with the totems of their office.

There were warriors with them, however: several muscular men wielding both stone-headed mallets and long clubs constructed of obsidian shards sandwiched between twin planks and held together with pitch. Ingrid imagined the awkward-looking weapons would be quite devastating when applied to the side of a head. Those glass teeth would have a bite.

There were no metal blades in evidence, much less guns. Ingrid didn't think these old Californians would understand a word of Spanish, either, which she figured put her at least five hundred years into her own past, if not considerably more. Guessing that this could be the year 910, a full thousand years before her time, didn't seem at all unreasonable.

At the center of the human knot, ringed first by priests, then by guards, was a woman. She was straighter and stronger than the old men around her, and her dark complexion and wiry hair led Ingrid to believe that she might be a captured member of another tribe, if not a traveler from distant lands. She looked African, frankly, while some of the men surrounding her could have hailed from the Orient or Arabia. They didn't look much like the native people she knew—the Lakota and Apache warriors-turned-showmen her family had traveled with as part of Buffalo Bill's Wild West Extravaganza, when she was a child. But then, there were hundreds of miles and centuries of descendants between them.

The dark-skinned woman carried neither weapons nor talismans in her hands, which were bound before her with fibrous yellow stalks. (This was also a strong indicator that these folks were not out for a late-summer picnic.) The party reached the top of the unseen staircase and gathered around outside of what, on Ingrid's side, was a door, but should have been nothing more than a hole in the sky from where they stood. It was obvious they hadn't climbed up a tree, however. A lot of things seemed different about this era already.

The priests pushed the dark woman into the room, then crowded in after her. The guards remained outside the door, wielding those jagged-edged cricket bats of theirs. They saw neither Mickey nor Ingrid, standing there in the second room, watching.

"What happens next?" Ingrid asked.

Mickey shrugged. "I have no idea," he said. "The moment is different for having you in it."

"You said she serves you, though." Ingrid nodded toward the bound woman as the youngest and meanest-looking of the priests twisted her hair at the back of her head to force her to her knees before the door to the Inner Sanctum.

"She is Califia, yes, a powerful priestess. She is queen of these people through my influence."

"She doesn't look like a queen right now!"

"You are correct in that," Mickey agreed, though he didn't seem troubled by either the fact or its implications.

The mean-looking priest, who was perhaps a weathered forty years old, held out his hand like a surgeon in an operating theater, and an acolyte slapped a black obsidian hand axe into his palm. It looked a lot like the one Mictlantecuhtli himself used to unflesh the dead.

These folks had influenced his act quite a bit, apparently. He seemed to like their style.

"Are they Aztecs?" Ingrid asked again.

"They do not use that name," Mickey said. "They are Nahuatlaca, speakers of Nahuatl, the people of Aztlán, sacred to the Left-Handed Hummingbird Huitzilopochtli, who calls them Mexica. To the tribes of the south these are the People Who Made the Hole in the Sky. Their priesthood of the Azteca Chicomoztoca built a temple that reached to the navel of the moon, and from its peak they called to me with the screams of ten thousand men, sending so many dead over to my realm from this spot that the boundaries between our worlds grew thin, and tore. They sated my thirst for blood and my hunger for flesh before they begged my favor, which their progeny enjoy in many subsequent iterations of the real."

Ingrid lost the thread, much less the sense, of what the King was saying well before he finished speaking. The bound woman snarled up at the vicious priest as he yanked her hair again to pull her head back, and placed the honed edge of the obsidian blade to her throat.

"Mickey," Ingrid said, looking back over her shoulder. "Your queen's gonna lose her crown in about thirty seconds here, and I don't want to see it."

"Then help her," the King said. "If that be your wish."

"Yeah?"

Mickey stepped aside and made a nonchalant 'be-my-guest' sort of gesture.

Ingrid drew her pistol from the sash of her robe as she stepped through the door between worlds.

She blasted the knife-wielding priest between the eyes at point-blank range. The look of dumb surprise on his face as he fell over backward, dead before he hit the floor, was almost comical.

The rest of the old men screamed like a pack of terrified schoolgirls at the deafening sound of the shot, dropping ceremonial artifacts as they bounced off the walls and off each other in their haste to get away. Ingrid's ears felt stuffed with cotton, the babble all around her nearly drowned out beneath a distant, high-pitched ringing.

The woman Ingrid had rescued, Califia, looked up at her with something like religious rapture in her eyes. For just a moment, before reason reasserted itself and she scrambled for the dead priest's blade. It was sharp as a scalpel, and a few swipes against it shredded the dried plant stalks binding her wrists enough that she was able to tear free of them and find her feet.

Califia bashed her commandeered hand axe right down into the forehead of the nearest priest, and he crumpled aside in a spray of blood. She whirled and shoved another nearby man through the door between the worlds. His flesh fell away from his bones when he staggered into the Inner Chamber. As he got up and looked himself over, the skeleton of the man Califia had just killed with the obsidian blade appeared next to him, with a sizable dent right in the middle of his bare skull.

If Mickey had performed his vivisection ritual on either of them, Ingrid hadn't seen it happen. Maybe he'd put on a special show with Cynthia Iverson, the soldier girl from the future. He didn't necessarily need time to do something that seemed to *take* time, either, she reflected. So she couldn't tell if his theatrics were mere stage dressing, or actual requirements of the death experience.

The important thing right now was that the expired priests were unable to cross back over into the realworld. Their bones couldn't rejoin the fight. Mickey, similarly constrained, threw them aside to continue watching the action through the doorway.

Califia bolted for the exit—for the door that led back out to her world.

The guards stationed outside it crossed their weapons and blocked her way. The intended sacrifice threw her chunk of obsidian, catching one of the warriors square in the face with it, even as Ingrid darted forward and kicked the second man right where it counted. Together she and her new friend shoved them back from the door, and both of the warriors fell—one rolling down the long stairway they'd all just climbed up; the other bouncing much more jarringly down the stacked levels of the tall mud-brick pyramid.

The first thing Ingrid saw when she and Califia exited onto the temple's top tier was that there was no Tree below the Hole in this era, some undetermined number of centuries before her ancestors ever imagined the Americas might exist. These people had (or *had* had) an artificial mountain instead of a sacred Tree, and Ingrid was humbled to think of how much time must have passed that there was no sign of it remaining in her own age. It was an impressive structure, too—the falling guards took the better part of a minute to tumble all the way down its side.

Neither of them moved after they thudded to the ground.

A crowd of tribesmen (and women, and children) at least several thousand strong looked up from the fallen warriors, to the pair of women standing at the summit of their pyramid.

The hush that fell over them was absolutely primeval. The only sound in all the world seemed to be a trill of distant birdsong.

Ingrid turned to the woman she'd liberated, who seemed to be at as much of a loss as she was, if not more. Califia looked up from the awed assemblage populating the plain below them and over to her redheaded savior, Ingrid, who'd appeared out of nowhere and now stood at her side like a vision made real.

Califia looked back down to the wide-eyed crowd, and then broke into a wicked grin.

She grabbed Ingrid's hand and thrust it into the air like she'd just won a prizefight and shouted something down at the people in their own language. They murmured and looked to one another in bemusement, not sure what to make of this unprecedented development.

The liberated sacrifice screamed down at them, quite vehemently. Their closest ranks shrank back. They still seemed unsure, not able to accept whatever she was telling them.

Exasperated, Califia picked up her trusty hand axe one more time, from where it lay near Ingrid's feet. She turned and strode back through the doorway built around what would be, in Ingrid's time, merely a hole in the sky. There were still two priests cowering in there. They and their former captive exchanged words, briefly, then one of the remaining two grabbed his counterpart and pinned his arms behind his back as he pushed the weaker prelate to his knees.

It looked to Ingrid like one of them had just accepted a new job offer, while the other was about to be, well... terminated.

She turned away when Califia carved into the struggling, shrieking priest's abdomen with the black glass blade.

The crowd below heard the screams too. Ingrid could feel their growing unease even from up here, rising toward her like a current of heated air.

She might've intervened to help the priest, as she'd helped his captive, but she had a harder time mustering pity for the adherents of a tradition that included the butchering of tied-up women as one of its rites. The religious authorities of her own culture had burned witches like herself alive as little as two centuries before her time, and the thought of it always made Ingrid's blood boil.

The newest priestess of Mictlan stepped back out of the pyramid's inner chambers with a raw and glistening human heart cradled in her hands. Her arms were coated with blood to the elbows. It looked like she was wearing long crimson gloves.

Califia took Ingrid's hand and smacked the heart into it. The damn thing was still pulsing, hopping in her palm like a captured toad, and Ingrid almost vomited, although she was not in general a squeamish sort of girl. The priestess raised her arm up for her again, thrusting the old priest's beating heart skyward with a resounding shriek of triumph. Ingrid could feel thick blood dripping from the fibrillating lump of muscle and down the length of her arm, but she was glad not to have to look at it anymore.

The last of the old priests dragged the heartless body of his colleague out of the pyramid's chambers and dumped it down the stairs. It left dark splashes of blood behind as it rolled.

The crowd below them fell to their knees in a wave, looking like nothing so much as stalks of grass flattening out as a heavy wind swept across a field.

Ingrid was awed by their reaction. She was a veteran performer; she'd received applause before and it always had an effect on her, but *this*, this sort of unalloyed supplication, veneration, and wordless-yet-palpable adulation…

This was something else again.

It was almost enough to make her forget about the human heart cooling in her hand.

The instant priestess and her new acolyte (the last priest standing) grinned at one another. The old man stepped forward and shouted something down at the assembled people. The only word at all intelligible to Ingrid was his last one:

"…*Califia!*"

The freed captive dropped Ingrid's hand and stood at the edge of the pyramid beside her aged servant in order to address the crowd. Ingrid caught the name Mictlantecuhtli in her speech, and then, apparently in reference to Ingrid herself, the name '*Mictlancihuatl*,' which was greeted with cheers as the crowd rose to their feet.

It was not a name she'd heard before, but Ingrid understood that she was being associated with the god, that she was being billed as either his queen or his consort. Califia was generating political credibility out of their brief relationship, right before her eyes. Like a goddamn candidate for office. Ingrid had seen such aspirants attach themselves to celebrities before, and her new friend Cali clearly wasn't one to waste an opportunity. Her life had just been publicly spared through the last-minute intercession of a magical being made out of moonlight and fire, to all appearances, and a more impressive endorsement than that was not likely to come along.

The human ruler of the Nahuatlaca knew it, too. Ingrid hadn't noticed him before, sitting atop his fancy litter near the back of the crowd, surrounded by servants and courtiers, but he stood up nervously when the rest of the tribe turned and looked at him, on Califia's command.

She screamed again, and the dethroned king jumped from his litter to run for his life as the rest of the tribe shouted *en masse,* and gave chase.

He didn't make it fifty yards before his former subjects ran him down and trampled him, crushing and kicking him as he screamed. Ingrid was glad that he fell quickly out of sight, subsumed by the mob.

Califia, the new priestess-queen of southern California, unexpected usurper of the throne, took her by the hand (not the one still clutching a twitching human heart), and led her down the steps of the realworld's ancient Pyramid of Mictlantecuhtli. The very one Mickey had copied for the sake of his own amusement and vanity, over on his side of the Hole in the Sky.

Ingrid wondered how far into the world of the past she should wander, away from Mickey, who could neither follow nor help her, but Califia was leading her along and making the most of her proximity to the apparent goddess. Ingrid could feel the crowd aching for her, yearning toward her, even as they cringed away. Droves of them fell to their knees and chanted prayers, afraid to look directly at her. Others could not help but gape. They all shied back from the foot of the pyramid as Califia and Ingrid reached the ground and stepped over the opened body of the former priest that lay in the dirt. Ingrid held up his heart and stared at it. It was still thumping erratically, unevenly, almost stopped. Califia was shouting at her people again, exhorting them to their feet and adapting their shouts and prayers into a call-and-response that Ingrid understood but two words of:

'Califia,' of course, and her own new, undeserved name, 'Mictlancihuatl.'

And the chant had its effect, despite Ingrid's constricted understanding of its meaning. She knew the people were cheering for her, or at least *at* her: their miracle, the goddess made flesh, too real and too witnessed for anyone to deny. She also understood, more distantly, that Mickey had some trouble with verb tenses. Every moment was somehow the present, to him. He'd delivered her into the instant when Califia *began* to be queen of the Nahuatlaca, not one in which she was already established, and it was only Ingrid's timely appearance on the scene that was allowing the dark-skinned woman to seize power.

And yet Mickey had known she *would* be queen. He'd assumed it, when the catalyst for it, namely Ingrid, had only just arrived in his realm herself. He'd even said that the moment was different for having her in it. So, Ingrid had to wonder, would Califia still have become queen by some other route if she hadn't shown up? Or would the priests be hoisting Cali's heart high at this very moment? Had the event played out differently in some other, overwritten memory of Mickey's?

It was a lot to contemplate, and her head was spinning. The fact that it was all so utterly real—the people, the sounds and the smells of them, the hot midday sun on her face, the feel of coagulated blood flaking off her arm—made Califia's version of the story seem almost more plausible than her own. Which one really made less sense, Ingrid wondered: a delivering angel or a rogue time traveler?

The entire world felt too bright, too loud, too crowded. Plus, she hadn't eaten anything other than Teonanactl mushrooms for the better part of two days, according to her body's confused internal clock, and she was hungry to the point of dizziness. Did the Goddess of the Dead need to eat, like a common mortal? In human form she did.

Ingrid, Mictlancihuatl, dropped the heart she was holding. She took a step toward Califia, her priestess and the people's queen, but her legs felt rubbery, like her knees wouldn't hold her weight for very much longer.

A moment later she was lying in the dirt, unconscious.

Chapter Three

BY the time she awoke, it was dark.

She needed some moments to remember who she was, and where, and by what manner she'd arrived. A nagging sense of memories receding just beyond her mental reach made her feel panicky, like she was drowning, but the feeling diminished as soon as she opened her eyes.

She was Mictlancihuatl, of course, the Goddess of the Dead, and she had come from the Pyramid in order to save the queen. The new queen. She remembered that much. She suspected the density of her assumed human form might be constricting her long-term recollections, and that was why she remembered next to nothing of the otherworld from whence she'd come. It made a certain sort of sense to her that this borrowed head should only contain as much as a physical mind could hold.

Outside, the people were celebrating the coronation of Califia, the foreign captive she'd saved from sacrifice on a whim. There were drums and there was singing. The shell rattles tied to every dancer's ankles sounded like ocean cataracts rushing and crashing in a danceable rhythm. Decorated bodies whirled past the open front of the tent in which the goddess found herself. She sat up and pushed her corona of fiery hair back from a face that looked as white and clear as the face of the fullest moon, when she looked it over in a polished obsidian mirror someone had left near her sleeping-pallet. Her hands, too, were bloodless and pale, just as a dead thing's should be.

She wondered from whom this form had been borrowed, what her natural life had been like, and thought again that she could almost delve into that missing woman's memories. Almost, but not quite. The whispers and fragments that recurred to her were troubling anyway, full of bizarre occurrences and facts too improbable to face. So perhaps her incomplete remembrances were a form of self-defense. She believed, then, that she was safest simply being who she thought she was... at least for the time being.

She stepped from her tent to join the throng, and the inebriated people crowded around their living miracle.

They pressed steaming tamales and corn cakes into her hands, and the goddess ate eagerly. She drank the leaf-cups of fermented juices they offered. Soon her head was buzzing and her body felt pleasantly nourished and warm, and the nagging sense she had of other memories looming, of a lost identity fighting for recognition, receded to a dull discomfort rather than escalating into the storm of panic that had threatened to overtake her right after she awoke.

They were in a village situated amidst a grove of oak trees. The pyramid was nowhere to be seen, but it might still have been nearby—the night beyond the peoples' ring of torches was as dark as the goddess's memory.

Califia saw that she was up, and approached her across the village center with a whole retinue of new servants, shamans, and sycophants in tow. All of them were drunk, discomposed, and thrilled to be alive, Califia herself being no exception. Her eyes were glassy from plant chemicals and her face was aglow from exertion when she lurched forward gracelessly, laughing, and kissed Mictlancihuatl full on the mouth, to the enthusiastic cheers of her new courtiers. Her body was hot and yielding as she pressed against her surprised savior. Her breath was cold with alcohol vapors. Her hair smelled of herbsmoke.

As one, the queen and the goddess began to dance. The rest of the people joined in and reeled around them, stomping the earth in time with the drums. The light of numerous crackling torches painted them in tones of orange and red. Feathered headdresses three feet high bobbed, shook, and stirred the smoke. They looked backlit and strange in the lurid fireglow, casting long, serrated shadows. The golden ornaments of the upper classes glinted as the bodies of the tribe swayed around the two unusual women at the center of it all—one of them darker-skinned and curlier-haired than any of the local people; the other one as white as death.

The tribespeople were slow to notice the unusual number of ants scrabbling up out of the dirt, over feet and up calves. Some shouted, flailed, and brushed at their legs, but the collective energy of the celebration shunted their individual expressions of revulsion aside... for a minute or two.

It took the appearance of spiders and wasps by the buzzing, scuttling score to finally break up the party.

The drums failed and screams replaced them. People fled, stumbling over each other in their haste to escape the sudden infestation. Small green mantises sprang about like drops of water flicked onto hot stones. Women tore wasps from their long black hair and wailed as their hands were stung. Children stomped on ants and spiders. Califia shouted to reassure them, though she clearly had no idea what was going on.

Only the goddess Mictlancihuatl understood.

"*Tzitzimime!*" she screamed, her shrill soprano voice cutting through all other noise. Both humans and insects forgot what they were doing and swiveled their heads in her direction. She continued to address the bugs in a language that was unfamiliar to the people, but which the Tzitzimime seemed to understand.

"Take form. I would speak with you," she said.

The horde of insects seemed to consider this request, wherever they were—under people's clothing, on their skin, or in their hair—before coalescing across the village center and clumping up into feminine forms as tall and shapely as the goddess's own. The crawling things' hard exoskeletons melted and liquefied, like bits of metal sintering together in a forge, and the Tzitzimime solidified into four points of relatively complex consciousness, rather than four million scattered fragments. Half woman and half bug, they each stood taller than any of the people.

Spider stepped forward. Her thorax was marked with red; her skinny limbs were as black as pitch. Her bristling mandibles worked as she forced out her contorted approximations of human words. The other Tzitzimime, Ant and Mantis and Wasp, hung back from her, glaring balefully around at the silent people.

Wide-eyed Califia edged closer to Mictlancihuatl.

"King... wants... you..." the stately arachnoid managed to chitter, with a visible effort. Grammar and syntax were a bit daunting to things like these, even at their most organized.

"The King can ask politely if he expects a response," the goddess said tartly. "Like anybody else."

The eight-limbed Tzitzimitl seemed at a loss. The people held their collective breath. The queen squeezed the goddess's hand.

"King wants you," Spider repeated, more decisively.

"I prefer not," the goddess said. "Now cease your molestation of my people. Return from whence you came, and trouble me no further, unless I should call for you. I am Mictlancihuatl, the Lady Death, and *you* show much disrespect to your superiors, little bug."

Spider stepped back, looking abashed. "Y-yes, Mictlancihuatl," she managed, hanging her multi-eyed head in shame and confusion as the other bugwomen shuffled behind her, like chastised children. They'd been sent to find the dead woman whose body this was, not a goddess. If she'd been playacting they would've felt it, and taken her, but her intentions were firm, and the authority of her name was absolute. She stared them down with her fierce blue eyes.

"We go," Spider said.

She was the first to fall apart, dissolving into a tumble of tiny scuttling bodies that spilled across the earth. Ant and Mantis and Wasp followed suit, crumbling into separate insects that disappeared off into the air or down into the dirt like water absorbed by the soil.

Within seconds they were gone, as if they'd never been.

Califia was looking at the goddess with undisguised awe in her eyes.

A collective cheer went up from the people, and if the drums were loud before, the drummers now redoubled their efforts. The queen threw herself against the living goddess and squeezed her with a fierceness and devotion that already ran unimaginably deep. It seemed to occur to no one that, while Mictlancihuatl had routed the bugs, they would never have come in the first place if not for her presence here amongst them. That fact unsettled her, but the people were simply grateful, and thoroughly impressed. What had been a party turned itself into an unrestrained orgy of dancing, drinking, and licentiousness on a tribe-wide scale—one that lasted through two nights straight and didn't even start to wind down until a second new day had dawned.

Chapter Four

WEEKS passed.

The embodied goddess and the new queen spent some days recovering from their first long nights spent together in genial debauchery. They took over an elaborate reed-roofed dwelling, a *xahcalli*, from the tribe's ex-ruler, the *tlatoani*, who no longer had need of it. *Cihuatlatoani* seemed to be the word for queen, and the new one brought but a single possession with her from her former life: a greenstone carving of a long-haired tribesperson wearing an agonized expression on its broad, flat face. It found a place of pride in their new home, near the fire, right next to a skeletal idol with staring eyes that had been venerated by the xahcalli's prior occupant. Mictlancihuatl recognized the old carving as an image of her own counterpart in the next world over: the tribe's ancient and bloodthirsty patron, King Mictlantecuhtli. Califia's humbler statue was named Tlazolteotl, and the goddess came to understand that this had been her new friend's guide through a previous career as a healer and semi-nomadic midwife.

Califia burned incense before the pair of totems every day, and would gaze upon them for long periods of time, lost in quiet devotion.

AFTER the goddess and the queen emerged from their new shelter, rested and restored, they were ever at each other's side. Each of them was striking in her own right, but Mictlancihuatl knew that as a pair they made for a compelling and seemingly meaningful vision, one of them pale and the other dark, like two sides of a single mystery.

They couldn't communicate well, as they didn't share a language, and yet it was plain to the goddess that Califia knew she was troubled. Mictlancihuatl didn't sleep well; she had nightmares and needed to be soothed in the darkness. While waking she would sometimes drift off, staring at nothing, her brow creased in concentration as she tried hard to remember or figure something out. Califia would nudge her out of such trances and stroke her sunset-colored hair until she smiled again, and reached for one of the delicacies or beverages the people took it upon themselves to always have ready for them, or else she might lead the queen off to the fern-shrouded spring in the foothills where they liked to bathe and lounge in the cool shadows all through the long, late-summer afternoons.

Califia had assumed her throne on the autumnal equinox, when day and night were of equal length and neither sun nor moon was dominant, and the weather began to turn cool not long after that. Stifling heat and the smoky scent of distant wildfires gave way to clear-skied days and cold wet winds that gusted in off the ocean a few miles to the west. The people needed fires to warm themselves at night, and not just blankets. They had harvests to attend to during the days, and other preparations to make in anticipation of the colder weather yet to come. It rarely snowed in this land, but the winters were still something to contend with.

THE bone soldiers came on a crisp afternoon in mid-autumn, on the first of the two days when this world and the next come into close alignment each fall.

Mictlancihuatl could tell that Queen Califia feared they'd come to take her goddess from her as soon as the first messengers arrived to describe this sight that had been seen by a number of people in the outlying fields and hunting grounds: a war party marching north toward the foothills, from the direction of Mictlan's Pyramid.

The soldiers were unlike any other warriors the tribe had encountered, though to the goddess they sounded oddly familiar. She'd picked up enough of the local language that she was able to catch the gist of the descriptions. The invaders' body-shaped vestments were said to be tan and gray in color, made from a heavy cloth that blended in with the scrubby chaparral landscape they marched across. Their feet were like enormous hooves. Each of the six who came carried a black staff that looked somewhat like a walking stick, though they never rested their weight upon them.

The messengers hesitated to explain that it was a war party *of* the dead, unmistakably—six fleshless, bleached-white skeletons in earth-colored clothes, marching with purpose toward the village. None of them had ever seen anything like it.

Califia decided she wasn't giving up her love without a fight. The goddess watched the resolution harden across her face.

The Queen of California summoned her own warriors and sent them out to meet the otherworldly interlopers with *atlatls* to hurl short spears, as well as with their *macuahuitls*—those heavy wooden club-swords with obsidian chips embedded in their sides that, when properly wielded, could rend a man in two.

Within less than an hour Mictlancihuatl, Califia, and all of her war advisors heard a strange stuttering thunder echoing back to them from out beyond the trees, and soon the queen's messengers were back with lurid reports of sorcerers' staves that coughed fire from their ends and hurled tiny stones so hard that they tore holes right through the bodies of the people who stood in the war party's way. The goddess understood but little of these involved descriptions, and yet some part of her recognized those sudden, repetitive blasts, and could picture the sort of machines that uttered them.

The queen's soldiers could not combat weapons like the ones she was imagining. All they could do was be killed.

One amongst the messengers seemed to be suggesting that the damage inflicted upon the queen's men didn't last; that they would get up, whole and unharmed, after about ten or twenty minutes, as if their injuries had occurred only in a dream—but that sounded insane, and it seemed like much too much to count on. The goddess's grasp of the Nahuatl language was really still in its infancy. She had to be mishearing.

Califia opted to flee. Both she and Mictlancihuatl were strong and well able to run, which they did, accompanied by a regiment of the queen's elite guards, whom the goddess thought of as the Shorn Ones, after their emblematic hairstyle. The company raced up the trail that was known for leagues all around as the Path that Led Past Death's Pyramid and headed toward the desert valley that lay beyond the hills. There were caves and arroyos in that direction—possible places to hide.

The dead soldiers overtook them before they reached the mouth of the mountain pass called Kawengna, not long after the sun had ducked behind the western hills. The war party was, by now, accompanied by a thick carpet of crawling insects that pointed the way for them. Flying bugs lent air support, spotting their quarry from the darkening skies, where a full moon already rode high and bright.

Califia's Shorn Ones dug in to make a stand. The Corpse Soldiers (and that *was* what they were, walking skeletons—Mictlancihuatl saw it with her own eyes, as did a shocked Califia) all pointed their walking sticks, and the queen's warriors went down in a brief but deafening hail of fire.

Only the goddess and the queen were left standing.

Califia stepped in front of Mictlancihuatl, shielding her love with her body.

"Will you two for Christ's sake just *wait a minute?*" said the leader of the Corpse Soldiers—a skeleton with long yellow hair and a female voice. "We have a message for you, and a gift."

But Califia would not wait a minute. She drew a stone-headed club from the belt at her hip and flew at the dead soldier girl, intending to crack her skull open.

The dead men's thundering weapons all but tore the queen apart.

The goddess howled and ran to her, falling to her knees as red blood bubbled out of Califia's body from a dozen different ragged holes. The Corpse Soldiers stood back as the goddess wept and screamed. Every one of them looked appalled by the tableaux they'd helped create.

"Tzitzimime," Mictlancihuatl said, softly, without ever looking up from the agonized face of her dying companion. "Destroy them for me."

The insects that had been leading the way paused—the wasps in midair, the ants in mid-march—then pulled together into four individual bugwomen.

They surrounded the Corpse Soldiers.

"Now, wait a damn minute…" the yellow-haired commander said.

"We dare not disobey," Wasp told her, angling her hips in order to brandish her two-foot-long, needle-sharp stinger.

The dead soldier girl ordered her men to defend themselves and their magical canes spat fire again, even as the bugwomen lunged. The demons were blasted back into showers of insects that fled to regroup at what they thought would be a safe distance. The bone soldiers gunned them down again as soon as they drew back into human-like forms, which they apparently had to do in order to think at all. Were the monsters to hit upon the idea of coming at them in bullet-permeable swarms, then the soldiers would have a bigger problem on their hands. But the bugs hadn't gotten there yet. They just couldn't reason very well after they'd gone to pieces.

"Lady, listen, will you please just *listen?*" the yellow-haired leader girl said, turning to the goddess. "Old Man Death said to give you this."

She took a small object from inside her coat and tossed it to Mictlancihuatl, who caught it reflexively, on the fly.

It was a fat, faceted garnet, about the size of an eyeball. A red gemstone that looked as black as a blood clot in the goddess's palm, under the brightening moonlight.

She cocked her head as she considered it. It seemed to mean something.

A red stone.

Redstone.

Ingrid remembered her name, and her world came slamming back into her head with a force like a blow from a sledgehammer. She swooned, almost falling. She looked down at herself, feeling some degree of wonder. Her breasts were bare, and her upper arms were sleeved in golden ornaments. Her simple skirt was fashioned from the remains of a flame-embroidered kimono. She still wore her knife, strapped to her left thigh.

Califia's slain Shorn Ones sat up, miraculously, and some of them fled. Those who didn't were gunned down again, even as the queen herself came back to life and threw herself at the corpse of Cynthia Iverson for a second time. Ingrid yelped in surprise, even though she *had* thought, earlier, that one of those messengers had been trying to suggest that something was wrong with the way people were dying. That the familiar rules of life and death were somehow out of kilter. She'd felt the news-carrier's confusion even then.

The soldier girl felled the queen with a decisive burst of fire and she died again, shrieking, for the second time in as many minutes.

"*Stop it!*" Ingrid yelled, balling her hands into fists. "All of you—leave them alone!"

"Better we shoot 'em than fight 'em," Private Iverson explained, as Ingrid dropped to Califia's side, ignoring the soldier's words completely. The queen's eyes were fixed and motionless, and that was all she cared about right now.

"Lady Redstone?" Iverson's skeleton asked uncertainly, even though Ingrid knew the deceased soldier had recognized her already. Or at least seemed to think she had. Ingrid supposed her current costume was probably a bit... unexpected.

"Yes, *what?*" she snapped, still feeling aggrieved by the queen's second painful demise. This had to be some stupid trick of Mickey's, the result of some loophole he was able to exploit, but it had still been as agonizing to watch as any real killing.

"The guns are from the other side," Iverson said, tapping her weapon against the side of her helmet. "Not real, dream things. It only looks and feels like these people are dying—they'll wake up in a little bit like it was all just a nightmare. But if we get into it hand to hand and we hurt 'em, that's real, and the injuries stay. Only our bones are really here. That's what Grimace McReaper said when he sent us out to get you, anyway. There's only these few days in a year when he can let us walk—that's why you had to wait as long as you did for a rescue op. What happened out here, anyway? The bugs couldn't find you or you sent them back or something? You lost yourself, the King said? Your memory?"

Ingrid didn't bother to respond. She was still holding Califia's slack hand.

"So..." Iverson said, "better we get the hell outta here while they're all still dead, and that way we won't have to kill 'em again. I don't like it any better than you do, believe me."

Ingrid nodded. She closed Califia's eyes.

Mantis clumped up out of the dirt behind a Corpse Soldier and took his skull off with her jaws. The rest of the unit scattered her to bugs in an instant with their guns, but she came right back, along with the other three insect avatars, forming a perimeter around Ingrid, Iverson, and the remainder of their armed skeletal escort.

"King wants *you*," Spider spat.

"With us..." Ant hissed.

"...you will come," Wasp supplied.

"All right," Ingrid said. "Let's go."

"First we eat soldiers," Mantis said.

"As goddess commands," Ant explained, as if to remind Ingrid of what she'd said a few minutes ago. One of Iverson's men shredded the bugwoman with a burst of rifle fire and she screamed, but her individual drones began to reform in another spot, right away.

They wouldn't stay down for long.

"You don't have to do that now," Ingrid said to the next bug down the line, who happened to be Spider. "I'm telling you. Let's just go, quick."

"*You* are not goddess," Spider said. "You are red stone."

"*You* give no orders, red stone," Mantis said, even though they were presently acting on one of her orders, if they'd stop to think about it. The lanky green demon snapped at another Corpse Soldier, and he shot her to pieces that broke down further and scrambled away as soon as they hit the ground.

The Tzitzimime had listened to Ingrid before because she'd believed absolutely that she *was* the goddess, but they weren't going to fall for that now.

"What happens if they eat us?" a bony soldier asked. "Do we stop existing or do we go back to where we started, like in a video game or something?"

"I have no idea," Ingrid said. She had no idea what a video game was, either, but it hardly seemed like the time to ask.

Califia gasped in a wrenching lungful of air, leapt to her feet, and ran at Iverson. When the men hesitated to shoot her again, Wasp cut one of them down with her stinger. Like the skeleton just decapitated by Mantis, this casualty failed to get back up. Ingrid saw his bones crumble to soft dirt within his uniform.

His comrades-in-arms burst Wasp back into a diffuse swarm with their gunfire.

Iverson's skeleton pushed Califia aside, but the queen came after her again, grabbing hold of her spine at the neck and doing her best to pull the dead girl's skull off. Cynthia broke her hold and decked her across the face with the butt of her rifle, which drove Califia to her knees but hardly stopped her. She grabbed Iverson's leg to pull her off balance and the private had to kick her aside.

The queen wasn't going to be able to hurt the dead girl, but she wasn't going to quit trying, either. Not even if she ended up hurting herself. So Iverson was right: better to kill her for a moment or two than beat her down in a way that would last. Ingrid couldn't watch any more of that.

"Do what you have to," she instructed Iverson. "Efficiently, please."

The yellow-haired soldier shot Califia professionally in the back of the head. The queen of the Aztecs' ancestors collapsed and lay still, instantly. Face down. Ingrid felt sick, and her eyes blurred with tears.

"I'm sorry," Iverson said.

"I don't want to see that again," Ingrid told her. "So let's *move*."

They did, Ingrid, Iverson, and the rest of her unit, now diminished by the two men the ladydemons had 'eaten,' or at least taken out, whose ultimate fates were still unknown. The remaining Corpse Soldiers kept the path ahead clear of Tzitzimime only with sustained gunfire, and still the bugwomen kept trying for them, spreading out into loose swarms to avoid the sting of bullets and then clumping back into humanoid forms to make a grab whenever they saw a chance for it.

The people who'd been cut down by the Corpse Soldiers' weapons, fearsome Shorn Ones included, were up again, and angry. Dying by violence couldn't be fun, even if you recovered from it twenty minutes later. They came after Ingrid and her military escort, wielding sharp or heavy objects, pounding down the foothill paths and then across the open prairies that surrounded Death's Pyramid, and more of the people joined them as they ran. They had the distinct advantage, both because they knew the landscape and because running was their primary form of transportation. Ingrid hadn't seen a single wheel in the weeks she'd spent in the village. The people were mere yards behind the Corpse Soldiers by the time the mud-brick pyramid came into view. Dozens of enraged men and women, maybe hundreds of them, all hellbent on murdering their tribe's attackers.

Califia was near the rear of the crowd, running after them. Ingrid glimpsed her when she looked back. She got over her deaths quicker than most of her people, but that wasn't so surprising. The queen had long since shown an unusual level of determination, and an ability to roll with the punches that matched.

Ingrid was going to miss her.

"I know you don't like us shooting them," Iverson said. "But…"

"No, do it," Ingrid panted. "As many as you can. Make it as ugly as you can."

"Huh? Why?"

None of the soldiers had any taste for that sort of action. The damage done by their guns may have been illusory, but it still looked as real as anything they remembered from their life experiences.

"So that maybe they'll tear down that fucking pyramid after we're gone!" Ingrid yelled, and Iverson nodded, seeing the point in that. They were barely a hundred yards from the structure in question.

She shouted an order and made a hand signal, and the Corpse Soldiers closed around Ingrid, all of them facing out. They opened fire in every direction, mowing down both Tzitzimime and the Nahuatlaca people indiscriminately. Iverson herself covered the skies with her rifle, ripping Wasp from the air as she dove out of the darkness with her glistening stinger thrust forward, meaning to impale.

Califia, on a hillside blessedly just out of range, went to her knees as she wailed in grief and terror, both for her love and for her people.

It tortured Ingrid to look at her. She had both hands clamped over her ears, and still the gunfire was deafening.

The people went down like ranks of toppled dominoes, falling away from the soldiers in concentric rings.

It didn't take but minutes to clear the field, though it felt like an hour. There was dark blood everywhere.

When the last of the people were either dead or scattered, the Corpse Soldiers stopped firing, and the ensuing silence seemed nearly as loud as their guns had been. Ingrid's abused ears rang steadily.

None of the people would forget this experience, even after their mortal wounds evaporated like holdovers from a nightmare.

Still, Califia came running across the fields, after her goddess.

"Get upstairs, and be quick about it," Ingrid said to Private Iverson. "Tell Mickey to call off his bugs. I'm sorry about setting them on you. I didn't know what I was doing at the time."

Iverson nodded grimly and signaled for her men to follow her up the side of the pyramid, back to the realm of the dead. They'd retrieved their objective; their job was done. Ingrid knew she was on her own now.

She turned to catch Califia up in her arms as the queen ran to her.

The former midwife was sobbing, keening, babbling hysterically at her in that odd glottal tongue—ancient Nahuatl—of which Ingrid had only picked up the barest rudiments during her weeks in the village. She hugged the dark-skinned woman and rocked her, trying to calm her, while remaining keenly aware that she should depart before the rest of the tribe returned or revived. Poor Califia had just died three times and watched the rest of her people massacred, however, and she needed a goddamn moment.

When she stopped pleading, weeping, and clutching at her, Ingrid pulled away. Califia mimed that she would go with Ingrid up the pyramid, and Ingrid shook her head. No, she didn't want that. She couldn't risk it. Califia's first affinity was with life, not with death. Mickey had told her so himself. Ingrid had no way of knowing for sure, but she felt in her gut that it was her deep attachment to the solid, physical, sensuous world— to all that might be symbolized by the element of earth, the substance from which all life arises and to which all life eventually returns—that accounted for her own mysterious free pass. An alignment with the fire of generation would tend to have the opposite effect, she feared, when one came to cross the threshold between the worlds. If Califia followed her back to Mictlan, she'd be stuck there for good as one of the dead, and Ingrid wasn't ready to take up permanent residence in the King's realm herself. She was going back to 1910, where the Queen of California could not follow.

Ingrid wouldn't have her give up the rest of her life just because they couldn't say goodbye.

Ingrid put a hand to her breast, indicating herself, then gestured toward the hundreds of motionless, bloodspattered bodies that littered the fields around the pyramid, claiming responsibility for them. Califia shook her head, vehemently denying a connection between her love and the shocking carnage on display all around.

Ingrid insisted, though, letting the queen know with her eyes that it was true. These things would never have happened if she (or Mictlancihuatl, who was not *quite* her) had never come.

Accepting it seemed to break Califia's heart, but Ingrid thought it might not yet be too late to help her, or at least to leave her with something that would help her carry on.

Ingrid picked up a stone-headed war club from where someone had dropped it as they fled from the Corpse Soldiers' guns. She bashed it against the pyramid, once, twice, and a third time, until a brick cracked, broke, and she could pull a chunk of it loose.

This pyramid could come down much more readily than the stone examples to the south that had yet to be built by these peoples' descendants, but which would ultimately survive into Ingrid's native time.

She threw the chunk of mud brick to the ground and handed the club to Califia. Her meaning seemed clear, and the queen nodded, though the sadness looked like it would never leave her eyes.

Ingrid embraced her, one last time, then started up the side of Death's original Pyramid.

Behind her, with a scream, Califia began to lay into the mud-brick mountain with her stone hammer, raining down blow after blow.

I T was a hike up to the top.
When Ingrid was a third of the way there she risked a look back. The people were just then beginning to revive, waking from imagined deaths with amazement and relief. Every chunk the queen tore from the structure seemed to resurrect another man or woman, and they joined her in beating at the temple's brick sides with clubs, rocks, or hammers, tearing it down from the corners in, following their monarch's example.

The climb was exhausting, and Ingrid had started it weary. By the time she reached the top, the stairs had shifted perceptibly beneath her feet. The pyramid was steep; with even a bit of support removed from the base, it was fast becoming unstable. A considerable portion of the building's west face avalanched away, scattering the shouting, excited people down on the ground below, even as Ingrid stood there watching over it all from the brickpile's precarious peak. More people were coming all the time, returning from hiding or waking from apparent death, and they all pitched in to help rip down the Pyramid of the Dead, seeming to think that the effort they were making was the thing effecting the tribe's magical restoration. They believed they wouldn't be safe until their artificial mountain had been scrubbed from the landscape. And Ingrid knew their queen wouldn't be safe—not until her access to the King's Chambers was cut off, for good.

Ingrid turned and stepped through the stone doorway that someone had long ago built without ever knowing it would one day frame a hole in the sky, a hole between worlds. Its lintels looked crooked now. Misaligned.

Mickey was waiting for her inside his Chambers, standing at the threshold of the door between the two rooms. That was as far as he could go, the very edge of his world.

"My love," he said sardonically. "Have you enjoyed your trip?"

Ingrid glared at him and looked back out the door as several tons' worth of the realworld structure's south side fell away with a resounding crash. The occurrence was greeted by the people down below with an equally resounding cheer.

"Return to me," Mickey instructed.

"In a damn minute," Ingrid said, without looking at him. The people were by now swarming the last of the pyramid, destroying it with whatever implements were to hand, all with the queen's vocal encouragement.

"Tzitzimime," the King said, sounding bored. "Escort her."

The bugs poured from the cracks in the room's brick walls. They came together quickly, congealing into armor-plated, multilimbed women. Wasp and Mantis and Ant fanned out to surround her, while Spider darted right in, meaning to subdue her and drag her back to the other side, probably bound up in some sort of disgusting webbing.

In a flash, with a motion as quick and graceful as that of a silver fish arcing from a glassy lake, Ingrid unsheathed the knife she wore on her thigh and threw it.

The blade caught Spider right between—or rather, right *amidst*—her multiple eyes.

The ladydemon's feet went out from under her and she slammed to the rough floor on her back, scrabbling at the length of steel lodged in her head with at least four of her eight limbs.

All beings Ingrid was aware of were organized on the intangible level as strings of subtle energy centers, and she'd bullseyed Spider through her uppermost point, the one she supposed would correspond to an *ajna chakra* on a human. It was the seat of intelligence and self-knowledge according to the Hindu system she knew—a point otherwise called the Third Eye. Half-visible blue energy seemed to spew from the bugwoman's bifurcated head, like an ongoing fireworks display, and the other three monsters shied back from their downed sister.

Even Mickey looked surprised.

Spider thrashed and shook on the floor like she was having a seizure. Her individual bugs exploded apart and tried to come back together again, but they couldn't seem to find the trick of it anymore. They scrambled into a headless suggestion of the humanoid form they remembered, but it wouldn't cohere. Finally the hundreds of tiny arachnids retreated into the walls as the Spider Tzitzimitl's top chakra deflated and dispersed like a ring of dark blue smoke. Her three remaining points of semi-perceptible light wiggled away together, through the doorway, past Mickey and back into the realm of the dead. Ingrid didn't imagine the damaged demon would ever be able to take on a humanoid form again.

She retrieved her knife from the stone floor.

"I *said* I'll come back when I'm good and ready, and not a *minute* before," she told the King as she slid the blade back into its sheath on her ivory thigh.

"As you would have it," he said, gesturing for the other three bugwomen to retreat. They did so gratefully, breaking down into insects to hurry past him, retreating into the safety of his realm.

Ingrid leaned against the side of the doorway that opened out onto the realworld, and she watched as the people of Aztlán demolished Death's Pyramid, right out from under her.

Within a few hours it was already losing the shape that defined it. The stairs fell away into sheer cliffs a quarter of the way from the top. The people daisychained the broken pieces away into the fields, and children smashed them up further with rocks before they scattered them far and wide. By the time the moon had crossed the sky the false mountain's summit was teetering, and just after dawn, it fell. Ingrid stood where she was as the roof and walls crumbled away around her, to the vocal astonishment of the people observing from below. The pyramid tumbled but the goddess remained, framed in a hole in the sky. One final miracle for all to see.

If the people wanted to believe they'd been resurrected because their goddess-made-flesh had restored some equilibrium between the worlds by leaving them, that was their business. They'd need a way to make sense of the things they'd seen.

"What happens to them?" Ingrid asked, back over her shoulder. "To her? Can you tell me?"

From his doorway, Mickey shrugged. "Under her leadership they migrate south, and there begin again. They remember this place and these happenings only in tales they half-believe. The first Spaniards will not hear of her legend for some six hundred years."

Ingrid nodded. She raised her hand in farewell, and Queen Califia, torch-lit on the distant ground, did the same. The pyramid would soon be gone but the Hole in the Sky would remain, as would knowledge of its location. Ingrid knew that before they left someone amongst the people would plant a tree to mark the spot. Someone would have to, if any of this were to happen.

Ingrid turned away and strode back into Mictlan, brushing past

Mickey and into the sacrificial chamber. "You figured out how the nows are meant to be arranged while I was away, didn't you?" she asked.

"One after the next, yes," Mickey said, with a razor grin. "It is quite beautiful, in its way. I thank you for the lesson."

Ingrid ignored his gratitude. "Did you know what would happen when I went out there?" she asked, meaning the amnesia, the inability to accept the truth of herself and her existence under the weight of social belief and apparent reality that had accompanied the loss of her name. She'd had to live out what the world around her would accept, as a way to assimilate her experience. It was how the realworld had defended its boundaries, by inclining her to believe what made the most sense, whether or not it was true. She knew that now.

"I did not know," Mickey said.

She held up the garnet Private Iverson had delivered. "But you knew to send this, to remind me?"

"I made an experiment, and I was rewarded," said the King. "You remembered yourself, and now you are free to walk at will, provided you carry your talisman with you."

"Well... thank you, anyway," Ingrid said, examining the dark red stone before looking up. "Where are the Corpse Soldiers, and Cynthia? I should thank them too."

Mickey looked mildly surprised. "My Tzitzimime needed to feed after their exertions," he said. "You did give permission, they said. They are not smart enough to lie."

Ingrid stared at him, appalled. "They're just gone, then?" she asked. "That girl? Her men? Just gone?"

"You did give permission," Mickey reminded, and Ingrid hung her head. Cynthia Iverson hadn't seemed all that satisfied with her lot in the afterlife, but all of the soldiers had balked at the thought of not existing, period.

Ingrid didn't know how to feel.

"I think I'd like to go home now," she said softly. "Can we do that?"

"All you need do is think of when you would go," Mickey said. "Imagine the span between that then and this now."

"That's all?"

"Will you not be satisfied unless it's complicated? Such things are merely a matter of perspective."

For you, maybe, Ingrid thought, but she closed her eyes without comment and quickly inventoried what she knew of the next millennium. The Crusades and the Dark Ages. The Renaissance. The New World. The American Revolution and the War Between the States. Westward expansion and electrical technology, right up to and including the very first movie shot in Los Angeles, in which Ingrid herself had played a small part. That had been more than a year ago, and a thousand years in the future. Four thousand individual seasons.

When she opened her eyes, the night sky out beyond the hole looked just the same.

"Did anything happen?" she asked.

Mickey nodded toward the far doorway and Ingrid turned, surprised to see a young man climbing up into the first room beyond the Hole in the Sky.

He was tall, big-shouldered and black-haired, perhaps a year or two younger than Ingrid. He seemed better equipped for the climb up the tree than she had been, laden as he was with ropes, packs, and fancy mountaineering harnesses. He still looked weary from the effort, though. His clothing looked appropriate to Ingrid's era—the electric dawn of the 20th century.

"Who is he?" she murmured.

"His family name is San Martín," Mickey said. "Called Oscar. He is pledged to me, as was his father before him. He comes to curry favor."

Oscar San Martín hauled himself up onto the floor of the first room and lay there for a moment, catching his breath. When he rolled over and saw both Ingrid and the King standing in the far doorway, he sat up quick.

"Mictlantecuhtli," he said, and Mictlantecuhtli tipped his cowled skull in acknowledgement. Ingrid hadn't even noticed the King changing forms, giving up his illusion of living skin, it had happened so quickly.

"You gonna be tormenting us with visions now?" San Martín asked of him, with a grin, as he rolled a salacious eye down the length of Ingrid's body. She remembered that her breasts were still uncovered, after the fashion of her proto-Aztec friends.

When Ingrid stepped out of the otherworld, across the threshold and into the first chamber, the young initiate named Oscar backpedaled so fast he was in danger of tumbling right back out through the Hole in the Sky.

"You—you crossed," he said, looking at Ingrid with eyes the size of dinner plates. "It's still three weeks before he can send anybody out."

"Then this is October?" Ingrid said.

"October eleventh."

"October eleventh, nineteen...?"

"You don't know what *year* it is, lady?" San Martín seemed understandably incredulous.

Ingrid just waited.

"It's 1910," San Martín said.

"Thank you."

Ingrid went to the door that opened onto the realworld and looked down. The familiar tree was there, its topmost canopy some three or four feet below her, its leaves silvered in the moonlight. She didn't know how in the hell she was supposed to get back down. Perhaps Oscar could be moved to help with some of his climbing equipment.

"Sure you don't want to get people to put up a building in this era?" she joked in Mickey's direction. "Maybe a nice skyscraper? Something with stairs, or even an elevator?"

"As you wish it," the King said, and when Ingrid looked back down, the Tree was gone.

Below her, far below, was a concrete foundation inset with steel girders. The metal skeleton reached up to and around the Hole in the Sky, like an exercise in perspective.

There was a building going up, just like that, out there in the realworld.

Because she'd made a joke about it.

Ingrid looked back at Mictlantecuhtli, astounded. Oscar San Martín was still staring at her with no less amazement, although something about him had subtly changed as well. He looked more... serious, somehow. Studious, maybe. She couldn't tell.

"How?" was all she said.

Mictlantecuhtli tipped his skull toward his human servant. "The subtlest alteration in the position of moments can have remarkable effects down the timeline, I have found," he said. "I have changed the history of this one, to make him a man capable of fashioning the thing you have requested."

"You changed his past?"

"In small ways, at key moments, yes. He studies 'architecture' now, with a passion. The art of building, which his ancestors amongst the old people knew as well. As you have seen. Does his work please you, my love?"

"It'll make it easier to come and go, I guess," Ingrid said, looking back down at her incipient skyscraper. "When it's finished."

She didn't dare to ask why it hadn't appeared complete, why it was still under construction. Had the old god miscalculated? She sensed that Mickey might not take perceived criticism very well, and kept her questions to herself.

"You will return to me, then?" Mictlantecuhtli asked.

"You know I will," Ingrid said, thinking only on her second take that he might *really* know—that he might be able to look into other moments and see if she was there. Plus, there were all the possibilities that knowing him opened up, as well as the lingering heat of her own physical attraction to his favorite lifelike avatar. (She was glad he hadn't chosen a blue one with multiple limbs, like some Hindu deity-made-flesh.) "How could I not come back here?" she asked, somewhat rhetorically.

El Rey de Los Muertos nodded. "My living servant will escort you down, if that be your wish," he said. San Martín seemed to pale at the suggestion.

Ingrid nodded, absently. She wanted to say something more, but she found herself at a loss. Since she knew she'd be back anyway, probably within days, she simply turned on her heel and walked away.

Outside the Hole, in the wan moonlight, she had to inch her careful way down a single girder to an 'elevator' at the corner of the new structure. The lift looked more like a cage that wouldn't hold a sickly dog than a sound method of conveyance, but there was room on its rattling platform for both her and Oscar, who clearly knew how to operate the thing, even though it hadn't existed ten minutes before.

He was staring at her, Oscar was, searching her face somewhat too avidly. She would've felt more comfortable if he'd been looking at her still-naked breasts.

"Who *are* you?" he asked. "That you can cross back and forth like it's nothing at all?"

Ingrid thought about it. Who was she indeed, that she could do such a thing? She had no idea, really. She was the one who'd done it, though, and maybe that was all she needed to be.

She looked out across the dark landscape as Oscar the architect started the elevator clanking downward. It was powered by a gasoline engine.

"Do you remember what you were before?" Ingrid asked, over the noise.

"What?" Oscar said, and Ingrid shook her head. She barely remembered what *she'd* been before. A performer, a thespian, and a singer, yes. A lost girl who'd abandoned the glamorous affectations and the self-abusive habits of her riotous life in London not when they became a detriment to her health or an unsupportable drain on her finances, but only when they failed to amuse her. Or, perhaps more truthfully, when they no longer were sufficient to distract her from the despair and meaninglessness that always threatened when laughter or lust ran out. From the fear that there was nothing more to do or know or focus on beyond distractions, and the games that people played.

She'd become an initiate of the ancient mysteries in response to that fear, becoming first a member of the Golden Dawn and then later of the Golden Chain—affiliations that others of her acquaintance cultivated in the name of slightly wicked fun, but which for Ingrid had involved a serious quest for obscure knowledge. She'd learned what those groups would teach her and stolen those secrets they wouldn't share, and then struck out on her own, looking for something she knew she would recognize only when she found it.

And now, as of this morning, she was a time traveler, perhaps the first or even the only one *ever*, as well as the lover of a god, the intimate of a queen, and a tourist just returned from a trip through the land of the dead. A Eurydice who'd brought *herself* back from the underworld, and done a better job of it than Orpheus ever had, in any version of the tale.

They reached ground level, and Oscar opened the elevator cage to let Ingrid out.

A second man was waiting, a rather tall white man, leaning against the front fender of a brand new horseless carriage that he'd parked at the far corner of what had been a field, and was now a cleared and graded lot. Though she didn't know his name, Ingrid recognized him straightaway, from the Temple of the Ordo Aurea Catena in downtown Los Angeles. She quailed for an instant, sure she'd been caught out (seeing as she *had* stolen her map to this place from the OAC archives), before she realized it was most likely that the tall man had done the very same thing in order to get here. Copied out the same old map, which meant he had the same call to worry about her that she did about him.

She figured she was safe enough from the gangly motorist, even if he recognized her too.

He saw her and Oscar coming and met them halfway across the lot, holding open a long duster coat so that half-naked Ingrid might slip into it.

"You must be cold," he said in a dry British accent.

Ingrid took the hammered cuffs of pre-Columbian gold off her arms before she shrugged into the coat, and gave one cuff each to Oscar and the Englishman, like a tip.

"Come for me, if I call for you?" Ingrid said, both to the Brit and to San Martín. The King's Men. "I'll want to go back up, after I sleep for about a year."

El Rey's human servants looked down at the brand new antiquities they'd just been given—a small fortune in precious metal and cultural history—and both of them nodded.

"But who *are* you, anyway?" San Martín blurted, as Ingrid let the tall Englishman lead her off toward his waiting motor car. The sky was lightening, a literal golden dawn moments away from breaking.

Ingrid Redstone paused and looked back at the King's architect, Oscar San Martín.

"I'm the greatest witch who ever lived," she told him.

NEXT TIME:
Episode Two
MAD GODS & IRISHMEN

MAD GODS & IRISHMEN

Chapter One

—Los Angeles, 1910

INGRID didn't wait so much as a week before going back to him.

She wanted to wait; she wanted him to see her as cool and aloof, even in the face of the wonders he offered. She knew that would've been the safest thing.

The problem was, she just couldn't do it.

She had her comfortable room downtown, at the Hotel Angelus, on the corner of Spring and Fourth. The tab for the suite was paid by the Selig-Polyscope Motion Picture Company, and even though Ingrid knew she was welcome to use it for as long as she liked without ever seeing a bill, she no longer felt entirely safe there. Like someone might be watching her. Or at least looking for her, thinking about her, if not actually on to her yet. She would wake in the night feeling exposed, certain she was somehow visible, and could only sleep again through many mental repetitions of her mantra-like banishing rituals. There was no evidence of surveillance by the light of day, no concrete reason for suspicion, but the sensation persisted, and presentiments of danger were never to be ignored, no matter how vague, unfocused, or frustrating they might be.

After yet another in a series of largely sleepless nights (during which she'd lain awake quivering less with paranoia, truth be told, than with carnal musings about her King), she called through the hotel's switchboard for Winston Watt, the King's Englishman, and instructed him to come fetch her at noon in his fancy new auto-mobile. He had the Model T idling at the curb in front of the Angelus a minute or two better than right on time, when she stepped out from under the grand arch of the hotel's wide front doors.

She knew he didn't want word getting back that he'd been anything less than conscientious in the performance of his duties.

"Lady," he said, and Ingrid acknowledged him only with a nod. Mr. Watt didn't know her name, and that was how she wanted to keep it. Learning his had been a matter of sneaking a quick peek at the registration papers he kept in his horseless cart's glove compartment, stuffed back behind an extra pair of goggles, when he'd stopped to re-fuel on the occasion of their one previous meeting. She'd memorized his exchange number at that time too, from the same document. Receiving a telephonic summons from her this morning had no doubt shocked him, but he'd turned up, motivated both by the golden Aztec artifact she'd bought him off with the last time they met, and by the sure knowledge that their King would expect no less.

Watt held his car's door open for her now, and took her kid-gloved hand to help her up into the back seat. She knew it irritated him that she wouldn't sit up front and converse, that she was once again making him chauffer her around like a goddamn domestic when he too was a fully-fledged initiate of the King's mysteries, and entitled to more respect. At least that's the way he seemed to have it figured. His take on the situation may or may not have been valid, but Ingrid knew better than to get familiar with Winston Watt. He was welcome to think of her as a haughty, superior bitch, if it maintained that valuable distance between them.

Besides which, didn't she have good reason to feel superior, when all was said and done? Wasn't she a unique creature? So far no other had come along to disabuse her of the notion.

The fact of the matter was, she could cross the barrier between the worlds, where neither Watt, the King's Englishman, nor San Martín, the King's young architect, would ever follow. Or *could* ever follow, not without forfeiting their lives, while Ingrid hopped back and forth between life and death like it was nothing at all. The King's men had never seen anyone pull such a trick before. She'd known it from the expression on San Martín's face the first time he saw her exit the Inner Sanctum with her flesh still on her bones. The doorway into the King's realm only worked one way for the rest of the human race, so far as any of them knew. All were free to enter, but anyone else attempting to leave by that portal was apt to find it quite impassable.

So didn't that entitle her to just a touch of personal pride?

Ingrid truly wasn't sure. How was one supposed to feel about an enviable feat performed effortlessly, one which others would never manage at all?

These were the sorts of thoughts that populated the landscape of her mind as Watt piloted them west down Beverly Boulevard, skirting the increasingly bohemian township of Hollywood that lay directly to the north.

THE construction site wasn't really so far from civilization, despite the troubles Ingrid and other supplicants continued to experience when trying to find it. The Tree that had grown on it for a thousand years was gone now, chopped into a Pyramid's worth of firewood, but the Hole in the Sky remained above the place where it once stood.

The web of hexes that had cloaked the old encino from profane eyes was still there too, in spite of the sacred Tree's unanticipated erasure from reality. Ingrid found herself disoriented when they were still a good ten minutes out from their destination, and she knew she would've lost her way, had she been navigating. Watt's solution to the problem of overcoming the wards' befuddling influence came in the form of tiny peyote buttons he chewed on as he drove, one by one, like they were hard candies. Ingrid knew how horrid the dried cactus flesh was apt to taste (she would've preferred a marginally more palatable mushroom to achieve the same end, herself), but its bitterness had no discernible effect on Winston's already sour expression. The plant's potent alkaloids did nothing for his disposition, even though Ingrid saw that his pupils had widened to quite an alarming degree when she happened to catch a glimpse of his eyes in the auto's rearview mirror.

How often had Watt come and gone from the King's Chambers that mescaline visions no longer impressed or disoriented him at *all*? That the psychoactive succulent's acrid, aspirin-like flavor didn't draw so much as a twitch or a grimace out of him?

She knew that Winston, for one, was deeply jealous of her unprecedented status, and that made her nervous. It wasn't the first time she'd ever been envied, but this resentment was of a different order than any of the backstage cattiness she'd experienced in her previous life as an actress. This ran deeper than life and death, for Mr. Watt. She didn't know if it was worth trying to explain to him that their King wasn't intentionally showing her special favor; that Mictlantecuhtli was as baffled by her unimpeded comings and goings as anyone else. She doubted Watt would ever believe her about that. Not now, when there was so much palpable animosity coloring his assumptions.

Her eyes kept wandering away from the bucolic farmlands he drove her past and onto the back of his balding head. She had to wonder what sorts of dark schemes might be rattling around inside that depilated cranium as it shone in the bright mid-day sun.

REACHING the build site in Watt's vehicle took them little more than an hour, where it might've taken a quarter of a day to get there on horseback. Ingrid loved riding and all things equine, but even she had to admit that the convenience offered by internal combustion technology had its place. She could have Watt ferry her downtown for lunch and still be back out here in time for afternoon tea, at this rate of speed.

Although, with her Mickey, in his realm, any time was teatime, if that's what she desired. Teatime or party time, a banquet or a ball, an afternoon stroll down a bustling metropolitan street or a night spent lounging by a mountaintop campfire, primordially isolated from all the worlds. Anything she wanted, whatever she might conceive. Nothing was beyond the talents of her King. Mictlantecuhtli was the ultimate set designer, bent on seeing every nuance of his elaborate productions realized in rich and convincing detail. He drew the imagery he based them on straight from the memories of his subjects: the dead of every time and place.

Only the skies above never really changed, no matter what Mickey did. The ceiling might darken from a pale silver to an ominous charcoal (depending on the hour being depicted), but one way or the other, the weather in the netherworld was eternally gray.

Ingrid squinted and adjusted the broad, beribboned brim of her hat when Winston held the door open for her and she stepped out of the motorcar, thinking that the denim-blue dome overhead made for quite a sharp contrast with Mictlan's eternal gloom.

To think, her Mickey had never seen a blue sky, and never would. Such things were not a part of his world.

THE building-to-be was just across the newly graded dirt street, miles away from anything else. Ingrid wasn't patient enough to wait for its completion. She felt all activity grind to a momentary halt as the work crews became aware of her. She looked up into the cross-hatching of steel beams that would one day soon be a skyscraper, shielding her eyes with her hand, and several men in flat caps and suspenders waved down at her, not quite salaciously. There were no whistles or catcalls. They feared the reputation of her lover, their boss, (whom none of them had ever met), far too much to be impolite.

But they were aware of her. Down to the last man.

Well, she had dressed to make an impression, hadn't she? She'd spent much of the previous afternoon with the tailors and hairdressers housed in the basement of the Hotel Angelus, depleting her savings by an unreasonable yet satisfying degree. The result had been a smart new suit, yards of creamy pinstriped linen cut to hug her every curve. The ankle-length skirt clung to the extravagant arc of her hips, while a belt of deep red silk that matched her plumed hat cinched in tight at her waist. Her collar was high, her sleeves turned back at the wrist, not a single inch of flesh on inappropriate display, and yet she might as well have stepped naked from the car like Venus from her half-shell for the hush that fell over the otherwise bustling site.

She hoped to have a similar effect on Mickey.

Oscar San Martín, the King's Architect, was the one who broke the silence. He came ratcheting down the side of the skyscraper-to-be in the flimsy-looking, gasoline-powered lift the workers used to ascend to their lofty yet menial tasks. He spotted Ingrid straightaway and scolded his men back to work in Spanish before he crossed the construction site and then the road to greet her.

"He said we should be expecting you," San Martín told her, nodding an informal hello as he walked up. He was aiming for nonchalance, and yet he stopped a few feet further back from her than social and conversational norms might dictate. He made an admirable effort to look her in the eye, though it made his stare feel a little too direct.

It was like he was afraid to stand too close, as if she were a fire and he feared being burned.

Ingrid had to admit he might be wise to feel that way. Their King was nothing if not the jealous type.

She took off her floppy scarlet hat, and the blazing red hair she revealed in doing so no doubt reinforced San Martín's inflamed impression of her. "Did you think there was a chance I wouldn't be back?" she asked. She supposed she'd done so rhetorically, but he had an answer for her nonetheless:

"I *thought* there was a chance you were something I dreamed."

His tone made it sound like he'd been hoping this might be the case. Like it would've made his life easier should she somehow happen to not exist.

Well, she was sorry to disappoint him. Except she wasn't, really.

Oscar San Martín seemed like a nice enough man. He was nice looking, anyway, embodying the sort of affable strength that might afford him the space to be thoughtful and kind. The handsome young architect with a builder's powerful hands might've quite fired Ingrid's imagination at another, earlier point in her life... but in comparison to Mickey, he barely registered.

She brushed past him, headed for the corner of the structure with the elevator attached. She was taller than him in her heels, she noticed. San Martín seemed to notice it too. She sensed him exchanging a glance with Winston Watt, behind her back.

"We mustn't keep el Rey waiting," she said, though all three of them were well aware of the absurdity of that particular statement. Time was little more than an interesting novelty to Mickey.

The King's Men dutifully followed after her, and that solemn hush washed over the workforce once again as she passed amongst the laborers. They were a paint-spattered collection of stout, muscular men in leather hardhats and coarse practical clothes—several dozen of them at least. Perhaps more than a hundred. The cumulative weight of all their eyes on her was considerable. Ingrid knew they talked amongst themselves, and that she was a regular subject of their gossip. To them she was *la Bruja Roja*, the Red Witch, an appellation she rather enjoyed, while Mickey was simply the King. El Rey. Speculation was rife regarding just what it was they got up to, all the way up there in the prematurely finished office suite, where only she, San Martín, and Winston Watt were privileged to tread.

Ingrid refused to let the whispers bother her. What did any of them know, about anything? Even Watt and San Martín, with their years of experience of the King, were woefully ignorant when compared with her, the old god's newest, truest intimate.

She felt a hollow quivery thrill deep in the pit of her stomach at the thought of seeing him again.

She stepped up onto the lift platform and turned around, holding up a hand to stop San Martín from boarding the contraption with her. "Just send me up from here. You can do that, can't you?"

San Martín nodded reluctantly. Watt looked smugly vindicated, though he did a masterful job of not letting it linger on his face for long. The elevator could only bear the weight of two passengers at once, and so he would've had to wait like a second-class servant for it to become available again before he could ascend and join them to see whatever there was to be seen. This way he'd still have to wait, but now Oscar would have to wait with him (and Ingrid would be through Death's door and long out of sight by the time they could follow her up to the modern room that now surrounded the fabled Hole in the Sky).

So the race for second place in Mictlantecuhtli's affections was well and truly on. The notion amused her and made her nervous, in almost equal measure.

"Good afternoon, then, Soror Bonum Irrumabo," Watt said, as San Martín drew the safety gate and depressed the button that started the elevator rising, and his words made her blood run cold.

He'd addressed her by the Latin motto she used as a name within LA's Ordo Aurea Catena, as did all initiates of the Order of the Golden Chain (as the organization was known in English). Nobody was supposed to know anyone else's real name, by tradition, and Ingrid had held fast to that rule in all of her dealings with the OAC, even though few other members did.

So she didn't think Watt could've learned her true name yet, though he was certainly letting her know that he'd been doing some detective work of his own. Trying to frighten her, judging by the self-satisfied smirk on his upturned face. San Martín shot him a funny look, having failed to understand the unfamiliar salutation he'd used.

Well, fuck him anyway, Ingrid thought. If knowledge of her secret ceremonial pseudonym was the only card Watt had to play, she didn't think he presented much of a danger.

Although that (like everything else) was apt to change, given time.

SHE turned her face away from the King's Men and squinted up into the cerulean sky as the lift raised her high above them. She could barely see her destination through the sun's glare: a boxy squirrel's nest of plaster and planks nestled high amidst the sturdy steel branches of the framework that had sprung up to replace the monumental Tree. It grew larger in her field of vision as she drew closer: one single suite of rooms at the heart of the top floor finished off well ahead of schedule, even before the corridor that would eventually lead to it. She'd have to scuttle down a long girder to get there, like some sort of remedial acrobat.

But to think, the last time she'd approached this place, her only choice had been to climb the ancient oak, as uncounted scores of supplicants had done before her, across the centuries. Watt and San Martín were only the latest of these, though San Martín's father had also served before him, apparently. (Ingrid managed to hear more gossip than anybody knew, given all of these men's reluctance to speak openly around her. It helped that she had more Spanish under her belt than anybody realized.)

Now, today, late in the year 1910, a visit to the Hole in the Sky involved nothing more than rattling, chugging, petroleum-scented modern convenience.

The combined effect of gasoline fumes and vertigo made Ingrid queasy as the car lurched and swayed, and looking up compounded the problem. She stared hard at the horizon to clear her swimming head, as she'd long ago learned to do aboard a rocking ship. She was gripping the rail at the side of the platform so hard her palms were starting to ache.

Then she was there, at the top. Alone in the sky. The elevator engine's relentless rumble died away, leaving behind only the whine of autumnal wind as it blew around bare girders. That and the muffled thud of Ingrid's own pulse, hammering palpably in her chest, in her throat, and in her ears.

She stepped off the elevator platform and onto the girder she'd have to shuffle down. Her red satin shoes looked incongruous against the thin steel beam. It wasn't unnecessarily thin, she understood, as building materials went, but it seemed miniscule when it was all she had to stand on, more than a hundred feet up in the air.

She shifted her foot an inch to the left, blocking out the sight of Watt and San Martín's tiny, upturned faces with the toe of her crimson shoe. That felt better, though she could still see all of the other workmen dotted around the site staring up at her in a similar fashion. It made her wish for a few dozen more feet.

Ingrid sighed and looked straight ahead. She took hold of the rope that was tied taut between the structure's two largest upright beams at chest level, then began her careful shuffle down the girder. Toward a Hole in the Sky that was now, through her own nearly accidental intervention, just a Door Between Rooms.

The poetry of it all had been damaged a bit by her last rewrite of reality. *Oh well*, she thought. *C'est la vie.* Or *c'est la vie après la mort*, as she supposed was more properly the case.

She kept her eyes level, fixed on the door to the suite, with no looking up, down, or anywhere around until she'd reached the office and gingerly stepped off the beam, into the first chamber. Her long legs felt far less substantial, at the moment, than the reassuringly solid floor she now had beneath her feet. She could've dropped to her knees and pressed both hands to that floor just to appreciate its carpeted breadth and its level dependability.

She didn't do that, however. It would've spoiled the entrance she wanted to make.

The King of the Dead was already waiting for her, framed in the door on the far side of the first room. The doorway that was really a portal between worlds, one through which Mictlantecuhtli himself could never pass. Ingrid had every reason to believe he was indivisible from Mictlan, the otherworldly realm that shared his name.

He'd dressed in anticipation of her arrival, this time around. Dressed both in pleasing flesh and in striking black tie. Mickey's shirt was as crisp as a sheet of new paper, and his silk jacket seemed to absorb the warm torchlight that flickered in the chamber behind him. His lustrous hair was brushed back from his brow in deep grooves. His almond eyes sparkled when he grinned. He looked as dashing as a movie star, and Ingrid applauded his efforts, quietly and politely, like a golf spectator. El Rey's fallback position was to appear as a bloodstreaked skeleton wrapped in a billowing cloak and cowl, so she knew this transfiguration meant he was happy to see her, as well as eager to please.

She tried not to let her delight with his choices show too much. His ego was easier to feed than a brushfire, and he was still wearing his traditional necklace of human eyes over his dinner jacket—a sight which helped to temper her enthusiasm.

"My love," he rumbled, in that sonorous tone of his that made Ingrid feel like licking her lips or shifting her weight from hip to hip, as if to twitch an invisible tail.

"Mickey," she said, crossing the first room to offer her hand. He took it, through the doorway, and kissed the back of her cream-colored glove as she asked: "How've you been?"

"I am as I am," the King replied, looking a little puzzled as he straightened up and looked her over from head to toe. He was as he'd always been, of course, and would forever be.

"That's good," she said, then trailed off, unsure of what to say next. A charged silence spun out between them. Mickey didn't seem at all uncomfortable with it. His sharky grin grew wider, if anything.

Ingrid drew her hand back and stepped past him, forestalling the first inevitable kiss.

She skirted the blood-darkened altar stone where Mictlantecuhtli unfleshed the recent dead, leaving him to follow. She didn't spare the grisly rock so much as a glance before stepping out through the chamber's far door and into the afterlife proper.

Mickey did follow, out into his realm's weak approximation of sunlight, and together they surveyed his expansive view.

MICTLAN seemed to stretch away forever, far below them. Mickey hadn't bothered to replace his Pyramid here in this realm, Ingrid noticed, despite the swapping of Tree for Tower he'd set into motion over on the realworld side of the SkyHole, at her request. He was now two structures behind the times as she perceived them, still mirroring the tribute the old people had erected in his name and then torn down again—also at her instigation. It was like a trademark, she supposed, a leitmotif: Mictlantecuhtli and his Aztec temple. He wouldn't have been himself without it.

Standing at its summit once again made her think of Califia, with a pang of regret. Mickey had assured her that the Queen would lead her people south, into present-day Mexico, where their descendants and their legends would be absorbed into the great Aztec empire, which wouldn't end (for them) for another six hundred years. It was a better fate than dying on an altar as a sacrifice, which was how the former midwife would have concluded her days, if not for Ingrid's timely and apparently divine intervention. She knew she could see her friend now, here, in Mictlan, if she wanted to, for Califia would've died her natural death almost a thousand years ago—but Ingrid wasn't ready for that. She preferred to think of the Queen as alive and vital, and that wouldn't be so easy to do over here in the realm of the dead.

So she set Califia aside in her thoughts, but not before making a silent promise that she would see her again one day. In one way or another.

The weather on this side of existence was foggy gray, wintery as usual, and the landscape that spread out to every horizon was as California's once had been: untrammeled, unspoiled, and unchanging, as far as the eye could see.

Except… to look at any one place down on the plain for more than a moment or two was to see the mists congeal into skeletons, many of them contorted by torment, all of them made tiny by distance. They went about their business in silence, often for no longer than a few minutes or even seconds at a time before fading back into indistinct grayness.

Ingrid thought she would never grow bored with this. It was like finding pictures in the clouds, and she could've watched the smoky skeletons come and go all day. Not that a phrase like 'all day' had a whole lot of meaning over here.

Mickey slipped an arm around her waist, sidling intimately close. The muscled thigh that came into contact with her hip felt as sturdy as a marble column. She shivered, and guessed the King was grinning again as he noticed her sensitive flesh pebbling up into goosebumps.

It was easy to soften against him and relax into his embrace, despite her catalogue of anxieties and reservations about returning here. But she did enjoy his games. She hadn't come because she didn't want to play.

She tilted her head back as she leaned against him and his lips were there, ready, eager, and she was no longer able to postpone the kiss that needed to occur. She turned and pressed herself into Mickey's arms. Their mouths collided; his strong fingers worked their way into her hair. The King could've worn any face or form he wanted, and he'd custom-tailored this body to fuel her desires. *Very successfully, too,* Ingrid thought as she slid the inside of her thigh up the outside of his hip in a most unladylike manner, abandoning her last pretense of reserve.

She couldn't tell if she felt robbed of her own volition around her Mickey, or if she felt so free to do anything and everything she'd ever dreamed of that it frightened her.

This wasn't the moment for trepidation, however. Not with Mickey's tongue in her mouth, and now with his hands on her ass. Though she would always need to take care around him, she thought distantly, as she became aware of his illusion of a heart beating firmly against her breast. He was what he was, ancient and vast, but social niceties and the nuances of etiquette were an undiscovered country from where he stood. The needs and assumptions of the living were foreign to him. If she made a hash of her experiences over here, in his world, either through failing to explain herself or by letting their games get out of hand, then she would have nobody but herself to blame.

Ingrid broke their kiss and stepped back demurely, as if they'd exchanged nothing more than a polite peck, and not something that bordered on a mutual grope.

"What can you show me today?" she asked, turning again to consider the fog-shrouded panorama at their feet.

"What would you see?"

Ingrid thought about it. It sounded like the simplest of questions, but it had the most enormous implications.

What did she want to see, anyway? Or who? An audience with some historical personage would be nothing at all for the King to arrange. So who might it be fun to sit down to dinner with? William Shakespeare? The ghost of the immortal bard would certainly have been her father's first choice. Joan of Arc also came to mind. Ingrid had been thrilled by Miss d'Arc's story since she was very small. Thrilled and horrified, that was, and the appalling parts of the tale were something that needed to be taken into consideration. If Joanie was still tortured by memories of the executioner's pyre, that might be more than Ingrid could bear to witness. Mickey wouldn't spare her anything, and he might not even know what was apt to upset her, so she had to be very careful about what she asked for.

Though it was all academic anyway. There was only one answer to the question el Rey had asked her.

"You," she told him, and realized how true the words were only as she voiced them: "All I want to see is you."

That seemed to please him. Flattery always did.

He stepped close to her once again, and Ingrid had to look up to meet his eyes, even in her heels. She didn't think she'd ever tire of that.

"I would see *you* as well, my love," he murmured, and Ingrid shied back, holding up a hand to halt his advances.

"Wait," she said. "Don't make my clothes disappear. I just got them."

Mickey nodded, and Ingrid began unbuttoning before his natural impatience could get the better of him. She sailed her big hat over to him, playfully, and he caught it. Then he tossed it again, this time right off the top of the Pyramid. A convenient wind seized it and sent it rising and spinning into orbit around them, at a distance of a hundred yards or so. Its red plumage fluttered in the breeze, making for a vivid splotch of color that stood out brilliantly against the silver sky. Faraway skeletons on the plain below looked up as it circled the giant step pyramid that always stood tall on their horizon. By the time the piece of airborne millinery floated boomerang-like back into Ingrid's outstretched hand, she was down to nothing more than her garters, her stockings, and her favorite pair of blood-red heels.

She perched the matching hat up atop her head, cocked far enough back that it must've resembled a big red halo. She put a hand on her bare hip and favored the King with a shameless smile. His salacious return grin told her he was very well pleased with her display.

"Your turn," Ingrid told him. "Entertain me."

Mickey didn't even look flustered. He looked ready, in fact, to put on a show. Like he'd been rehearsing for some time and was now eager to perform. It was a look Ingrid knew well.

A theatrical spot suddenly illuminated him, glaring right down out of the gray sky from no apparent source. The rest of the otherworld faded into gloaming, like an auditorium as the houselights went down and the curtain rose on a radiant stage. The King's black hair and his tuxedo jacket reflected the hard white light in just the same way, as though they were somehow made of the same smooth material.

"Join me and I will," he said, and Ingrid discarded the last of her uncertainties. She took el Rey's outstretched hand and stepped into the light beside him.

Chapter Two

THE world around them was different as soon as she hit her mark. Gone were the Pyramid, the plain, and the silver sky. Even the spotlight itself disappeared, as if some unseen stagehand had switched it off from the wings.

They were indoors now, inside a lush and dimly-lit parlor. Lord Mictlantecuhtli had also changed, along with their surroundings. Changed his clothes, at least. Now that he'd generated a location his evening wear might've been suited to he'd given it up, in favor of the costume of an Aztec king. His long, strong body was adorned only with a loincloth that tied in the front, golden armbands, and the elaborate skull-and-feather headdress that made him look about nine feet tall. The tips of his regal feathers were bent awkwardly against the room's low ceiling.

The two of them must've made quite a sight, but the frowsy-haired skeleton that drifted into the room, absurdly clad in a bustle and corset, seemed not the least bit taken aback by their appearance.

"Milord," the cadaver said in a coarse London accent, swiveling her skull from one of them to the other as flesh filled in over her facial bones. The middle-aged woman the skeleton morphed into was powdered, perfumed, and colorfully made up. An impressive décolletage found itself restrained by her previously-empty corset, and her skirts now seemed to swaddle fleshy thighs instead of flapping emptily around a pair of stick-like femurs.

"Yer rooms await," the newly voluptuous matron told Mickey, with a graceless curtsey and a deferential angling of her eyes down toward the rich Persian carpet that lay beneath his incongruous double-thonged sandals.

Ingrid had heard that particular Cockney croak before.

"Lucy?" she asked, as she and the King followed the older woman across the front parlor and toward a dim hallway at the rear of the room. "Lucinda Swire!"

Their dead hostess stopped and turned around, framed in the door to a long corridor that receded back into gas-lit gloom. Ingrid *knew* she'd recognized the woman, Lady Swire, as she'd been called back in the day. They'd known each other a bit in London, through mutual acquaintances in the Hermetic Order of the Golden Dawn.

"I didn't know you were dead," Ingrid told her. Perhaps tactlessly.

"Nor I you," Lucinda replied, looking Ingrid up and down with one eyebrow arched by the tiniest increment.

"Oh, I'm just visiting," Ingrid said. She'd almost forgotten she was wearing little more than her hat and garters, like Félicien Rops' infamous portrait of the goddess Pornocrates. That explained Lady Swire's unspoken critique of her attire. Though really, Lucy was hardly in a position to judge, given the nature of the entertainments she specialized (or *had* specialized, Ingrid corrected) in arranging. "When did you get here?" she asked, taking off the ridiculous red hat and smoothing her hair, as if that somehow made her nudity less brazen. She tossed the hat onto a nearby chair. "It hasn't been that long. Last we saw each other was what, two years ago?"

"Wouldn't know about that, would I?" Lady Swire said, sneering like Ingrid had accused her of something. "Time's not what it was, over here. Nor nothin' else neither, I dare say."

Ingrid nodded. Conditions for the dead were rather more like lucid dreaming than full waking consciousness, she was coming to understand. Continuity and consistency mattered less, over on this side of things. Symbolism and personal meaning were all important. The deceased acted out their inner needs, whether or not they'd acknowledged those needs within their lifetimes, and those who knew themselves the least seemed to suffer most (although there were obvious exceptions to that rule). Only Ingrid's continuous banishings held her mind together and kept her cogent within this environment. Otherwise she might've drifted off into a heaven or a hell of her own devising and stagnated there—the way los Muertos seemed to, by and large.

"You must've gotten here by some route, though," Ingrid prodded. "Do you remember how?"

"I may be dead, but I ain't daft, am I?" Lucinda Swire said, scowling and looking affronted. "Course I remember."

Ingrid waited for her to share. Mickey stood behind her, still as a stone monument.

"I know yer thinkin' it were the opium pipe what finally done me in. I know it. I can see you thinkin' it. But it weren't nothin' like that."

"All right," Ingrid said.

"And I weren't stabbed to death by no customer, nor brainrotted from the clap, nor nothin' else you'd expect for the likes o' me."

That 'Lady' title always had fallen somewhere between an affectation and a joke.

"Then what?" Ingrid asked, beginning to feel genuinely curious.

Still, Lucy hesitated. "I want you to promise yer not gonna laugh."

"You *think* I'm going to laugh over the way you *died*?" Ingrid said, and was wounded to see Lucinda shrug. She hadn't imagined she'd left a great impression, especially considering the manner in which she'd departed London, but she might still have expected a little credit for basic humanity. Apparently she hadn't earned it. Not in Mistress Swire's eyes.

"All right, then," Lucinda said. "I'll tell you. I tried to heat up me bath with one o' them new electrified wires what just got put in for the lights."

Ingrid raised both eyebrows, and bit her tongue. "That's shocking," she said, and her lips felt stiff with the effort of stifling involuntary giggles.

"Fuckin' hell, I knew I shouldn't have said," Lucinda pouted, crossing her arms over her ample bosom and glowering up at Ingrid. "It weren't that stupid to think, neither," she went on, defending herself and her dubious application of the scientific method. "That bulb gets bloody hot in that socket. Burn yer fingertips to touch it. So stick it in water, why shouldn't that get hot too?"

"Irrefutable logic," Ingrid said. "Mickey, please restore Mistress Swire to life. There's been a terrible oversight. I think she also deserves a patent on her very safe and efficient electric water heater, but that's all up to her once she's back on the other side."

Lucy sneered, but caught herself and turned her eyes away from the King, who was also standing right there. "I- I know it don't work that way, yer Lordliness," she said to him.

"It does not," Mictlantecuhtli confirmed. He dipped his chin and the feathers in his towering headdress scratched at the plaster-and-beam ceiling like quills in the hands of agitated scribes.

"Mistress Swire and I knew some of the same people in London," Ingrid told him, by way of explanation.

"I know," Mickey said. "Your image lives in her memory. Vividly."

"Oh," Ingrid said. Recalling what *sorts* of images must've been living there made her say it again, involuntarily. "Oh!"

"Yes," the King said.

She found it disturbing in the extreme that he'd been through dead peoples' memories of her. All her experiences had been her own choices and she wouldn't have tolerated anyone standing in judgment of her because of them—but that didn't mean she didn't blush under her King's knowing gaze. She turned back to Lucy Swire before he could make her fidget.

The aging purveyor of all things that dare not speak their names looked as real, solid, and unwholesomely vital as ever. It was hard for Ingrid to imagine that everything Lucinda had been in life was now just another aspect of multifaceted Mickey.

"Hey—you weren't some sort of a secret Aztec, were you? Religionwise?" she asked aloud, even as it occurred to her to wonder. It seemed like a stretch to think that Lucy might've been a practitioner of suppressed native American rites, but far from an impossibility. Their ring of acquaintances back in London Towne had included adherents of quite a wide range of arcane beliefs, including but hardly limited to Egyptian revivalism, Himalayan shamanism, and West Indian *vodou*. Even the famous Irish poet Mr. WB Yeats, perhaps the most esteemed intellect amongst them, had maintained a staunch belief in the Fair Folk of Celtic lore.

"I weren't never nothin' but a proper Christian lady." Lucinda sniffed, doing her best to look offended by whatever she thought Ingrid might be trying to imply.

"Then what are you doing *here*?" Ingrid asked. The portion of Mictlan visible around them may have looked like an outdated and threadbare Victorian drawing room, but Mictlantecuhtli himself, in his loincloth and feathers, was a vivid reminder of the pre-Columbian mythology these dreams were built on.

Mistress Swire herself only shrugged, seeming again to not really understand the question, or even Ingrid's reason for asking it. She was dead, so she was here. What more was there to know?

Ingrid assumed her King would have to have some answers, what with being a god and all. She turned and looked up at him. "Do *you* know what I mean? Why you and your world, Mickey, and not Saint Peter at the pearly gates or Satan in his pit, for the people who expect that sort of thing?"

"We are Death, and we wear as many faces as does Life," Mickey said cryptically. He put a large hand over his current visage and pulled it right off, in order to contemplate it for a moment or two. The flesh came away from the bones with a wet sucking sound that made Ingrid want to cringe.

"Few fail to recognize this face, whatever they choose to believe," he said, meaning, as he indicated by gesture, the grisly grinning death's head underneath his illusion of skin. It did seem to be his default choice. He only bothered to look alive when Ingrid came to visit.

"But the living men, *and* the women," (the King here made a point of grandly including Ingrid's gender, in light of her unique accomplishment) "all of those who come up to my Chambers at the Hole Between Worlds, they understand and expect this."

He was now referring to the slack face of an Aztec king that he held in his hand.

"The lore they hand down in secret recalls the name of Mictlantecuhtli, which their fathers gave to me a hundred centuries before your birth."

Ingrid nodded absently. "Will you please put it back on?" she asked, gesturing toward the rugged mug the King was still holding up for general admiration while she did her best not to look right at him. This without appearing rude, of course. It was no mean feat. Death's eyes bulged grotesquely from the sockets they'd stayed lodged in when his eyelids peeled away, and the red striations of muscle that moved his jawbone when he spoke were rather unpleasant to see. He looked as though his barber had gotten wildly overzealous with a straight razor while giving him a shave.

Mickey glanced between the detached face and his revolted guest, looking as surprised as a moron asked to stop picking his nose. The lidless googly eyes lent a particularly idiotic aspect to his unfleshed expression, so Ingrid was much comforted when he smoothed his caramel-colored features back into place over the bones.

She also noted that his understanding of living anatomy had improved markedly since she first taught him how to imitate a pulse. Skeletal systems came naturally to him—little surprise there—but there'd been a sharp learning curve when it came to the intricacies of muscle, cartilage, and connective tissue. Previous drafts of his flesh had been undifferentiated all the way through, lacking in nuances like tendons, nerves, or circulatory apparatus, with the dreamstuff he worked in molded over the bones like so much warm modeling clay. His new endeavors, however, seemed informed by an improved understanding of the body's internal architecture. It was like noticing the insightful leaps a young artist had made in his sketchbooks during a first serious study of the human form.

"You look like a page out of Gray's Anatomy under there," she said, looking her King in the eyes again now that the rest of his features were back in their proper places. "It's impressive."

Mickey grinned, and Ingrid realized he'd been showing off. Seeking her approval, in his own weird way. He'd pulled his face off as a demonstration of his recent efforts, so that she might acknowledge both his hard work and the ever-increasing physical sophistication that resulted from it.

"Ahh, yes, Henry Gray," the King mused. "You have a 'good eye,' as the living say. Your Gray did as well. Two of them, in fact. This, here, was his," Mickey said, holding up one of the deflating orbs that was strung on his omnipresent eyeball necklace, then turning the long garland to locate a second lump of gristle that matched the first. "And this as well." He angled the glistening vitreous mass so that its blue iris caught the light and gleamed like a raw sapphire. "These eyes saw much and looked deeply, far beneath the surface of things. I value them for all they retain. Would you know Gray, my love? I will summon him upon the instant, if that be your wish."

"No, that's all right, I think I'll pass," Ingrid said, figuring the renowned anatomist's conversation was more likely to spoil her appetite than anything else. "I like what you're doing with his knowledge, though," she said, complimenting the King as she reached out to touch his arm, with its dark, unblemished skin and textbook-perfect musculature.

Lucinda Swire snorted, behind her. "Cor, I just *bet* you like it," she muttered, almost under her breath, as Ingrid turned around and settled her hands onto her gartered hips.

"Is there something you'd like to say to me, Lucy?"

"No."

"Because it really seems like there is."

Swire stared down at the floor and shuffled her feet, exhibiting all of the surly yet servile diffidence Ingrid remembered from her in life.

"There ain't a single bloody goddamn thing I got to say to the likes o' you, Ingrid Redstone," she said, steadfastly refusing to meet Ingrid's eyes. "And that's a fact."

"I don't remember doing anything to you," Ingrid said. "And I always paid my bills. Or at least made sure somebody paid them."

"Who said it were me you done it to?"

"Then who?"

"Don't you even *know*?" The stout woman couldn't help but glower up at Ingrid as she stepped in toe-to-toe and hissed the question through gritted teeth. "Ain't you got no *conception* of the mess you left behind in yer wake when you departed without so much as a fare-thee-well, you self-centered, ginger-headed edifice?"

"Well, clearly *not*," Ingrid said, beginning to feel more exasperation than she could be bothered to contain. "And I may just have my own side to whatever story it is you've been telling yourself, Lucinda Swire. Have you stopped to consider that?"

"No side o' no story you could ever tell is gonna mean two shits to me, considerin' what happened to poor Doctor Pagán."

"Finn?" Ingrid said, feeling startled by an unexpected jolt of concern. Doctor Phineas Pagán was her employer's stage name, though his real name, Peter Finnegan, was far more humble. "What happened to Finn, what are you talking about?"

Lady Swire further narrowed her already beady eyes. "You really don't know, do you?"

"For fuck's sake, *no*, Lucinda, I really do not!"

"Yer precious 'Finn' up and kilt hisself after *you* went swannin' off without a word." Lucinda looked well satisfied with her work when she saw the revelation hit Ingrid like a fist to the gut. "*That's* right," she spat. "That's what happened. You happy, then, now you know?"

"No…" Ingrid said, shaking her head as if to negate what she'd just heard. "No, that can't be true. Can it? Mickey?"

She turned around to face the King and found him eyeing her solemnly, with his arms folded across his chest.

"Mickey?" she said again.

"Would you see your 'Finn?'" he asked, and even through her shock she caught the new note of menace in his low-pitched tone.

"I… ahh… no," Ingrid said, even though every fiber of her being shrieked for her to answer yes, yes of course, bring him here right now and let me hear these things from him, from his perspective and in his words, in the likely vain hope they'd make more sense that way. "Maybe later," she managed to say in a dismissive tone, even though breathing had become difficult, like she'd had the wind punched out of her.

Mickey was scrutinizing her with his small, humorless eyes.

"That… that isn't what I came for," Ingrid told him, swallowing hard before attempting a smile.

"Who was this man Finn to you, my love?" Mickey asked in that same slow, quiet rumble.

She knew he could sense her inner turmoil, despite her efforts to conceal it.

Lucinda stepped up next to the King, tutting and shaking her head, with undisguised disgust scrawled across her face like an epithet written on a water closet wall. Ingrid wanted to swat her.

"Poor bedeviled bugger goes and does hisself in from the pain of unrequired love," the squat old whoremonger said, between *tsks*, "flings hisself into the Thames with rocks in his pockets because o' *you*, Ingrid Redstone, but you can't bother yerself to look at him. Don't hardly know what to say about that, me."

"Then maybe you should shut up," Ingrid suggested, and Lucy responded with a disdainful scowl when she found herself unable to produce a rejoinder in time to make it sting.

"I expect an answer, Ingrid Redstone," the King murmured, in a voice that barely rose above a whisper. "Who was this man Finn to you?"

"Finn, he's—well, he *was* my… my employer, in a manner of speaking," Ingrid managed. "And don't *you* say a fucking word," she added, jabbing a finger in Lucinda's face in anticipation of the next crack she figured the curvilinear harpy was apt to make.

"He was a magician, Mickey," she hurried to explain. "Not a magick with a 'k' kind of magician. Just a stage performer. A prestidigitator. 'The Paranormal Phantasmagoria of Doctor Phineas Pagán' was how they billed him. I was part of the act, but sex was never part of the job." Ingrid glared down at Lucy. "No matter what this one wants to think."

"Weren't it, then?"

"No."

"So we're meant to believe that bouncin' yer boulders around a stage and flashin' yer pretty thighs to divert them punters' roving eyes weren't *exactly* the service he paid you for?"

"It was," Ingrid said. "More or less."

"So?" Lucy smirked, as smugly as a prosecutor resting an airtight case before an agreeably angry jury. "Ain't that the same as sellin' him yer sex?"

"By several orders of magnitude, no, it isn't," Ingrid said, though Lucinda continued to look gleefully unconvinced.

"I reckon all o' that tuppin' backstage were off the books, then?" she taunted, laying things right out there in front of Mickey. "Strictly '*pro boner*,' as the legal people say?"

Ingrid had to wonder if Lucy'd intended the pun, or if the odds merely dictated that one malapropism in a million was going to sound like it meant something. Probably the latter. She figured she had it within her character to ignore the dead woman, and looked up at their King instead. Lady Swire was now a part of him, technically speaking, his subject in every way, so if she felt free to speak her mind it could only be because he wanted to hear the things she had to say.

"I get it, already," Ingrid said to him. "You know Finn and I slept together. The secret's out."

"*Sleeping* is not the act that interests me."

"I don't remember telling you I was a virgin, Mickey."

The King continued to stare at her coldly.

"All right, we fucked," Ingrid said, crossing her arms and mirroring his closed-off posture. "Frequently, athletically, and climactically. Is that what you want to hear? I don't see what difference it makes, when you know all about it anyway."

"I would know what the repetition of this act meant to *you*, Ingrid Redstone. This is what I would hear of."

"Did I love him, is that what you're asking me? Were we in love?"

The King waited for her to continue. Ingrid understood that much now hinged on her ability to provide an acceptable answer to that very question.

"No, of course not," she said, responding in a clear and steady voice, even though the words hurt like swallowed sewing pins that lodged in her throat. "We had a fling because there was no good reason not to," she explained. "Finn was hardly my first."

Ingrid bit down on her runaway tongue before it could gallop any further ahead of her brain.

"And here's you, tryin' to convince us you weren't no whore," Lucinda said.

This time Ingrid did raise a hand to slap her, but the corpulent courtesan ducked behind the King's hip with an angry hiss before she managed to lower the boom.

Mickey never moved. He only tracked them with his coal-black eyes.

Ingrid stepped back, forgetting about Lucinda. She tossed her hair out of her face and looked up at the King, squaring her jaw in defiance. Her initial shameful sense of being caught out was rapidly giving way to one of irritation. Even anger. Mickey had ambushed her with Lady Lucy and her mnemonic index of sordid sexual secrets, arranging for her to learn of a former lover's sad demise in just about the most demeaning and upsetting manner possible. And this was no social *faux pas* on Mickey's part, either. He'd done it as an experiment, to gauge the depth and intensity of her response. Ingrid knew deliberate machinations when she experienced them. She knew when someone was trying to turn her own feelings back against her, like twisting her wrist when she was holding a knife.

She felt wounded, all right, and it was nothing she appreciated.

"This is absurd," Ingrid said. "I came here to be with you, Mickey, but I'm not your possession and I never will be."

"Never say never, my love," Mictlantecuhtli said, curling his lips back in a sinister and knowing snarl. She would die eventually, like anybody else, and the fact of it rendered all her individualistic boasting null and void.

"Well, I'm not your subject yet. And if all you want to do is comb over my past for imaginary challenges to your dominion, then you can escort me right back to the Hole in the Sky and I'll be happy to leave you alone with your delusions."

Mickey paused and thought things over for a moment or two, rubbing his chin as he ruminated.

"I would not prefer this," he said at last.

Ingrid inwardly wilted with relief. "Well, then?" she scolded, taking care to keep her sternest scowl plastered across her face as she rebuked him. "Quit acting like a jealous judgmental jackass and do something to make me glad I came."

She wondered immediately if she hadn't gone too far and almost winced, but she put her hands on her hips and didn't so much as blink when Mickey glared back down at her. She got the impression no one had taken such a tone with him in centuries, if ever, and she wondered what it would mean in practical terms if she should happen to die while sojourning in the land of the dead.

"Do my efforts not please you?" Mickey asked finally, in a much more conciliatory tone of voice than Ingrid might've expected.

"Don't try to tell me you brought Lucinda here because you thought I missed her."

"Do you not?" Mickey said. His consternation seemed genuine enough, which only served to confuse Ingrid further. She frowned as he explained: "According to the Swire's memories, you spent hours enough here to make into days. Or rather you spent them in the realworld's equivalent of this place. Her place, the Lady Swire's. You came time and again, both in company and alone. I have reproduced it for you from her mind in its every detail, and even now I sense a desire stirring within you, I believe, to recapture something of those times?"

"Do you understand what I did there, Mickey? Or here, or whatever?"

The King shrugged. "You slept lying on your hip, drowsing in the catacomb that lies beneath this house, and smoked from time to time with a carved-bone pipe you heated over an oil candle left ever burning at your side. This I believe is the Rite of Da Yen, the Big Smoke, and this is what the Swire saw."

"I smoked opium, yes, with Finn," Ingrid said. "That's what was down in Lucy's basement. Not a catacomb, an opium den."

While the upper portion of the property had served as a brothel in the guise of an inn; a gaming hall used for cards, billiards, knife-fighting, or what have you; an occasional clearing-house for stolen or smuggled goods; and even an ordinary public house, called the Cock & Bull, where workers from the nearby docks drank themselves into imbecility every night in the establishment's sawdust-floored tap room.

Its lounge bar, by contrast, had enjoyed a certain trashy cachet with Ingrid's more bohemian and theatrical set, both for the ready access to extralegal products and services it offered, and more importantly for the disused music hall stage that took up the rear of the room. There'd been a battered and jangly old piano back there too. A dozen or more drunkenly extemporaneous productions had broken out upon those creaking boards on any given night, with their obscenity quotient rising in direct proportion to the lateness of the hour. Ingrid had been a minor star up on that stage, always greeted with lascivious cheers when she got up to shake her ass and sing popular songs with the lyrics rearranged to include references to a wide range of sexual arcana—a practice she'd discovered she possessed a sharp and ready talent for.

No doubt she could've made the Muses prouder with more distinguished performances delivered in more venerable venues, but in truth she'd never taken more simple pleasure in the act of making a spectacle of herself than she had under that shabby proscenium arch.

"You made this for me, to entertain me?" she asked of Mickey, dubiously. "The whole place is here? Even the stage downstairs?"

"Every board and every nail is here," the King confirmed. "The chipped pint glass on which you once cut your mouth can even now be found behind the bar."

"Good to know you kept on using that," Ingrid said to Lucy. She tongued a thin seam of scar tissue inside her lower lip, remembering. "What's a little facial laceration amongst friends?"

"I ain't stayed in business thirty years by throwin' away glasses," was Lucinda's only statement in her own defense. She offered it with a harrumph that implied Ingrid was putting on airs by suggesting she might've done otherwise.

"What about the people?" Ingrid asked of Mickey, thinking of others she'd known. Her London friends had been an opium-smoking, hashish-eating, absinthe-swilling kind of a crowd. It was entirely possible that more than a few of them had preceded her here. "Is anybody else I know already dead?"

"But the two," Mickey replied. "Thus far."

Ingrid hesitated, thinking of Finn. She didn't want to discuss him any further. Not now. Not yet (although she *would* need to see him, she knew that she would, just as soon as she could figure out a way to arrange it without inciting Mickey's ire). She noticed Lucy had a critical eyebrow arched in her direction, letting her know that she was thinking of Finn as well. Ingrid had never known the fat little captain of criminal industry harbored such fond feelings for her former lover. It struck her as more than a bit weird.

"You will meet ancestors here," Mickey assured her. "Not descendants. None who have yet to perish as of the day you came to me, in your 'Year 1910.' I would know time as you know it, Ingrid Redstone. Your living body remains a soft clockwork, full of cycles and rhythms, and I have made my time to match it. I see no more future, beyond yours. Even now I find I would have to make an effort to still this body's beating heart, especially when in your company."

He double-tapped his sternum, mimicking a cardiac cadence.

"Mickey, that's... that's very sweet," Ingrid said. It was sweet, in its way, especially coming from an archetype more generally associated with rapacity than sentiment. So much so that she found herself feeling warmly toward her King once again, heated from the inside out—the way she'd come over here wanting to feel.

She stepped closer, into the circle of his arms, and laid her head against his chest. Mickey took an awkward moment to understand that she wanted him to hold her, but he figured it out soon enough. He even stroked her hair once he'd gotten the picture, and she thought that was nice. She got the impression he'd be willing to stand there indefinitely, cradling her against his shoulder until she was ready to break the embrace.

That was nice, too.

"Thank you," she whispered into the crook of Mickey's neck, squeezing him and relishing the feel of being all but crushed by him in return. "I think your gift is lovely."

When she glanced past her King Lucinda was there, still standing a few yards behind him with her hands planted on her ample hips. The dead woman was silent for the moment, but judgment and venom were evident in her eyes.

"But you need to understand I have a past," Ingrid warned Mickey, breaking off eye contact with Lucy to look back up at him. "I've had lovers, several of them, and I've done a lot of other things a lady isn't supposed to do. I haven't even tried to be good, by the conventional measure. The thing to remember about all of it is that I might never have found my way out here to you if I were any other sort of woman than the one I am. All right?"

The King thought about it, and finally nodded. It wasn't the strongest affirmation Ingrid might've hoped for, but it was a place to start.

She was more confused and wearied by his covetousness than she wanted to admit. Her dealings with Mickey were apt to swing from wondrous to dangerous faster than the winds could change. She was also having trouble believing Lucinda's presence here was really the result of an innocent oversight, and not a ploy to goad her into a reaction. Death seemed to like it when she got emotional, perhaps because his realm could be so desultory and gray when she wasn't around to liven it up with her colorful example.

"What would you experience next, my love?" Mictlantecuhtli asked, looking earnestly into her eyes. "The entertainments and the amenities you remember from this place are all available, as you desire them."

Ingrid wished there was a dressing room backstage where she might nip off for a nap between acts, just long enough to regroup and sort out her feelings. But there was no back to Mictlan's ever-changing stage. At least not that she'd discovered so far.

"Can we just, I don't know… lay down for a while?" she said. When the King frowned, as though this were far too trifling a test of his abilities, she added: "Have you tried sleeping yet, Mickey? You know the living spend about a third of their time doing it, and not just because it's mandatory. We take pleasure in it."

Mickey's frown rolled over into a thoughtful nod. "I know this to be true," he murmured. His curiosity was piqued. Ingrid saw it in his expression when he arrived at a decision, approximately half a second before he announced it. "I will attempt your 'sleep,' if you will instruct me in the art."

"I suppose I can do that," Ingrid said. She turned around and looked down at Lucy, who was still skulking about behind them. "Mistress Swire, show us to your finest suite, if you please. The one with the four poster bed, hmm?"

In an aside to Mickey, she murmured: "I won't mind if the linens are fresh, though. Not every detail has to be exactly the way it was."

Lucy scowled, but she seemed strangely ineloquent all of a sudden as she curtsied before the King and his consort and then turned once again to lead them out of the dusty formal parlor and up the staircase that led to the guest rooms on the next floor. So Lucinda's voice *did* come and go according to Mickey's whim. This observation further confirmed Ingrid's notion that the lady of the house was not here merely as a part of the stage dressing. Lucy had been summoned (and this scenario had perhaps been chosen in the first place) specifically so that she might articulate all of the things Mickey wanted to dredge up but didn't want to take responsibility for.

Ingrid felt her jaw start to tighten with slow-simmering anger as she followed a huffing and laboring Lucinda up the stairs. Mickey followed after them both. His weight made the old wooden risers underfoot creak and pop.

As much as she might have wanted to let it go, she was still out of sorts over the news about Finn's suicide, not to mention Mickey's method of delivering it. Finn hadn't been the sort of twit to romanticize self-slaughter, but he had been given to bouts of melancholia that few of his associates and none of his public ever saw. Ingrid had been closer to him than anyone, for a time, and she'd been in a position to witness more than most.

She was glad she'd managed to talk Mictlantecuhtli into dabbling in the mysteries of slumber. She may have lain awake nearly till dawn the night before, restless and inflamed over the thought of being with him again, but right now she couldn't imagine 'sleeping' with him in any sense other than the very most literal. It was the best she could do after the way he'd attacked her with news he knew would hurt.

Lucy opened the door to the suite she'd requested. Ingrid followed Mickey into the room and looked it over. The King took off his skull-and-feather headdress and set it on an end table near the bed.

"I'll be leavin' you to yer business, then," Lucinda said from the doorway, wrinkling her nose in Ingrid's direction, then looking solicitous again as she turned back to Mickey. "That is, if there ain't nothin' more yer gonna be needing, Milord."

"You are dismissed," her lord told her, with a wave of his fingertips, and the lady of the house backed her bustle out of the room, pulling the door closed behind her.

Ingrid and the King were all alone.

Mickey came around the massive four-poster bed to stand before her, not quite coming into contact, but so close to her that she had to look up to meet his gaze. The knotted front of his Aztec-style loincloth brushed against her navel. She gulped as he clasped her hand to his bare chest and murmured:

"Shall we commence our ritual of sleep?"

Ingrid felt almost as flustered by his abstruse choice of words as she was by his overwhelming nearness. He was too tall for these low-ceilinged chambers, really. The finials on the extravagant bedposts stood whole inches below his eye level.

"Is this space appropriate to the performance of the act? I have done my best to make it right."

She looked around and saw that he really had attempted to please her, according to the criteria she'd laid out. The room was dim, lit only by a faint warm glow from a fire in the hearth that had burned down almost to the embers. A driving rain lashed at the windows, slashing down out of a leaden sky. A gas lamp on the deserted street below seemed to float in the gloom, framed by a single warped glass pane in the window's bottom corner. The feather bed beside them looked deep and inviting, and the air was crisp enough that sharing body heat beneath the sheets would be an exquisite pleasure. The conditions for deep, soothing sleep had all been maximized—at least as far as Ingrid's personal wants and needs were concerned. The room and all of its details were calibrated to comfort her, personally, in the same way that Mickey's physique had been designed to entice. She realized with a mild start that she wasn't even naked anymore. A soft cotton shift that clung comfortably to her curves had at some point materialized to cover her stockings and garters. It was so light and loose she hadn't even noticed its arrival.

How Mickey could be so vengeful and cruel in one instant but then turn thoughtful, observant, and almost sweetly eager to please in the next remained a significant mystery.

"Do you find this setting acceptable?" he prodded, wrinkling his brow out of concern over her slow response, which must have seemed ambivalent at best. "Adjustments may be made as you desire them."

Ingrid nodded vigorously, to reassure him. "It's fine, Mickey," she said. "It's more than fine, I mean. It's perfect. I'm just... sort of overwhelmed by it all, I guess."

The King grinned, choosing to read this as a compliment, as Ingrid supposed he should.

She peeled back the bedclothes and kicked off her blood-red shoes before hopping up onto the mattress. She patted the spot next to her, indicating that Mickey should join her there. He climbed up onto the high bed somewhat awkwardly and then settled down as if he wasn't quite sure of how best to arrange his limbs. Ingrid nestled back against him, fitting her shoulders and bottom against his warm plank of a torso. Then she pulled the arm not pillowing her head over herself, as though Mictlantecuhtli were more blanket than man. He allowed these things to happen with a certain complacent bemusement, like a family pet being dressed up in doll clothes by a mischievous child, and Ingrid could tell he was assimilating his new experiences, cataloguing them and comparing them against everything else that existed within the vast and eternal archive of his mind.

"We don't just lay here, do we?" he asked after a moment or two. The novelty was wearing thin for him already.

"No, of course not," Ingrid said. "You've seen me sleep before, Mickey. Did it look like that's all I was doing? Just laying there?"

Mickey said nothing. Ingrid suspected he would've shrugged, had they not presently been laying down.

"Sitting still and doing nothing while you're awake is called meditation," she attempted to clarify, as his large hand found its way to her breast and cupped it. "Not everyone does that. Sleep is something different. Living people need it as regularly as we need to eat, for one thing, or else we go mad."

She knew she was rambling, if not babbling. This had been a stupid thing to ask for—there was no way she could really hope to fall asleep.

It was merely the first wish that had popped into her head, and so she'd voiced it.

Dammit, Mickey, she thought fleetingly. It was almost like he'd gone out of his way to spoil this for her.

She sighed involuntarily, then caught herself and covered it up by yawning, stretching, and snuggling back more firmly into el Rey's embrace—something he seemed more than pleased to participate in. He shifted his weight and wedged one of his legs a little bit more firmly between her thighs. Her King was a male creature, all right—she could feel the anatomical bit that defined him as such beginning to plump against the curve of her bottom.

Laying here with him should've been comforting and cozy, but her memories of Finn were wide awake, stirred up by Mickey's mouthpiece Lucinda and her ugly accusations.

Her former employer was the only man with whom she'd ever grown comfortable sharing a bed. They'd performed together as many as seven nights a week, back in her London days (which sometimes meant a total of eight or even ten shows in that time frame, if their engagement included matinees), so sleeping side-by-side had been almost a matter of convenience. Sheer exhaustion had made it easy. They would tumble headlong into the sack together in the wee small hours, bleary-eyed and still buzzing from the effects of applause and champagne, and then hibernate well into the next afternoon. Their feet wouldn't touch the floor again until long after the ordinary working world had roused itself and trundled off to its myriad occupations.

Those late, lazy mornings were when they'd tended to have their fun. They'd often hired this very suite of rooms (or rather, they'd hired the real version, back in the realworld—the original example Mickey had based this re-creation on). Lady Lucinda's Cock & Bull had been the pub most local to the warehouse space where 'Doctor Pagán' had designed his illusions and then rehearsed them alongside 'Miss Ruby,' his lovely assistant. They could've slept at the workshop, and sometimes did (its upstairs loft-space contained a Japanese-style *futon*, amongst other apparatus), but they'd both preferred the relative comforts of the public house.

How many times had they lain together in this very bed, socked deeply and warmly into the goosedown mattress, letting their hands wander beneath the sheets as they swam back to consciousness after sleeping off yet another long night?

Too many to count.

Finn hadn't been patient by nature so much as fascinated with her in a tactile way, and nearly as attuned to the evidence of her arousal as he was to his own. He'd known how to electrify the surface of her skin with the barest brush of his fingertips, and had liked to hold her close while his touch made her shiver and jump. He'd known all of her especially sensitive spots, like the nape of her neck, or the tender pockets just inside the bends of her elbows. Perfectly chaste places to touch that nevertheless set her nerves to singing. Even the palms of her hands could drive her into rapture when softly stroked in just the right way, and Peter Finnegan had been an undisputed master of the technique.

When she couldn't bear any more, she would guide his talented prestidigitator's hands lower, southward, down the shallow incline of her belly... down to where those nimble fingers might perform their very best trick of all.

Ingrid surfaced from her reverie with a small gasp. Her King's member had become a rigid presence against the back of her thigh while she'd lain in his arms, remembering another man. She could only imagine how much that would infuriate him, if only he knew. El Rey kneaded her breast, sparking a cascade of goosebumps all down her back, and Ingrid realized she was ready to do the thing he wanted.

Physically ready, if not emotionally so.

Never mind about that, she told herself as she rolled first into Mickey's arms and then on top of him, all while pulling her internal banishings as tightly as she could around the most secret center of her mind. El Rey seemed surprised by her burst of enthusiasm, but his massive hands landed on her hips like a pair of vise grips and she shuddered when he began to rock her back and forth in a firm, inexorable rhythm.

Ingrid fell forward, crushing her breasts between them, and kissed desperately, questing after his tongue with her own. Mictlantecuhtli's torso flexed like a running horse's back beneath her, but she wasn't thinking of her King as she rode. She was remembering Finn. Tall, broad-shouldered, affable Finn, with his reddish-blond beard and his scruffy Irish charm. Ingrid made sure it was his image and no other that stoked her desires and finally ignited a climax so explosive it should've caused a shockwave.

Imagining a different lover may have been a petty sort of revenge for the way her King had hurt her, but it was hers and she took it.

Mickey finished moments later. Ingrid slid off of him and rolled away as soon as he was done, offering him only her back.

"What do we do now, my love?" El Rey asked after a few long moments of quiet consideration. He sounded uncharacteristically uncertain.

"Now, we sleep," Ingrid said. "*Really* sleep. No living man I've ever met could do anything else, after that performance."

She sensed Mickey nodding, even though she wasn't looking at him. His hair rustled against the pillowcase.

"For how long?"

"Eight hours should do it."

"As you would have it, Ingrid Redstone," Mictlantecuhtli said.

And then he was unconscious, just like that.

Ingrid rolled back over to look at him, and saw he really was asleep. Asleep and snoring softly. He'd dropped into slumber like a stone might drop down a well, at the barest hint of a challenge to his ability to do so.

Convenient, Ingrid thought as she stored away that useful kernel of knowledge for future reference.

She lay there for some time, watching her King's face and waiting to see if he would wake, or if she might fall asleep herself. When she felt reasonably certain that neither event was imminent, she eased herself out of bed and padded over to the washbasin in the corner, where she absently sponged off and then dried herself with a folded towel that had been positioned next to the white ceramic water pitcher. She could hear rain on the roof, as well as distant, muffled voices mixed with bursts of raucous laughter, and from these she inferred that the bar downstairs was already open for business. Or maybe it was always open, and always would be.

Could there be a last call in a place where time never passed?

Ingrid wondered if the deceased patrons down there believed they were in heaven, or in hell. Or if they stayed drunk enough not to think about it.

She looked again at Mickey, sprawled out across the massive bed, and thought about what she ought to do with herself for the next seven hours or so. Finally she decided she might as well go downstairs.

Chapter Three

THE only thing she had to wear (besides her bright red shoes and the matching hat she retrieved from the parlor on her way down to the bar) was the loose cotton nightgown Mickey had made for her. It was a bit dusty now, from having been cast off onto the floor during their athletic little liaison, and it was so thin it left almost nothing to an active imagination, but nobody down in the crowded lounge seemed to take any special notice.

Not of her outfit, anyway.

The first thing Ingrid did when she entered the room was to look around for Finn, though the faces gathered at the candle-lit tables all seemed unfamiliar to her. Maybe they were conscripts from nearby afterlives, called in to pack the house, or maybe the dead who still had a taste for this sort of environment wandered in of their own accord. Everybody looked alive, at any rate. There wasn't a single skeleton to be seen. All of the extras were in costume, as their King had decreed, in the name of her amusement.

Ingrid spotted Lucinda, who was busy drawing off a pint of stout behind the bar while listening over her shoulder for another order, but neither Finn nor his alter-ego Doctor Pagán were anywhere in evidence. The not-so-good Doctor had been a regular customer here in his own right, and other barflies had often failed to realize that Finn and Phineas were actually the same man. That sort of amazed Ingrid, but once he was in costume Finn never broke character, not even for an instant, and his performance had consistently fooled many of those around them.

Ingrid might've guessed that Mickey would exclude him from this scenario. The King wasn't going to let her see him before she'd jumped through a few more hoops, and jumped through them in just the right way, at that.

Well, that was all right. She wouldn't have known what to say to Finn right now anyway.

Her déjà-vu-like sense of visiting her own past was shattered when an entire shoal of tiny winged creatures buzzed by her, making her duck instinctually and flail at them for fear they'd get caught in her hair. Ingrid's first startled thought was that they were iridescent green hummingbirds—new world natives that had no business being here in London, not even in this re-created sliver of it. It was only after her initial surprise passed that she saw the little fliers for what they were: tiny green women with opalescent skin and spun-sugar hair, not a one of them longer than her index finger, all the way from head to toe. Their quick, translucent wings chirped and whirred like impossibly intricate clockworks as the entire mass of them turned in the bar's smoky air, all at once, like birds of a feather flocking in the proverbial manner. Then they broke apart and flitted away to different corners of the room, one of them flashing a bright smile and a glitter of emerald-chip eyes when she zipped past the tip of Ingrid's nose.

A half-mocking giggle made her turn her head even as the miniature women were alighting on shoulders and landing on shadowy tabletops all around the hall.

"You *see* them," the source of that sly little laugh declared, with some surprise. It was a woman: small, blonde, and perhaps a few years younger than Ingrid. She sat alone in a high-backed booth that seemed to swallow up what little light the lone candle on her tabletop managed to project. "And now you see me too. What in the worlds are you?"

"Not dead," Ingrid said, feeling this was explanation enough. "What's *your* story?"

The elfin blonde laughed again—a delicate, pretty sound. Ingrid took a moment to look her over. She sat lengthwise in her booth, with her legs stretched out in front of her on the bench seat as she leaned back against the far wall. She was wrapped in a loose, light tea gown, and lounged far too comfortably to be corseted underneath it. Cute black boots with short, squared-off heels poked out from under the ruffled mass of her skirts. She had a drowsy, self-satisfied expression on her face and wore her straw-colored hair piled up atop her head in a frowsy Gibson Girl mass.

She appraised Ingrid as well, and the corners of her lips curled mischievously.

Ingrid slid into the booth across from her and looked her right in the eye.

"Call me Poppy," the blonde girl said, offering a hand as slight and pale as a lily petal across the table, as if she expected Ingrid might kiss it.

"Do I know you?" Ingrid asked, ignoring the gesture. There *was* something oddly familiar about this Poppy, she thought as she set her un-worn hat aside. Something about her mannerisms or her attitude, although she couldn't quite put her finger on it.

"Have you been here before?" Poppy asked, sitting up straight and turning to face Ingrid properly. She leaned in, cupping her chin in both hands and propping her elbows on the tabletop as she smiled. The pupils at the centers of her lovely purple eyes looked overly large and excessively deep. "Downstairs, I mean," she teased. "Spent an afternoon or two drowsing and dreaming of bejeweled worlds that never ever were? Hmm?"

Ingrid nodded reluctantly.

"Then I suppose you know me."

"Why don't I remember you?"

Poppy shrugged. "Your memory for names and faces must be as poor a thing as my own," she said. "People come and people go, and it's quite beyond me to remember them all. Still, one like you would tend to stand out, I'd think. I don't suppose you came very often?"

Ingrid shook her head. No, not so often. Not as often as Finn.

"Well, some don't," Poppy said with a dismissive sniff. "While others can't bear to be away."

That made her think of Finn too. She couldn't stop, all of a sudden, when she'd forced herself not to think about him for so long. Her dismay over what he'd done probably would've snowballed into grief and anger already, if not for the sure knowledge that even in death her former love wasn't entirely out of her reach. Mictlantecuhtli's patronage had changed life's most fundamental rule, and that was what she needed to remember.

Poppy was smiling that knowing smile up at her, from across their stained and scarred tabletop. She reached out and clasped Ingrid's hand in both of her own, earnestly, like she meant to either confess or confide.

"*Do* say you'll go downstairs with me," she begged. "Oh, please do say you will! It's ever so crowded up here, and loud," (although Ingrid, personally, thought the room was only at about a dull roar), "—and the noise is starting to hurt my head!"

Ingrid wanted to draw her hand away, but Miss Poppy held on tight, as if in real desperation. The girl's hungry eyes had also fallen right to her chest, in classic mannish fashion. But then they also stopped on her throat and even bounced all the way up to the center of her forehead before leveling to meet her gaze, and Ingrid understood that Pops was fixated not on her physical endowments, but on the subtle energy whorls that ran up and down the median of her spine.

Poppy was eyeing not her body, but her soul. Which seemed like even more of an intrusion, in a way.

She hopped out of the booth but slid right back in again, on Ingrid's side of it this time. The aggressive waif pressed in tight before Ingrid could say anything at all, backing her into the booth's furthest corner, as though the bench they now shared had shrunk to less than half of its actual size. In such close quarters the girl smelled both stale and sweet, like she might've chosen a liberal application of perfume over a bath at some point in the recent past, but even as Ingrid wrinkled her nose and recoiled she knew that she didn't find Poppy's rudely-imposed nearness to be an entirely unpleasant thing. The woman radiated a bizarre sort of magnetism, and Ingrid's head swam with the effects of it. She thought she could just as easily have leaned in, rather than shying away, in order to catch this compellingly sordid little stranger up and gather her into her arms...

Instead she made a quick hand sign that recalled a moment in her magical education when, under the influence of various spirits and in the company of experienced guides, she had attained the ability to see the subtle energy systems that operate within entities of every kind.

That ability came back to her now—just a flash, triggered by the mnemonic gesture—and she looked into Poppy the same way Poppy had looked into her.

The first thing she saw was that this 'Poppy' person wasn't a person at all and never even could have been, as she possessed the wrong number of *chakra* points for it. Ingrid counted only five, all of them a seething, ember-like orange, as opposed to her own rainbow-hued collection of seven. So Poppy wasn't one of the dead (whose root chakras appeared burnt out and black, like cigarette scars on a tabletop). That revelation didn't tell Ingrid what she *was*, exactly, but it provided a hint that the pseudo-girl might not be playing by all of Mictlan's ordinary rules. The entity calling itself Poppy may have been no more bound by the letter of Lord Death's authority than she was.

"What are you?" she asked again, pushing Poppy back from herself with a hand placed on the creature's bird-boned shoulder. Her (or 'its') glassy eyes shone from pits of oily, bruised-looking flesh. When she grinned up at Ingrid now, it looked more like she was baring her teeth.

"Why, *I* am Lord Death's guest, just the same as you must be," Poppy insinuated. "Isn't that right?"

Ingrid didn't hurry to respond.

"He asked us here specifically, you know," the girl said. Tauntingly, Ingrid thought, like she was trying to get a rise out of her. "King Mictlantecuhtli, that is," Poppy breezily explained, as if she could possibly have been referring to anyone else. "Not that he could really forbid us, when we have our rightful claims upon so many of his sad old souls. Still, acceding to his little wishes seemed like the polite thing to do, wouldn't you say?"

"We?" Ingrid queried.

"Why, the Green Fairies," Poppy said, like it was the most obvious thing in the world. "As well as myself, of course. Darling Mickey said these were the aspects of our being that his newest concubine remembers fondly, whosoever she may turn out to be."

"Oh, Mickey did, did he?" Ingrid said, feeling a hot coal kindle deep in the pit of her stomach upon hearing Poppy so casually drop the nickname she'd given to her King. That's right, *her* King, she reiterated, emphasizing the personal pronoun in her head. He was hers and she would not share. Mickey's petulant display of envy over the content of Lucy's memories may have been an ugly enough thing to behold, but it was nothing compared to her own sudden resentment of this half-real brat beside her.

What a pair we make, Ingrid chided herself as she compared her emotional response against the King's. *Jealous enough between the two of us to set the worlds on fire.*

"But he must surely have invited *you,* too," Poppy said. "Unless... Oh, my." She clapped both hands over her mouth in an expression of mock surprise. "You wouldn't be *her,* would you?" she asked with wide eyes, from behind a steeple of pressed-together fingertips.

"The aforementioned concubine, you mean?"

Poppy giggled, but it sounded wickedly amused rather than nervous or abashed. "A living girl, this time—I hadn't expected that, to be sure," the coquettish creature purred, stroking Ingrid's arm and giving her shoulder a quick experimental squeeze, as if to verify her solidity. "How absolutely star-crossed."

Ingrid declined to comment. She was nearing the end of her tolerance for Poppy's particular brand of bullshit. "I'd like to know what you are," she said, "and I'd like to know right now."

"Come downstairs and see for yourself," Poppy breathed into her ear, as her hand found its way to the chakra centered in her solar plexus. "We can better enjoy ourselves down there, I'm sure."

Ingrid pinched what should've been a pressure point in the girl-thing's wrist and twisted her arm back, slamming her down against the tabletop while levering her small shoulder close to the point of dislocation. It was a maneuver known to wring hot tears and profuse apologies out of full-grown men, but all Poppy did was cackle like Ingrid was tickling her. Pissed off now, Ingrid responded by increasing the torque on the girl's pale, frail arm, mashing her face down into a scum of spilled beer until something audibly cracked in the back of her neck. It was far more vicious behavior than the situation called for, but Ingrid felt she'd been toyed with enough for one day, and the meanest, nastiest part of herself—the part that only came out when she was exhausted and frustrated beyond all reason—wanted to hear smug little Poppy squeal.

She couldn't pay it back to Mickey, so taking it out on one of his so-called 'guests' was going to have to do.

Her moment of cruel satisfaction was not to be, however. Ingrid's hand sank right through Poppy's shoulderblade and touched the splintery, damp surface of the tabletop before she gasped and yanked it back, thinking for an instant she must've somehow killed the tiny woman (even though she knew such a thing wasn't strictly possible). The fingers pinning Poppy's wrist closed in on themselves, cuffing nothing but empty air while Poppy, still laughing, dissolved into misty smoke that floated up from the table in lazy blue streamers. The fumes smelled rich and resinous, sweet and earthy and vaguely sexy all at once, and Ingrid recognized the scent immediately.

It could only be opium vapor.

Her head seemed to wobble on its axis from the accidental lungful of Poppy's essence she inhaled. She slumped back in her seat, coughing out the smoke and feeling a wave of relaxation wash over her that was so profound she had trouble keeping her eyes focused. She blinked hard, forcing her gloomy surroundings back into relative clarity.

Poppy's string of five orange chakras arced over the tabletop like water poured from one glass to another and landed on the far bench, one atop the next. They drew their thin fog of narcotic dreamsmoke along in their wake and it coalesced around them, swirling back into a very convincing simulation of a beaming, languorous, drowsy-eyed young woman.

"*You* remember me," the reconstituted Poppy said, leaning back in imitation of Ingrid's posture. She stretched her arms across the back of the booth and let her head loll bonelessly to one side, like it was too much effort to hold it up. Her grin was all teeth. "You remember me very well, I think."

Ingrid nodded. Yes, she supposed she did at that. Her mind was beginning to race even as her muscles unwound, in a very familiar fashion. Choosing words to say aloud was becoming a bit of a chore, when such a plethora of them suddenly seemed present and available inside her echoing head.

"So you're… what, like a plant spirit?" she barked, too loud. Her thoughts seemed to stretch out like pulled taffy before looping back on themselves. "The Opium Ghost or something? Like Mickey's Tzitzimime?"

"Not merely." Poppy sniffed, straightening up her spine a bit in response to the perceived challenge to her pride. "Do I look like some simpleminded necrophage to you?"

Ingrid shrugged, and Poppy scowled.

"I am Nepenthe: daughter of Nyx, Lady Night, and Hypnos, the Face of Sleep," she said. "I am sister to Morpheus, Ikelos, and Phantasos: the Oneiroi Dreambringers. I am Hul Gil, the Plant of Joy, and Ahi-phena the Venom Flower, companion of physicians and magicians for five centuries of centuries and more. My blossoms wreathe the shoulders of gods. My milk so eases the agonies of living flesh that the incarnate pledge themselves to me, body and soul, in the desperate hope of knowing my mercies. *I* am not of this realm, though not even your precious Death can banish me from it, as my reach transcends mortality. Something you and I would seem to have in common, hmm?"

Ingrid nodded again, absently, thinking that these otherworlders sure could yap, especially when they felt offended. Mickey was the same way, as soon as you failed to react with visible awe to whatever he happened to be doing or saying. It was frustrating enough to give her a headache, as was the effort required to process Poppy's tiresome listing of traits and titles.

She became aware that the half-crowded pub now seemed uncomfortably loud, although nothing but her own perspective had changed.

Poppy was watching her, curiously and quietly, with that eternal Mona Lisa smile dimpling the corners of her rosy-pink mouth. She'd asked a question of some sort, hadn't she? Maybe a rhetorical one, but Ingrid had failed to acknowledge it in any case, and now she couldn't even recall what it had been. Not that she thought the girl really wanted to chat. It was more a question of her knowing what sort of effect she was having, and in that regard, Ingrid could tell that prescient Poppy was very well aware.

She wished they were downstairs already, where they could be alone with the slow-burning glow of the lamp over which they were meant to heat their long pipes. She'd spent hours with Finn in just that manner, so many hours that multiple days had sometimes slid by them like a slow black river, broken only by infrequent meals and the performances of their act they'd managed to surface for. Submerging herself like that had frightened her back then, and yet she ached to give herself over to Poppy now, as completely as she could. She longed to be pulled down into her depths. It would've been so *easy*…

But then Ingrid happened to notice one of those green fairies, one of the tiny women with the hummingbird wings and the eyes as bright as bottle glass, and it drew her gaze away.

She watched the fascinating creature land like a tame thing on the collarbone of a very drunk dead woman who was sitting alone at a table across the room, just as she poured water from a carafe into a tall footed glass about one-quarter filled with an emerald green liqueur. The absinthe turned cloudy and pearlescent as the water swirled in. The tiny green woman and the rest of her flock were absinthe fairies, and Ingrid didn't know why she hadn't recognized them before, as there were fanciful artists' depictions of them in half the posters tacked up onto the plaster walls of this very bar.

While she marveled at the green fairy it tipped its head toward the deceased alcoholic's neck and drew blue energy from its host's throat chakra when the woman raised her glass to drink, funneling it off in a ghostly stream. Others of its kind were doing likewise, all around the room.

The fairies were feeding on the dead. The winged women were little more than tiny green vampires, carrion vampires, and Ingrid jerked when the understanding hit her. She yanked her hand back from Poppy with a gasp and shrank from the opium eidolon as it hissed up at her in frustrated rage.

"*Oh*, for fuck's sake!" Poppy barked, slamming her small fist down on the tabletop. "Quit *pretending* you don't want me!"

Ingrid scrambled out of the booth, away from her, almost tripping over her own long nightgown. Her limbs felt leaden and sluggish and she stumbled against the nearest table, catching herself on the back of a chair. Two startled absinthe fairies chirped angrily as they buzzed off from their perches in search of other prey. The seated dead couple they'd been feeding on looked up at her with bleary, besotted eyes, but neither of them said a word. Perhaps they couldn't, so soon after having the ragged remainders of their souls violated by beings they couldn't even see.

Everywhere Ingrid looked, jade-skinned fairies were sating themselves, sipping delicately from ethereal energy pools that closed and swirled back toward their own centers once the parasites withdrew. The punctured chakras continued to look depleted and unhealthy—blocked in ways that were sure to be a source of torment to their deceased owners. Ingrid felt her stomach drop away and she broke out in a cold sweat, as if she'd smoked too many pipes too fast and would now be violently ill as a consequence. The Lady of the Poppies tended to punish a careless performance of her ritual quite harshly, as Finn had taught her in a past that wasn't as long ago as it felt.

"You're making a perfect ass of yourself, you know," the flower's flirtatious blonde avatar said. "You might want to sit down before you fall down. Really, you might."

Ingrid knew the sound of good advice, but she wasn't about to take it from a parasitic plant phantom. She sensed it would be an enormous mistake to do anything Poppy wanted. Acquiescing to her wishes would surely be the first step toward winding up in her thrall.

"You... you *feed* on them," Ingrid croaked, making no attempt whatsoever to hide her revulsion.

Poppy shrugged. "Why let them go to waste, just because they've passed their expirations? What's left over can still be squeezed for nourishment. They are unpleasantly stale, it's true, but they last practically forever."

She drew her lips back from her small, sharp teeth in what was probably meant to be a smile, but wound up looking far more lurid and sinister.

"The ones you owned in life still need you over here? All of them?" Ingrid pressed, wondering sickly if Finn was out there being 'squeezed' right now, somewhere within the vastness of Mickey's realm. "You don't ever let them go?"

"Well, they still want us, in any case," Poppy said. "And being wanted is what really counts in the end, now isn't it?"

Ingrid hardly felt qualified to say. Her nightgown was plastered to her back, down between her shoulderblades, and her brow felt beaded with sweat. The lounge's atmosphere tasted thick and noxious, like it was composed more of cigar smoke than oxygenated air.

In the next instant Poppy was out of the booth and standing in front of her, having crossed the intervening distance like a breath of mist before coming back together without so much as a whisper. She pressed close and laid a hand on Ingrid's sternum.

"And you still have your beating heart, too," Poppy murmured, stroking at Ingrid's chest with velvet fingertips. "All hot and red and wet. It's no wonder whatsoever that dried up old Death is so utterly mad over you."

The *Genius flosculus*—the little flower spirit—pressed in closer, and her small belly felt as taut as a drumhead against Ingrid's own.

"I can keep you happy," the eidolon swore to her, in a low, pleading tone of voice. "We both know I can. Be mine, here in Mictlantecuhtli's realm, and that living heart of yours might stay fresh and full and ripe for me till all the worlds turn black around us."

"Thank you, no," Ingrid heard herself saying, even though her tongue felt far too thick to form words. Her skin sang with wild chills anyplace Poppy touched her. The seductive thing was second cousin to a succubus. To give in to her now, Ingrid understood, would be bliss. Pure ecstasy, and it would never have to end, not if she didn't want it to. Not over here. The only catch was she'd be trapped, for all eternity.

Pulling away from Poppy took almost more effort than she was able to make, but somehow she managed it.

Managed it only to promptly trip over her own hem and go sprawling, gracelessly and painfully, onto her ass in the middle of the floor.

Poppy's peal of laughter over the pratfall was harsh, bright and discordant, like a windchime dashed against a wall. She clapped her hands to her mouth and bent over double with the sheer force of her hilarity. Dead drinkers all around the room joined her in sarcastically toasting Ingrid's lack of coordination. Most of the chortling corpses were unknowingly studded at their necks and torsos with gluttonous green fairies: tiny leeches that consumed precisely the sort of pain and fear these people had spent their lifetimes trying to drown. The dead seemed not to have the first inkling that they were being farmed, for all intents and purposes, by Poppy and her ilk. Lucinda Swire's Cock & Bull was a closed loop for them, seamless and inescapable, where their torment was exploited for the entities' enjoyment. That knowledge made this place where Ingrid had spent so many hours feel stifling. Oppressive. All she could think of was getting out. Every other concern was shunted away to the periphery of her consciousness by a sudden need for fresh air, and she thought her chest would explode if she couldn't get to it right away.

Poppy was beside her in an instant, materializing out of nowhere like she did. The eidolon offered a hand to help her up, but Ingrid batted it aside. It was important not to accept Poppy's help or give in to her wishes, in even the tiniest of ways. Ingrid made it to her feet before the silver-tongued spirit could speak and shoved past her, reeling blindly across the room, through the crowd, and—she hoped—toward some sort of escape.

SHE almost didn't know how it happened, but moments later she found herself outdoors, in the deserted street outside the public house, with the heavy front door slamming shut behind her. She was, miraculously, still clutching her huge red hat, like it was some sort of floppy and ill-designed shield. The night's rain-scrubbed chill hit her like a slap after the humid human warmth inside the bar, and the raucous noise emanating from within already sounded distant, abstract, and unconnected to her. She felt dizzy and poorly balanced when she tried to walk in her red pumps, too tall, like her legs had somehow stretched just enough to affect her sense of equilibrium. She could smell the flat, muddy, mineral scent of the Thames, mere blocks away, and it made her stomach clench like a fist inside her.

Ingrid braced herself against a lamp post halfway down the block from the Cock & Bull and vomited garish yellow bile into the gutter, an act which, while wrenching and unpleasant, also had the effect of clearing her head so thoroughly that it almost came as a relief. The post's cold wrought iron felt wonderful when she laid the side of her flushed face against it, after she was done throwing up and all was blessedly quiet once again.

When she opened her eyes and looked around, she saw that neither Poppy nor anyone else had followed her out of the pub. She had the entire street to herself—if not the entire city.

It looked as much like gaslit London as any of her very clearest memories, down to the glistening cobblestones at her feet and the narrow brick buildings across the way that stood jammed together like a row of uneven teeth. Ships' masts with furled sails lashed to them rose up behind the rooftops. The docks were that close by.

Ingrid supposed the illusion's persistence meant that Mickey was still asleep upstairs, true to his word as a god and a gentleman. She probably had about six hours left to go before he'd wake. She wished she could crawl back into bed with him now, but she didn't feel like she could go back inside. She wasn't ready to risk facing Poppy, or Lucinda, or anybody else again so soon.

She turned around and was only partially surprised to see the Temple of Mictlantecuhtli—that monumental step-sided adobe pyramid—standing incongruously against the leaden sky. It was the tallest building in the neighborhood by a good margin, and it seemed to be located only a few blocks away, to the north, positioned behind dark dockside warehouses and precarious stacks of low-rent flats. Its surreal, imposing presence was the only visual reminder that this gray and misty place wasn't actually London's east end at all, but a suburb of Mictlan, the great necropolis.

Ingrid spat some more of the sourness out of her mouth, smoothed down her unruly explosion of hair, and started toward the Aztec temple on the near horizon, mostly for lack of anything better to do.

S HE found her new suit of clothes lying in a pile of crimson pinstripes right where she'd shed them, up on the Pyramid's very top level, outside the door to the temple's inner sanctum. She kicked her pumps aside and pulled her clammy, sweat-stiffened chemise off over her head, then took the time to dress. Knickers and camisole first, followed by a high-collared shirtwaist and a thin red necktie that she knotted and pinned into place. Then the suit itself went on. First the narrow, ankle-length skirt that made her legs look about a mile long and was supposed to be the very latest thing for the coming season, topped by a double-breasted paletot jacket that was trimmed in scarlet silk at the lapels and belted at the midriff. Finally she stepped back into her blood-colored shoes and worked her slender fingers down into her tight white kid-leather gloves.

By the time she'd bound her chaotic hair into submission with a stray satin ribbon and settled her red hat with its shoulder-width brim back up onto the crown of her head, Ingrid was starting to feel like herself again.

She already regretted walking out on Mickey while he slept, without so much as a thank you for his efforts or even the courtesy of a proper goodbye. She'd been on the receiving end of similar treatment once or twice before and she knew it didn't feel especially good. Not good at all, really, but it couldn't be helped. She needed time to think, and she wouldn't be able to do it over here.

When she looked back one last time before stepping into the altar chamber, London was still spread out down below her, in a dark wedge that expanded out from the Pyramid's base. She could make out and even hear the Cock & Bull, lit up and rollicking as it was. Then there was the river beyond it, twisting through the cityscape like a dark, muscular serpent. The cone of visible city looked as though a stiff gust of wind might have just then revealed it by parting Mictlan's curtain of omnipresent fog. The familiar black-limbed, leafless trees hung half-obscured in the smoky mists that continued to roil beyond the diagonal edges of the cleared zone. It looked like it could close up again at any instant, erasing the metropolitan mirage King Death had called into being.

He'd done it either to please her or to tease her, and she still hadn't figured out which.

"Mickey... you unbelievable shit," Ingrid muttered, shaking her head and sighing as she turned away from his realm to enter the inner sanctum of the pre-Columbian temple he maintained over here, on his side of the fabled Hole in the Sky.

S HE walked right past the round limestone altar in the center of the room and went straight to the far door, the one that opened onto the first chamber and from there led back out to the living world. The antechamber looked exactly the way she remembered leaving it, circa 1910: with the old adobe walls freshly plastered over and painted, with electric light fixtures in the place of pitch-soaked torches, with new carpet laid down on the floor and gleaming pressed copper tacked up onto the ceiling, making it almost the same warm color as her own autumnal hair. The chamber's exit door (the newly-fashioned frame around the actual holy SkyHole itself) was still open to blue daylight, and that seemed somehow wrong to Ingrid, when she could turn around and look out onto a cloudy night through the door immediately behind her. It was like walking out of a darkened nickelodeon and back into the same sunny afternoon on which she'd bought a ticket, having been so wrapped up in the picture show that it felt as though days if not lifetimes should've rolled by while she watched. The surreal sensation left her feeling a step out of sync with the rest of the regular world.

Ingrid therefore closed her eyes and turned the hours forward, mentally, the way Mickey had taught her, in a half-considered attempt to better align her perceptions with her expectations. She figured she might watch the sun come up on the next new day, then borrow a horse for the ride home to Los Angeles when the work crews arrived soon after dawn.

This would be the first time she attempted to visit her own future, but Mickey's rhetoric led her to expect it was possible. The realm of the dead lay outside of time, the way he told it, and so its orientation to the living world need not be strictly chronological.

Right?

It all sounded good, except it didn't work.

That isn't to say something hadn't occurred by the time she opened her eyes. Something quite clearly had. She just didn't know what it was.

The sky beyond the door hole had turned a deep twilight indigo, for one thing, verging on a royal purple, when she'd aimed for a black nighttime hour that would approximate the current conditions in Mictlan. Tabulating moments in time like beads on an abacus was far from an exact science, but Ingrid was still surprised to have missed her mark quite so badly. She wasn't even sure if it was dawn or dusk she was looking at out there.

More than the hour felt off-kilter, but it was only when she stepped into the antechamber that she perceived the subtle changes it had undergone.

The walls, previously painted in a mellow shade of mint green, were now colored only by an amazingly uniform layer of lichen and moss. The carpet underfoot had turned to sod, as neatly manicured as a golf course putting green. The new ceiling had changed into varnished wood, although it remained carved in the same floret pattern that had been pressed into the now-vanished copper tiles.

Ingrid clutched at the fat red garnet Mickey had given her the last time she'd gone out traveling—the talisman that let her remember her name and herself in spite of prevailing chronological conditions—which she'd carelessly left behind in one of her jacket's concealed pockets. Thank whoever might be appropriate that it was still there.

She waited with bated breath to see what would happen, but her mind and her memories remained unscrambled inside the fragile eggshell of her head, while the weird new environment around her remained all too vividly real.

Her heels sank seed-hole divots into the spongy turf-carpet when she hurried over to the living world's door and looked out, into the crepuscular violet stillness that had shown up in place of the starry night in 1910 she'd aimed for. She'd meant to hop five or six hours into her own future. It should have been as easy as daydreaming. But the sight that greeted her only served to deepen the mystery.

Ingrid found herself near the top of a partially completed skyscraper, exactly as she expected, only this building wasn't under construction, founded on concrete, or even framed in steel. It was all made of wood— of living, rooted wood—and it was somehow being *grown*.

She could see four separate trunks stretching down toward a perspective point from either side of her perch. Laddered rungs of horizontal limbs grew together all the way up, meeting and merging to form the rudiments of floors, doorways, and window frames. Both bark and branches seemed to be taking on a curiously smooth, almost fluid quality, like surf-polished driftwood, as they came into architectural focus on a slow organic timetable. Ingrid suspected the decorative florets on the ceiling might actually have blossomed there, rather than being carved. She had little doubt that the entire structure would be realized in comparable detail within a few more fruitful growing seasons.

The total effect was dizzying, and she stood back from the doorway, fearing she might swoon with vertigo and go tumbling out.

What the hell was going on here?

She twisted her ankle into a bright bolt of pain when she turned on her heel to flee and it dug down into the sod floor, upsetting her balance. She crossed the antechamber in one long careening stumble and fell to her knees once she'd made it back across the threshold between life and death, only barely managing to avoid dashing her teeth against the stone altar when she fell.

She squeezed her eyes shut and was pulling back the hours before her scraped palms had even stopped their stinging, before her pulse had stopped hammering in her throat and temples, before she'd even thought to get up from the kneeling crouch in which she'd rather painfully landed. She thought she felt time's great wheel turning, but the sensation was so internal and subjective that anxiety made her doubt it.

The first chamber and the clear blue sky she glimpsed through its open doorway looked normal enough again by the time she dared to take a peek. This felt like the moment she'd started off from, sure enough, right back in plain old 1910. She could hear the faint clanging, clattering, and banging sounds of construction work rising up to her from far below. She could hear the flimsy mechanical service elevator ratcheting up toward her unfinished floor as well, no doubt bearing an unwelcome payload of the King's Men: nosy Mr. Winston Watt and the affable architect Oscar San Martín.

Ingrid did not feel like dealing with them at the moment. Not with either of them. The thought of making even the most minimal conversation wearied her beyond all reason.

Besides which, she needed to know if what had just happened with the metaphysical machinery that aligned the worlds was a one-off fluke, or something she should worry about further. She'd dropped back to her starting point so easily that she had some hope of finding everything settled back into its proper working order when she spun the worlds and tried her luck again.

So she closed her eyes and concentrated on moving time forward by a tiny little bit. Just until silence took over from the distant noises of a realworld skyscraper being assembled by busy human hands.

Ingrid un-scrunched her eyes and saw what she feared she might: more purple sky out beyond the door. The air again felt heavy with a charged and ominous stillness, like the pent-up breath of a storm that hadn't yet begun to howl. Things were by no means back to normal.

The antechamber had changed again.

Gone was the natural wooden warmth the office at the top of the topiary tower exuded. The bright copper ceiling was back in place, however, as was the green paint on the walls. Thin wires snaking out from under the red metal plates overhead had been gathered into fat cables and strung along the moldings to the room's corners, where they stretched down to the floor and disappeared beneath non-conductive porcelain tiles that had sprung up in place of the green grass rug.

Ingrid's heels clicked on the insulated floor when she crossed to the exit portal. Each unglazed ceramic square underfoot was embossed with the same ornamental daisies that were stamped into the sheet-metal ceiling above. She could already hazard a guess at what she might see when she looked down from the Hole in the Sky again, but the intricacy of the astonishing artificial tree that had swapped places with the organic building was more than enough to take her breath away.

Its canopy of foliage was sparse, perhaps due to the season, and yet Ingrid could see a smattering of translucent leaves on display a few scant feet below her vantage point. Green glass leaves veined with filaments of copper and gold, lovely things more finely wrought than jewelry. She was tempted to flatten out on the floor and see if she could reach down far enough to pluck one. The tree's trunk was a braid of thigh-thick iron cables, as big around at its base as the original oak had been, and its trailing ends plugged right into the earth like a root system. The twisted limbs it thrust up at her were crusted in bark-like flakes of reddish-brown rust. Individual threads within the cable-branches looked sprung, snarled, and dangerously sharp, giving Ingrid a sense that trying to climb down this tree would be a fool's gamble against tetanus, at best. She saw clumps of tiny white lightbulbs hanging like milky glass mistletoe berries. The whole apparatus hummed in a frequency so low it felt more like a pressure on the eardrums than an actual sound. But the electrical sconces on the walls were lit, so she knew the elaborate 'power plant' had to be doing something.

Ingrid turned away from the vision without attempting to pick a leaf and hurried back to Mictlan. A sharp pain stabbed through her left ankle with each step, surprising her, and she had to think back to remember she'd twisted it a few moments ago. This crazy-quilt of overlapping timelines had her that disoriented.

It was again no problem at all to dial herself back to the instant she'd come in from, right before this latest visit with Mickey and all of his fascinating friends.

But the future was broken. Bifurcated. Ingrid had seen two realities, each attempting to fill a single slot in space and time with both a Tower and a Tree. Mictlantecuhtli had wedged her new skyscraper into the realworld with little regard for cause and effect, and now the slow road forward seemed to fork around it. Time had split in two at the moment of her last departure from the living world, and the doubled-up information now became jumbled when she tried to jump ahead.

The unseen elevator's mechanical racket reached its zenith then died away to an almost grateful-sounding silence, leaving Ingrid to conclude that Winston Watt and San Martín had finally joined her up here on the incomplete skyscraper's executive floor. They'd be starting their vertiginous shuffle down the bare girder and toward the King's Chambers, las Cameras del Rey, even now. Her entire visit to Mictlan— the reunion with Lucinda, the introduction to Poppy, and the bitter grappling with Mickey all included—had taken place within the span of their dozen-story, ninety-second elevator ride.

At least it had from their point of view. Disillusioned and weary as she was, Ingrid had to smile over that.

The approach of the King's Men also meant that time had resumed passing in its proper fashion. The globe was spinning on its axis and the white winter sun had resumed cutting its way across the top of the sky. The *blue* sky. Below her would be most of a steel-framed building, swaddled up in ancient hexwork and wards, where once there had stood a magnificent millennial tree.

It looked as though the living world would still run, Ingrid concluded, as long as she was in it to live the moments forward personally, in their proper sequential order. Picking up where she left off seemed to be the key.

That would have to do, for now. She could ponder the meaning of it all later.

Oscar San Martín swung himself off the girder and into the room—into sight, at last—just as she was straightening her skirt. Mr. Watt was not far behind him. Ingrid now felt absurdly glad to see them both—as representatives of normalcy, if not as individuals. San Martín's broad shoulders blocked out most of the sky while he stood in the doorway, gawping at her. Watt shuffled in around him and stood aside, back against the wall, folding skinny arms across a scrawny chest.

"Ready when you are, boys," Ingrid told them.

"But... you can't be done," Oscar said, his expression blooming into a grin that withered to a puzzled frown as soon as he realized she wasn't joking. "Not already…?"

Watt glared at her, but she was getting used to that, as she supposed everyone who dealt with him eventually must. Not the most personable of people was Winston Watt, and he seemed to know it as well as anybody. Ingrid saw no reason to take his habitual churlishness especially to heart.

Both men were taking stock of her, their brows ticking together in consternation over what they saw. The discrepancies were subtle, such as wrinkled linen where her suit had previously been pressed smooth, as well as the scuffs and smudges of dried blood around her knees, where she'd scraped them against the temple's floor in her fall. Her big feathered hat could only do so much to disguise the damage done to her expensive coiffure. She wouldn't have been surprised if the kohl she'd painted around her eyes that morning had smeared badly enough to make her look like she'd been punched in the face. She smelled of sweat, sex, and opium too.

"*What* is going on here?" San Martín asked, softly and semi-rhetorically. "It hasn't been a minute."

"The Time of Men does not equate with the Time of Gods," Watt intoned, as portentously and pretentiously as Mickey might have himself. Ingrid heard every emphasized capital. She found herself nodding, agreeing with him that no, it sure as hell did not, though she declined to share her thoughts aloud. Of the two acolytes, Mr. Watt seemed a bit faster on the uptake, at least when it came to envy and suspicion. "She might've spent a week on the other side and still come back to right now," he elucidated, with no small degree of condescension, for the benefit of his baffled colleague.

Oscar nodded as his remedial comprehension of the impossible event filled itself in. Dead time was not the same as living time, not by a damn sight. He knew that. Knew it intellectually, anyway, as astronomers and navigators had once known the world must be round, despite the evidence of everyday common sense. Ingrid watched these notions shimmering across the architect's guileless face like sunlight on a shallow river bed.

Watt continued to regard her with the same sneer he aimed at pretty much everything.

"Where… where is el Rey?" San Martín ventured, his voice catching on the first syllable. He craned his neck, attempting to peer around her and into the torch-lit shadows of the sacrificial chamber, like he thought Lord Death might be playing peekaboo or some goddamn thing. "Mictlantecuhtli?"

"He's napping," Ingrid said.

"*Napping?*" Mickey's servants repeated in unison, their incredulity on full display.

"But he… he's… I mean, he doesn't…" San Martín sputtered, trying to start a sentence before he had a firm enough grasp on his objections.

"Death never sleeps, as we all well know," Watt supplied, in a dark and accusatory tone. "So don't tell us. No, no—it's all right," he said, dismissing her budding protestations with a wave of his hand. "Keep your secrets. And we'll keep ours, as we always have."

Ingrid rolled her eyes. She really couldn't help it. All of this intrigue and infighting was so unnecessary, except that Watt seemed to require it for some reason, and uncertain San Martín was being pulled along in the wake of his mistrust.

She didn't know how to combat those sorts of misgivings, or if she should even try. She wished things could've been different between herself and the King's Men. They were her closest peers, after all.

Looking into Watt's face, though, she knew she might as well have wished for a pot of gold and a functioning pair of fairy wings. She'd stolen enough from them already simply by showing up, according to his interpretation.

"Have it your way, Mr. Watt," was all she chose to say.

Watt nodded once, sagely, like he'd expected no less and was now seeing his worst theories about her confirmed. San Martín looked from her to Watt and back again, with something like sadness darkening his clever, gentle eyes.

The King's Men stood there, waiting for her to make the next move.

"Right," Ingrid said, attempting to sound decisive when she felt anything but. "Shall we?"

"Shall we what?" Watt asked.

"Um… go?" Ingrid suggested. "Back to Los Angeles?"

"Back to *Los Angeles?*" Watt repeated, as if he couldn't possibly have heard her correctly. As if she'd demanded a ride to Chicago or to Paris or maybe all the way up to the moon instead of a city less than an hour's drive to the east. "But we've only just arrived."

"You've only just arrived, Mr. Watt," Ingrid reminded him. "I've been here for some time, as you were good enough to point out to Mr. San Martín. And I would like to go home now, if you please."

"But I have business with the King," Winston insisted. "I need to see him."

"You might be waiting for a while," Ingrid warned. "He really is asleep."

Watt sneered, as though he were too sharp to believe one word of *that* bullshit script, no matter how often she quoted from it. "I believe I'll chance it anyway, if it's all the same to you."

"Well, actually..." Ingrid had no intention, herself, of standing around for the next five or six hours, while the sun went down and the night turned frigid around them. Mickey wouldn't be awake any sooner.

"I can drive you," San Martín offered, well before she had a chance to finish her sentence. When both Ingrid and Watt turned to look at him, he offered a sheepish half-shrug. "I'm going downtown," he said. "It's no trouble."

"Fine," she said to Oscar. "Thank you." And then, turning to Winston: "Say hi to el Rey for me, if you would. Tell him..." *Tell him I'm sorry*, she almost said, then thought better of it. "Tell him I'll be back. Soon. And I hope you left a jacket in your auto-mobile, if you intend to stick around till he wakes up. You're going to need it."

Winston nodded but made a face, both acknowledging and dismissing what she was telling him. He seemed secure in his belief that she had to be winding him up for her own mean amusement. Ingrid expected Watt would abandon his vigil and drive home long before the King awoke. He'd probably interpret Mickey's failure to appear as the capper to her elaborate gag and use it to stoke his anger against her, even though she'd told him nothing but the unvarnished truth about what to expect.

So stupid, all of this posturing and distrust. So pointless. But it was the hand they'd been dealt, and now it seemed they had little choice but to play it out.

San Martín stood aside, offering her first use of the exit portal. He couldn't hold the door for her, gentleman or not, as he had yet to hang one.

Ingrid was outside, on the girder and in the breeze, with nothing but bright blue sky above her and the King's Architect following right behind, before Winston lobbed his parting shot.

"Were I you, I'd enjoy my privilege while I'm able," he said, coming to the doorway to lean out after them, although it wasn't clear if he meant to address Ingrid, Oscar, or both of them together. They paused and looked back together, suspended a few yards from the waiting lift and a hundred feet above the earth.

"Don't forget," Watt warned, raising his voice over the breeze that sang through the building's bare superstructure, and what he said next filled Ingrid with a deep premonitory chill, one that wouldn't thaw out again for a good long while:

"—Black Tom is coming home."

Chapter Four

B LACK Tom?" Ingrid said, turning on the truck's bench seat to watch San Martín's face as soon as they'd lost the construction site behind the scrim of brown dust their wood-spoked wheels kicked up. They were the first words either of them had spoken since Winston Watt made his enigmatic threat.

"It's just a name," Oscar hedged, keeping his eyes on the rutted road ahead. "A nickname."

"I didn't think it was a brand of baked beans." The young architect surprised her by wincing, as if the barb had actually contained some pith. "Who is he?"

Oscar hesitated. "You're not from here, are you?" he asked. "From Los Angeles? Originally?"

Ingrid shook her head. She'd been born in San Francisco but she didn't say so. A policy of not volunteering more information than was asked for seemed wise.

"Most operators in town know that name, but a lot are still afraid to say it," the architect said. "Ten years ago he made a deal with el Rey to, um, destroy the inner order of the Aurea Catena."

Oh. Ingrid *had* heard that story, or the outlines of it. Her acquaintance with the surviving members of the exclusive and secretive Order of the Golden Chain hadn't been long, yet she'd had time enough amongst them to sample their favorite gossip. The bloody demise of the previous generation was something they whispered about like kids around a campfire. "Slaughtered them, was how I heard it described."

San Martín didn't deny it. Their motorized truck, a Garford by make, coughed like a tubercular wildcat as they bounced over divots and stones in the wheel-worn track. Ingrid had to hold on to her hat, literally, as Oscar had the truck chugging along almost as fast as a horse could gallop by the time he eased it into third gear.

"Why is he coming back? Why now?" She had to raise her voice to be heard above the vehicular clatter.

"Deal they made."

"This Tom and Mictlantecuhtli?"

San Martín didn't respond. So he didn't want to talk. Maybe he was wising up.

"Did you know him?"

That earned a glance in her direction. "Since I was little," he said. "He was my father's friend. Like an uncle to me. I even called him that, growing up. Tio Tomás."

"He's not in the past tense, if he's coming home."

"No. But my father is."

That was a sore spot, then. One Ingrid could prod. "Recently?" she asked.

"Not very."

"What happened to him?"

"He went over," Oscar said, looking at her as he downshifted. "To Mictlan. Same as you. Only he never got to come back."

So others had made the experiment within the span of living memory—only with more predictable results than she'd achieved. "How old were you?"

"Not quite thirteen."

"You must miss him."

Oscar shrugged, unconvincingly. "I've seen him since. Talked to him. His bones, anyway, at the door between the rooms."

"That's more than most people get, I suppose."

"I suppose," the King's man echoed. "That's maybe gonna change, though."

Now he was baiting her. That was fine—distrust worked both ways.

"What happened ten years ago?" Ingrid asked. "From your point of view? I've heard the OAC's version."

"Their 'version?'" Oscar's voice had gone ice cold. "Their *version* mention they killed someone Tio Tomás loved? Trying to learn what he knew? What our grandfathers and their grandfathers knew? Trying to steal what they couldn't buy, our secret, handed down from before white people ever knew this continent existed?"

Ingrid shook her head. No hint of culpability on their end had ever figured into the OAC's telling of the tale. But she didn't want to stop Oscar talking, now that she'd gotten him angry enough to be honest.

"Well, they did. They started it. That's my version. And Tio Tomás? He called on Mictlantecuhtli for his revenge."

"Do you know how many people died that night?"

"None that didn't have it coming."

Ingrid wasn't prepared to weigh in on that. He might not have been wrong. There were certainly some pieces of work amongst the Aurea Catena's current membership. "What deal did they make? What happens when this Black Tom comes home?"

Oscar shook his head. "I'm sure el Rey wants it to be a surprise."

"You don't know, do you?"

"We'll all find out, on el Dia de los Muertos."

The day after Halloween, then. Next Tuesday. Ingrid sat back, letting San Martín think he'd talked her to a checkmate. Neither of them said another word, not until she stepped down from his grumbling truck in front of her glittering hotel, and they exchanged a businesslike goodbye.

A WALKER between worlds she may well have been, but that didn't mean she could walk out on her responsibilities. She'd tried when she left London, and they'd followed her halfway around the world.

Ingrid couldn't sleep that night, not even hours after Oscar San Martín dropped her off in front of the Angelus, her temporary nomad's home. She felt more at ease in hotels than she did in houses by this point in her life and career, but rest eluded her.

The question of why she could return from the land of the dead when others could not was finally beginning to trouble her in earnest (as it probably should have done right from the start). But she had no answers. Her every intention had somehow gone awry on this last visit to the otherworld, and she'd felt like she was behind the beat at every step of a dance. Her first heady experience of Mictlantecuhtli and his realm may have led her to behave a touch incautiously this time around, blundering into mysteries she couldn't hope to understand.

Or maybe that was too harsh an appraisal of her own conduct, she told herself as she rolled over on her brass bed's feather mattress for about the fiftieth time since lying down to sleep. The acquisition of new knowledge required risk. That's all there was to that. To start feeling otherwise now might be the first step toward regretting ever having come west to Los Angeles at all, and Ingrid wasn't ready to entertain any such admission of defeat.

THE next morning was the soonest she could set her nascent plan to rescue Finn into motion. She'd decided in the night that she meant to try. Imagining the torments Mickey and his guests might be inflicting on him even then was more than she could tolerate. She didn't have a lot of time to prepare, though. The Day of the Dead was almost upon her, and the kind of opportunity Mickey's mysterious 'surprise' presented might not come again.

She wasted too many hours nosing around the dirt streets of the Chinese quarter east of Alameda, where she stood out amidst the mostly-male population like a flamingo roosting in a colony of gulls. She managed to overpay for what looked like a ball of inferior hashish and a lump of resinous incense before understanding that the local criminal element wasn't going to supply such a conspicuous outsider with the substance she wanted. Rip-off and runaround were the best she could expect. But Lucinda Swire's opium supply had always come in straight from the London docks, as far as she remembered, so as a plan B she boarded a train at the Arcade Depot and set out for San Pedro—the coastal enclave that supported the Los Angeles harbor.

Her luck was better along the waterfront, but the twenty-mile trip out from the city ate up a large portion of the afternoon, and it was almost dark by the time she managed to arrange a meeting with a pair of sailors in a back booth at a place called the Union Saloon. They sold her three pea-sized balls of dark brown gum wrapped in waxed paper, weighing less than an eighth of an ounce. She'd have to eat them, as she had neither a pipe nor a lamp for smoking, but that was all right. She and Finn had eaten the drug as often as they'd smoked it. Laudanum would've been available from any pharmacist, much easier to acquire than the recently-banned opium, but Ingrid didn't think a cheap substitute would do.

She decided to take a room at the nearby Hotel Spokane rather than rush back to Los Angeles, and she ate a leisurely dinner at the restaurant next door. Front Street was a bit wild on a Saturday night. Snatches of up-tempo music drifted in from nearby bars, as well as occasional shouts and cheers that still sounded good-natured this early in the evening. Ingrid liked the sounds of boisterous life going on around her. Not so long ago she would've wanted to be out there, immersed in it, but not tonight. Her experiences in Mictlan had left her feeling separated from the ordinary flow of things.

The idea of slipping one of her recently acquired opium balls into her cup of tea surprised her with its intensity and persistence. She'd bought more than she needed, and could easily have spared it. But she hadn't bought it to enjoy it. She'd quit the habit when she quit London, and let her shipmates on the journey over to New York mistake her obvious discomfort for seasickness compounded by a miserable cold.

She sat for a long time after finishing her meal, inconspicuously meditating, letting her desires arise and then dismissing them without prejudice. Doing that and nothing more required all the force of will she could bring to bear, and still an hour passed before she was certain she had her compulsion to revisit opium's midnight shores under her control. She left the smoking paste in the hotel's safe that night anyway, concealed under the pad in a velvet ring box. She didn't want to have it nearby if she happened to wake in the small hours, when its promise of easy narcotic bliss might prove too powerful to ignore.

All this, and Ingrid's relationship with the Big Smoke had never run half as deep as Finn's. If any entity other than Mickey had the power to connect her with whatever remained of him out there in the aether, the Lady Poppy would surely be that creature.

AFTER a second fitful night's sleep, she decided not to go back to Los Angeles at all. San Pedro would make as good a staging ground for her planned operation as any other place, and it offered her the added bonus of anonymity. Nobody knew she was here, and nobody here knew her. A little deflective hex should be enough to keep the King's men from tracking her down, even if Mictlantecuhtli ordered them to try. As she expected he would.

He'd want an audience for the unveiling of his latest effort to become more human.

Ingrid had little doubt about what he was up to. He wore his obsessions like medals of valor, and it wasn't hard to know his mind. He might've engineered this deal with 'Black Tom' quite recently, delving back decades along his servant's timeline and making whatever changes his purpose required. Her solid memories of the Aurea Catena and their tales of carnage on a long ago Halloween night might only just have sprung into being.

The important thing, though, was that Mickey hadn't said anything to her about his plans. He couldn't fault her for her absence when he hadn't offered an invitation. He'd be angered when his men failed to retrieve her, for sure, but she'd have the grounds to take an indignant stand. And if she was right about what he meant to do—that he meant to slip into a human skin and stalk the realworld for a night, same as he'd done a decade ago—then it was worth risking his displeasure.

Because if Mickey was distracted on the Day of the Dead, if his oceanic perspective and millennial consciousness were condensed down into the volume of a single human skull, then he might never be the wiser if she pried open a back door and slipped into Mictlan for a couple of hours.

S HE spent Monday morning, All Saints' Day morning, making final preparations for a clandestine visit to the land of the dead. Gathering supplies and steeling her nerves. By noon she'd checked out of her cheap room with its sagging brass bed and hired a horse from a local stable, intending to take a long ride up the coast.

She set out across the grassy dunes wearing a new pair of scandalous blue jeans and a sheepskin coat bulky enough to stave off the autumn chill, both purchased in San Pedro from her dwindling supply of cash, along with a broad-brimmed man's hat to tuck her conspicuous hair under. She wore her pistol on her hip and kept her favorite knife tucked into her belt at the small of her back.

If anyone disturbed her operation this evening, she wanted to know she could insist on being left alone.

Around mid-afternoon she found what seemed like a suitable location: a deep cove, with lots of dry sand above a high-tide line marked by driftwood. The cove became a cave the further back she pressed. A shallow one, at the bottom of a sheer cliff face, yet deep enough to keep her out of the wind. The already-rising tide would cut off any escape as it rolled in, trapping her between two un-scalable outcroppings of friable sandstone and isolating her from the rest of the realworld completely.

It would make a fine ritual space, once she set up her wards and performed her banishings.

Ingrid strapped a feedbag onto her rented mare and set about gathering driftwood to build herself a good warm fire.

SHE swallowed the first of her opium pellets just before dusk, and chased it with a few soda crackers to spur digestion. While she waited for the drug to take effect she used a stick to write the names of the four cardinal angels around herself, at the four quarters of the compass, according to Golden Dawn specifications. She drew their associated pentagrams in the air with the tip of her knife, imagining them incised into reality as glowing lines of light, each colored according to the classical element it represented. Ingrid was an accomplished imaginer. The stars blazed bright—yellow in the east, red in the south, blue in the west, and green in the north—and they remained as visible to her as the fire crackling near the mouth of her cave, even when she stopped concentrating on keeping them there.

Within half an hour she felt the narcotic resin's presence creeping in. Her acquaintances from the docks hadn't cheated her. The paste she'd bought from them was what it appeared to be: a good-quality smoking preparation, *chandoo*, as its London aficionados called it, which had not been adulterated with morphine-heavy dross scraped from the inside of a used pipe bowl. That common practice resulted in leaden limbs and a swimming head for the user—a generally stultifying experience. The clarified gum, by contrast, sharpened her perceptions and excited her mind. Funny ideas and fantastical images began tumbling through her head, too fast for her to catch or consider them. She wanted to dance to her memories of music, which played unbidden in her head with a fidelity no phonograph could match.

This was how she'd fallen in love with Finn, in just this altered state of mind. Flirting and philosophizing, laughing at meaningless private jokes, lost in a mutual dream nobody else could penetrate.

Ingrid sat cross-legged in the sand above the tide line with her back to her bonfire, contemplating the blue pentagram that hung in the air above the breaking waves as they came clawing their way up the beach. High tide would strand her in the cove overnight, unless she wanted to swim, but the thought reassured her more than it troubled her. The wind off the ocean grew frigid as the sun descended, but the fire behind her heated her shoulders, right through her heavy coat.

She wondered who amongst the King's Men had been sent to fetch her, and whether he'd be in a frenzy by now, unable to find her and rightly terrified of disappointing his patron. Or maybe Mickey had sent creatures. Tzitzimime, or something worse. These were the days when the dead could roam, if el Rey allowed it. Many traditions acknowledged the alignment of worlds and the blurring of boundaries that occurred this time of year.

But it didn't matter. Ingrid knew how to drop out of sight—even second sight. So the dead wouldn't find her out here any more readily than the living.

S HE was gambling that Mickey would time his operation to coincide with the peak of the seasonal grace period, when the worlds most closely overlapped, like the moon and the sun at the apogee of an eclipse. That would give him the greatest chance of success. Ingrid was following his lead, but she hoped the timing would work to her benefit as well.

It was far from unheard of for the dead to make contact with the living, or for dreamers to visit the land of the dead. There was a road to the otherworld that old souls had traveled, quite separate from her secret shortcut beyond the Hole in the Sky, and Ingrid meant to walk it tonight.

As soon as her guide showed up.

She paced around her fire as the sky went dark, turning the ocean from a picturesque postcard to an implacable black void that churned at the mouth of her cove and hissed up the sand as if grasping for her, straining to catch her and drag her from the sliver of rocky beach she clung to.

She was considering swallowing more opium or else falling back on a formal conjuration to hurry this bullshit along—either the Golden Dawn's wordy medieval entreaty or the first of the tongue-twisting Enochian Keys—when she heard a familiar giggle behind her.

Ingrid turned around to see Poppy sitting backwards astride her horse, with the wind making a storm of her frowsy blonde hair.

She leaned forward, planting her elbows on the horse's haunches and resting her chin in her hands. "I figured I'd hear from you sooner or later, but I didn't expect so much *ceremony*."

"I was thinking maybe you needed more."

Poppy smiled. "Don't worry, pretty witch. Your call compelled me. You're still at the top of your game."

Ingrid narrowed her eyes. The things Poppy said were almost compliments, yet they dripped with condescension. Ingrid needed her, though, and this would go so much easier if she chose to cooperate. "Thank you for coming," she said.

Poppy shrugged. These were niceties. They both knew that Ingrid could force her or any other spirit to appear within her ritual circle, but once here, Poppy's behavior and her attitude still had to be bargained for.

"You must want something truly unusual, to go to all this trouble."

"I want to make… an arrangement," Ingrid said.

"Do you mean a deal?"

"If you like."

"You know my price."

"You don't know what I'm going to ask."

"Doesn't matter. My price is my price and it's always the same."

"For anything?"

"For everything. I want you, Ingrid Redstone. Body and mind, heart and soul. I want your lust, your love, and your longing, for as long as you persist, in this world or any other."

Ingrid had, in truth, anticipated this, and she had a plan in mind: to make the deal now and renege on it later. Its beauty was in its simplicity.

"All right," she said. "*If* you can do what I ask."

"I have built fortunes and I have raised empires," Poppy said, straightening up. "I have given voice to poets' dreams. There is no limit to what I might do."

That was good, to get her bragging. She wouldn't want to lose face now, even if it meant defying Mictlantecuhtli.

"I want you to take me to someone. One of yours. I want you to help me find him."

Poppy beamed. "Anywhere in the wide world."

"Not this world. The next one."

Poppy hesitated. "You must have loved him," she said. "To risk that."

"Do you know who I mean?"

"Peter Finnegan," Poppy said with defiant certainty. "Your 'Finn.'"

"Can you take me to him?"

"Not as you are." Poppy sniffed, wrinkling her nose in disdain for Ingrid's current corporeal state. "He's moved beyond material things."

Ingrid dropped to the sand, folding her legs into a lotus position and touching her thumbs with her ring fingers even as she let go of her body, sending her mind straight up into the cloudy night sky—while taking care not to breach the ring of symbols she'd erected around her cove.

She settled back into a gossamer image of herself, standing beside her own empty body, and nodded to Poppy that she was ready to travel.

"Showoff."

"You can take the girl out of the theater…"

"This is your birdcage," Poppy said, feigning contempt for the quartet of blazing pentagrams Ingrid had projected from her heart chakra to fence them in together. "You'll have to open it."

"Which direction?"

"Which do you think?"

Ingrid looked around. The red and green glyphs burned against the walls of the cove. The blue one, out in the west, hung above the black nighttime surf.

The yellow star, in the east, blocked the mouth of that shallow cave.

"That one?"

Poppy rolled her eyes like she was dealing with a novice.

Ingrid let go of the yellow pentagram and it dissolved on the wind like a wisp of smoke. The cave yawned in the negative space it left behind.

Poppy reached down to help Ingrid's spirit up on to the horse's back. Ingrid—who was practically a valkyrie when compared to waiflike Poppy—wound up seated behind the smaller woman, with blonde hair blowing in her face. The horse whickered and shuffled uncomfortably beneath them. This all felt real enough to Ingrid (even though she could look down and see her own body sitting in the sand, beside the fire), but who knew what the poor animal might be feeling, with a pair of apparitions perched on its back?

It responded well enough when Poppy nudged it with her heel, flattening its ears back but carrying them uncertainly forward, into the cave that gaped behind the leaping bonfire.

INGRID had judged that cavern to be about ten or twelve feet deep when she scouted it earlier in the afternoon. Not much more than a windbreak, really. But now, at night, she couldn't see to the rear of it. Their horse trudged ahead blindly at Poppy's urging, farther than it should've been able to without bumping its nose. Ingrid winced, expecting an impact that didn't come. When she un-scrunched her eyes and looked back over her shoulder, the comforting fire crackling at the mouth of the cave was already far behind them, flickering in blackness like a candle tucked into a niche.

Her head swam. For an instant she feared she might topple off the horse, which was absurd, seeing as she wasn't really on it. Everything she felt now was the product of her mind and the imagination—even more so than usual. But it might as well have been 'real.'

Poppy giggled, as if she knew what Ingrid was thinking. And maybe she did. These were just the sort of intoxicated thoughts her chemical incarnation was known to inspire.

"You certainly chose your moment," she said, needling Ingrid by alluding to Mictlantecuhtli's big plan. Without explicitly mentioning it, of course. "That was clever of you."

Ingrid didn't hurry to respond. Her eyes were adjusting to the darkness, beginning to pick out the broad shapes of their surroundings.

"Nobody much takes the old road anymore," Poppy said. "But it's still here, a part of Mictlantecuhtli's old stories."

Ingrid knew a bit about this. She'd read up when she first began searching for the Hole in the Sky, inspired by the Golden Chain's legends. There'd once been a road of trials that deceased souls had to brave before they reached the place where Mictlantecuhtli claimed their skins and consumed their hearts. Ingrid recalled descriptions of two obsidian mountains that crashed together, winds that rent the flesh, and a Styx-like river that had to be crossed. When she looked up, she saw a ribbon of charcoal sky above and realized they'd come out the far side of the cave and had been hiking between two glacial slabs of volcanic glass for some time already. The high chasm walls were close enough to touch on either side, but Ingrid yanked her hands back with a hiss when the jagged obsidian sliced her ghostly fingertips. She and Poppy and their unfortunate horse could be mashed to a paste in the event of seismic activity, even a tiny tremor. Yet the ground felt stable, and Poppy seemed blithely unconcerned. They rode out from between the now-stilled gnashing mountains and onto a plain studded with arrows that had been loosed long ago, by departed archers, and then passed through a silent, misty jungle where hungry beasts no longer prowled. It seemed the small gods set over these obstacles had all fled, with no living believers left to hold them in place. Academic memory kept the path demarcated, but the torments the Aztec dead once faced no longer had any bite.

It must have been Mickey's small clutch of devotees that kept him at his station, when the rest of his pantheon had long since faded from relevance. He'd held on to his final, eternal circle of hell, and the contemporary dead were welcome to find him via whatever routes their personal religious suspicions led them to invent.

Before Ingrid knew it they'd arrived on the bank of a broad, slow river. She could see the familiar gnarled trees and endless fog of the Mictlan she knew on the distant shore.

"I thought it would take longer," she said to Poppy. "Four years, I think I read?"

"Dreamtime," was the opium eidolon's dismissive reply, delivered with a wave of her hand. "Nothing's what it used to be. But we've ridden as far as we can. We're on our own from here."

Poppy swung herself down off the horse and dropped to the ground. Ingrid did the same. The black river before them slid past in eerie silence.

"Last chance to turn back."

Ingrid shook her head.

"It's your afterlife at stake," Poppy said with a lazy shrug. "There's little enough your King can do to me."

That was true. She was risking so much. And what for?

"Let's go," Ingrid said, shrugging off her doubts. "Mickey won't stay distracted forever."

THE river was broad, but not deep. They were able to wade across it, and the water never rose above Poppy's waist. Her loose tea gown billowed around her hips like pigment blooming from an artist's brush dipped in turpentine. The black water only climbed about halfway up Ingrid's thighs, but it was bitterly cold. Her shivering stopped by the time they reached the far bank, but the chill remained, as if it had settled into her bones.

This was quite a different experience of Mictlan, visiting in spirit only, with her warm-blooded form checked at the door like a fancy coat. Her psychic projection of a body stayed cold all the way through, but soon enough even that ceased to bother her.

"I'm ready when you are," Ingrid prodded.

Poppy was looking around, her small face creased with consternation. She appeared to be scenting the air.

"Poppy?"

"Shh."

Ingrid was only so willing to be shushed by something she'd conjured. "You *can* find him, can't you?"

"Yes, if you'll shut up a minute."

Ingrid stood back and put a hand on her hip. "Well?"

Poppy scowled. "I don't understand. Is this some sort of a trick?"

"I was wondering the same."

"He exists. I feel his need. I just can't locate him. He must be hiding, somehow."

"Really." Ingrid's patience was wearing thin.

"Yes, *really*. Is that so impossible? While you're in the very middle of sneaking past the King of the Dead?"

"Is Mickey hiding him?"

Did he know they were coming?

"I don't suppose I'd know, would I?" Poppy sneered, looking irritable. They both knew Ingrid wasn't bound by a pact the eidolon couldn't deliver on.

"Is this what happens when people escape from you?" Sometimes they did. She had.

"He *hasn't* escaped. And no, this is not what happens." Poppy softened. Her confusion seemed real. "When they truly escape I lose all track of them. And I haven't. He wants me, and I feel it. But I don't know where to start looking."

Ingrid frowned. "I might have one idea."

T HEY found the inhabitants of the Cock & Bull trudging through another dreary morning. Or maybe it was evening—Ingrid couldn't tell and didn't care. Few heads turned when they walked through the door. More stayed face-down on the tabletops. Among the upright was Lucinda Swire. Poppy may not have known where to find Finn, but leading Ingrid straight to Lucy hadn't been any trouble at all.

"Renewed yer old acquaintance, I see," Swire grumbled from her accustomed perch behind the bar, giving ghostly Ingrid and her new companion her usual judgmental once-over. Naturally she found them wanting. "That didn't take but half a minute."

"Look. Lucy," Ingrid said. "I know you always hated me—"

"Now what would've ever given you an idea like that?"

"I don't know what made you feel that way, but I suppose you have your reasons, and I didn't come all this way to talk you out of them."

Lucinda harrumphed, letting her know there was little enough chance even if she tried.

"I also don't know what relationship you had with Finn or why you care about him, but I believe you *do* care, and I think you know he's in danger. Even if he's hidden, he's in danger."

"If he is, it's only because of you."

"That may be. And you can despise me for it, or you can help me do something about it."

Lucinda narrowed her eyes in suspicion. "And what is it you think you can do?"

"I have a plan. But I need you to tell me how I can find him."

INGRID suspected it was Lucy's desire to prove she had a secret that led her to acquiesce, more than any genuine wish to be of assistance. It didn't matter. If Mickey's subject had useful information regarding Finn's whereabouts, Ingrid didn't give half a damn about her motivations for coughing it up.

They didn't have all the time in the otherworld, and she was feeling a need to hurry this thing along.

Lucinda led them outside, into the muddy London streets. The city of memory was hallucinatory in its crisp detail, but as still as a graveyard. The avenues were as empty as a poet's wallet. Even the normally bustling docks were deserted. The Thames they jutted out into was a slow-moving ribbon of mercury, reflecting a tarnished pewter sky.

Ingrid looked away, toward the river's far bank. There were no boats on the water that she could see. "Do we have to swim?"

"Not hardly," Lucinda said, and before Ingrid could press her for an explanation, she stuck two fingers into the corners of her mouth and whistled, the way she might've done when calling for last orders in the pub. Poppy winced at the strident single note, which died away over the water without an echo, smothered by the dream-city's sepulchral silence.

What now? Ingrid was about to ask (as there was no sign of anyone anywhere around them), when the water about thirty yards out in front of the dock they stood on began to bubble and roil. Ingrid took a step back and Poppy took two, but Lucinda stayed right where she was. She looked back and up at Ingrid from the edge of the quay, grinning with mad delight. She was practically bouncing on the balls of her feet.

Ingrid had never seen her behave this way in life, not even once. Lucy's excitement was almost as odd as whatever was going on in the river.

Within moments a mechanical leviathan breached the surface, a submersible craft that heaved itself up from the depths of a waterway that looked much too shallow to contain it—and would have been, back in the realworld. Here in Mictlan, rivers ran as deep as required. Lucinda applauded like she was part of a throng celebrating the return of an ocean liner from faraway ports.

The submersible ship was unlike anything Ingrid had ever seen, outside of the illustrations in a Jules Verne novel. The sort of fantastical novel Finn had always loved to read. The realworld's military submarines, as far as she knew, were neither this big nor this advanced. The gargantuan steel cigar before her rode high in the water, towering above the dockside warehouses, with the dregs of its emptied ballast tanks still gushing from vents above the waterline. A short, squared-off structure topped the torpedo-like hull, looking something like a blunt dorsal fin and running about two-thirds of the ship's length. Its flat top had a railing all the way around, and this seemed to be the vessel's only exterior deck. They heard the clang of a hatch being thrown open up top, out of view, and the submersible's crew of perhaps two dozen hands filed out to line up at the rail, one by one, as if for inspection. Their uniforms were dark and simple—so much so that Ingrid thought they looked more like stagehands than sailors.

Last to emerge was Finn himself, dressed in the flaring black frock coat with the crimson lining he'd always worn on stage. His blond hair and beard were both a bit shaggier than a gentleman's should be, and his silly grin was just as she remembered. Enough so that it made her heart ache.

"Ruby!" he shouted, spotting her down on the quay and pushing a bug-eyed pair of smoked-glass goggles up onto his forehead. "Where the hell have you been? I was worried about you."

Ingrid bit back a laugh that could as easily have come out as a sob. "Worried about me, were you?"

Finn kicked a rolled-up ladder made of chains and iron rungs down the side of his ridiculous ship, letting it unfurl with a resonant series of bongs and clanks. He hopped over the rail and scrambled down onto the dock with simian agility. Then he yanked Ingrid into his arms and kissed her before she could say another word.

NOBODY applauded. Lucinda and Poppy watched them in critical silence, while Finn dipped her and Ingrid flailed in unbalanced surprise. She swatted at his shoulder until he set her back on her feet.

Of all the greetings she'd imagined, nothing like this had made the list. She'd come here expecting torment and tribulation, only to find him sailing the seas in a ship from a fantasy story? She couldn't fathom it.

Did he even remember committing suicide?

"Finn," Ingrid began, after wiping her mouth with the back of her hand. "You're looking well."

"I'm not the only one," he replied, eyeing her ass in the tight denim pants she still imagined herself wearing (and *was* still wearing, back on the beach, in a reality far from this one). "My compliments to the wardrobe department."

She meant to retort, but one of the hands up on the submersible's deck interrupted her. The officer was a rather breathtaking East Indian woman with a long fall of lustrous black hair. "Doctor?" she called down at Finn.

"Aye?"

Ingrid raised an eyebrow. That title had never been more than a decoration for a stage name, though nobody in this scenario seemed aware of it.

"We've picked up a reading. We don't have much time."

"Thank you, Commander," Finn said, then turned back to Ingrid and her unlikely spirit guides. "Ladies. It is my pleasure to invite you aboard the mighty *Paracelsus*."

"Finn, we need to talk."

"And we will. When we're underway."

"It's important."

"So's leaving, love, and sooner'd be better than later."

The crew, as if on cue, rolled three more chain ladders down the side of the ship. Lucinda grabbed hold of one eagerly and began hauling herself up the hull's pronounced curve. Finn's raven-haired officer helped her over the rail when she reached the top. Poppy also climbed, after shooting a mistrustful glance in Ingrid's direction. No doubt she wanted to retain the claims they'd bargained over, and could feel them growing less certain the more the situation changed.

"Ruby?"

Again with the stage names. "Oh, all right," Ingrid said, when Finn gestured toward one of the unfurled ladders. He only paused to watch her going up it for a moment or two before following after, which led her to think his show of urgency might be genuine.

"Doctor!" the beautiful first officer shouted, in her musical accent. "Incoming, six o'clock position!"

Ingrid, with her hand on the ship's rail, looked down in time to see Finn whip his head around. She followed his sightline across the docks and down the alleys beyond. Something was coming—something she couldn't quite see. The 'shapes' rocketing toward them looked more like disturbances in the air, heat shimmers or dust-devils, than physical things, and they were visible only for the way they distorted the structures and objects behind them. Ingrid didn't know what the hell was going on, but Finn's shouted exhortation to hurry seemed like a capital idea.

The lovely lieutenant and another deckhand (this one a burly, bearded pirate-type) hauled her more than helped her over the railing. Poppy had already dropped out of sight, down into the belly of the mechanical whale, and Lucinda was still stuffing herself through the hatch in the center of the deck. As soon as she popped through Finn herded Ingrid and the remainder of his crew down the spiral staircase that led below, then slammed the hatch shut after them, sealing out his horde of half-seen enemies.

COMMANDER Doshi, the bridge is yours," Finn said, coming down the wrought-iron stairs like all was well with the world. "Take us out of here."

Finn's first officer nodded smartly and strode away, presumably in the direction of the submersible's command center. The pirate and other black-clad hands of varying descriptions also slipped away to perform their duties. An uncharacteristically speechless Lucinda shrank back against the conning platform's wall, looking over-awed by their surroundings. This was modern technology on a scale she'd never dreamt of.

Poppy merely crossed her arms and glared.

Someone or something (if not a great many somethings, by the sound of it) began pounding on the outside of the hull. The noise they raised was an insistent thunder, as of dozens or hundreds of fists raining down on resonant metal. There were no voices raised in accompaniment; no shouts or threats. Just that furious, arrhythmic knocking.

Engines thrummed to life and the deck trembled beneath their feet. Finn, standing at the base of the spiral stairs, looked up at the rushing sound of ballast tanks taking on water, and grinned. The pounding on the hull unnerved him as much as anyone—visibly, at least for a moment—but Ingrid saw his old confidence surge back to the fore when the *Paracelsus* pulled away from its mooring on the imaginal Thames and angled to dive. She felt the deck swing on some invisible gimbal that held it level. The angry hammering died away as the ship outpaced its pursuers, plummeting down into darkness and silence.

"C'mon," Finn said, like this was all in a day at the office. "Let's have the grand tour, then."

INGRID and her tiny entourage followed when he descended the next staircase, leading them down to an impressive glass-walled observation deck. It was either that or be left up top to man the periscope. She had no more interest in the layout of his made-up boat than he had in answering her questions, but she posed them anyway. A few of the more immediate ones, at least.

"What *were* those things? Back on the dock? Finn?"

"Dunno, love. And it seemed like a bad idea to wait around to ask."

There was no arguing with that logic. "How long have you been running from them?"

Finn shrugged. "Awhile. We're days or weeks ahead of 'em, most of the time." He rapped on the inner hull with his knuckles. "This old girl's a good bit faster than whatever they travel by. Don't know how they caught up with us so quick, this time."

He kept his tone light, almost flippant, but Ingrid could tell by the furrows in his brow that his concern over the question ran deeper than he wanted to admit.

"Finn… do you know where we are?"

"Observation deck of the *Paracelsus*, the wonder of the seven seas."

A school of luminescent jellyfish began blooping past the picture window behind him, as if to underscore his point. There were leather club chairs from which to appreciate the undersea wonders, warm wood paneling on the interior walls, and a wet bar to provide libations. A bolted-down grand piano stood in one far corner.

"Beyond that, I mean."

Finn turned and looked out the window himself, into the deep undersea twilight. "Middle of the Channel by now, halfway to Calais. Why, Ruby?"

"You know that's not my name."

Something hit the side of the ship, hard. That hidden gimbal system absorbed some of the shock, but not all of it, and the impact sent everyone lurching for balance.

Finn caught hold of a handrail and punched a button on a panel set into the wall. "Bridge!" he barked into a wire-mesh circle in the panel's corner. "Situation report, please."

Commander Doshi's posh accent came crackling back from the speaker. "We're under attack, Doctor. Something has attached itself to the hull."

"What has?"

"I don't know. We can't see it, not from any quarter of the ship. But it's slowing us down. I believe it means to stop us."

"Like bloody hell it will," Finn said with a snarl. "Reverse engines, full power."

"But Doctor—"

"Don't argue, just do it!"

Another violent lurch spilled Lucinda onto her ample bottom. Finn grabbed her hand and hoisted her back to her feet. Poppy dropped her pretense of physicality and floated a few inches above the deck rather than endure further undignified jostling. Finn whooped like a cowboy when the *Paracelsus* jerked loose from the grip of whatever held it and squirted away in the opposite direction. The jellyfish outside the windows parted like a curtain and then were gone, lost behind them as the submersible accelerated.

"Quick, Ruby," Finn shouted, dashing down a corridor without even bothering to look back, so certain was he that everyone would follow. He seemed to be having no end of fun, despite the apparent danger. "Let's get to the bridge!"

W HAT'S wrong with him?" Ingrid murmured to Poppy as they hurried down the ship's twisting passageways after the mad doctor, who had a decent head start on them. "Why doesn't he remember?"

"I really haven't the slightest."

"Is this why you couldn't find him?"

Poppy scowled. "I found him for you. He's right up there."

"But you couldn't find him, not at first. Not without Lucy."

"He's found now, so what does it matter?"

The opium eidolon wasn't going to say anything that might negate her claims. Ingrid wasn't going to get a straight answer out of her. Not that it was certain she had one to give. In truth, Poppy looked as confounded by all of this as Ingrid felt. Mickey might have been able to explain what had gone wrong within Finn's mind, but not wanting to ask him was the entire point of being here.

"What do *you* know about this?" she said to Lucinda. "More than you're saying, I'm sure of that."

"Like that one said." Lucy thrust her chin in Poppy's direction. "He's found, so who gives a fig?"

"I do," Ingrid said, almost to herself.

THE bridge of the *Paracelsus* was, if anything, even more daunting than the observation deck had been. That portion of the ship was designed to impress, like a well-appointed luxury liner; this section assaulted the senses with its technical complexity. Dials spun and gauges clicked, lighted buttons throbbed with urgency and toggle switches bristled from every surface. Various members of the crew attended to them while Finn stood before the main window, conferring with Commander Doshi.

"We've got multiple readings on the echolocator," she was saying when Ingrid and company entered through a pair of hydraulic doors, "but they're... distorted. I can't make any sense of them."

"Doctor Pagán," another crewman at a nearby battle station interjected, this one a ginger who spoke with a hard Scots' burr. "There's somethin' up ahead, twelve o'clock position. And below. Also at three and nine, and closing in. And of course the first group of hostiles, still pursuin' at six."

"Initiate evasive maneuvers, Helmsman. Let's make a leap, shall we?"

"Aye, Doctor."

Ingrid wondered what sort of maneuver would outfox an enemy that had them surrounded from all sides, but she didn't wonder long. The *Paracelsus* shot upward when the redheaded helmsman threw a lever, propelling all the fluid from the ship's tanks and causing it to break the channel's surface like a breaching whale. For a sickening moment the main window showed nothing but gray sky, before the near-vertical vessel tilted back toward the horizon and slammed down into the water with all the force of a falling skyscraper. Ingrid didn't know if the intention had been to vault over their foes or to smash them senseless with the full weight of the ship. Either way, Finn cackled with glee and the *Paracelsus* dove again, straight down into midnight blue.

Ingrid decided she'd had enough of this game. It would never end unless she ended it.

"Finn!"

He, Miss Doshi, and the rest of the crew looked up at her. Various alarms continued to sound, but all chatter on the bridge ceased.

"What, Ruby?"

"Say my name."

"I just did."

"Say my name, Finn. My *real* name."

"Doctor—" That damn Scot again. The lights on his array of instruments were flashing madly.

"He knows," Ingrid told the officer, cutting him off. "We all know. Blips on your echo-scope or whatever it is, closing in from everywhere. Right?"

"That's about the substance of it," the helmsman conceded.

"This really isn't the time, Ruby."

"It's the only time there will ever be. Now say my name."

Finn gaped at her. Something slammed into the side of the ship.

"Doctor!" It was a chorus this time—Doshi, the Scottish pilot, and several other hands all had dire data to impart, relayed from every end of the submarine.

"I know!" he shouted back, still holding eye-contact with Ingrid. "Ruby…"

"I'm not Ruby, don't call me that. And you're not Phineas Pagán."

The psychotic knocking resumed, like a thousand fists hammering the hull. It grew louder by the second.

"Of course we are, Ruby," Finn insisted. He looked like a man half-mired in a dream and struggling to wake. "Who else would we be?"

The *Paracelsus* groaned around them, like the steel superstructure itself was twisting in the grip of titanic forces. The lights flickered, and the bridge's ingenious electrical apparatus began to smoke and throw off sparks. Small leaks sprang from the ceiling, shocking Ingrid with cold seawater and promising a deluge to come.

"Peter Finnegan," she pleaded, seizing his hand. "*Say my name!*"

"Goddammit, Ingrid—" Finn thundered, reaching for the old power of command that had riveted audiences during his life and drawn a crew of lost souls around him after death… before he snatched his hand back and clapped it over his mouth at the realization of what had just come out of it.

Ingrid's name. Her true name.

An acknowledgement of their true past.

Long-denied memories flooded Finn's sanctuary, ripping open seams all down the length of the ship's hull to let in the crushing black waters that choked and drowned the *Paracelsus*.

INGRID came to on a stretch of lonely beach. The sky above churned with black stormclouds. Mictlan's sky, not the realworld's. Not yet. The water before her was placidly calm and smooth as glass, and it stretched all the way to the horizon.

"Did you know what would happen?" Finn asked, from behind her.

Ingrid turned. He was sitting on a rock, still dressed in his sodden show coat, though at some point he'd lost his bug-eye goggles. She shrugged. "I suppose I had some idea."

"Should I bother asking why?"

"Do you know where you are now? Do you know what happened?"

Finn looked around as well. They'd fetched up on an island. A tiny one, not much more than a rocky spur. A skinny tree stood at one end, and closer by, a small, simple house. Its peaked roof was shingled with dark blue tiles. Finn's crew was here too, most of them huddled around the building. A few rivet-studded bits of the wrecked submersible poked up out of the shallows, near the waterline. "Died, didn't I?" he said, considering the evidence. "Drowned in the Thames. And this is what comes after."

Ingrid nodded. "We're in danger here, Finn. Both of us."

He greeted the news with a weary smile and looked back out to sea, like he hadn't really heard her. "Never believed in anything after," he mused. "Not really. I pretended, back in the orphan pen, or else the Sisters would've slapped me stupid. But deep down... not really. So this is all gonna take a bit of gettin' used to."

"Don't bother," Ingrid said. "We won't be here long."

He laughed, without much humor in it. "And where is it we're meant to be going?"

"Back from where we came." She hesitated. This was the part of the plan that required salesmanship. "You won't have a body. You'll be a ghost. But you'll be safe." She had a talisman prepared back in the real, an old gold coin he'd used in his act. She'd kept it as a souvenir of their time together. It would make a solid anchor for him, being both physically durable and loaded with personal associations.

He grunted in response to the idea. "Felt safe enough these past few... well, however long it's been. What's changed?"

Ingrid didn't know where to begin. What had changed? What hadn't? Her fundamental understanding of life, death, and time, for starters. "It's my fault," was what came out when she opened her mouth to explain. "The important thing is I'm here to set it right. As much as I can, anyway."

He looked her over, reconsidering. "You talk like you caught a cross-town train. Are you not just as dead as me?"

"No," Ingrid said. "I'm alive, completely alive. My body's waiting for me in a circle on a beach in California. I snuck in here without it, and we can sneak back out again. Together."

Finn took some time to process this. The revelation seemed to take the starch out of his spine. "It was always real to you, wasn't it?" he said at last. "The magic. You always believed."

"I never believed anything. I learned. And then I knew."

"Because you *did* it. The rituals and the reading and the sittin' around crosslegged like some Himalayan holy man. While I played at it and pranced about on stage and tricked earnest people into believing things I never could."

"You entertained them. You didn't lie. We put on a show."

"But I laughed at them. Sneered at them for their need to touch something beyond the everyday, same as the most cynical 'spiritualist' fraud rappin' on a wealthy widow's table at a feckin' séance. I took their hard-earned money and blew it on hashish and champagne."

...and opium, Ingrid thought, but didn't say. Poppy stood many yards away, glowering out at the placid sea, but who knew how far earshot stretched for a thing like that?

"I laughed at you, too." Finn couldn't look at her when he said it. "Inwardly, but still. For taking it serious. For spending time with those gobshites from the Golden Dawn. For thinking that mystics and magicians and their dusty weird books might be pointing the way to something true."

"I know," Ingrid said, and was sorry to see him wince. "Look, we can talk later, about everything, but now we need to go. We've pushed our luck too far already."

"Maybe so, love," Finn agreed, looking past her even as the shipwrecked members of his crew began standing up and pointing toward something behind her, out on the water. "Seems we've got company."

Chapter Five

NGRID whirled. She knew what she would see, and her brief prayer that it wouldn't be so went unanswered.

Mictlantecuhtli was coming.

The King stood at the rear of a long, low boat while a team of perhaps sixty skeletons poled it smoothly across the shallow water, toward the tiny island. The war canoe, or *acalli*, had been dug out of a single massive spruce trunk, and it dwarfed the similar crafts Ingrid had once seen her proto-Aztec friends employ. Mickey himself had never looked more fearsome, with shells at his ankles, feathers at his brow, and gold on his biceps. His double-looped garland of harvested eyes stared every which way, and his red leather cape seemed to be made of fresh human skin, artfully flayed and turned inside out to expose the bold crimson color.

"Oh, fuck," Ingrid murmured.

"Friend of yours?" Finn asked, and Ingrid shot him a glare that shut him right up. This was not the time for his sense of humor.

She felt sick, but she stepped forward to greet her King just the same.

Rain began to fall before el Rey's royal acalli could touch the shore. It pelted down in driving sheets, without so much as a smattering to foretell its arrival. Ingrid and the rest of the castaways from the *Paracelsus* were soaked through in moments, although Mickey, curiously, seemed to stay dry.

The rain was falling on the island, but not on the water around it. The surface of the sea remained unmarred by falling drops.

El Rey noticed this and snarled. He held up a hand to order his crew of bony oarsmen to a halt when they were still several yards from shore.

Ingrid felt someone step up next to her and turned, thinking it was Finn coming to her side.

It wasn't. It wasn't anyone. Rain sizzled off an empty man-shaped space, through which Ingrid could view one baffled Finnegan, the rock he'd been sitting on, and the rest of his soggy, confused crew.

The rain-man seemed to incline his head toward her, perhaps in a polite nod of acknowledgement. It was hard to tell with nothing more than a hazy silhouette to focus on. Water coursed down over the creature's broad shoulders and dripped from its unseen arms. It looked back to the canoe and said in a rumbling, resonant voice:

"Mictlantecuhtli. You will not pass."

"Tlaloc," Mickey said, barely bothering to conceal a sneer. "Cousin. I had no idea you still existed. But you will not keep from me what is mine."

"These are none of yours. All have died by water, and so belong to the House of Rain."

"Tlalocan is a level of Mictlan. I am your lord."

"Tlalocan is the highest of the hells and the lowest of the heavens. It is the place where above becomes below, and so belongs to neither kingdom. You are not my master, Mictlantecuhtli, not in this. And you will not pass."

Mickey's eyes narrowed and his lips curled back from his straight white teeth. "Ingrid Redstone," he said, fixing her with an acid gaze. "You have betrayed me."

Ingrid found she had no defense to offer.

"Tlaloc," Mickey said. "Release this one to me. You have no claim upon her."

"Nor do you, cousin. The red witch yet lives. She is neither of ours to command."

"D'you know what's happening?" Finn murmured, stepping up on Ingrid's left, opposite to the empty man, the anti-man, the creature Mickey had addressed as 'cousin.' "'Cause I for one am at a total loss."

Ingrid shook her head, but Tlaloc explained (or attempted to):

"Mictlan lies at the end of the road you travel. There are stops along the path where some chosen few are made welcome. Those who pass between worlds by water are honored in the House of Rain."

"Does he mean drowning?" Finn said. "What, like people who die by drowning get a reward? What's the sense in that?"

"Would you risk war?" Mickey demanded of Tlaloc. "Time has come and times have changed, cousin. The governors of the other shallow realms have fled their posts or perished, as I believed you had. Will Tlalocan's faded strength stand against the wrath of Mictlan?"

"Though much is taken, much abides," Tlaloc said thoughtfully, hunching his rain-spattered invisible shoulders into a bit of a shrug. "Try us, if you would know."

"They about to fight or what?" Finn asked.

"Shut *up*," Ingrid hissed at him. As long as the eidola continued to squabble over their unfathomable politics, she still had a chance to figure a way out of this catastrophe.

"Lady of the Poppies," Mickey said, trying an ominous new tack.

"What deal has Lady Redstone made with you?"

"Her devotion in perpetuity, in exchange for my help in finding this one amongst the remains of my slaves." Poppy sniffed in Finn's general direction.

"Then assert your claims and bring the man Finn to me, and you will have the devotion of ten thousand souls."

"Done and done," Poppy said.

"No!" Ingrid and Tlaloc shouted in unison.

"Now you wait a bleedin' minute," Lucinda said to Poppy, looking like a half-drowned rat in Tlaloc's selective downpour. Ingrid had almost forgotten she was there. "Handin' him over weren't no part o' what we agreed."

"Persist in this and you will have your war, Mictlantecuhtli," Tlaloc warned. Thunder rumbled to underscore his point. "You will not steal from the House of Rain."

"*Oi!*" Finn shouted over the argumentative babble, causing every head to turn in his direction. "Do I get any say in this? It is my afterlife under discussion."

"No," Mickey and Poppy said together, without an instant of consideration. Poppy crossed her arms, Mickey planted his hands on his hips, and both of them continued to scowl.

But Tlaloc's outline turned in the rain to look Finn up and down. "Make your wishes known," the small god said to him.

"I want to see if I've got this straight. The reason I'm here is you take in anyone that happens to drown? Regardless of who they were or how they lived?"

"The House of Rain has always done so, as the House of the Setting Sun once claimed warriors fallen upon the red fields and the House of the Rising Sun claimed mothers lost in childbirth."

Tlaloc spoke like this should have been obvious.

"So the *Paracelsus* and all those times, fightin' the Sanguinox Horde and chasin' the Petrichorians under Antarctica, that was all some sort of *reward*? For me having died a particular way?"

"The dreams were your own," Tlaloc said bemusedly. "I did not script them."

"We all of us feared for our lives, you know," Finn gestured around at his nodding audience, mostly made up of his former crew. "Which seems pretty ironic now."

"You discovered in your realized imaginings opportunities for ingenuity and valor, did you not?" Tlaloc said. "You fulfilled yourself in them."

"So the person I should've dared to be in life is the person I got to be in death?"

"Such is the gift of Tlalocan."

Finn turned to Ingrid. "And you came to rescue me from that?"

"This isn't what I expected." The old road she'd come in by had looked so disused. She'd never guessed that Aztec remnants other than Mickey might still be clinging to their ancient spheres of influence. She'd read about Tlaloc, the god of rain, same as she had with Mictlantecuhtli, but never anticipated meeting him.

"So I suppose my only other question," Finn said, "is what the hell is going on? How did I wind up in the middle of this?"

"Ask *her*," Mickey said, in a tone so petulant anyone other than a god or a child would've been embarrassed to use it.

Finn turned to Ingrid. "So?"

"It's all my fault," she repeated.

He grinned, in the way that had always tugged at something in the core of her. "Think we're all in agreement there, love. But maybe more specifically?"

"Do you remember when I told you about the Tree Below the Hole in the Sky?"

"What, that silly old story about the Aztecs your Golden Dawn twats liked to kick around? Fairy tale, wasn't it, like your Atlantis or your Shangri-la."

"It's there, Finn. The Hole in the Sky is there, and it has been for a thousand years."

"You went looking for it? All the way to California?"

"I *found* it. And I went through it. And I came back again, which nobody else has ever done."

Finn was starting to look suitably impressed. Yes, she was a woman of unique accomplishment. It may have been petty, but it pleased her to know he understood that.

"What was on the other side?" he asked.

"Him," Ingrid said, pointing. "Mictlantecuhtli. El Rey de los Muertos."

"The King of the Dead," Finn translated.

Ingrid nodded.

"But not the king of all the dead?"

"I am," Mickey said.

"Though the governors of the provinces have their rights," Tlaloc added.

"And so do I." Poppy wasn't about to let them forget it.

"I still don't see how this all comes down to me."

"She betrayed me," Mickey told him, "for love of you."

"What, d'you mean like…?" Finn looked back and forth between Mickey and Ingrid. "You mean you and him…?"

Ingrid nodded.

"But isn't he a god?"

"Have you read *any* myths?" Gods had never been known for chastity, or discretion.

"All right, I take your meaning."

"She chose you over me, dead man, but you are mine by right," Mickey said to Finn, "and when I have you, you will suffer like you have never imagined."

Finn swallowed hard, but stood firm.

"The drowned man belongs to the House of Rain," Tlaloc said.

"Our claims together outweigh yours," Poppy told the man-shape cut from a curtain of driving, stinging rain, stepping in front of it to side with Mictlantecuhtli. "So we'll be taking him."

"I got a claim, too," Lucinda Swire said uncertainly. "So if I was to throw in with no-body here," —she cocked a thumb at Tlaloc— "would that be like a stalemate?"

"It would," the rain god said. "The man Finn stays where he is."

"What claim do you have? Lucy?" Ingrid took the squat woman by the shoulder and spun her around, but Lucinda set her jaw in defiance. She didn't feel the need to explain anything, not to the likes of Ingrid. "Mickey? What claim does she have? Somebody tell me what she's talking about."

"Her claim is maternal," Tlaloc said impatiently. "The drowned man is her child by blood."

Finn jerked like he'd been slapped in the face. Ingrid's reaction wasn't much different.

"What?" Tlaloc said, innocently. His grasp of human priorities seemed as shaky as his skeletal cousin's.

"Goddamn you, Ingrid Redstone." Lucinda balled up her fists as she turned red with shame. "I didn't never want him to know."

"Wait a minute," Finn said. "You're my real mother and you knew about it? You *always* knew about it?"

"Yeah, really," Ingrid said, "how much opium did you sell him over the years?"

"What? It were a gentleman's habit. Healthful too, so long as you don't smoke the dross, and I made sure he never did."

Ingrid shook her head, but she supposed that wasn't really the salient point. "You knew where he was this whole time?"

"No. But I felt like I could reach him if I called."

"You knew the Russian, didn't you?" Finn asked of Lucy. "The Great Volta. You paid him to take me on as his apprentice."

Lucy nodded. "Theater people were thick as thieves in the pub. I knew acts that toured all around the Continent, and Ireland too. See, I always had word of you, growin' up. County Down ain't that big a place. Old friends from me nine months in the girls' home would drop notes in the post now and then. I knew when the Sisters placed you with old John Finnegan and his brood, down on his farm. I knew when you got high marks in school. And I knew you never missed a fair or a festival or a traveling show, from the time you could sit up straight and watch players on a stage. So when you got a little older and I had money laid by, I sent Mr. Volta to take you on and teach you his craft. If you wanted to go, that was."

"I was fifteen, with a head full of books and stories. It was an offer I couldn't refuse."

"And ten years later you were headlinin' yer own act. I bought a ticket the first time you came through London, and every time there after."

"Volta told me I had a 'wealthy benefactor' who'd known my parents, but had to stay anonymous because of their position. Like some shite outta Dickens. Tightlipped old sod never told me anything more. I used to make up all sorts of tales about who you might be."

"And all o' them was better'n the truth."

"You could have told me."

"Told you what? That the bankroll for yer costumes and yer props came from girls and absinthe and opium? Would you have believed me? You'd have thought *I* was angling for money, by then."

"I never even knew your names. You or my father."

"I didn't know his either. I'm sorry, but I didn't. Michael, but I only ever met him once and I never learnt his last name. I were only fourteen meself when it... when I... well, you know what I did."

"What happened?"

"What happens is what happened. What else? Yer grandfather sent me off to 'visit relatives' back in Ireland, but really to the nuns to give birth and keep quiet. Then, for all his pious noise about how I'd sullied his name an' all, he married me off to Edgar Swire almost the minute I came home. For financial security, right, 'cause old Swire owned the public house. And ran the tarts, and moved the swag what came in off the docks, and were generally the biggest criminal in the whole neighborhood. But Mr. Swire were also twenty years older'n me, and never in good health. So when he keeled over, everything was mine. And I made more out of it than old Edgar ever could. That ain't much in the way of accomplishment, maybe, but knowin' you got to make a name for yerself out in the world always made me proud. For what it's worth."

Finn nodded. Ingrid couldn't tell what he might be thinking. Mickey, too, had watched the whole exchange with quiet interest.

"You didn't know where he was when you sprang Lucy on me, did you?" Ingrid said, turning to look at her King. "You wanted to see if *I* knew. You couldn't find him any more than Poppy could, when I asked her to try. Because he was here in Tlalocan."

"I believed you had hidden him," el Rey confessed, "through some exercise of witchcraft. I thought the Swire might goad you into revealing your trick. I never thought to find your Finn sheltering in the House of Rain."

Ingrid sighed. She would never have been moved to hatch this stupid plan if Mickey hadn't leapt to his conclusions. Though she supposed she hadn't given him much benefit of the doubt, either. So who was at fault in this? Or did it come down to both of them together? "I thought you'd be angry if I wanted to make sure he was all right. That's the only reason I did this."

"I am sorry," Mictlantecuhtli said, surprising her almost as much as Lucinda had surprised Finn. "That is the word, is it not? Sorry? I should have trusted in you."

"I... I should've trusted you too."

"Would you still take him back to the real?"

"Not if he can stay where he was happy. All I ever wanted was for you not to hurt him."

"The drowned man must remain in Tlalocan," Tlaloc said. "He belongs to the House of Rain."

"It matters naught to me," Mictlantecuhtli said. "But Lucinda Swire will return to her proper place."

"Can she not stay as well?" Finn asked. Pressing his luck.

"No." This time it was Tlaloc and Mictlantecuhtli who spoke in a chorus.

"She is a *guest* of the House of Rain," Tlaloc said, "defined by her departure."

"She belongs to Mictlan. I have eaten her heart and taken her skin. Her absence would make us less."

"What if I switched with her? Could she have my place here if I filled in for her... wherever?"

"Finn," Ingrid said, "I'm not sure you know what you're doing."

"Puttin' myself at the mercy of your man there. I know that much. But I'm willing to trust him, if you are."

"You don't have to prove anything."

"Don't I?"

"Mictlan finds no objection to this arrangement," el Rey said, after several moments of deep rumination. "What say you, cousin?"

"She is not drowned," Tlaloc said.

"She did die in water," Ingrid mentioned.

"But not *by* water."

"No," she admitted. "By electricity."

"E-lec-tricity?" Tlaloc repeated, as if unsure of the shape of the new word. "What is it?"

"It is fire," Mickey said. "Blue fire that travels on filaments of red metal, to make lamps burn."

"It's maybe a little more like lightning," Ingrid said carefully. "Man-made lightning, contained and controlled."

"Lightning is lightning, manmade or not," Tlaloc said, considering.

"Natural creatures cannot make unnatural things," Mickey agreed.

"Lightning falls under the aegis of Tlalocan." A bolt of it flickered on the far horizon, like a distant synapse firing in some all-encompassing brain, marking a decision made. "The House of Rain will accept your Swire in trade."

"But I don't want to stay." Lucy spoke to Tlaloc, but tipped her head toward Ingrid. "Like this one said, he were happy here, on his ship an' all." She turned to Finn. "I'm not havin' you give that up on account o' me. I'm *not*. Why would you want to?"

"Because this place is a dream, and so's everything that happens in it. That means doin' something for you right here and right now might be the last chance I ever have to do anything that matters."

Lucinda didn't look any less dismayed by that reasoning, but she didn't know how to respond.

"Are we agreed?" Mictlantecuhtli asked of Finn, before anybody else could throw in an opinion.

"We are."

"Then wake, Finnegan. Your dream is at an end."

SEVERAL things happened then, all at once. Tlaloc's selective rain switched over from falling on the island to falling on the water. The ground beneath Ingrid's feet dried out and crackled within an instant. Mickey's team of skeletal oarsmen extended a ramp from his war canoe to the arid, grayish beach, allowing their King to come ashore with all due pomp and ceremony.

As soon as he set foot on shore el Rey stepped up to Finn and swept his obsidian blade upward, opening his new prize from crotch to forehead. Finn's memory of flesh fell away from his bones like two halves of a torn suit. Mickey reached under his exposed ribs, gripped his heart, and gave his still-standing skeleton a rude shove, ripping the fist-sized organ loose as the bare bones staggered back, off balance.

Lucinda wailed in protest as Mictlantecuhtli turned toward the far side of the island and raised the heart above his head. The waters of Tlalocan parted around the spit of land he stood upon and drained out into the sea behind him, sweeping away Lucy, Finn's crew, and even the rustic little house with the steep blue roof. Perhaps the House of Rain itself, for all Ingrid knew.

Only she, Mickey, Finn, and Poppy remained where they stood, on dry and solid ground.

What the rushing cataracts left behind was a familiar misty landscape of low rolling hills dotted with dead, twisted trees. Mictlan. The beach stretched away to either side of them, as far as the eye could see, and the sea lapped the shore at their backs. Rain pelted the churning waves and clouds roiled overhead, marking out the indisputable border of Tlaloc's realm.

Finn's skeleton bent down to retrieve his coat, the long black one with the crimson lining. Dr. Pagán's coat. The articulated bones shook it off and shrugged back into it. The way the red lining showed through between Finn's ribs made Ingrid think of Mickey's royal cape, fashioned from flayed skin turned inside-out.

Mickey bit into the heart he'd claimed like it was some bloated piece of fruit and munched on it contentedly.

"Are you all right?" Ingrid said to what remained of Peter Finnegan.

He nodded his skull and straightened his cuffs. "Think so, yeah. Bit cold, I suppose."

Ingrid nodded. That was only to be expected. She turned to Mickey. "What happens now?"

"Go and return to me in your whole form," he said, waving a hand through her like she was made of smoke. It was a strange sensation. "I miss the substance of you."

"What about Finn?"

"What would you have me do with him?"

"I… I'm not sure." She wondered how someone who'd died by suicide was apt to fare in Mictlan, even if its jealous king could be talked out of making a special effort to torment him. The rules here were different than they'd been in Tlalocan.

"We will discuss it when you return. My cousin will escort you back to the border of the real, and there I will send for you."

"What about my rights, Mictlantecuhtli?" Poppy spoke up. "You gave my property away."

El Rey turned to her, a girl-shaped thing barely half his height. "The Swire was more mine than yours," he said.

"Still, I had my claim. And now I can't reach her. Tlalocan is opaque to me. So I demand reparation."

"What reparation would you have?"

"You promised me ten thousand souls."

"On conditions you failed to meet."

"Yes, but—"

"Besides which," Mickey went on, "you violated Mictlan's borders when you brought this shade of Lady Redstone over. And for that, I nullify your compact with her. She owes you no devotion, neither in life nor in death."

"You can't do that. You haven't the authority."

"I can destroy every soul you lay claim to within my realm. I can feed them to my creatures, all at once, in an orgy of gluttony the like of which they have never known."

"You wouldn't."

"Why wouldn't I?"

Poppy didn't have a good answer for that. "Fine," she said to Ingrid. "You're off the hook. It's good to do the King, isn't it?"

Ingrid didn't bother to retort, although she couldn't help smirking a little bit.

"So I'm to have nothing?" Poppy said, turning back to Mickey and planting her hands on her hips. "While your strumpet gets away with everything? What justice is that? I have a right to be made whole."

"Take this one as your servant, then," Mickey said, nudging Finn's remains toward her. "If that will shut you up."

"Oh, Mickey, I don't know," Ingrid said.

"Why?" el Rey asked. "It is no worse a fate than he earned on his own."

Ingrid supposed that might be true. Such an arrangement would also keep Finn from falling prey to Mickey's whims in the future. "What will you do with him?" she demanded of Poppy.

"Why, keep him close forevermore," the opium eidolon replied, taunting Ingrid with her saccharine smile. "Few of my slaves are as cogent as this one. He'll be of great use to me. Not that you have any say in the affairs of immortals, witch. We'll strike whatever bargain we choose."

You're not so immortal, either of you—just old, Ingrid thought but didn't say. There was no percentage in it.

Mickey was scrutinizing her. Gauging her reactions. "Is this exchange acceptable to you?"

"I won't see him again, will I?"

"No," Mickey said.

"Never," Poppy confirmed.

Ingrid took a deep breath and let it out as smoothly as she could. She'd been ready to throw so much away on Finn's behalf. She'd loved him completely at one time and loved him still to some degree—enough that she didn't want him annihilated, especially if she was the cause. But the fact remained that she'd left him before he died. She'd already chosen to move on. And Mictlan, by way of California, was where she'd arrived. Did she want her adventures here to end because of someone who'd mocked the very possibility that other worlds could truly lurk behind the thin fabric of the real? When she'd been brave enough to light out in pursuit of those territories on her own, to see what she might find?

She gave her assent to Mickey's proposal with a single nod of her head.

"Then let it be so," el Rey pronounced, and Poppy broke into a grin.

"Sounds like this's goodbye then," Finn said, turning to Ingrid.

"I think so."

"D'you know what I loved most about magic when I was a lad?"

"No." She shook her head. It wasn't a question she'd expected.

"The illusion of it all. Not the illusions themselves, exactly, so much as the way they came together with the patter and the costumes and the stage dressing to suggest another world, a bigger, more exotic world, where secret knowledge could put the bold and the brave into contact with levels of being that everyday reality never dares to imagine. Learnin' it was all built on cheap tricks, and that conjurers are only characters, was a cause for despair."

"I'm sorry, Finn."

"Don't be. That's not what I'm sayin.' You tried to tell me the world could be like that, like I wanted, but I couldn't let myself hope for it, not by then. Not anymore. I'd learned better. I'd grown up. And yet, there you were. Right beside me, right on stage. Real, in the way I used to dream of. And I never knew. If I'd have been able to open my eyes to what was right in front of me, who knows what might've been?"

Ingrid nodded a thank you. Her throat was tight. She had to swallow before she could speak. "I'm sorry about your submarine," she whispered. Not to mention everything else that went along with it.

Finn shrugged. "You came to help. Even if it didn't go accordin' to plan."

"Time's up," Poppy said. To Ingrid: "Don't look now, but your ship has come in."

Ingrid did look, out to sea, and saw a massive shadow moving toward shore through the fog. It resolved into a hulking three-masted frigate, painted black and bristling with mismatched cannon around its upper deck. Its square-rigged sails were dyed blood red, and a black flag emblazoned with skull and crossbones flew from the tallest mast, snapping and dripping in the rain. The intimidating ship dropped anchor out beyond the jutting wreckage of the *Paracelsus* and the crew lowered a rowboat down to the waterline. Its oars creaked as a large sailor muscled it into the shallows.

Finn spotted a familiar figure standing up at the bow of the pirate ship and he raised a bony hand to wave. Lucinda waved back. This was a trimmer, younger-looking woman than Ingrid remembered, wearing a tri-corner hat and a brocaded frock coat. The Lucinda that might have been, in another time and place.

"I'm glad of that, y'know," Finn said, tipping his skull in Lucy's direction. There was no way to read his expression. "I think I did a good thing there. Something real."

"Me too."

"Wish I'd got to say a proper goodbye. Will you tell her that for me?"

"Of course I will." Ingrid wanted to say more, but Poppy was making a show of looking bored, sighing and shifting her weight from hip to hip. It was just as well. The skiff from Lucy's ship had reached the shore, scraping its bottom into the wet sand.

"Cap'n Swire of the *Black Rose* wishes to welcome the Lady Redstone aboard," the rower said, standing up while lowering his gaze in deference. "On the orders of Tlaloc, governor of this province and master of the House of Rain."

"Guess that's my ride," Ingrid said.

"Then let's all be on our way." Poppy stepped up next to her new acquisition. "Mictlantecuhtli, it's been a pleasure. Ingrid Redstone... it's been what it's been."

She offered el Rey a quick curtsey, seized Finn's hand, and then they were gone. Just gone, without so much as a bang or a puff of smoke to distract attention.

No magician had ever made a cleaner exit from a stage.

And Ingrid was left alone with her King, standing on an endless, empty beach, under his world's dreary sky.

He offered her his hand, but Ingrid couldn't take it. Her insubstantial fingers passed right through his.

"Go, and return," he said, "as a properly invited guest. I will wait for you."

Ingrid nodded, then turned away and stepped into the surf, and into the rain. From Mictlan to Tlalocan. It was like stepping out from under a sheltering roof. Lucy's crewman took her hand and helped her into his boat. He offered her an oilskin slicker but she shook her head to decline. The downpour was frigid, but it wasn't the sort of cold that could hurt her. It was just there to be observed.

Mickey waited on the shore, beyond the wall of rain, growing smaller as her gondolier rowed out to the ship he'd called the *Black Rose*. El Rey waited while she climbed up a rope ladder and was helped aboard. He was still there when the ship set sail and came about, headed out to sea, and Ingrid watched him standing on the beach until distance and weather blurred, then faded, and finally erased him from her sight.

THE *Black Rose* sailed through the night, but her captain didn't come to see Ingrid until the last hour before dawn.

Tlaloc's rain had eased off to a drizzle. The pirate-type she remembered from Finn's dream had brought her a steaming cup of lapsang souchong some time ago, and the porcelain still felt warm between her palms. The big buccaneer looked better suited to this milieu than he had to the *Paracelsus*. They'd talked a bit, enough for Ingrid to learn that the *Black Rose* was crewed by privateers—pirates licensed by the Crown to capture slave ships and set the cargo free. It sounded like something that might've excited Lucy as a girl. She hadn't seen Miss Doshi, and was wondering whether Finn's former first officer had been transferred to a different psychodrama when Lucinda emerged from the navigation room on the sterncastle deck and joined her at the rail.

"Won't be long now," she said. "Then we'll be shut of each other once and for ever, Ingrid Redstone."

"I didn't mean any harm, Lucy."

"Well, meanin' and doin' ain't hardly the same, is they?"

That was one of the truest things Ingrid had ever heard her say. "He was proud to give you this," she said, meaning Tlalocan. "He wanted you to enjoy it."

That sounded absurdly insufficient even as she said it.

"Thing of it is, I will," Lucy said. "I have been. See, I got two sets of memories at the moment. I feel like I been on this boat for years, but another part o' me knows it's been about five minutes. I remember what happened back on that beach, *and* I remember bein' Lucy the Pirate Queen. Only I got a sense I'm like to forget one of those things when you step off my ship. The rains wash everything away. So I been writin' down what I remember, as best I can. To try an' hold on."

She opened her coat to show Ingrid a thin sheaf of pages she'd folded over and tucked into her belt, next to a flintlock pistol, as if defying her or anyone else to try and steal them. Ingrid wondered how durable those memories would turn out to be. Rain could wash ink away so easily.

"He wanted to say goodbye. He asked me to tell you that."

Lucy nodded. "You ain't got no idea how it feels to have somethin' so precious snatched away, do you? Not once but twice, now."

"No," Ingrid admitted.

"Maybe you will someday," Captain Swire said. Then, with a lift of her chin toward the horizon: "Land ho."

Ingrid looked out over the water to see tall seaside cliffs looming through the fog as the *Black Rose* drew close to shore. The sandy embankment running along the cliffs' base looked washed out, cold and scrubbed of color in the early light... except for a hazy dab of deep warm auburn Ingrid recognized as her own shock of ginger hair.

They'd sailed all the way back to the edge of the real.

Even as she realized it she jerked awake with a gasp and found herself sitting cross-legged in the damp sand, on the beach. Her knees felt stiff as rusted hinges when she uncrossed her legs to stand up, and her back ached fiercely. Her fire had long since gone out. The chill here was a more menacing thing than it was in the otherworld, and she felt it even through her thick sheepskin jacket.

Her horse hadn't made it. Probably it had died at the instant Poppy led it into the cave and onto the old road. The tide had taken it when it receded—Ingrid could see the half-submerged body rolling in the desultory waves.

Out beyond that, a shadow that could have been a departing ghost ship dissolved into the morning fog.

Ingrid brushed a lock of salt-stiffened hair off her brow. She was calculating how long the walk back to San Pedro was apt to take when she heard herself addressed from the clifftop above.

"Lady Redstone?"

An eager skull was peering down at her, over the cliff's edge. Three others joined it.

"Who wants to know?" She was only being sarcastic, but Mickey's emissaries seemed not to register it. Today was All Souls' Day, the last hours in the year when el Rey could send the dead out into the living world, and he had said he would send for her.

"We have been instructed to escort the Lady Redstone back to the

Hole in the Sky. By, um, Mictlantecuhtli."

"How did he know where to find me?"

The spokesman amongst the animated skeletons pointed to the horse corpse tumbling in the surf behind her, leaving Ingrid to infer that Mickey had somehow spotted her in the dead animal's last memories. He must have been looking hard.

It was unsettling to know he could do that.

The skeletons rolled a rope ladder down the side of the sandstone cliff. The rungs on this one turned out to be made of human femurs.

Ingrid did the only reasonable thing, under the circumstances. She stepped onto the lowest bone and started climbing.

Chapter Six

THE build site was empty of workmen and eerily silent, for a weekday afternoon. The weather had turned temperate just these few miles inland. The half-finished tower stood still and silent under a china-blue sky mounded up with mashed potato clouds, looking like a ruin in reverse.

Ingrid found a dead cat when she crossed the bare concrete foundation. It was gray, scruffy, and looked as though it had fallen from a significant height. She wondered what had happened as she stepped over the small body, but didn't pause to speculate. El Rey was waiting, after all.

His servants had carried her all the way from the coast in a royal palanquin, of all ridiculous things, like the *cihuatlahtoanis* of old. The four skeletons had taken up the ends of the poles that supported Ingrid's tiny, private compartment and set off at a brisk pace, like an ironic team of pallbearers. One of them still had the tattered remains of Aztec shells rattling against his ankle, so she guessed these to be some ancient bones indeed. But the ride they provided was smooth. The old ones were masterful cross-country runners, as might be expected of people whose technology had never included the wheel.

She wondered why neither Winston Watt nor Oscar San Martín had been sent to fetch her in an automobile, but the answer became obvious as soon as she reached the room at the top of her incomplete tower.

The King's Men were dead, both of them. Oscar's body lay on the floor in a pool of dried blood, as lifeless as the cat down at ground level. It looked like he'd been shot through the liver. But his bones stood in the doorway to the next room, under the hand-hewn limestone lintel. Watt was there too, similarly ossified and leaning against the opposite jamb. His realworld remains were nowhere in evidence, but they were undoubtedly as dead as the exsanguinated architect on the carpet, if he was stranded on the Mictlan side of that doorway. Ingrid could only identify the new skeletons by their clothes. Watt wore his customary tweed and starched collar, while Oscar's reconstructed bones wore the same suspenders and workshirt with rolled-up sleeves as his sorry, stiffening corpse.

Ingrid balked at the idea of stepping over him more than she had for the dead cat. "Black Tom?" she asked, from the plain modern doorway that now framed the legendary Hole in the Sky.

"He got away," Oscar said.

"The duplicitous son of a *whore* betrayed us all," Watt snapped, without bothering to conceal his anger. "He cheated Mictlantecuhtli and he murdered us."

"He didn't murder us. We pretty much killed each other," Oscar said to Ingrid.

"Well, he *got* us killed," Watt grumbled, and Oscar didn't argue any further.

"You had a family, didn't you?" Ingrid asked. His body had a wedding ring, anyway.

Oscar's skeleton nodded. He looked as miserable as bare bones could. "My wife is pregnant right now."

"I'm sorry," Ingrid said. It didn't seem like anywhere near enough. She was setting a record for emotional understatement.

"He was angry you weren't here," the ex-architect told her. "We tried to find you."

"If he wanted me here he should have invited me."

Oscar shrugged. They both knew Mictlantecuhtli wouldn't see it that way. Logic only had so much effect on his perspective. Besides which, Ingrid *had* been playing a game, hiding out until she knew Mickey was in the middle of his big project and then sneaking around his territory in search of Finn. Though el Rey had been playing the same game back from the opposite direction.

"He expects me to finish the building. When I can't go any further than this door. Never mind looking like this." He waved bare phalanges in front of his empty eye sockets. "What am I supposed to do?"

Ingrid skirted the body in the middle of the room. "I can help a little bit. Here, give me your hand."

Oscar hesitated, but let Ingrid take his brittle fingers. Reaching through the door, across two worlds.

"Now close your eyes."

"I don't have any eyes."

"You remember how it feels, though. Pretend. Try."

Oscar bowed his head. Ingrid could study the seams where the plates of his skull had fused together.

"Now think about looking in a mirror. Think about combing your hair, or shaving your beard."

Pretend flesh swirled together from fine dust, covering his bones as he concentrated. "What's the point of this?" he murmured.

"Look."

He raised his head to look at his hands, and the surprise showed on his reconstructed face. That visage could blow away again as easily as a mandala made of sand, but at least now he'd be able to direct living workmen from this doorway, as inefficient an arrangement as that might prove to be.

"Well, thank you for that," he said, running a hand back through his hair in the same nervous way he'd always done when talking to Ingrid. She nodded. It really wasn't much. Would've happened anyway, as Mictlan took on the shapes of his regrets around him.

Watt had watched them with a sneer that transcended his lack of lips. When they turned to look at him he stood up straight, balled his fists, gritted his molars, and forced his dour old grimace back into being, apparently out of pure spite. Skin bloomed from his bones like some pale fungus. When the restoration was complete, he doffed an imaginary hat at them. His bald head was shinier than his bare skull had been. "Go on," he said, showing Ingrid the way with mock gentility, like a bitter butler. "Mustn't muck about with the help any longer than necessary."

She might've told him to go to hell, but it would've been redundant.

Instead she stepped through the door, joining the King's Men in Mictlan. On a whim she turned around, closed her eyes, and attempted to roll time forward by a few weeks, then months, then years, as an experiment.

And this time it worked. Each time she checked, the antechamber's new carpet had thinned and the fresh paint on the walls had faded a little bit more. Sometimes the furniture changed, but the office itself never did. The door on the far side of the room either stood closed or opened onto a dim hallway, but never the open sky.

The broken time-stream that once resulted in a choice between a flowering tower or an electrical tree had been mended. A finished building existed in her future—because Mickey had made up his mind about whether or not he wanted it there. Ingrid had suspected as much when Oscar told her he was still expected to complete the project, despite his new limitations.

She left the builder and the butler gawping into the silent decay of the late 20th century, and went to find her King.

H E'D parked his Pyramid on the endless beach, beside the sea, where Tlaloc's rain stippled the water but never touched the sand. He'd brought back Lucy's Cock & Bull as well, plucking the pub from memories of London and providing it with a new ocean view. There were no other structures to be seen.

Ingrid supposed she was meant to climb down and join him for a drink.

S HE found him sitting at the bar, with his tall feathered headdress propped up on a stool next to him. She took a seat on the opposite side. They must've made a surreal sight amidst the colorless crowd of regular drinkers—a redhead in blue jeans meeting a bare-chested Aztec king.

It sounded like the setup to a joke whose punchline might prompt a psychotic break.

"I meant to join you in the realworld," Mickey said without looking up from his pint of ale, like a caricature of a morose drunk. "It was to be a surprise. But you knew that, didn't you?"

"Yeah." There was no sense in denying it. Watt and San Martín were his creatures now—he would know from their memories everything they'd told her about Black Tom's homecoming.

But it didn't seem like a topic Mictlantecuhtli much wanted to discuss.

"I was surprised by what he did," el Rey ventured, steering the subject away from his failed plans. "Your Finn."

"For Lucy?"

He nodded.

"Me too," Ingrid said.

"You never divined the nature of their relation?"

"Never even guessed at it. Though it does help explain why she never could stand me."

"Because she believed you would cause him misfortune?"

Ingrid shrugged. "She wasn't wrong."

"You never meant to. And his final choice was brave."

It was odd to hear Finn complimented by someone who'd meant to expunge him from existence.

"The Lady of the Poppy needed to be appeased," Mickey added, when Ingrid didn't respond right away. "Her compact with you had merit."

"No, I think he'll be all right with Poppy," Ingrid said, feeling acutely aware of the gold coin in her hip pocket. Poppy would keep him occupied, all right. Dr. Pagán was custom made for the stately pleasure domes of her subjects' imagination. The two of them would make a fine double-act. Poppy wasn't cruel, so much as selfish and vindictive, and her influence *could* be conquered. If she wanted to swipe at Ingrid by torturing Finn, she might not find it so easy to manage.

The palanquin ride in from the coast had taken a couple of hours. There'd been plenty of time to coat the coin she'd prepared as a link in lacquer-layers of potent wards. One final conjurer's trick. Poppy would still own him—Ingrid couldn't undo what Mictlantecuhtli had done—but she could protect him from malice. The opium spirit would keep the power to compel his presence, but she would never be able to trade him away, control his actions, or dictate his words. All she'd have in Finn was a jester who could heckle her without any fear of retribution, unless she chose to cut him loose from her service. And if she did that, he'd still have an anchor in the realworld, well out of Mickey's reach.

Ingrid dropped a hand to her thigh, touching the outline of the coin through her jeans. She was almost surprised Poppy wasn't here already, demanding redress for the damaged goods the King had unknowingly pawned off on her.

"When I was angry," he said, unaware of anything she was thinking, "before I understood the mistakes we made, I wondered if I wanted our... our 'thing' to continue."

"And now?" Ingrid asked, knowing full well that if he'd made up his mind to finish the building, he'd also made up his mind about her.

"I find myself feeling... relieved," he said, selecting his words with care, "that so much was based upon misunderstanding."

Ingrid didn't ask how much her abandoning Finn had also contributed to his newfound peace of mind. She simply nodded in honest agreement. "You should pay Oscar San Martín's wages, if he's still working for you," she said. "To his wife. Will you have Watt see to it?"

"I will," Mickey said. The afterlife would hold no rest for the King's Englishman. Somebody had to manage the accounts, and now Watt could do it from the office at the top of the tower until the end of time.

"And provide for his child when it gets older?"

"On that score, you must have no doubt," Mickey replied with a grin that was a touch too broad for comfort. "The descendants of San Martín will always know my patronage."

That sounded almost more like a threat than a promise, somehow, but Ingrid let it go. It seemed they were going to try taking each other at their word, for a change.

More or less.

"Can we get rid of this place?" she asked, wanting suddenly to be almost anywhere else—any place the memories weren't as thick as the layers of tobacco smoke that hung in the pub's stale air.

"Does it no longer please you to revisit?"

"It's part of my past. I'm ready to leave it there."

Mictlantecuhtli, el Rey de los Muertos, stood up from his barstool and offered his hand.

Ingrid accepted, stood, and took one last look around. She hadn't known quite how ready she was to close the book on this chapter until she heard herself say it aloud.

"Will you 'miss' him?" Mickey asked.

She considered. "I'm glad I saw him. But I was mad at him, for what he did. For putting it on my conscience. I only came because I felt responsible. You know that, don't you?"

His actions had nearly spoiled everything she'd sought for herself in Los Angeles. She realized she'd never even spoken to Finn about why he'd done it, though it hardly mattered now. He'd atoned where he could, made the most of his limited second chance, and that would have to be enough for both of them.

Mickey picked up his feathered headdress and tucked it under his arm. "His choices were his own, and your obligations are self-imposed. I say you are free if you choose it."

"I do," she said. "I have."

"Then let us go."

"Yes, let's." Ingrid took Mictlantecuhtli's gold-banded arm and accompanied him to the door, like any everyday couple embarking on an afternoon stroll.

IN a nearby booth, one located out of sight of the bar, Finn sat back frowning while Poppy buffed her nails on her sleeve and inspected the shine.

"What did she mean, 'mad at me for what I did?' What am I meant to've done?"

"I'm sure I have no idea."

"Does she think I killed myself?"

"Didn't you? Lucy thought so."

"No, I never did! I got thrown in the river. By two American 'detectives.' Men who were lookin' for *her*. For Ingrid. For her and some map she's said to've stolen."

"Really?"

"I didn't tell 'em anything. Didn't know anything to tell. But that won't have stopped them looking."

"How absolutely fascinating."

"I thought she knew. I thought… oh, to hell with what I thought. Come on, we have to warn her!"

Finn bolted across the tap room, shoving his way past a pair of lumbering drunks who were being battened on by unseen whisky angels, thirsty for more than their share, and he made it as far as the front door's threshold before Poppy raised a hand to halt him in his tracks.

The door swung shut in front of him, cutting off his view of Ingrid and the King as they meandered up the beach.

Poppy was at his ear in the next instant, murmuring: "She hexed you up, lucky man. Cheated me, or else you'd be demon-feed already. I can't crush you, and I can't command you. All I can do is keep you on a very short leash, but it turns out that's really quite enough. I just *knew* I'd find some way to get back at her, if we came back here."

She meant to let Ingrid walk away without a warning about the murderers on her trail, and let fate take its inevitable course. Finn gaped while Poppy smirked, then he turned and kicked the door back open, so hard it cracked against the exterior wall.

"Ingrid!" he shouted after her… at the instant Mictlan's re-creation of the Cock & Bull crumbled to ash and swirled away on the wind.

"DID you hear something?" Ingrid paused and looked back the way they'd come. The Pyramid was there in the distance, its foundation stones only yards from Tlaloc's steady rain and lapping waves, but Lucinda's old establishment had been scrubbed from the landscape.

El Rey cocked his head, listening. "Nothing but the voices of the wind and the water," he said.

Ingrid nodded uncertainly. The beach they stood on could have been any isolated stretch of California coast, bleak and beautiful under a stark winter sky. They seemed to have it all to themselves.

If there was trouble creeping up behind her, Ingrid couldn't see it.

NEXT TIME:
Episode Three
SILENT TOWER

~EPISODE THREE~
SILENT TOWER

Chapter One

—September, 1912

WHEN Ingrid Redstone stepped out the front door of the
finished Silent Tower for the very first time, the weather was
warm and bright, and the golden late-summer landscape
looked as drowsy and peaceable as a picture on a postcard
for miles all around.

The new Tower loomed behind her, a misplaced man-made monolith
that blocked out the sun, and there was nothing else like it anywhere in
sight. The lone thirteen-story building had arrived ahead of history, in
anticipation of a city that had yet to spring up around it.

Construction of the oddly-situated skyscraper had begun more than
three years prior, in the summer of 1909 (on the very same day Ingrid's
first moving picture had premiered, synchronistically enough). She'd
used the stage name 'Silent Tower' in the credits of that film (the first
theatrical venture to be shot entirely in Los Angeles), and now she
couldn't help but assign the same eccentric title to the brand new building
her influential lover had caused to be erected for her in the middle of a
broad sheep pasture, some miles south of a blossoming residential
development called Hollywood.

That's how it had happened in this new version of reality, anyway.

When Ingrid first found her way to this spot back in 1910 there had been a massive oak tree growing in this field—a tree that hadn't been disturbed in centuries. That, and nothing more. No building, house, encampment, or hermit's hut, not for leagues in any direction. No construction, no workmen, no nothing. Ingrid remembered it clearly.

She'd climbed the sacred Tree and crawled through the Hole in the Sky she found above it. When she emerged from the world that lay beyond the Hole, less than an hour later by the clock, enough of the skyscraper had magically sprung up that she was able to ride a mechanical service elevator back down to *terra firma*.

The past had changed while she was gone. The Tree she'd climbed up had been cut down months before she ever got there.

The paradox was still enough to make her head spin.

Now, today, late in 1912, the Silent Tower was finally complete. The modest brick office building with beaux-arts crenellations that had been grafted onto the pristine landscape made for quite a surreal sight, standing tall and rust-red against the flawless blue of a California sky. It fronted on a street that was only paved for a few dozen yards in either direction before devolving back into a rough dirt track. Grasses and dandelions sprouted along the hump between its wheel ruts. Nobody but the crews employed to build the Tower ever used that path, and now their work was finished. Nobody had arrived on site this morning, for the first time in a long time, and nobody was coming. The nearest active road would be the ancient *Camino Real*, the Royal Road, sometimes called the *Carretera del Rey*, and it lay about a mile to the north.

Ingrid breathed deep of the cool, fresh air of a rewritten world, adjusted her broad-brimmed hat to shield her fragile redhead's complexion from the sun, and started off toward what she thought of as the King's Highway, on foot.

S HE sort of enjoyed the trek, though she'd never let her King know it. He was better behaved when he was somewhat chagrinned. It shamed him that the Tower had taken years to complete, when he'd intended that it should appear instantaneously before her. The building in the realworld was a fledgling effort, a first attempt at extending his reach beyond the boundaries of Mictlan, the Aztec realm of the dead. But he'd miscalculated, and the unaccustomed sense of limitation had flustered el Rey into humility for a time.

Two of his best men had died in 1910 during a fight with a third, who subsequently disappeared, and the resulting lack of living minions had adversely affected Mickey's degree of influence in this world. One of the dead was his homegrown architect, Oscar San Martín, the building's designer and construction foreman, and losing him had been a significant blow. Progress had slowed to a crawl. Oscar (an affable, handsome young man Ingrid had found rather attractive but never dared to get close to) hadn't cared for being dead at all. He'd left behind a wife and a young son, and his mind stayed troubled on their behalf. He had difficulty keeping his thoughts coherent enough to oversee the completion of the work he'd been charged with, especially given the hindrance of never being able to leave the inner office of the executive suite at the top of the building. Those two rooms, long known as the King's Chambers, *las Cameras del Rey*, had lain beyond the Hole in the Sky for centuries—until the day Ingrid's Silent Tower rose up to enclose them.

With the last proper initiates of his cult either dead or fled, el Rey de los Muertos was down to employing thugs and henchmen who had no inkling of his true nature. They were dealt with by Winston Watt, the other servant who'd died in Mictlantecuhtli's debt. The independent contractors expected to see their boss rarely if ever, as they were led to believe he was the head of a powerful underground syndicate, and Ingrid supposed there was more truth in that than they imagined.

Miguel Caradura was the name the realworld knew him by, these days. Ingrid had suggested it, after a saying she'd picked up in the bustling markets downtown. '*Cara dura*' literally meant 'hard face,' and it was the haggler who kept the harder face who came out on top in a negotiation. Unless her Mickey made a special effort to the contrary he still tended to appear as a shrouded skeleton wearing an extravagant garland of human eyeballs around his collarbones, so the name fit on a literal level, and not just as a description of his personality.

The part she found funny was that his new recruits, Spanish and English speakers alike, had already adopted 'Mickey Hardface' as a nickname for the kingpin in the office at the top of the Tower.

They'd all soil themselves in terror if they ever learned just how hard—ossified, in fact—the man's face truly was.

The thought never failed to make Ingrid smile.

She supposed she was a necromancer, nowadays, and that in its most romantic sense. Her relationship with the King had opened up new realms, but it also set her apart from both the living and the dead. Only women in myths had experiences like hers.

Who could the time-traveling lover of a god expect to confide in, though? And loneliness was nothing new. The connections she made with people were often intense, but they also tended to be brief.

That said, she did still have a few friends back here in the realworld, and she meant to call on them at her earliest convenience. She missed the warmth of living company.

Ingrid crested a low rise in the deer track she'd been following, stepped out of the trees, and found herself within yards of the old Camino Real. Its winding dirt course had been packed down smooth by millennia of foot and wheel traffic, although it was empty right now, in either direction.

The road looked like a thin, pale scar on the landscape that the earth had never quite managed to heal (though it never stopped trying). Trees reached for each other across the top of it, and the scrub brush along its sides was thriving. No other sign of civilization intruded upon the countryside's primeval quiet. It was hard to believe that the increasingly cosmopolitan *Ciudad de los Ángeles* itself, with its tall buildings, its rumbling motor cars, and its palatial theaters all ablaze with electric light, could lay just a few miles to the east.

The shirtwaist, skirt, and heels that had come back with her from Mictlan were hardly appropriate for an extended hike. She missed the simple woven sandals that the old people, the Nahuatlaca, the Aztecs-to-be, had introduced her to a thousand years ago. She could've strolled to San Francisco and back in a pair of those.

Ingrid stood by the side of the ancient track, weighing her options in the clear morning sun, and presently she heard a distant clop of hooves and a rumble of wagon wheels headed her way. That was fortunate. She shifted her weight from one hip to the other and stood back to see who might come around the bend in the road.

It turned out to be a dairy wagon, heavily laden with two-foot-high metal milk cans and pulled by a team of four. The teamster—a careworn old fellow sporting a handlebar moustache that looked as wilted as his posture—sat up a little straighter on the headboard when he saw Ingrid standing there. She must have been a sight: as elegant a lady as any you might see in the salons of Europe, alone in the middle of the California nowhere. The dairyman didn't take his eyes off her even once in the two minutes or so it took for his team to reach her.

When he pulled his cart abreast and reined the horses to a stop he still seemed at a loss for words, so Ingrid took it upon herself to fill in the awkward silence:

"Headed downtown?" she asked. "Los Angeles?"

The old teamster nodded.

"Good." Without further ado Ingrid took hold of the rail and swung herself up onto the headboard, depositing herself right next to the driver on his bench. He couldn't have looked more surprised if a bear had walked out of the woods to offer him brandy and cigars. But he didn't ask her to get down.

"Shall we?" Ingrid said, favoring the little man with a bright smile. "Allons-y?" she tried, when he continued to gape at her. She didn't have a Spanish equivalent for 'let's move, pal.'

Finally she put the reins he'd dropped back in his hand and gestured toward the road ahead, and her new friend at last seemed to get the point. He clucked to his team and they resumed their southeasterly trudge, unmindful of the extravagant new passenger on board.

Chapter Two

THE milkman glanced over at her repeatedly during their journey into the city, but only once or twice at her expansive décolletage, and Ingrid was prepared to accept this as gentlemanly behavior. She favored her driver with a combination of warm grin and cool blue eye-contact every time he looked at her, and the droop seemed to leave his crooked spine by gradual increments as they approached Los Angeles proper. By the time they reached the fashionable neighborhoods at the top of the scenic Loma de Mariposas (the Hill of the Butterflies, known officially as Bunker Hill for many years now, though Ingrid would always prefer the older name), he was sitting up ramrod straight on the headboard, calling to and waving at startled acquaintances like he was piloting the one single float in a personal parade.

Ingrid hopped down from the wagon at the corner of Temple and Broadway, still some considerable distance away from the busy markets along San Pedro Street, before her happy deliverer could stir up more gossip amongst his peers than he'd be able to live down back at home. Ingrid didn't want to be the cause of trouble for him when he'd done her a kindness. She waved from the concrete curb as the milk truck rattled away down the packed-dirt street, borne along with the flow of traffic. The unruly tide was composed of horsedrawn trucks; rail-bound trolleys with angry, clanging bells; and more rumbling, honking motorcars than Ingrid had ever seen in this town before.

Her driver swiveled his head to watch as his ember-haired vision receded behind him, without ever having said a single word to her.

THE hotel she kept a room at, the Angelus, was still a few blocks away, at Fourth and Spring. She might have gotten a little closer to home base before hopping off the milk wagon, but she felt like taking a walk down Broadway, so that she might pass by the numerous jewelry stores that always had exquisite gems on display in their front windows.

There were the Southwest Turquoise Company and H.J. Whitley's, both currently plastered in signage offering credit or boasting of the outfit's prominence on the West Coast gem market. Hephaestus H. Harris & Sons had a sapphire and diamond necklace featured in their main show window, and Ingrid shivered at the thought of its cool silver setting touching her skin as a sales clerk fixed it at the nape of her neck.

She loved stones, jewels, and metals of every kind. Not for monetary value or social status, but because they were the tangible result of earth meeting fire. Gems were objects forged in the furnace of the world's molten heart, and they excited something within Ingrid that she couldn't quite define. Their colors were so much like candy they made her salivate, for one thing. But she also felt the engulfing vastness of time when she contemplated the millennia of heat and pressure that had gone into forming them, and that thrilled her. She saw natural magic in the jewels' cold gleam.

Ingrid had an eye-sized garnet in her handbag, dark as a clot of blood. It had been a gift from Mickey, and wasn't a real gem at all, but an artifact of the otherworld. Her red stone. She wanted suddenly to have it set; set in the silver she so much preferred to gold, both because it complemented her mother-of-pearl complexion and for the lunar associations it evoked. She could picture the faceted red rock mounted in her favorite moon-metal and strung on a chain, made into a necklace she would never take off again. She almost went inside and placed an order for what she envisioned, before remembering she had no money whatsoever, not even a coin for the streetcar. Setting her stone would have to wait, as the garnet was far too valuable a thing to leave as its own collateral. She'd want to stand by and watch while the jeweler did his work.

Ingrid turned away from the window, attuning herself to the noise and bustle of Broadway once again, and sighed.

The street had changed while she was 'away.' There were fewer trees and houses than she remembered, to say nothing of the conical roofs and lightning-rod-capped spires that had been emblematic of the last century, but which were now disappearing fast. The low old buildings with their charming cupolas and Moorish details were being replaced by taller, boxier structures with ornamented facades and plain brick backs, not unlike her own Silent Tower, which stood so many miles away, out in the middle of nowhere. These buildings were packed together like uneven teeth in a concrete jawbone, and they all had advertisements painted on their whitewashed sides. Mostly the names of the businesses housed within, but Ingrid spotted a few bright, temporary show posters interspersed up there as well.

There was no one to see the Silent Tower, not out where it stood, and therefore no reason to scrawl messages upon its virgin walls.

It might be best if it remained that way, but Ingrid didn't think that was apt to happen. With Los Angeles mushrooming the way it was the Silent Tower might be engulfed by urban sprawl in a matter of a few short years. She was seized by an urge to hurry back there as fast as she could and hop forward in time to see how long it would be before the city filled in the empty spaces around her lonely office box, but she didn't know what point such an exercise would serve. She didn't know what to do about the situation.

There had been a great deal of warding built up around the Tree Below the Hole in the Sky when Ingrid first discovered it. The deflective glamour had been reinforced by the old peoples' shamans in every generation, and much of it remained in place despite the dramatic change in the landmark it protected. As conspicuous as the skyscraper in the field south of Hollywood seemed to Ingrid, she knew other people would have a devil of a time finding it, even if she drew them a map. *Especially* if she drew them a map. The clearer your idea of what you were looking for, the more trouble you'd have locating it. (Work crews seemed curiously exempt from such disorienting effects, perhaps because they came seeking only their paychecks and bore no knowledge of the Hole in the Sky.) So the old hexes might continue to work even as the population exploded, if she was lucky, as people walked past buildings without really noticing them every day of their lives.

During her hike to the Camino Real, Ingrid had been sure to pick a few of the sacred mushrooms that would guide her back to the Tower when she consumed them. This remained the only reliable method she knew for finding it again.

So the Silent Tower wasn't apt to be discovered on this particular afternoon, and she was glad to be back in the realest world she knew. She'd been a guest in Mictlan, where all was in flux and nothing was fixed, for far too long.

Ingrid had skipped over 1911 altogether. She'd decided to jump forward by a span that seemed more or less equivalent to the unquantifiable number of 'months' she'd spent vacationing in the otherworld, and the day after her Tower's completion seemed as good a time to return as any. Her experiences in Mictlan (her exchanges with Finn and Lucy and Poppy especially) had affected her enough that she wanted to feel like she'd been gone for a while. But now she was back in town and back in time, moving forward minute by minute and day by day, just like anybody else.

She longed for the familiar things she'd enjoyed in this neighborhood before. Perhaps a cup of green *sencha* at the indoor tea garden on the second floor of Yamato's import shop, or maybe a pint of beer and one of those 'French dip' sandwiches at Cole's café. Food and drink were to be followed by a minimum of ten hours' sleep in a bed at the Angelus that would stay lumpy all night long and make no effort whatsoever to reconfigure itself in the name of ensuring her perfect comfort, as everything in Mictlan always did.

The harsh reality of a sprung mattress sounded like paradise, just then.

Ingrid knew this sentimental fixation on the details that proved she was alive and awake in this time and place wouldn't last long, but right now they stood out with exquisite clarity, and she cherished that. It was a gift Death couldn't know he'd given her.

She turned and headed east on Fourth, toward the Angelus, now just a block away.

Ingrid paused in front of the hotel, checking the time on the big clock set high up into the masonry on the building's southeast corner, and then stood there for another moment to gaze up and across Spring Street, at the imposing edifice known as the Continental Building.

The decade-old office tower was so like her own Silent Tower, both in height and design. Perhaps Mickey had pilfered an image of it from her head and delivered it into the dreams of Oscar San Martín, or maybe the architect had seen this building himself and drawn his inspiration directly. At thirteen stories it was one of the first really tall structures in this city, and it had been quite a curiosity in its day. Tourists had traveled for miles to stare at it. Now the neighborhood was shooting up to match it, with newer structures growing taller every season, rivaling the increasingly-humbled Continental for skyline supremacy.

The same way it was sure to happen out in Hollywood.

Ingrid turned on her heel and strode into the cool, lush lobby of the Hotel Angelus.

HER room was kept on the tab of the Selig Polyscope Motion Picture Company. It was a holdover from the production of her one movie, titled *The Heart of a Race Tout*, which her Uncle Frank had generously arranged for her. Uncle Frank, otherwise known as Francis Boggs, her director, wasn't really an uncle by blood but merely a close old family friend, whom Ingrid had known since early childhood. She'd traveled from London to Los Angeles to play a small but vital role in his film, which they'd shot in the rear yard of a Chinese laundry right over on Olive Street.

Well, that had been part of her motivation for coming out to California. The legends of Mictlantecuhtli and the Hole in the Sky had provided the rest.

The hotel's lobby was vast, with a mirror-polished, black-and-white tile floor that her heels clicked against. Two long rows of Moorish arches ran all the way down its length. Potted palms lined the center of the space and plush sofas hugged the walls. The faces of the clerks behind the front desk were unfamiliar to Ingrid, but then she had been absent for a spell.

She walked right up and requested the key to Mr. Boggs' suite, thinking she might freshen up a bit before going out for that sandwich. Or maybe stay in and order up some room service. The dining room here served an excellent rack of short ribs, if she remembered correctly.

The clerk she'd addressed frowned and checked a list, then turned away to look over a pegboard festooned with brass keys on numbered tags. He stepped away to consult with a gray-haired man in a crisp gray suit, who seemed to be a manager of some sort.

The manager glanced at Ingrid, then sent his clerk away and came over.

"May I be of assistance?" he asked, rather coldly.

"I'm a guest of Mr. Francis Boggs," she said. "Of the Selig Polyscope Cinema Company? I seem to have misplaced my key."

Most people perked right up at the mention of the fascinating and novel moving-picture business, but the manager of the Angelus remained stoically unmoved. "I'm sorry," he told her. "But we have no such person registered here."

"But that can't be. Uncle Frank—I mean, Mr. Boggs—always keeps a room in this hotel. The same room, since 1908. Number 422. He keeps it so his out-of-town actors have a place to stay."

"I am afraid that his name is not in our register today, Miss."

Ingrid was at a loss.

"I've stayed here for months at a time," she said.

"Be that as it may," the unsympathetic manager replied. He ticked his eyes past Ingrid's shoulder and another man—a taller, slimmer one, though also clad in a nondescript gray suit—folded the newspaper he'd been perusing and stood up. Ingrid caught the movement from the corner of her eye.

House detective.

They thought she was a prostitute, is what that meant. Ingrid felt her cheeks burning with anger. That's why they wouldn't give her the key. Nobody around here seemed to recognize her at all. She hadn't expected quite so much staff turnover in only a year.

"All right," Ingrid said, before that house dick could be called over and she could be escorted out. "I must be mistaken."

The manager nodded and looked down his nose at her as she turned away, putting her back to both him and the glorified thug with the newspaper, who still hadn't approached. Ingrid's heels tapped out a measured rhythm as she strolled back down between the lobby's double rows of white arches, toward the front doors.

She wouldn't let herself hurry.

OUTSIDE again, on the street, Ingrid didn't look back until she reached the south-western corner of the hotel building. Behind her, the liveried doorman held the door again and the tall detective stepped out, onto the sidewalk, trying to keep an eye on her without making a scene about it.

But he looked north first, up Spring Street, toward Third and away from her, and Ingrid seized the instant to duck into the alleyway behind the big hotel.

She felt at once like she'd stepped into a different world.

It was dark back here, in the artificial canyon between tall buildings, and surprisingly quiet, considering the bustling thoroughfare wasn't but a few yards behind her. Ingrid had effectively disappeared from the reality at her back. Nobody (except maybe for that house detective, if she didn't hurry this up) was apt to notice anything she did back here.

She cast her eyes up and over the black iron fire escapes that zigzagged across the hotel's white side.

They were the sort with a last section of ladder that was meant to telescope down, so as to remain unreachable from ground level. One of them, though, had come loose and slid down partway. Ingrid thought she might be able to reach it and hurried over to try.

The bottom of the ladder turned out to be a maddening few inches beyond her reach. She tensed her legs to jump, then thought better and pulled off one of her shoes instead. She gripped it by the pointy toe and, balancing on one long leg like an exotic bird, hooked the heel over the ladder's lowest rung.

The fire escape came rattling down with just a tug. Ingrid had to duck out of its way.

She slipped her shoe back on and started to climb. Her heels were no better suited to ladder ascension than they had been to cross-country hiking, but Ingrid was nimble. She'd been dancing in front of audiences since she was thirteen, often in footwear far more outrageous than what she had on now.

She was up on the fire escape's first narrow iron balcony before she knew it, outside an open window situated at the end of a second-floor hallway. The corridor looked deserted. There was a maid service cart parked some doors down, but no maid in evidence.

Ingrid slithered in through the window and looked back just as the tall house detective in the unassuming gray suit rounded the corner into the alley below, clearly on the prowl for her.

She ducked back from the window before he could look up and spot her.

Or so she hoped. She had no way to be sure without looking out the window again, and she wasn't going to risk it. She didn't know if the lowered ladder would escape his notice or not, although there was nothing to be done for it now, one way or the other.

Ingrid hurried down the hall, sidestepping that service cart as she headed for the stairs. She didn't want to risk drawing the attention of an elevator operator (or anyone else, for that matter) until she could sort out the situation here.

SHE didn't expect to find her Uncle Frank upstairs, as he kept the rooms in question strictly for her use and left his own benefactor, Colonel William Selig, to pay the bills in turn.

She'd also lied to the clerk downstairs about having misplaced her room key. In truth she knew exactly where that key had gone. Mictlantecuhtli had requested it as a tribute, same as he had with her cash money, a pistol, and numerous other articles of clothing and jewelry. Lord Death had become an avid collector of realworld artifacts since first meeting his living love. The miniature bas relief portraits on coins captivated him, or else he might spend what seemed like hours running a single silk stocking through his hands, wholly absorbed in his experience of novel sensations. Mickey would pout in his angry way if Ingrid didn't give him the things that caught his eye, and she generally found it easiest just to hand them over. Such bits of everyday ephemera were of no use to her on the far side of reality anyway, and were therefore easy to forget about.

Now she wished she'd made more of an effort to hold onto that key.

No matter, though. She was handy enough with a couple of hairpins, and certain she could get into the suite. Then she'd have fresh clothes (she'd left a number of things in the closet), and twenty dollars or so, assuming no overzealous housekeeper had discovered the bills Ingrid had rolled up and stashed inside one of the hollow posts of the room's big brass bed, for emergencies.

She could also attempt to telephone Uncle Frank. She didn't have an exchange number to reach him at (as he'd been in the process of finding a more suitable film-production facility than the drying yard of the Sing Kee Laundry the last time they talked), but she was sure a switchboard operator would be able to connect her to the offices of the Selig Polyscope Company, wherever in the city they may have landed.

This would all be easy to straighten out then. She wasn't really worried about it. At the moment she was mostly miffed that the indulgence of Mickey's juvenile obsessions had resulted in embarrassment and inconvenience for her.

SHE'D broken into a light sweat by the time she emerged from the narrow stairwell and into a quiet fourth-floor hallway. The only sound was a subtle whoosh of moving air that would suck away to total silence as soon as she closed a room door behind herself.

Ingrid hurried down the hall to her accustomed suite.

She extracted two spiral hairpins from her coif and bent one of them out to a ninety-degree angle, recasting it as a makeshift tension bar. The pins' wavy shapes made the other one suitable for use as a rake without any modification at all.

Ingrid dropped to her knees to assess the keyhole above the doorknob and the complexity of the locking mechanism that lay behind it.

The knob turned before her eyes, of its own accord, as she was beginning the application of her clandestine skills, and the door opened from the inside. The gray-haired manager from the front desk nearly walked into her, and Ingrid found herself staring up the gray flannel front of him, from a position that lacked dignity, to say the very least.

Wonderful. If he hadn't made up his mind about her already…

"*You* shouldn't be here," the manager said, offering a hand to help Ingrid to her feet. She took it and stood, then demurely straightened her long black skirt and reflected that he seemed somewhat less startled by her kneebound presence in his hallway than she might have anticipated.

"This isn't what you think," Ingrid assured him.

"I know," the manager said, then shook his head and began again. "I mean, I *do* remember you. From several years back. I believe a champagne bottle thrown from your window during a celebration hit a passerby, and the police were called?"

"Oh," Ingrid said. "Right."

She still didn't recognize this particular supervisor, but she knew the incident in question had occurred during an impromptu soiree thrown to commemorate completion of principle photography on *Heart of a Race Tout*. Ingrid's own recollection was a hung-over blur, but she thought her hard-drinking co-star Tom Santschi had been the one to launch the infamous projectile, while her Uncle Frank smoothed things over with the bombarded couple on the street below. First by inviting them (as well as the cops they'd summoned) up to the ongoing wrap party, and then finally to the exclusive premiere of the movie itself.

That had been in the autumn of 1908. Four years and one reality ago, by Ingrid's reckoning.

"Really, you *mustn't* be here," the manager restated, but then instead of either shooing her from his hotel or yelling for his detective to come and help, he surprised her by grabbing her arm and yanking her into the room, then glancing down the hall in either direction before closing the door. That subliminal rush of air from the corridor did indeed evaporate into stark silence before the lock Ingrid had meant to violate with hairpins engaged behind them with a soft, definitive *click*.

Chapter Three

Y OU won't be able to hold me here," Ingrid said, turning around calmly, even though her heart was clamoring against her ribs like a trapped animal in a cage. "I'll go quietly if you like, but I won't wait around for the police. Or anybody else, for that matter."

"Like the Pinkerton downstairs, you mean?"

"Pinkerton?" Ingrid said, with genuine surprise. "That man in the lobby, who followed me out the door?"

The manager nodded.

"I thought he was your house detective."

"No hotel can afford a house detective like that," the manager said. "Though he might as well be ours, for all the time he spends here. He's kept room for the better part of a year and done little more during all that time than lounge around in our lobby."

"That must be costing somebody a fortune." Ingrid wondered who might be behind it, and what if anything it could possibly have to do with her.

"I would imagine so, yes," the manager said sourly. "I'm Mr. Kittering, by the way. Herman Kittering, the general manager here. We've met, but only briefly."

Ingrid nodded. Her rising tide of panic was ebbing away already. Kittering seemed a bit too buttoned-down to go acting out his baser passions, despite the fact that he was taking some rather unprofessional pains to buy them this moment of privacy. His discomfort on that score could not have been more evident. He was probably worried that if one of his staff happened to find him like this, in here with *her*, then he might never be able to live the resulting scandal down.

He seemed like a worrier, this Mr. Kittering.

"Why are you doing this?" Ingrid asked. "And what is it you think you're doing? Which side of this thing are you on?"

"I'm warning you," Kittering said. "And saving your skin, I expect. That detective showed up right around the time we realized your Mr. Boggs was no longer paying his bills."

"Wait. When was this?" This was beginning to feel like more than a misunderstanding. Perhaps a lot more.

"Nearly a year ago," Kittering said. "Your, er… your 'friend' had been in the habit of attending to his obligations in advance, so it was some time before we realized anything might be amiss. We held the suite for him for an additional six months after his deposit ran out, in deference to our longstanding relationship. As you said, your Mr. Boggs has kept a room here steadily for a number of years."

"But what *happened*?" Ingrid demanded, shocking a flicker of wistfulness off Kittering's face. She could hear that her tone had sharpened. "Do you know?"

Kittering shook his head. "I don't. His checks were always drawn on the account of the Selig Polyscope Company. When we attempted to contact them, they simply settled his account without a word of explanation."

Ingrid frowned as she struggled to absorb the facts. "And the Pinkerton? Where does he fit in?"

"Well, he requested the room right next to this one, which I didn't think much about. Not until one of my maids told me she thought *this* room might have been broken into. It was nothing we could prove, of course," the gray little manager said. "Nothing we could be certain of. The lock did show some evidence of tampering, and my maid believed some of this room's contents may have been moved around, although she couldn't be certain, as it's our policy to give a room only a light housekeeping turn every two weeks when a guest is not expected to be in residence. But it got me thinking," Kittering explained, in detail, as he seemed wont to do, with or without being prompted. A thorough man, was Mr. Kittering. "I also looked into who was paying the bills for the man in the next room. Once I knew he was an investigator I started to wonder who he might be waiting for. Until today, that is, when both of us took note of *you*." He fixed Ingrid with a cold, managerial sort of scrutiny. "So now there's no more wondering, is there?"

Ingrid swallowed, and the sound of her dry throat clicking was plainly audible in the quiet.

"I'd hoped you might get away before he had a chance to follow you," Kittering said. "But that didn't happen, so I came up here to see if he might come back to his room. To see if he'd bring you back with him."

"What would you have done if he had?"

Kittering shrugged. "I really don't know. Called for the police, maybe, if you looked like you were being coerced. Not that it would've done much good."

Ingrid supposed he was probably right. The local police weren't going to interfere too much with the affairs of an organization like the infamous Pinkertons. Their reach and their influence extended much too far.

She appreciated Kittering's concern, as much as it surprised her. "We must've done something to make a good impression on you," she said, though she had no idea what it might have been.

"Oh, no," Kittering responded, looking almost startled by the assertion. On the verge of an uncharacteristic laugh over it, even. "God, no!" he repeated. "You people were horrid, to be quite frank. A continual torment to my staff *and* the hotel's other guests, what with your constant parties and your in-room rehearsals and your, your... your *midnight assignations.*"

"Then why are you helping me?"

Something about Kittering's somber demeanor turned... somberer. Especially serious. "What do you know about the Pinkertons?" he asked.

Ingrid shrugged. "Not much, really, I suppose." She knew they were a private detective agency, but her understanding was they often functioned more like hired thugs. A legitimized mob.

"'The Eye That Never Sleeps,' they call themselves," Kittering told her. "They're employed by the Federal government as well as by private industry. They're used as spies and strikebreakers and labor Union infiltrators, amongst other things."

Ingrid nodded. That accorded with what she'd read in the papers. She couldn't for the life of her imagine what the 'Pinks' might want with her. "Seems to me like you might not want to meddle into the affairs of a group like that yourself," she said, casting a glance toward Mr. Kittering. "So why are you?"

"My brother was a labor organizer. *Was,*" he repeated.

"Oh," Ingrid said.

"All Peter ever wanted to do was build a better, fairer world," Herman Kittering said. "And they killed him for it. The Pinkertons and the people they work for. They murdered my only brother in the name of nothing more than money. But I can't very well go throwing bombs over it, now can I?" the middle-aged manager said, his face reddening with the stress of an old and irresolvable frustration. "I had a family of my own and a bad back even then, back when the... the 'event' occurred. But if there's anything I can do today to foil, hinder, or otherwise vex that band of miserable *cocksuckers,*" (Ingrid thought the very proper Mr. Kittering looked on the verge of a hemorrhage from the unaccustomed strain of swearing, as he paused to draw in a deep breath) "—then it's *more* than a duty to do so," he finished emphatically. "It is, in fact, I would say, a very deep and abiding personal *pleasure.* A little something just for me."

Ingrid smiled at this strange, brave little man, then bent to give him a spontaneous kiss on the cheek. The aging factotum blushed all the way to the crown of his shiny head.

"Good man, Mr. Kittering," she murmured, as he nodded his uncomfortable thanks.

"Yes, well then," he said, clearing his throat for emphasis. "You should be off, before our friend returns. I'll take you downstairs in the service elevator. There's a tunnel from the basement that exits half a block away, up Spring Street. We use it for deliveries. The public doesn't generally know it has any connection to the Angelus at all. You should be able to make a proper getaway from there."

As Ingrid was nodding along and about to express her gratitude, she noticed the briefest wink of light near the corner of the framed landscape that hung over the room's big brass bed.

Just a flash, as if—perhaps—an eye had moved away from a peephole.

The Eye That Never Sleeps.

"Run," Ingrid suggested, entirely too casually.

"What?" Kittering looked confused.

"*Run!*" Ingrid repeated, with much more force, as she grabbed the older man's hand and dragged him out the door, back into the hallway.

The door to the next room over banged open, gouging the plaster wall behind it with its knob, and Kittering yelped as not one but *two* new Pinkerton detectives burst into the corridor after them. Ingrid had no doubt as to their associations. They were both wearing those same plain suits.

And who knew how many more of them there might be?

Ingrid stepped out of her heels—both because they made fleeing difficult and because there was a dim chance that one of the Pinks might possibly trip over them—and together she and Mr. Kittering sprinted for the service door at the end of the hall.

Chapter Four

O NE of the detectives did stumble over Ingrid's abandoned shoes, for a wonder. She heard him curse as he crashed into a narrow table topped with a vase full of fresh flowers set against the corridor's wall. Glass shattered and table legs snapped behind her.

The other Pinkerton barely missed a stride. Ingrid heard his footfalls hammering the carpet all too closely behind them. Kittering had his keys out and he used them deftly, unlocking the service door and throwing it open as only a man who'd performed the same action day in and day out for many years could. Ingrid knew she would've dropped those damn keys in the heat of the moment, herself.

She slammed the door behind them, catching Pinkerton fingers and eliciting a yowl from their owner, as Kittering threw open a service elevator's accordion gate at the rear of the small supply room. He thumbed a button that started the platform down toward their current level.

The pursuer with the crushed fingers kicked open the door behind them and Ingrid danced back from it with a shout. Kittering wheeled around as the elevator platform was still noisily descending, and stood his ground.

"Now see here!" he said, with surprising authority. Despite his discomfiture around Ingrid, he was obviously a man accustomed to being not only listened to but immediately obeyed. "I won't have this sort of thing in my hotel!"

"Fine by me," the Pinkerton said, before he stepped forward and nonchalantly shoved Mr. Kittering into the elevator shaft.

The manager fell away into darkness with a shout that abruptly cut short, much to Ingrid's horror. She was shocked speechless. An instant later the elevator platform Kittering had summoned rattled past them, headed down.

The so-called 'detective' was unprepared for the right cross from Ingrid that greeted him when he turned around, intending to deal with her.

The blow drove him backwards onto the descending platform, where he stumbled over his own feet and fell hard against the back of the shaft, banging his head against the cinderblocks that looked to be rising upward in relation to the platform's downward motion. Ingrid kicked him in the face with the ball of her stocking foot, just for good measure, as she hopped onto the moving lift after him. She felt the bridge of his nose crunch and he began to gurgle blood as it gushed between the fingers he clapped over the injury. She felt grimly satisfied by that, after what he'd done to Mr. Kittering.

Ingrid looked up to see the second Pinkerton staring down the shaft after them. His wide-eyed face disappeared when he ducked back from the opening, presumably racing off to find another downward route by which he might intercept her.

Best not to let that happen.

Ingrid stopped the service elevator a few levels above the lowest floor of the sub-basement, alerted by the shouts and warnings that echoed up the shaft from employees down below. They'd realized that Kittering, their manager, had fallen, and probably believed it was some sort of accident. Ingrid didn't know if he was dead or terribly injured. There did seem to be some sort of a rescue underway down there, so perhaps there was hope for Mr. K.

Ingrid racked open the elevator's gate and shoved her battered Pinkerton out into the hallway before her, where he fell to his hands and knees. She used the control box to raise the platform back up by a couple of feet, the way she'd seen Kittering do it. Then she yanked the stunned detective backward by his coat collar as he was trying to rise and threw him to the floor once again, flipping him over one locked and extended leg. He landed hard enough to bruise his spine.

Ingrid shoved his head into the shaft and had the platform lowered back down to within a hairsbreadth of decapitating him before he realized what was happening.

He started screaming as soon as he did. The lift platform muffled him a bit.

"You'll want to shut up and answer my questions," Ingrid said. "All I have to do is press a button to quiet you down once and for all."

The Pinkerton did as she suggested and managed to quit yelling, though he was still visibly panicking, beating his fists and heels against the floor and audibly on the verge of hyperventilation. Ingrid could hear him snuffling unpleasantly against the underside of the lift.

"Who are you working for?" she asked.

"Name's Vreke," the trapped detective gasped.

"Freak?" Ingrid repeated. It wasn't easy to hear him from underneath the elevator's reinforced floor.

"Yeah, yeah!" the trapped man yelled. "James Vreke, with a *v* and a *e* at the end! People call him Jimmy the Freak, though, like it's got a *f*!'"

"Are you kidding me?"

"You think I'm playin' games when you're gonna crush my fuckin' *head*?"

Ingrid had to agree that it did seem unlikely. "What's this Freak want with me?"

"I don't know! We don't ask! It don't matter to us, a job's a job!"

"That's not much of an answer."

"It's the only one I got," the almost-headless henchman whined. He'd given up pounding the floor, but his breathing was still harsh and loud. Ingrid could see tension and terror in every rigid line of his body.

She didn't think he was lying.

"Who is he, then, your Jimmy the Freak?" she asked. "I assume you've looked into him, if he's paid you enough to wait around this hotel for almost a year."

"He's... some rich guy," the Pinkerton snuffled. "Makes a fortune importing raw ingredients for patent medicines. Opium from central Asia and Mexican hemp, all that sorta thing."

Ingrid frowned. She supposed she might know someone who fit that profile, though she knew him by a different sort of name. A Latin one. 'Deus Es Canis Inversus.'

"Where can I find him?" Ingrid asked. "Do you know?"

"His company's gotta office up near Chinatown and a warehouse down by the harbor in Pedro. Vreke Pharmaceuticals. But he spends his time at some weird gentlemen's club offa Wilshire and Seventh. Place with some weird name. Latin-like. I can't remember right now, I ain't a Catholic so I don't know a whole lotta Latin, okay?"

"The Templi Aurea Catena?" Ingrid suggested quietly, fearing the answer even though she pretty much knew what it would be.

"Yes!" the hired goon cried. "Yeah, yes, that's it! So you know it, then? You can find it on your own?"

"I suppose I can," Ingrid said.

"Then you got no need to press that button on me, right?"

"I suppose I don't."

Ingrid scowled and folded her arms as she stood there and considered her options. Then she turned around and walked away. Left him there. She wasn't going to kill the Pinkerton in cold blood (even though he'd done as much to Mr. Kittering, at least in terms of intent), but she wasn't about to let him loose while she was still within his reach. He was probably armed and certainly dangerous, so freeing him wasn't an option.

If someone summoned the service elevator down before they called it up, he'd be fucked, in no uncertain terms. But there was only so much responsibility Ingrid was prepared to feel on a casual murderer's behalf. She hoped he enjoyed a gamble, as his odds of survival were no better than he'd get on the toss of a single coin.

She hurried down the nearest stairwell, keeping a wary eye out for that other Pinkerton detective.

A T the bottom of the stairs, down in the hotel's deepest sub-basement, a crowd of employees continued to gather. Ingrid stretched to see over their heads when she emerged from the stairwell, back behind the general mass of them.

A burly man in cook's whites and a pair of painters in overalls had joined forces to hoist a badly-damaged manager out of the elevator shaft. Both of poor Kittering's legs were crumpled in a way that hurt just to look at, but he was alive and conscious, despite the jagged length of fractured femur sticking out through a tear in his left pant leg. He was even holding onto the belt someone had cinched around his upper thigh as a tourniquet, keeping pressure on it himself.

He spotted Ingrid near the back of the employee throng.

"Bring that elevator on down here," the big cook supporting Kittering said, over his shoulder. "We gotta get him up to the doctor fast."

A coverall-clad custodian standing nearby helpfully prodded the switch that would bring the platform down.

Ingrid started to shout a reflexive word of warning, but it was too late. She heard the lift contraption's engine strain for a moment, over the sound of a muffled shout, and then there was a distant, wet crunch, as of a green branch breaking. A moment later a spherical object tumbled down the elevator shaft and landed in the shallow well at its bottom with a hollow splat.

A chambermaid with a far better view of the scene than Ingrid's shrieked at full volume. That helpful janitor turned aside to vomit explosively, splashing the baseboards with his breakfast.

Ingrid might not have been able to see down into the deepest part of the shaft, but she did see a dark cascade of blood pour from the top of the service lift's double-size doorframe. Kittering craned his neck back to see what his employees were gasping and pointing at.

When the agonized manager looked back to meet her eyes his face was pale and his grin was strained, but it was enormous and triumphant, too.

He shooed her away with the hand not holding his tourniquet, off down the corridor and deeper into the bowels of the Angelus.

T HE hotel's network of subterranean chambers was vast and confusing. Ingrid knew it covered more acreage below ground than the building itself did above. There was a bowling alley down here somewhere, as well as the hairdresser's she'd visited before, not to mention a tailor, a florist, a tobacconist, and any number of other service providers who might be of use to guests of the Angelus. A shoe store might've been welcome, as Ingrid was still in her stocking feet, but she was below the basement's commercial levels already, and this was hardly a time to shop.

She scurried past the occasional delivery man pushing a dolly as she searched for the long service corridor Kittering had spoken of. The one that would let her out somewhere down the block, well away from the hotel and out of sight of anyone who might be watching its exits.

It took her a few minutes to find what she was looking for, behind a door marked AUTHORIZED STAFF ONLY, but to Ingrid it felt much longer. At least there were no employees hanging about who might give her the hairy eyeball. By the time she located the almost-secret tunnel, everyone who had business in this part of the labyrinth had drained away to the far corner where not one but *two* people, including one of their managers, had apparently fallen down an elevator shaft.

Ingrid knew that was more show than any crowd could resist. So it looked like she might be able to pull a vanishing act after all.

T RACKING down this Vreke, Jimmy the Freak, was her next order of business. She hurried up the elongated, ill-lit, and low-ceilinged service corridor, already cogitating.

She was certain by now that she knew the man, the Freak, from the halls of the Temple of the Golden Chain. The Templi Aurea Catena, where he was known formally as Frater Deus Es Canis Inversus, the Outer Head of the Order itself.

Well, she supposed she should've known the Aurea Catena would have something to say about her theft of their secret map sooner or later. She'd taken pains to avoid letting anyone within the organization know her real name (even before she 'borrowed' the map to the Hole in the Sky), but apparently her precautions had not been sufficient.

According to Mr. Kittering, her Uncle Frank had left off paying his bills here at the hotel almost a year ago, and that wasn't like him at all. Not that he couldn't be as flighty as any show person Ingrid had ever known, if and when a new inspiration seized him. But he had never neglected a promise to her, to Ingrid, *his* Silent Tower, not once in her entire memory.

If he'd run afoul of the OAC on account of her, then she was acutely worried for him.

But Kittering had also told her that Selig Polyscope had picked up the remainder of his tab, so perhaps old Colonel Bill, the producer Uncle Frank worked for, was the first man to seek.

If anyone could tell her what had happened to Francis Boggs, William Selig would be that man.

She could also run for the safety of Mictlantecuhtli's Silent Tower, if she had to, but she wanted to get a better grip on this situation before doing so. If she was being watched by some unseen cadre of hired Pinkertons, then she might well end up leading Jimmy Vreke and all of his cronies from the Ordo Aurea Catena straight to the Tower's front door. And who knew what manner of disaster might result from that? There were some spiritually advanced individuals involved in the OAC, despite their preponderance of nasty nihilistic habits. (Learning from their example that Gnostic experience doesn't necessarily result in saintly behavior had been one of the fundamental surprises of Ingrid's own mystical career.) Imagining the sort of nightmare deals they might try to strike with the King of the Dead made her shudder. Worse still was the thought that one of them might be able to cross between the King's Chambers the same way she did, and then to time-hop, or commune with the dead, or what have you. Ingrid didn't want anyone moving in on her territory. She was jealous enough of Mickey and the Tower he'd made for her that she didn't care at all for the thought of competition.

S HE made it to the end of the secret service corridor, breathing hard from the effort of hurrying up its pronounced grade, and pushed the door she found there right open. A blinding wedge of sunlight angled into the dim concrete corridor, making her squint. She heard familiar traffic sounds—the soft clip-clop of hooves against a hard dirt street overlaid by an irritated blatting of motor carriage horns—but for a long moment she could see nothing at all through the day's bright white glare.

The pain began to subside and she stepped tentatively out onto the streetcorner where the tunnel came up, shielding her throbbing eyes from the sun.

The tunnel's secret door slammed shut behind her.

Before she could whirl around a large hand clamped down hard over her nose and mouth. Cupped within it was a cloth soaked in vaporous chemicals. A different sort of white light overwhelmed Ingrid's vision when she gasped involuntarily and her head spun right off its normal axis. The strength drained out of her limbs and the only thing she could do was sag back into the arms of her assailant.

She was marginally aware of something happening to her as one of the detectives she hadn't decapitated heaved her slack form into the back seat of an auto-mobile that squealed to a well-timed stop at the curb, then threw a blanket over her to hide her from general sight. Her kidnapper jumped into the car's front seat and barked at the driver to move, and despite her best efforts to remain conscious and possibly have a chance at saving herself, the chloroform and the rhythmic rocking of the motorcar conspired to drag Ingrid under, down into a dreamless sleep.

Chapter Five

BY the time she came to it was dark out beyond the bedroom's windows, and she had what felt like a monstrous hangover pulsating deep inside her skull. It took her a moment to recall how she'd acquired it, but then memories of her abortive attempt at escape from the Angelus began to fill themselves in.

She'd never been chloroformed before. She didn't think she'd care to repeat the experience. She felt like someone had put a chisel between her eyes and tried to crack her head like a block of marble. It was worse by far than anything either absinthe or opium had ever done to her in the past.

When she sat up on the bed, her stomach took an unpleasant lurch. She leaned over, staring down at the floor between her feet (which were still partially wrapped in ruined silk stockings). A chill seized her even as she broke out in a prickly, all-over sweat, and she thought for certain she was about to be sick. But the feeling passed with a few deep breaths, and then she was able to look up and evaluate her surroundings.

At first she couldn't tell where the Pinks had brought her, exactly, but the room they'd placed her in was lush and meticulously appointed. The sheets beneath her were silk, and the mattress was stuffed with down. The carpet on the floor was Persian. There were fresh flowers in crystal vases adorning every flat surface. It was as fine a room as one could wish to occupy. The only thing spoiling it for Ingrid was the nagging suspicion that she wouldn't be allowed to leave.

Then she noticed the tiny insignia embroidered onto the corners of the pillowcases. Three golden ovals, linked together in a chain, which she recognized as the sigil of the Ordo Aurea Catena.

That got her motivated. Ingrid leapt up and tested the door and all of the windows, but they were locked tight, exactly as she'd known they would be.

She was a prisoner in a fancy cell, a captive of the OAC. Her best guess was that they were holding her somewhere within their building on

Wilshire Boulevard. The gray granite edifice served them as a temple, a private club, and apparently on occasion as a jail. But this was no time to let herself panic over it.

A candlestick-style telephone apparatus stood on an end table, but when Ingrid unhooked its receiver and held it to her ear it seemed not to be in operation. Little surprise there. Almost as an afterthought she tugged open the table's small drawer, and inside found a recently-printed telephone directory for Los Angeles and its surrounding environs.

She snatched it up and flipped to the S's, hoping Selig Polyscope would have a listing. And it did, right there under William Selig's name. Ingrid found the new studio's telephone exchange number and its street address, out in some place called Edendale, a suburb she'd never heard of before. Under 'type of business' it read, simply: 'Motion Pictures.'

Ingrid grinned, despite the sour ache in her head. She tore the page out of the directory, folded it, and tucked it away up inside her sleeve.

The sound of a key in a lock prompted her to chuck the book back into the drawer and close it. She flopped back down on the mattress and lay still, trying to breathe steadily and quietly, like she was sleeping, in spite of her jackhammer heart rate.

The door eased open on softly creaking hinges, and someone stepped into the room.

INGRID heard him breathing as he padded over and stood near the bed. She was faced away from him, but she could see his bulky masculine shadow on the wall. He stood over her for what seemed like too long a moment. Finally he put a hand on her shoulder and rolled her over.

Ingrid sat up like a jack-in-the-box and punched him square in the throat. Hard enough that she felt some rubbery bit within the structure of the man's neck pop against her knuckles.

Ingrid knew how to fight when she had to, and more importantly, she knew how to *win*. Even against long odds.

The punched thug's eyes reddened and bulged as his hands flew to his crushed esophagus. His face twisted into a caricature of shock as he lurched aside and fell over, where he flopped face-down on the floorboards and fought to drag air into his lungs through what looked to be a hemorrhaging larynx.

It was an ugly thing to see. Ingrid didn't know whether or not she'd killed him, this big bastard she recognized as the second Pinkerton who'd been lying in wait for her at the Hotel Angelus. When he began to convulse she heard a crunch and smelled chloroform again, which made her want to gag. Her victim flipped over onto his back, and Ingrid saw a dark wet patch spreading out around the breast pocket of his suit, where his glass vial of knockout drops must have broken.

When she looked up, a youngish man who'd once been introduced to her as Brother Deus Es Canis Inversus was leaning in the open doorway.

He grinned at her, utterly unmindful of the Pinkerton who continued gasping like a landed trout and drooling blood onto his elegant carpet. The private investigator was nothing more than an expensive pawn in this game, one sacrificed by an employer with brains enough to avoid being the nearest person to Ingrid after she woke up.

"You haven't been easy to find, and I've had men looking on both sides of the Atlantic, Soror 'Bonum Irrumabo,'" the Outer Head of the OAC said to her by way of greeting, and Ingrid cringed. She hadn't been addressed by the stupid Latin motto she'd selected as a ritual name upon her initiation to the Order in quite a while. (Mickey's man Winston Watt had been the last person to do so, in fact, before he died.) Few members of the Order knew much of the dead language beyond the phrases they appropriated from old books for use as sobriquets, but Deus Es Canis Inversus spoke like he enjoyed the benefits of a classical education. The wry way he was eyeing her made it plain that he knew Ingrid's chosen name, loosely translated, meant Sister 'Good Fuck.'

All she could say about it now was she'd found it funny enough when she picked it.

"Or maybe you'd rather I call you Miss Redstone?" her brother initiate offered.

"Only if I get to call you Jimmy the Freak," Ingrid quipped, even though her heart sank upon hearing him say her real name, which settled the question of whether or not he knew it. "Or maybe JTF for short?"

Deus Es Canis Inversus nodded. He was perhaps thirty and approximately Ingrid's height, which put him at about six feet, although she guessed he outweighed her by a good twenty-five pounds. He had devilish blue eyes and a shock of brown hair. He dressed well too, with the sort of casual sophistication that money makes easy. His suit looked like it had been cut for him yesterday.

It wasn't the first time Ingrid had ever noticed him, though it unsettled her to learn he'd also been aware of her.

"My men told me you were a handful," he said, glancing over at the hypoxic detective still writhing tortuously on the floor. "I'm thinking that was a bit of an understatement. Did that other one tell you my name before you killed him? Is that how you know it?"

"I didn't kill him, I just… didn't make sure he'd live," Ingrid said, a touch defensively. "How did you figure out *my* name?"

"Why, I saw you at the picture show, my dear!" her captor said brightly. "Up there on the silver screen, as big as life and twice as lovely."

"You're gonna make me blush, Mr. Freak."

Deus Es Canis Inversus—Jimmy—laughed out loud at that. "It'd take a lot more than flattery to bring out *your* shy side, I'd think."

"I didn't use my real name in that movie," Ingrid said. "So you've only given me half an answer."

"No, they billed you as '*Silent Tower*,' didn't they? Kind of a weird stage name. I've been meaning to ask about it."

Ingrid planted her hands on her hips. She'd been unusually tall and exceedingly quiet as an adolescent, and Silent Tower had been a nickname applied by her Uncle Frank, Francis Boggs, then a dashing young performer only fifteen years her senior. The gentle mockery was meant to cajole her out of her shell, to get her to snap back at him with the quick wit he knew she possessed, and he'd always cackled with unfeigned delight every time she did it.

Not that she meant to share any of this with Jimmy the Freak.

"Tell me how you learned my name," Ingrid said. If Jimmy's method had included bringing any sort of harm to Francis Boggs, he was going to regret it. She had powerful friends in the lowest of places, these days.

"I contacted the production company," Jimmy said, shrugging like this was the most obvious solution in the world. Which, Ingrid reflected, it sort of was. "I asked your director how I could find you. Frank Boggs? He did nothing but sing your praises."

"I don't believe you," Ingrid shot back. "He'd never betray me like that."

"Well, I don't know that he felt like it was a *betrayal*, exactly," Jimmy said, holding up both hands and taking a step back. "I do look like an eligible young millionaire to some people, you know. I'm pretty sure he thought he was doing you a favor."

Ingrid nodded, slowly, unwilling to abandon her mistrust. The Freak didn't look to her like he was lying, but that might only have meant he was a good liar. "What is it you want from me?" she asked.

Jimmy grinned again. He seemed genuinely tickled by her. "I think you know the answer to that."

Maybe she did, but she was still going to make him say it. She saw little benefit in volunteering information, as a general rule.

"You have something that belongs to me, Ingrid Redstone," Jimmy the Freak accused. "To the Order of the Golden Chain, I mean. You took it and you disappeared more than a year ago."

"I didn't take anything," Ingrid said. She'd only copied the old map and its accompanying verses, leaving the original document behind. Even her reproduction had long since been burnt. "I know you had your men search my room, and probably me as well, while I was passed out? So you tell me, were they able to find anything?"

She straightened her rumpled shirtwaist. If she'd been frisked her searcher hadn't done a good enough job to find the handful of wild mushrooms tucked away in a small secret pocket sewn into the lining of her skirt. She could feel the wax-paper bundle nestled against her hip.

The garnet Mickey had given her was presumably still in there with them, but she wasn't about to draw attention to it by checking now.

"Let's call it 'intellectual property,'" Vreke said. "Knowledge."

"Knowledge belongs to everyone, Jimmy," Ingrid opined.

"Bullshit," he said in response. "Knowledge belongs to those who keep it, protect it, and transmit it across time. And some of yours, my dear, is really *ours*."

"Have you got some plan for pulling it out of my head?"

"I could pull everything out of your head. Maybe with a hacksaw and an ice cream scoop. That would do the job, for all intents and purposes."

He said it lightly, even jokingly, and yet Ingrid knew a real threat when she heard one. Cold adrenaline dispelled the last of her chloroform hangover, and her mind suddenly felt as clear as a diamond point. They were playing for keeps now, so she had to be on her very best game.

"Of course, if you were to simply tell me how to find the Hole in the Sky, I'm sure we could work something out," the Freak said, idly toying with his watch fob.

"You don't know how it's done, do you?" Ingrid didn't bother to suppress her amusement. If the haughty old-world ceremonialists of the Inner Order had any regard at all for the local style of witchwork (*brujería*, as it was known in Spanish, a tradition rooted in old shamanism), they would've known the invocation of the necessary nature spirits was accomplished by picking samples of their namesake plants right out of the earth and chowing down. There was no more ritual involved. It figured the over-educated elitists of the OAC had never made such a basic leap.

"You're thinking I don't know about the mushrooms right now, aren't you?" Jimmy asked, startling her, and she allowed herself the raise of a single eyebrow in response.

"Pharmaceuticals!" Vreke declared, like that explained everything. "Rare herbs and proscribed roots, powdered barks and sticky resins—I grew up in warehouses full of them. I know all about the secret graces and hidden virtues of the natural world, you see. Unlike my self-deluded colleagues, with their ranks and their grades and their elaborate hedges against ever having to put their illusions of arcane power to the test, I've been well aware for quite some while now that Mescalito and Teonanactl—the spirit names specified by the author of our map, as I believe *you* very well know—are old names for the peyote cactus and the *Psilocybe mexicana* fungus, respectively."

"Then why haven't you taken a nature hike, Mr. Freak?" Ingrid's voice stayed calm, but inside she felt sick and hollowed out. He knew so much more than she was comfortable with. "X marks the spot, you know."

"Please, call me Jim," Jimmy said. "Mr. Freak was my father."

Ingrid nodded.

"And who's to say I haven't done that?" 'Jim' said, referring in a lower tone of voice to a hypothetical trek out to the Tree. "Gone out there, I mean, or tried. Since your thievery brought that old map to my attention, I've staggered all over those hills with my mind so open that my brain near fell out, and all of it for nothing. The Tree That Grows Below the Hole in the Sky, which offered itself up so readily to you, won't reveal itself to me. No matter how many cactus buttons or mushroom caps I've stuffed down my craw in the course of any given expedition."

The *Tree*. That was it, then. The one and only thing keeping this Freak from finding the King's Chambers was the fact that he was still looking for an ancient oak tree.

"Some over-ambitious idiot seems to be building a skyscraper out there, of all ridiculous things, out in the general vicinity of where the Tree ought to be," Jimmy said, confirming Ingrid's theory. He had no idea how close he was to the truth. "And yet the Hole in the Sky remains veiled to me. All I can think is that the author of our map left off some key piece of information, to obfuscate the truth and divert us from our goals."

Vreke made direct and meaningful eye-contact with Ingrid. He'd been leaning casually against the door jamb all this time, like they were old friends chatting.

"A key *you* seem to have found," he said to her.

Ingrid said nothing—just folded her arms and waited for him to make his point. She knew it frustrated people when she did that, which was precisely what made it fun for her.

Finally Jimmy stepped from the doorway and into the room itself, letting the door shut behind him. "We could be partners, you and me," he said, in a lower, confiding tone of voice.

Ingrid snorted.

"Oh, don't be obtuse!" he barked. "Would you have come if I'd engraved an invitation?"

"No."

"Where would I have sent it, anyway? 'Care of the Angelus, Hold Indefinitely?' Or would I have done better to forward it on to the Land of the Dead?"

"That's crazy," Ingrid said, unconvincingly.

"Is it?" Vreke asked. "Is it really, considering every odd thing we must've experienced, between the two of us? I know you've been on the other side, Miss Redstone. I know because you brought something back."

Jimmy reached into his pants pocket like he was scrounging a coin for a cup of coffee and pulled out Ingrid's fat, faceted garnet.

Mictlantecuhtli's gift. Her red stone.

"Give it back," Ingrid demanded, all too quickly. She winced at the immediacy of her reaction, the way her hands flew to the secret pocket in her skirt, which still contained her mushroom stash but had been surreptitiously relieved of one precious gem.

Jimmy smiled. "I believe you know my terms."

"Yeah, well, to hell with that and to hell with you," Ingrid said. Even though it pained and panicked her to utter the words, she added: "That's just a rock."

"Don't try to make a living playing cards, Miss Redstone."

Ingrid quietly fumed, clenching her jaw. The Pinkerton fading on the floor behind her was likely armed—a pistol in a shoulder-holster would've been her guess. If she dove for it, she could have it in her hand in two seconds. She could have a bullet between Jimmy's eyes in three.

But if she did that, she doubted she'd ever make it out of here. The sound of a shot would be more than enough to draw an unwelcome sort of attention. The Templi Aurea Catena was nothing if not well-guarded.

Jimmy the Freak grinned at her like he knew what she was thinking. He held up her garnet and turned it so it glinted in the room's bright electric light.

"Interesting thing, this," he said, eyeing the stone. "I feel it here in my hand. I see it with my own two eyes. But if I put it on a scale, it doesn't register, like it weighs nothing at all. And when I hold it up to a mirror," —which he did, for the sake of demonstration, moving it close to the glass on the dresser beside him— "it has no reflection at all. Like it isn't even there."

He was right. Ingrid saw Jimmy's empty hand in the mirror, his thumb and forefingers curled into a 'c' shape like something should've been clamped between them. But nothing was. Ingrid had never noticed that weird property in her stone before. The garnet was an artifact of the imagination, though. It could be both here and not here. That was precisely the value of it—the magic quality that reminded her of who she was and where she came from, no matter where she might happen to roam.

"So I feel it even though it has no weight and I see it even though it reflects no light," Jimmy said, looking up from the stone to meet her eyes. "How can that possibly be?"

Ingrid shrugged, feigning boredom. "Must be a miracle. Or a magic trick."

"Magic, yes, but not a trick," Jimmy said. "This is the real McCoy, as they say, and I mean to know how you came by it."

"It was a gift from a friend."

"What sort of friend?"

"A good friend."

Jimmy smirked. "Of that I have no doubt," he agreed. Then, before Ingrid could retort: "Look, this doesn't have to be contentious. I'd rather make an offer than a threat. It's less complicated that way. So there must be something in this world you want, and I do have many resources."

Ingrid paused, frowning as if she might be considering this. Jimmy was quite wrong in his assumptions. There was nothing in this world, nothing at all, that she valued above her relationship with Mictlantecuhtli and the privileged knowledge of his realm that came along with it. There was no deal to be made between her and the Freak, but letting him think she might have an interest in his offer seemed like the easiest way to buy a little time.

"What is it you think I can give you, Mr. Vreke?" she said finally, when it became clear that Jimmy could play her to a draw in the awkward silence game.

"An introduction," he said. "To your 'friend.' That's all I ask."

"And what do I get in exchange for that introduction?"

"This stone, for starters," Jimmy said, bouncing the garnet that wasn't really there on his palm. "Money, if you want it. That's nothing to me. And you know you'll have to find some way to trust me if you ever want to leave this room again."

Ingrid shook her head. "Have you ever even *heard* of irony?"

Jimmy assumed the question was rhetorical and didn't respond to it.

"What do you want with that place anyway?" Ingrid said, in frustration. "What would you do if you went up there? What sort of deal would you try to make? You already have two of everything the world has to offer and money enough to buy a third. What more can you really want?"

"Something new," Jimmy said. "An experience."

Ingrid could understand that. It didn't mean she sympathized. "If you're that hellbent on meeting Death you could always go up to the roof of this place and jump off. That's still the express route."

"I don't have a death wish, Miss Redstone," Jimmy said. "Just a little death... curiosity."

"*Le petite mort?*" Ingrid murmured coyly, as she glided closer to him, catching him off guard. She trusted that Jimmy the Freak would pick up on her French euphemism, man of the world that he was.

Jimmy made her garnet disappear back into his pocket and he swallowed hard when her thigh came into glancing contact with his.

"You're not the only one with resources, Jimmy," she whispered to him, now that they were close enough to kiss and she could feel his heart accelerating. "Maybe I can interest you in a... different experience, instead of that introduction? Hmm?"

He seemed far from disinterested, if Ingrid was any judge. She slid a hand around to the small of his back, drew him closer, and kneed him decisively in the gonads.

He sank to his knees with a hollow moan and keeled over onto the carpet, crossing his arms between his legs.

Ingrid bent over the still-wheezing Pinkerton splayed out next to him and whipped a chloroform-sodden pocket square from the breast pocket of the man's plain gray suit. Fragments of broken glass vial came along with it.

She spun back to the Freak and crammed the wet rag down over his contorted, purpling face, before he had a chance to shout for assistance. He struggled against the chemical fumes, same as she had, but even so he was dead to the world in half a minute, insensate and drooling peacefully.

Ingrid slipped a hand into his pants pocket to retrieve his keys as well as her stone. The garnet looked and felt as solid as it ever had. She tucked it away, into her secret skirt pocket.

"*There's* a little death for you," she said to Jimmy, though he was no longer listening. "Or something like it. No need to thank me."

Ingrid stepped over him and exited the room, silently, without drawing any notice, using Jimmy's keys to open the door and then closing it gently behind herself. The lock engaged with a firm click and Ingrid walked away, leaving an unconscious Jimmy the Freak behind as the newest inmate of his own plush prison.

Chapter Six

IN the end she walked right out the front door of the downtown Temple of the Aurea Catena without incident. She even greeted a few of her old acquaintances by their Latin mottos as she passed them in the corridors and clucked with them over how much time had passed since they'd last seen one another. Two years, was it? Three? Where *did* the time go, and we simply *must* meet for cocktails, mustn't we?

Ingrid agreed that yes, of course they simply must, and not one amongst the knot of neophytes she ran into showed any interest in restraining her, or even seemed aware that she'd been accused of raiding the Order's secret archive.

About halfway through her interview with Jimmy the Freak—right when Jim closed the room's door to lock himself in with her—Ingrid had begun to suspect that Mr. Deus Es Canis Inversus might not be sharing the fruits of his investigations with his fellow initiates. He'd been searching for her on his very own dime. Finding the Hole in the Sky was a personal project. Tracking her down and holding her captive had never been an Order-wide directive, so nobody was bent out of shape over seeing her walking the halls.

Still, it wouldn't do to linger. Not when Brother Deus Es Canis Inversus was apt to wake up at any moment, with tandem agonies throbbing in his chloroformed head and traumatized groin. Ingrid couldn't imagine she'd exhausted his supply of privately-hired goons, either.

So she hurried downstairs and out onto Wilshire Boulevard, as quick as she could do it without appearing to flee the scene.

SOME blocks away from the OAC's multi-story mausoleum of a social club was a bar called the Golden Shoe that Ingrid knew to be a popular celebration spot with racehorse owners, trainers, and jockeys. The movie she'd made with her Uncle Frank had been set in the world of racing, and they'd immersed themselves in it in the name of research.

Tonight a knot of celebrants had gathered out in front of the bar to crowd around an impressive chestnut stallion whose apparent owner had brought him down from a motor-pulled trailer to preen in the street before his delighted and tipsy admirers. He was the only un-hitched horse anywhere in sight.

Ingrid walked right up to him.

The horse's owner was tallish, on the verge of elderly, with thin gray hair that receded from a round forehead. His moustache was waxed, his collar starched, and his four-in-hand tie was made of rich red silk. Ingrid glanced down at his mirror-polished wing-tips.

"Bet I know where you got those shoes," she said without preamble. When the men grouped around the stallion merely gaped at her in silence she continued: "I'm serious, boys. I'm proposing a wager."

"For what stakes?" a shrewd-eyed jockey still clad in racing silks piped up.

"For the horse, of course," Ingrid said, eliciting a round of uproarious laughter.

"Do you know what horse this *is*, little lady?" the incredulous owner asked (though in point of fact Ingrid was taller than him by a good four inches—not little by any measure). "This is Fair Play! Sired by Hastings, grand-sired by Spendthrift. His lineage is more rarefied than royalty."

"Winner of the Brooklyn Derby in 1908, right?" Ingrid said, and felt the assemblage's appraisal of her rise to a new level. She'd kept up her interest in the sport since stealing shots for *Race Tout* at the Santa Anita racetrack in Arcadia with Frank Boggs and her co-stars (before security got wise and threw them out). "He's earned more than eighty thousand dollars in his career, if I'm not mistaken," she said, nodding toward the horse as he whinnied and shook out his lustrous black mane.

"That is right, my dear, that is very right, and I am very impressed," the overdressed owner said, beaming at her and starting to enjoy this chance to so publicly interact with a lovely woman a third his age. "I'm August Belmont, by the way."

"Ingrid Redstone," Ingrid said. Even though she'd only hopped across a year this time, she still didn't dare to give a false name, lest she forget herself again. She didn't know if it would be a problem now, since she had her garnet, but she didn't want to chance it.

"So, Miss Ingrid," Belmont said, "since you plainly know the value of the animal you wish to win, may I ask: just what is it *you* intend to put up?"

"If I'm wrong," Ingrid said, unleashing her best bright and promising grin on him, "I'll let you name your own prize, August."

That was just too good to be true, the sort of thing that never happened outside of perhaps a movie, and the crowd murmured approvingly. This was probably better than some plays they'd paid to see.

"All right, all right, I'll bite," the horse man said, playing to his crowd and holding up his luxuriantly-shod foot for them to see before once again addressing Ingrid: "Where do you think I got these shoes?"

"You got 'em on your feet."

In the moment of silence that followed her inane revelation, Ingrid gently took Fair Play's reins from his former owner's hand. As the crowd burst out laughing and hooting and the old man stood there, stunned and gaping, Ingrid tapped one of the younger fellows on the shoulder and got him to give her a boost. She swung her leg over the horse in one swift and elegant motion. She didn't have any more time to waste. She suspected Jimmy the Freak's hired goons were like rats or roaches—meaning that where she saw one, there were apt to be another half dozen hanging around. She didn't see them yet, but that didn't mean they couldn't be after her already.

"Jesus, Auggie, you ain't gonna let her ride off with him, are you?" someone from the crowd said, and a trainer shouted: "Somebody get her the hell offa there! Come on, now, a joke's a joke!"

"Leave her be!" Belmont barked. To his trainer he said, "don't be an ass," and then, a little louder, to everyone: "A bet's a bet, isn't it? And I am a man of my word."

"That's very gracious, Mr. Belmont," Ingrid said. She offered her hand, and the old breeder kissed it. "I'll send him back to you if I can."

Belmont nodded, looking bemused, bereft, and bewitched all at the same time, and then Ingrid was off, spurring her new ride away up Flower Street.

Chapter Seven

THE champion thoroughbred she'd commandeered was ready to run like a scalded dog at even the slightest urging. Without the benefit of a proper saddle, Ingrid really had to hold on. She guided the horse back up the Loma de Mariposas, past the mansions that looked awkward and old in the glow from their new electric lights, out of the city proper and then up the old Carretera del Rey, with dust flying from her mount's hooves.

She had her red stone and her head was still attached, so she was making a mad dash for the Silent Tower while she could. It would always be home base in her recurring games of time-tag. She chewed one of her mushrooms while Fair Play galloped—just enough to help her find her way. It wasn't lost on her that Jim must have left the dried caps in her pocket on purpose, perhaps with the intention of tailing her when she rabbited. Maybe letting her escape had been a part of his plan all along. He was crafty enough for that. Though her kick to his crotch had seemed to come as a genuine surprise...

After ten minutes of hard riding with no apparent sign of pursuit, either physical or astral, she allowed herself to hope that she might have gotten enough of a head start to fox anyone who might be chasing her.

But no. She heard the sound of their engines first, as there were several bends in the road that kept the attached vehicles out of sight for a while.

She looked back over her shoulder when she reached the straight stretch of road that led up toward the Cahuenga Pass and there they were, four beams of light stabbing after her from a distance of perhaps two miles back. Two vehicles. When the road curved again the moonlight fell on them and she got a glimpse of the cars themselves: a pair of low-profiled roadsters with large spoked wheels. Built for speed, and coming fast.

They didn't look like casual motorists out for an evening drive.

Ingrid yanked the reins and steered Fair Play off the dirt road, into the chaparral. Visibility was decent—the crisp night was silvered with moonlight. And it was time to veer south for the Tower anyway. She hoped her racehorse would prove as surefooted in the brush as he had on the road. It was important that she reach the building well ahead of Jimmy the Freak's Pinkertons. She needed to get inside and disappear before they saw her do it. Jim knew the building was out here; he just couldn't wrap his mind around the fact that it had replaced the age-old Tree. The detectives wouldn't even have to tell him where it was, exactly—only what he needed to look for.

Letting these people see her enter the Silent Tower would be a disaster.

The trouble was, she didn't have any place else to go.

The headlight beams behind her bounced and swung wildly as the roadsters left the road and came after her overland. They'd already spotted her, then.

Fuck.

Ingrid dug her heels into Fair Play's sides and shouted to urge him on. Headlamp beams slashed at the black foliage around them, making it flash green and gold as Ingrid ducked and dodged past trees, trying to make pursuit as inconvenient as possible. The cars' motors bellowed behind her. Small animals' eyes glinted from the darkness ahead as they took one look at the glaring unnatural nightmare coming their way and ran for it.

Fair Play leapt over a downed tree trunk and Ingrid dug her hands into his mane, clutching it to avoid being jarred loose from his back. There was a moment of relative darkness as both cars swerved around the obstacle. Then the headlamps were back, following her like spotlights across a stage.

Her thoroughbred sailed over a shallow gulch Ingrid hadn't seen in the darkness. Spotting obstacles the driver didn't was one thing a motorcar would never be able to do. Even as she glanced back one set of lights nosed out of sight. There was a thud, an engine screamed, and Ingrid was rewarded with the moonlit sight of a brand-new roadster flipping end over end and flinging two screaming henchmen helplessly into the air like ragdolls.

The car landed twenty feet behind Fair Play, upside down, with an almost anticlimactic crunch.

The horse never missed a stride.

Ingrid heard no agonized howls from injured men, which she hated having to consider a good thing. She didn't feel quite as bloodthirsty as these people required her to act.

Still, that was one car down. There was only one to go. Surely she could think of something, some way to handle them before she reached the tower.

But she couldn't. She hadn't even figured out how to lose the first car; she'd just gotten lucky.

All she could do was continue to run.

And now it was too late. As soon as she rounded the ridge up ahead, the last gasp of the foothills before they sank away into the Los Angeles basin, she'd be in sight of Mickey's building.

It was hard to miss it out here. There were no other structures for miles. Just the lone, boxy skyscraper.

And wouldn't Jimmy the Freak laugh his ass off when his Pinkertons revealed his mistake to him? He'd waste no time at all in taking the elevator right up to the King's Chambers.

When Ingrid sighted the Silent Tower, she realized that maybe leading Jimmy's men out here wasn't the worst idea in the world after all.

Not if she could get them to follow her all the way up to the top.

She nudged Fair Play with her heel, begging for a last burst of speed, and pointed him straight at the building. They pounded across the plain toward it, as the roadster behind them closed the gap down to a few dozen yards.

Chapter Eight

IMPOSSIBLE lights came on in the windows of the Silent Tower (impossible because there was no electricity out here, not yet), and the front door opened of its own accord as her horse raced toward it. A fan of buttery warm illumination spilled out like a welcome mat.

Ingrid had never loved Mictlantecuhtli more. He was stretching his reach to its absolute limit, no doubt alerted to her predicament by the dead men from the crashed automobile she'd left in her wake.

She didn't rein Fair Play back at all—instead she rode him right through the open door and straight down the entry hall, still at a full gallop.

She heard the remaining roadster screech to a stop outside, tires squealing on the few yards of paved road that fronted the building. Vreke's men got out and ran after her, shouting warnings and threats to which she paid no attention at all. Fair Play charged across the empty lobby in about a stride and a half, and Ingrid guided him into the open central elevator car, where he reared and danced around, causing her to bump her head on the roof, not quite hard enough to hurt.

She pressed the button for the top floor with her toe and waved to the pair of Pinkertons gaping at her from the lobby as the doors slid closed. The last she saw of them before her car began to grudgingly ascend was the angrier-looking of the pair sprinting for the elevator to her right and hammering on the call button, with his uncertain partner trailing behind him.

Then she was rising. She and her horse. Cables groaned and the lift's engine labored. Fair Play snuffled and neighed, and Ingrid patted his neck.

The Pinks beat her to the top. Their elevator managed to rise a touch more swiftly, for fairly obvious reasons. But Fair Play reared again when the doors opened, and one of his front hooves caught the more aggressive of the two henchmen square in the face. Blood burst in the air like someone had mashed a tomato with a mallet and the detective was driven back against the hallway's wall, from there to slump bonelessly to the floor.

His partner drew a gun and started firing.

Ingrid kicked out and knocked him down as Fair Play, quite spooked by now, exploded out of the elevator car and shot down the corridor, headed for the King's Chambers.

The door marked with the name MIGUEL CARADURA opened before them. Ingrid could see the stunned skeleton of her most recently killed adversary standing framed in the *next* door, gawking. The Door Between Worlds, that one was—impassable for the deceased. Rounds fired by the dead man's still-living partner whined past Ingrid's head and tore divots out of the jamb.

Fair Play knocked the Pinkerton skeleton aside like a set of bowling pins as he charged on through, still bearing Ingrid on his back. She had to duck to avoid receiving an unscheduled facial rearrangement courtesy of the lintel. The horse's muscled sides deflated between her legs as his flesh dusted away and he too was reduced to bleached white bone.

He reared again, inside the sacrificial chamber, and Ingrid hooked her fingers into his empty eye sockets to keep from sliding right off the back of his suddenly denuded spine.

She reined him in and turned him around. The last of Jimmy's thugs was still out there in the first room, watching the events occurring in the second one with stark terror written all over his face. He was young, probably not more than twenty-five.

When Ingrid's eyes landed on him, he raised his gun again.

"*Yahh!*" Ingrid shouted, kicking at empty air. Fair Play's remains understood her anyway, and leapt forward powerfully.

The hammer of the young man's pistol clicked over empty chambers when he squeezed the trigger, and Fair Play's articulated skeleton came apart when it crossed the barrier back into the realworld, of which it was no longer a part. Ingrid's feet hit the floor as her mount disintegrated out from under her. His large horse bones scattered and clattered into the corners of the room, like they'd been cast by some gargantuan necromancer. (If there was meaning in the patterns they made, Ingrid couldn't fathom it.)

She skidded to a stop with her face less than a foot from the young Pinkerton's still-upraised revolver.

She took it gently out of his hand.

The quiet seemed enormous now, after all the tumult and noise of a few moments before.

The last Pink standing broke it when he sucked in a lungful of air and let it back out in a violent, full-throated scream. Ingrid flinched. The kid screamed again, and then again. She had to wonder if he ever intended to stop. Some key part of his psyche seemed to have gone on the fritz. It took her a minute to realize he wasn't even looking at her, but rather over her shoulder.

When she turned she saw the reason for all the shouting: Mictlantecuhtli had come to the door, a fresh skeleton under a heavy black cowl, garlanded with moist and slowly deflating human eyes.

Dressed for a day at the office, that was.

"You should run, before he gets you," Ingrid said to the brainburnt Pinkerton, and the young man was happy to take her advice. He turned and sprinted, yelling and babbling all the while. Ingrid could hear his screeching echo back up the stairwell as he fled.

She didn't think there was enough left of his psyche for him ever to give a coherent report about this place and what he'd seen here to Jimmy the Freak. The ancient site's wards should also muddle his ability to direct others to it, now that he knew what was up here. It might've been safer to kill him, but she didn't have the heart for it. In the heat of a fight was one thing, but she'd had more than her fill of violence tonight.

She turned back to face Mictlantecuhtli.

Fair Play stood behind him again—at least a new, ghostly image of the thoroughbred's skeleton did. The bones on the floor of Ingrid's chamber were his real ones, his actual physical remains, while the animating bit, the part that counted, the horse's 'soul,' remained in Mickey's world, and would forever. He neighed at Ingrid, shook a mane that was no longer there, and trotted out into the gray light that fell through the far door.

Out to stud in the otherworld.

It pained Ingrid to watch him go. More than she would've expected. Her throat felt tight and she knew that if she tried to speak, she would cry. Which she hadn't done in quite some while. But she could've curled up on the floor and wailed like an infant over that damn dead horse. She figured it was all the accumulated stresses of the last few hours seeking a ready channel for release.

But she *could not* break down in front of Mickey. It would never do to show him that depth of vulnerability. If she ever allowed herself to be totally unguarded with him he might be able to violate the screen of constantly-repeated banishing rituals that kept the inner core of her mind private. Once Mickey got that deep into her head, she'd never get him back out again. He'd own her, and she wasn't ready for that.

The hooded figure of Death watched her, and waited, without a word.

"I feel bad about the horse," Ingrid said, when she was able to do so in a steady voice. "He was borrowed. I told his owner I'd send him back if I could."

Mictlantecuhtli nodded, and in a flash he became Miguel Caradura, Mickey, her tall and handsome Aztec lover. His broad chest was bare, his skin the color of bronze. She wanted to run to him and hide in his arms and give herself over to him so that he might obliterate her every other concern… but she didn't dare to do it right now. She was still feeling too raw.

"Bring me his skull," Mickey said.

Ingrid retrieved the object in question from the corner in which it had landed. She brought it to the door and handed it over to el Rey.

Mickey held it up and peered into the ex-equine's brainpan through an eyeless eye socket. He looked thoughtful, like he was figuring something out. "He had a name?"

Ingrid nodded. "Fair Play."

"And an owner?"

"Belmont," Ingrid said. "His name was Auggie Belmont. August."

"Good," Mickey said. "Catch."

He tossed the horse skull back to her. Ingrid almost dropped it. But she didn't.

"Hold it there," the King said. "Think of him."

Ingrid held the dry, bleached horse cranium up at about the level it would've sat had it still been situated at the proper end of a living spinal column. She held it facing herself, and felt like Girl Hamlet addressing an unusual Yorick.

After a moment or two she felt a faint breeze or draft stir her hair. There were no windows in her chamber, so the air had to be moving in from Mickey's side of things, through the doorless portal behind him that opened onto the land of the dead.

Dust began to swirl. Ingrid had to squint to keep it out of her eyes. It rolled and coalesced into bones, which seemed to grow backwards from brainstem to tail, and then into smooth, solid flesh. Mickey's copy of the racehorse named Fair Play stood rendered in shades of ghostly gray for a moment, before the chestnut color of his coat filled in and his mane and tail turned black. His eyes were the last thing to return, the sockets filling in with balls of dust which darkened, melted, and warmed to a living, liquid brown. His eyelashes seemed half an inch long.

He looked as good as new.

"It's not really him, is it?" Ingrid said.

"It is a copy, better than perfect," Mickey said. "It remembers 'August Belmont' and will return to him, in fulfillment of your vow."

"It can do that? It isn't, I don't know, bound to your realm? Like dead people are? It doesn't have to wait till Halloween?"

"It is, as you say, not really him. It is an image from your mind, rendered in worldly dusts and bound together by my will. It will last for fifteen human years, and never disappoint its human masters. Is this acceptable to you, my love?"

"Yes," Ingrid said, unable to see a way in which it wasn't. The rebuilt horse could not be distinguished from the real thing. It was something like the servitors made by the Aurea Catena for a variety of purposes.

False ghosts created by intention. 'Taskers,' the OAC called them, and they could be quite surprisingly physical, though only about as smart as a clever dog. So this solution worked out well. "Yes, Mickey," she repeated, looking over at him. "It's wonderful. I appreciate this."

And she did. She felt practically limp with magnified gratitude, though she wouldn't have felt safe sharing that with him.

The King nodded, looking pleased with himself, as he always did when he knew he'd managed to make her happy. Sometimes his attempts at interpreting her needs and wishes went wildly wrong; but at other times, like this one, he hit the mark precisely.

Ingrid realized she was still holding the horse's reins in one hand and that last Pinkerton's gun in the other. She tossed the empty pistol into a wastepaper can and fitted the bridle onto the artificial thoroughbred. She petted his velvety nose and patted the side of his muscular neck. He felt just like the original had.

"So do I just turn him loose, or what?" she asked of Mickey.

"As you like," he said, and Ingrid nodded.

She looked one more time into the imaginal animal's large, gentle eye, and saw herself reflected there in miniature.

"Go on now," she said. Fair Play (or maybe that should be Fair Replay) shook out his mane, snorted at her companionably, and trotted off. Ingrid watched him clop on into the elevator down at the end of the corridor like it was a familiar stall. She trusted that Mickey's limited reach into the realworld would be sufficient to press the button to send him down.

She turned back to face her King.

"Thank you," she said.

Mickey offered his hand. "Would you care to join me?"

She did want to—she wanted to lose herself in the ecstasies only he could make her feel—but she wasn't going to. She didn't trust herself at the moment. She wanted to go back to the realworld, to be alone for at least a night and to think things over, though Jimmy the Freak wasn't going to make it easy.

Well, she had a way around him, too.

"Not yet, Mickey, if you don't mind," she said in response to his invitation. "I still have things to do so that my life on this side doesn't fall to pieces. I have business back out there, and relationships to maintain."

"Of course," the King said, forcing himself to be gracious. "You must attend to the necessities of your being. I will leave you to them. Return to me as it suits you."

And like that, he was gone.

Ingrid stepped through the door, across the border between worlds, and into the sacrificial chamber. Mickey kept his growing collection of her things in the corner, and she reclaimed a pair of kitten heels to replace the shoes she'd abandoned at the Angelus, hours ago. It had been a long day. She made a bit of an effort with her wild hair, peering into a mirrored compact. The telephone directory page she'd taken from the Aurea Catena's guest room (the one with the Edendale address of the Selig Polyscope Company) was still tucked away in her sleeve, as was her multifaceted garnet. Ingrid wrapped the stone in the page and slipped them both into one of several small pockets she'd sewn into her skirt some time ago. The skirt was part of her traveling ensemble—clothes she'd selected for the relative timelessness of their style. What she really needed to do was get that damn rock strung on a chain, so she'd never be in danger of losing it again.

She then closed her eyes and willed the seasons forward by thirty years or so—which she was getting better at all the time—and stepped back out into the first chamber. The lobby of the real, eternity's waiting room, where others' journeys ended and her adventures began.

She figured three decades ought to be enough to fox Jimmy the Freak. Thirty years into the past, before either of their births, might've made a better insurance policy, but the Tree would still be standing back in the nineteenth century, and Ingrid felt too tired to negotiate the long climb down to the ground. Even contemplating it was enough to give her a headache.

So thirty years into the future it was. The idea of seeing what the 1940s might look like had her curious. She could get a meal there and enjoy a good night's sleep, safely out of phase with her native timeline, and then pop back in later to continue her investigation.

To track down the address on that directory page.

She rode downstairs in the same elevator she'd watched Fair Play the racehorse take, three decades ago.

Outside the Silent Tower, it was nighttime again. Foggy, quiet, and rather cold. Many of the old building's new plethora of neighbors now rose higher than it did. The few cars parked along the curb looked larger, rounder, and more enclosed than the ones she remembered, their white-sided wheels small and plump like odd rubber doughnuts.

Ingrid's head swam as she started down the block and she staggered. She had to steady herself against the back of a bench marked 'bus stop' until she felt less wobbly.

"That was strange," she muttered, when her head cleared.

A discarded copy of the *Los Angeles Times* lay neatly folded on the edge of the bench, left behind for whoever else might like to read it. Ingrid picked it up and checked the date beneath the masthead. It read December 6th, 1941. She figured it was currently after midnight, given the quietude in the streets, so that made this December 7th.

The date was still in its infancy.

Ingrid's equilibrium again threatened to desert her and she moaned, sinking down to the sidewalk as the world seemed to spin and reel around her. A horrible idea occurred to her, and she fumbled her garnet out of her pocket, almost dropping it into the gutter in the process.

It looked all right. It felt real.

But then it was supposed to, wasn't it?

Ingrid stumbled over to the nearest car and held the red stone up to its window. There it was, reflected in the glass, just like a real thing should be.

The reflection troubled her, and for a sickening moment she couldn't fathom why. Then she remembered: because this stone wasn't supposed to *have* a reflection. It was an imaginal thing, perceptible without properly existing, like that copy of a horse Mickey had pulled together. It should have had neither reflection nor measurable weight, and yet it did. Which meant it wasn't *it*, anymore.

Which meant Jimmy the Fuck had switched stones on her. That was the only explanation. He must have stashed the ringer in his pocket before she awoke, expecting her to steal the special rock back from him. He'd fooled her with simple sleight-of-hand, the most basic of prestidigitator's tricks, and changed out Mickey's precious gift for a useless chunk of crimson crystal.

And now she was screwed.

A third devastating wave of vertigo overwhelmed her, driving her to her knees behind the bus bench. She grabbed for a stub of pencil she spotted laying underneath it, against its leg, and had trouble putting her hand into the right place to pick it up. She did get it, though, and was able to use it to scrawl her name, INGRID, in big shaky block letters across a torn telephone directory page she found in a fold of her skirt. She hoped it might be enough to help her remember herself when she came to. Whatever that meant. The sense of it was already going. She hoped it would work, because it was only December and Mickey wouldn't be able to help her for ten whole months. Not until All Souls' Day, when he'd be able to send the dead to fetch her.

But who knew if they'd ever find her, after that much time had passed?

Consciousness began to desert her. She felt like she was deflating as the cold concrete sidewalk rose up to catch her.

She was still clutching an ordinary red rock and a page with two important names on it when she blacked out, although she hadn't the slightest idea why.

Chapter Nine

—*December 7th, 1941*

SHE woke when a middle-aged woman opened the back door of a car parked some yards down the block, leaned out, and vomited into the gutter. The lady was dainty, well-dressed, and probably quite attractive at one of her finer hours. She turned her head and saw the redheaded girl lying on the sidewalk beside a nearby bus stop bench, watching her like she was enacting an ugly piece of street theater.

The anti-alcohol advertisement ducked her head back into the car and pulled the door shut.

A few moments later she got out of the vehicle, looking much more composed and demure. She was tiny, barely five feet high, with a pert (if somewhat mussed) hairdo and a bright button of a face. A white and brown terrier bounded out after her and sat at her heel, watching everything with avid and cheerful interest. The small woman regarded the girl behind the bench critically before removing a silver flask from her handbag and taking an extended, burbling swig.

"Strictly medicinal, you understand," she explained, when she'd completed the day's inaugural tipple and wiped her lips with the back of a gloved hand. "Don't be shocked."

The girl who'd just awakened cold and stiff on a sidewalk that felt about as comfortable as a coroner's slab could only shake her head. No judgment here. Her own mind was so muddled at the moment she could hardly recall her own name, and the white winter sunlight was enough to make her eyeballs ache.

Instead of re-capping the flask, the tiny inebriate held it out in offering. The girl on the sidewalk sat up and took it, but only sipped politely. The liquor inside burned her tongue.

"Go on, finish it," the flask's owner said. "You look to be in more need than me. At least I had a roof over my head last night, such as it was."

The sidewalk sleeper, who still hadn't remembered who or where she was, did feel like she'd spent the night at the bottom of a ditch. The back seat of a car would've felt like a palatial suite by comparison. She gulped the flask's contents down obligingly, hoping a stiff drink might do something to rouse her and jog her memories.

The scotch tasted like a doctor's office, and exploded in her gut like some sort of incendiary device. She sputtered and coughed till her eyes blurred and tears streaked down her cheeks.

The small woman cackled wickedly.

"It does taste medicinal, doesn't it? Laphroaig, from Islay: a single malt distilled on some uninhabitable sea-swept Scottish island. That piquant bouquet of alcohol swab and liniment oil was the justification for importing it legally back during the dark days of the Volstead Act. I suppose I acquired a taste for it then. Makes a first-rate eye-opener, I've always found."

The girl who'd awakened behind the bench nodded her agreement with that assertion. Her eyes were wide open, but she still hadn't caught her breath well enough to respond verbally. She handed the empty flask back to its rightful owner.

"I'm Dot, by the way," the tiny woman said, as she re-capped her silver canteen and returned it to her handbag. Her diction had a bored, formal, finishing-school drawl to it, though she seemed generally less well-mannered than her breeding might incline one to expect. She held out her hand. "Mrs. Dottie Parker," she said.

The girl who couldn't sort out her memories shook the proffered hand, weakly.

"And your name would be...?"

She honestly didn't know. She had something clenched in her left hand, however. It seemed to be a reddish gemstone, perhaps a garnet. Rather large and faceted, but otherwise unremarkable, except for being wrapped up in what looked like a page torn from a telephone directory.

The page had a name heavily scrawled across the front of it in pencil. Nearly engraved in pencil.

"Ingrid," Ingrid said, and it felt right on her lips, though precious little else about who 'Ingrid' was supposed to be filtered in along with it. She figured it would all come back as she came to in a more comprehensive way. "I'm Ingrid," she told Dottie.

Some other, larger package of memories threatened to fall into place when she gave her name... but then didn't. It remained tantalizingly out of reach. Ingrid looked at the red stone there in her hand, but the sight of it unlocked nothing for her. She didn't even know why she had it. It wasn't even strung on a chain to wear.

She slipped the big garnet and the defaced directory page into a pocket of her long and voluminous skirt, which looked to be of a rather antiquated style in comparison with Dot's form-fitting calf-length number. Slept-in, rumpled, and covered with wiry terrier hair, it still looked sleeker than the black sack Ingrid had on.

Dot nodded, still giving her that critical look. "Are you all right?" she asked in a low and serious voice. "Did something happen to you, dear?"

"I… I honestly don't remember."

"You look reasonably whole."

"I feel all right," Ingrid said. "But I can't remember much of anything."

"Occupational hazard, I suppose," Dottie commiserated, squinting in the morning light and rubbing absently at her own temple. "You're an actress I assume, looking the way you do," she stated rather than asked. "It's a waste if you aren't, dear."

"Yes," Ingrid said, and knew it was true. She'd been on stage, and on camera. She felt sure of it. So some part of her remembered these things—just not the part currently belted into the driver's seat of her psyche.

She stood up and found that she towered over Dottie by at least a foot. Both the diminutive drunk and her little dog looked up and cocked their heads.

"Well. We are statuesque, aren't we?" Dottie purred, as she fitted a long cigarette into an ivory holder and set it between her lips, which she barely moved when speaking. She lit up and exhaled a swirling cloud of cool blue smoke, and Ingrid had to wonder if she'd been paid a genuine compliment or dealt a jealous jab.

Perhaps a bit of both.

"Are you working on a picture, dear? Some historical thing? Your wardrobe department's going to be livid with you, I expect, wearing that getup off the lot and straight into the gutter."

Ingrid didn't quite know what to say. She had an embarrassed sense of having completely misjudged the occasion she'd dressed for.

"Well, we can offer you a ride, if you know where you're going. Or you can come have breakfast with us."

Us? Ingrid wondered if Dot was referring to her dog. She didn't know where she was going, and food sounded wonderful. Her stomach growled audibly.

Dottie nodded, her mind made up. "Alan!" she shouted over her shoulder, startling Ingrid. She didn't seem to be addressing the dog. "Alan, wake up! We're going to breakfast."

Someone sat up in the front seat of Dottie's car. Ingrid saw him through the rear window, before he got out on the driver's side.

'Alan' was almost as tall as Ingrid, with wavy brown hair and an affable, open face. He was well dressed in a light tweed suit, and his tie was still properly knotted even after a night spent passed out in the car. He blinked and squinted and shaded his eyes, looking down at Dottie and her dog.

"All right," he said. "Who's this?"

"My new friend Ingrid," Dottie said. "She's a refugee from a period piece, and it's our duty as socially conscious people to feed her and give her a ride. Don't you agree, dear?"

"Sure," Alan said. "Of course, Dot, if that's what you think."

He turned to Ingrid, gave her a quick appraisal, then took her hand and kissed it.

"Nice to meet you, Ingrid," he said, looking her right in the eye. "I'm Alan Campbell, better known as Mr. Mrs. Parker."

"Oh, stop it," Dottie frowned. "Don't be a shit."

"Please don't use that word, dear," Alan said, wincing slightly as a subtle apology for his wife's surliness.

Ingrid nodded, still looking into Mr. Campbell's kindly eyes. She didn't know why a married couple wouldn't share a married name, but this was an unusual pairing. Alan was handsome and dapper, as well as several years younger than snarky little Dot, though he was solicitous of her and obviously enamored.

In any case, Dottie's offer of hospitality seemed real enough. The mean little woman's incongruous offer of kindness was Ingrid's only touchstone right now, and she was reluctant to let Alan and Dottie drive away without her.

"Breakfast *would* be wonderful," she said. "If you really don't mind."

"Of course not," Dottie said. "Far be it from me to abandon a wayward goddess on the street. That would be 'bad karma,' as the Hindus have it. Don't you agree?"

Ingrid quailed at being referred to as a goddess, not out of some sense of modesty, but because it sparked a disquieting memory. She seemed to recall basking in the adulation of a worshipful multitude. She could almost hear an echo of their chants, and see the shadows of their tall feathered headdresses waving in smoky firelight.

She managed to nod.

"Well, come on, then," Dottie said, clicking her fingers for her dog. At least Ingrid thought it was for the dog. Alan seemed more responsive to the command, hurrying to hold open their car's rear door, admitting first the sprightly terrier, then Dot.

"Miss Ingrid?" Alan said, as formal as a butler, smiling brightly to make a joke of his habitual subservience.

She slid into the car, next to Dot on the back bench seat, and Alan closed the door behind her. Dottie's terrier hopped into her lap and licked at her face as Alan settled in behind the wheel, and they drove off, headed west.

Ingrid felt for a moment like she was leaving something important behind, like maybe it would be a good idea to remember her way back to this location, but the busy city streets were so unfamiliar that she wasn't able to keep her bearings.

Chapter Ten

BREAKFAST was conducted at a restaurant called Tom Bergin's House of Irish Coffee, where Dot and Alan each downed several cups of the namesake beverage, with Dottie taking a clear and early lead in the consumption challenge. Ingrid had one to be polite, as well as a big plate of steak and eggs. The restaurant didn't have specific breakfast items on the menu. More like pub fare, though the chef was nice enough to make her something that didn't feel too much like lunch. Alan had a Caesar salad, while Dot ordered French fried potatoes and a grilled cheese sandwich. Dot's terrier, Ernest, curled up under the table in their wood-paneled booth and slept after consuming a surreptitiously-delivered hamburger patty. When she wasn't eating, Dottie knitted with yarn and needles pulled from a large woven bag.

They were screenwriters, Ingrid learned, currently under contract at RKO, which she assumed was a movie studio, though she had no sense of ever having heard the name before. Dottie had recently been loaned out to another studio, called Universal, which had engaged her to supply choice scenes and bits of dialog for a film to be called *Saboteur*, being directed by an import from Britain called Alfred Hitchcock. Ingrid intuited that she was expected to recognize the name and be impressed by it, and she feigned both reactions with ease.

Alan, it turned out, was on loan to someone called Samuel Goldwyn, for whom he was writing a biopic about a sports figure named Lou Gehrig (whom she also clearly should have been familiar with). Before long Ingrid surmised that Alan and Dottie had started work on the picture as a team, but Dottie got herself fired. Instead of letting Alan go, the studio surprised them by replacing Dot with another woman, a younger rival named Helen Deutsch. Dot would only refer to Alan's new partner as Helen Ditch, if not by other, even less flattering epithets. Always delivered with a snarl and a smile.

Ingrid thought that the sanctity of Dottie's marriage was relatively safe, at least on the Helen Ditch front, though she didn't put her opinion out there. She couldn't imagine it would be appreciated. Besides, it was all 'water under the bitch' anyhow, as Dot delicately phrased it.

Eventually, perhaps inevitably, the conversation came around to Ingrid—though the Campbell-Parkers (or Parker-Campbells) were happy enough to talk about themselves that she had reason to hope it wouldn't.

"So what picture is it you're working on, again?" Alan asked, making an effort to be polite after realizing he and Dottie had been competing for attention.

"It's... I... I don't actually know," she said.

Dot and Alan exchanged a look.

"I mean I don't remember. I don't know why I don't. It's like I'm locked out of certain parts of my brain."

"You *did* take a knock on the head, didn't you?" Dottie asked.

"Maybe." Ingrid prodded at her scalp with her fingertips to see if anything seemed bruised. "It doesn't feel like it, but I don't know."

"Well," Dottie said, lighting another in an endless chain of cigarettes. "That's a mystery then, isn't it?"

Alan looked more concerned. "Do you have any ID? Did you have a purse? Maybe someone robbed you and knocked you out."

"People do know when they've been clocked on the skull, dear," Dottie said. "There tends to be a lingering headache."

"I have this," Ingrid said, ignoring Dot's sarcasm and putting the big garnet from her pocket on the table between them. She also smoothed out and set down the phone book page it had been wrapped in. "And this. And that's all."

Alan picked up the gemstone and held it up to the light. Dottie scrutinized the directory page with the letters I N G R I D ground deeply into its fibers, at a right angle to the pre-printed names and addresses.

"This is old," Dottie said, squinting at the type. She thrust the paper in front of Alan's face. "Look at this font."

"It *looks* old," Alan agreed. "The type does. Uneven. But the paper's white and brand new. I'd expect it to be brittle and yellow."

"What does that mean?" Ingrid asked.

"If you can't tell us, dear," Dottie drawled, "then I'm sure we have no idea. Unless it's a prop, of course."

"Oh, it *could* be a prop, couldn't it?" Alan said. "That makes sense."

Ingrid had to admit that it did make sense, though it didn't feel right to her, as explanations went. She saw no benefit in saying so, as Alan seemed quite excited by the idea.

"We could probably call around and find out who's shooting a turn-of-the-century piece," he said, mostly to Dot, who had put on her reading glasses to examine the names on the old phone book page and was ignoring him.

"Look, here—" she said, pointing out an entry to both Ingrid and Alan. "Selig Polyscope, a motion picture production company, in Edendale."

"Never heard of it," Alan said. "The studio or the town."

"'Edendale' has been absorbed by Glendale, I believe," Dottie said. "Out where the aircraft factory is supposed to be in Mr. Hitchcock's script. I expect this is a filmmaker's in-joke. Some sort of *homage*."

"What about Selig?" Ingrid asked softly, taking the page back as Dot handed it to her, looking at the entry printed beneath the deeply-inscribed letters of her name. The name Selig seemed to mean something to her, and that sense of almost being able to remember was as maddening as an itch she couldn't scratch.

"Well, there was the old Selig Zoo, if I recall," Dottie said. "East of downtown. Remember, dear?" She gave Alan a nudge. "Luna Park? With all the concrete animals at the entrance? It's long since closed down, though."

"Do you think there's a connection there?" Alan asked.

Dottie shrugged, affecting her habitual boredom as she resumed her knitting. "Perhaps," she said, clicking her needles. "But I think I know someone who would know for sure." She looked Ingrid over yet again, in that way that made her feel like she might soon be marched up onto an auction block. "He'll be pleased to make your acquaintance," she finished cryptically. "We have a meeting this afternoon anyway. I'll take you to see him as soon as Alan has paid the check."

Alan didn't have to be asked twice (or even once, really). He hopped up from the table and headed off to the bar. Ingrid had an impression that Dot might not have handled cash in quite some time. All the mundane tasks in their world had been delegated to the practical Mr. Campbell.

Ingrid was about to ask who it was they were going to see when an angry shout from the bar startled her. Both women looked over in that direction. Alan looked back at them, and his eyes were wide.

"Everybody, *shut up!*" the bartender roared. He was a gray-haired, grizzled Irish sort. A wood-cased radio set stood on a shelf behind him, and the barman turned up the volume as far as it would go.

"*Lissen*, for cryin' out loud, alla you!" he demanded, as every head in the room swiveled his way. "We're at goddamn war, here, people!"

THE pub's mix of late lunchers and early drinkers congregated at the end of the bar as the story began to pour out of the peak-roofed radio whose shape reminded Ingrid of a cathedral arch.

She and Dottie stayed in their booth while Alan stood at the bar with the rest of the men, though they listened to the news just as avidly. Dot's chronic ennui had evaporated. Her eyes were as bright and engaged as little Ernest's, and she even abandoned her knitting needles. The corner of the scarf she'd been working on was soaking up a small spill of Irish coffee, and she paid it no mind at all. Ingrid twisted the whiskey and cream out of the yarn and set the work-in-progress aside on the booth's padded bench for her.

It seemed that just after dawn, while Ingrid was unconscious on a Hollywood sidewalk, successive waves of Japanese 'planes' had bombed a naval base in Hawaii. At first she had no idea what that meant. She imagined a bombardment would have to be launched from ships, outside the harbor, though the anguished and anxious descriptions by the radio's newscasters made it sound as though the Japanese were attacking from the air. And that was mad. There were balloons and dirigibles, of course, and those Wright people on the east coast had managed to strap a gasoline engine to a giant kite, but the Pacific Ocean was surely too vast to cross in such contraptions. Aviators as Ingrid knew them were closer to sportsmen than soldiers. An irrational mental image of an imperial army blotting out the dawn with leathery, rustling batwings unnerved her, to say the least. It sounded like something from *The Wonderful Wizard of Oz*. One of the not-so-wonderful parts. She didn't know how any army could hope to defeat an enemy that could take to the skies.

Others in the bar were more than unnerved. Some were near hysterics, certain that a murder of airborne aggressors would be roosting on the rooftops of Los Angeles by nightfall. Dot, for one, was so focused on the news that she fairly vibrated. Other patrons (not all of them men) were furious, red-faced, pounding on the bar and shouting, voicing righteous calls for revenge.

Alan suggested they should be on their way. The world was still turning; they were still professionals (*believe it or not*, Ingrid couldn't help but think), and they had their obligations. "I'm sure Mr. Hitchcock will have a schedule," he mentioned strategically, attempting to exploit the pride Dot clearly felt in regard to her assignment. But he pronounced 'schedule' like it had no 'c' in it—'*shed*ule'—and Dot could never resist an opportunity to mock an affectation.

"Ignore him," she muttered to Ingrid. "He's full of skit."

"Dottie, really," Alan said, displaying a rare flash of exasperation. "*Please*, don't use that—"

"I didn't, did I?" Dot said, curtly and irrefutably, as she gathered up her knitting supplies and returned them to their bag. "But we can go, if you're ready. There's a radio in the fucking car."

Chapter Eleven

T HE streets, like the bar, were growing increasingly tumultuous as news of the surprise attack on Pearl Harbor spread across the city like a chaparral fire. Ingrid could only stare out the window of her new friends' bulbous Packard, aghast, while Alan drove them north.

Stores selling radios were mobbed, with men in hats and women with rolled hair straining to hear the news reports that crackled out of the inventory. The latest information was daisy-chained down block after block by word of mouth, and people snapped up extra editions of the *Times* as quickly as corner newsstand vendors could pop the twine on the just-delivered bales. The city itself looked so large and strange that it overwhelmed Ingrid almost as much as the angry furor engulfing it. She had no idea where she was or how to find her way back to where she'd started, and she still had a worrisome sense that she might need to do that, at some point. She was scared, and quite simply relieved that the Parker-Campbells (or Campbell-Parkers) hadn't opted to cut her loose back at the restaurant. She wouldn't have known where else to go.

Alan drove them through narrow, bungalow-lined Laurel Canyon and down into the San Fernando Valley, home of a filmmaking facility known as Universal Studios. As they drove through the front gate (with the security guard in the booth barely glancing at Alan), a giddy and distracted part of Ingrid's mind wondered if other galaxies had actually been consulted before the selection of the studio's name. She doubted it, though in a world where aviators flew around in metal birds to drop explosives on one another, she couldn't be sure of anything. Maybe radio communication between the planets of the solar system was considered as unremarkable these days as the technological miracle of aero-planes.

She didn't know why she should feel so startled over things other people took for granted. Not knowing what she didn't know was quite upsetting, but even so she was able to keep her composure, while others all around were losing theirs.

Reactions to the news of the bombardment made for strange tableaus around the studio backlot as Dottie led her between the sound stages and toward the production offices, with Ernest the terrier bounding along at their heels. Alan went off to park the big red convertible, with plans to rejoin them shortly.

Extras in Marine Corps uniforms mingled with a troop of harem girls straight from the Arabian Nights, all of them grouped around a radio someone had placed face-out on an office windowsill. It seemed that several battleships had been sunk in Hawaii, and that in some cases the Japanese were even flying their planes right into the American vessels, making themselves into living, targeted bombs.

Ingrid hoped the reports were exaggerated, news hyperbole, as the idea of it horrified her anew. It was even worse than her initial vision of armed men beating the air with mechanized wings as they swooped down out of a rising sun.

A knot of girls dressed for a dance rehearsal blocked the entrance of the office building Dottie meant to enter. She forced her way through, dragging Ingrid along by the hand like an oversized child. In the hall, a fraying mummy had his bandaged ear pressed to a portable radio while his nemesis, a tweedy archaeologist, read a wire service report aloud to a gaggle of assorted grips, secretaries, and technicians. Some of those departments probably never crossed paths, but now they were all in something together.

Dot muscled past them, as well.

She led Ingrid upstairs and down a carpeted corridor that felt strangely deserted and still after the tide of rage and agitation that was rising down below.

Ernest ran ahead and bounced up and down happily before a door at the end of the hall. Another tiny woman with glasses and pulled-back hair opened it. She greeted the dog cheerfully and by name, but acknowledged Dottie with only the barest of nods, while holding the office door open for the new arrivals.

"Alma," Dot said as she strode into the room.

Alma narrowed her eyes at Ingrid. "Alma Reville," she introduced herself, holding out her hand.

"Ingrid," Ingrid said, shaking with the suspicious lady.

"How do you know Dottie, Ingrid?" Alma asked.

"We picked her up off the street this morning, dear," Dot explained. "Completely at random. She's a natural thing to point a camera at, don't you think? I couldn't imagine not showing her to Mr. Hitchcock."

Alma looked like she might have more to say about that (Ingrid sensed an immediate tension between the two diminutive women, though she couldn't guess at the basis of it, other than Dottie's general abrasiveness), but a man Ingrid assumed to be Mr. Hitchcock himself stood up from a drafting table he'd been leaning over in order to scrutinize a designer's work.

"Good day, Mrs. Parker," he said, in a cultured English accent. He wasn't much taller than Dottie or Alma but he was exceedingly round, and clad in a double-breasted suit. His thin hair was slicked back from his brow. His protuberant belly made him resemble a ship with a strong wind in its sail. "You've heard the news, I assume?"

"Yes," Dottie said. "Those devious bastards."

"Indeed," Hitchcock agreed, illustrating the famous British flair for understatement.

He then looked up at Ingrid.

"Charmed to make your acquaintance," he said, taking her hand and kissing the backs of her slim fingers, all the while looking into her eyes. "I'm Alfred Hitchcock."

Ingrid repeated her name. Alma folded her arms, while Dottie grinned. Ingrid registered both behaviors from the corner of her eye. "Alfred is my father's name," she said, absently, as the fact popped into her head.

"Then I hope you'll find it easy to remember," the rotund little filmmaker said. He then turned back to Dottie. "Mrs. Parker, you know Mr. Boyle…"

The young man at the drafting table glanced up from his sketches and offered a quick raise of a hand before returning to his work.

Another, older man stood up from a small sofa in the corner of the office. Ingrid hadn't noticed him there, but something in her midsection went cold when she saw his face.

She didn't know why. She couldn't place him. But it was all she could do not to rip her hand away when he took it to kiss it, just as Mr. Hitchcock had.

"I don't believe you've met Mr. Vreke," Alfred said, mostly to Dottie, even though all of Vreke's attention was trained on Ingrid, like a searing light focused through a lens. "He's a recent investor in the studio."

"Miss Ingrid," the aging financier said. Somewhat cautiously, it seemed.

"It's a pleasure to meet you, Mr… Freak?" Ingrid said, though the statement was an unalloyed lie. Her initial shock was fading, though. She found the fear hard to hold onto without an obvious reason for feeling it, like an experience of déjà vu. "Though I think we might've met before?" she ventured.

"James Vreke," the unaccountably intimidating man said. He grinned again, and Ingrid tried to let herself be reassured. "Vreke with a 'v,' that is. You can call me Jimmy. And I like to think we'd remember each other, if our paths had crossed already."

Chapter Twelve

ESPITE the horrible news that continued to trickle in and the various wound-up colleagues who stopped by to exclaim over it, the mystery of Ingrid managed to compel some attention.

Much of it came from Mr. Hitchcock. Alfred.

"I thought one of you might be able to help her," Dot said, to Alfred and Alma both. "She has amnesia, but she's plainly in costume and she had a turn-of-the-century prop in her pocket. It's like something out of one of your suspense scenarios, don't you think?"

Alma and Alfred exchanged a glance. They were clearly fascinated, at least with the narrative possibilities of Ingrid's situation.

"Besides that," Dot continued (as Alan appeared after parking the car but shrank back against the wall with only the barest nod of greeting to the colleagues assembled in the production office), "—between the two of you, I'm sure you're aware of every studio project going before the lens right now. Maybe you can put your learned heads together and figure out what production this poor lost lamb is meant to be attached to?"

"Sort of a 'gay 90s' setting, I'd imagine, given her outfit," Alan tried to contribute, while Mr. Hitchcock and Miss Reville both frowned and almost literally put their heads together to mutter about it.

"I might be of some assistance, there, as well," James Vreke said. "May I see the 'prop' you had in your pocket?"

Ingrid produced the telephone directory page—old type on fresh paper, with her name scrawled across it in pencil so dark it screamed of desperation—and handed it over. Vreke frowned at it.

Hitchcock sidled over and took it out of his hand. "Do the names other than your own mean anything to you?" he asked, looking up at her.

Ingrid shook her head.

"One of the entries looks like it's for an old production company," Alan spoke up. "Something Polyscope?"

"Selig Polyscope," Alfred said. "I noticed it."

"Does it mean anything to you?" Dottie asked.

"I've heard of it, yes," Alfred said. "William Selig was quite the pioneer, in his day. His films were some of the very first shot in Los Angeles."

Ingrid nodded. She was listening attentively. That seemed to please Mr. Hitchcock, who was all too happy to play to her interests. Miss Reville, suddenly shoved to the same periphery as Alan Campbell, scowled and seemed to sulk. It troubled Ingrid that Alma was made uncomfortable by the way Alfred fixed the spotlight beam of his attention on her and her story, even over the war news, but she was also desperate to hear anything that might shed new light on her odd situation.

"Selig Polyscope was the first studio to attempt an adaptation of Frank Baum's Oz story, years before MGM," Alma said, eliciting interested murmurs with her bit of film trivia and catching Ingrid's attention.

"*The Fairylogue and Radio-Plays*, in 1908," she said automatically, feeling excited, and almost added 'I remember,' though she didn't see how she *could* remember a thing like that. She wasn't old enough for memories from 1908, surely. Not if this was 1941.

She frowned, and shut up.

Alma, too, was frowning. "I believe it was called *The Wonderful Wizard of Oz*, like the original book," she said, and Ingrid didn't want to press the point.

"Oh! I had this, too, wrapped up in the page," she said, remembering the faceted garnet, which she produced and held up for general inspection. It looked as black as a lump of coal in the artificial indoor light. "I have no idea why. It isn't jewelry, or… or anything."

Vreke seemed to straighten up upon seeing the stone. "May I?" he asked, and Ingrid handed it right over.

James Vreke took the red stone and held it up against the window, squinting hard at its pale reflection in the glass.

"I know a bit about stones, you see," he explained.

"Is it valuable?" Ingrid asked.

"I'd say it's exceptionally ordinary."

He handed it back. Ingrid felt disappointed, for no reason she could think of.

"Are you a geologist, Mr. Vreke? Or a jeweler?"

"Please, just Jimmy. And no, I'm nothing of the sort. Just someone with an interest in minerals."

"Could the page be a prop from one of this Selig's productions?" Dottie speculated.

"Oh, no, I wouldn't imagine," Alma said, perhaps a little too quickly, in her eagerness to shut the caustic Mrs. Parker down. "Selig Polyscope became insolvent years ago. Decades. Their holdings were sold off to the Fox company, if I'm not mistaken. Some time before 1920, this would've been."

"A Fox production, then," Dot suggested. "Employing an historically-minded property master?"

"I won't say it's impossible," Alma said. "But I'm not aware of any current project that would fit the bill."

"Me neither," contributed Boyle, the young art director in charge of the 'storyboards.' (Storyboards were an unfamiliar concept to Ingrid, though the logic behind the little comic strips that blocked out a film shot by shot was immediately obvious.)

"Well, I don't think she fell out of a hole in the goddamn *sky*," Dottie said, meaning Ingrid, making Alan wince, as he did every time she swore in public. It was a wonder he didn't suffer from a chronic facial tic by now. His angry little wife had resumed her knitting at some point, and Dot now clicked her needles irritably.

"Certainly not," Alfred agreed, looking Ingrid up and down. "She came from somewhere, and the story will likely prove rather prosaic in the end. The excitement of a mystery lies in that illusion of possibility, doesn't it, as if the world may in fact be larger, stranger, and more interesting than it generally appears."

"Yes, I'm sure she's really rather dull," Alma said, glancing pointedly at Ingrid and then away. "Her origins, I mean, where she came from. Not you personally, of course."

"Of course," Ingrid said. Alma wasn't confrontational enough to meet her eyes again. Dottie had a smirk on her little face.

"I do seem to recall this Selig's name being linked to a rather lurid murder case," Alfred mused, raising an eyebrow as he noted the subtle tension amongst the women. "He was wounded and one of his directors killed when their studio groundskeeper ran mad, if I'm not mistaken. This was many years ago."

Ingrid noticed that James Vreke looked uncomfortable, like the room was a bit too warm.

She didn't have time to speculate about it, because a scene painter in color-spattered coveralls stuck his head through the door and announced that reports were coming in of a Japanese submarine off the coast of Santa Monica. He disappeared, racing off down the hall to repeat his message of encroaching doom as many times as possible. Ingrid heard shouts and noise from outside as well. There seemed to be a growing sense that the surprise attack on Hawaii might have been only the beginning of a much more widespread and devastating assault.

"Will the Japanese bomb California now, the way the Germans have Britain?" Alma asked quietly, of Alfred.

The adipose filmmaker took her hand and held it, but didn't answer, Ingrid noticed. Nobody knew what would happen now.

"Maybe we should go see what's going on out there," Alan suggested. "People sound pretty worked up."

"They're whipping themselves into a frenzy based on slivers of information," Dot said.

"Still," Alma said, "I'd like to know what people are saying. Maybe there's news we need to hear."

"Yes, quite," Alfred said. "Shall we, then? I think work has been effectively cancelled for the day."

The assembled troupe—Alan, Dottie, Alma, Jimmy Vreke, Boyle the art director, and Ingrid—all filed out the office door after Mr. Hitchcock.

Chapter Thirteen

VREKE hung back until he was strolling along beside Ingrid, as the little group of filmmakers wended their way between the lot's boxy beige soundstages.

She noticed Dot noticing this. Dottie had Ernest the terrier cradled in her arms, and their eyes sparkled with a similar sort of avidity. She stuck close to Alan, just as Alma cleaved to Alfred.

It seemed as though everyone employed by the studio was milling about, exchanging rumor, gossip, and fragments of facts. The local radio stations carried no confirmation of the sub-off-Santa Monica story, though word of mouth kept the notion vividly alive. Seeing squadrons of enemy planes overhead would have shocked everyone but surprised no one, right then.

None of these people knew what their world would look like tomorrow.

"Mr. Hitchcock said you're a recent investor in his project, Mr. Vreke? Jimmy?" Ingrid said for the sake of saying something, if the man in question was going to insist on paying her such obvious attention.

Jimmy smiled. "Yes he did. I own a controlling interest in a company that develops optical technology, you see, and I figured it was high time I got a sense of how the tools I make are really used, by the artists and technicians they're made for."

"That's admirable," Ingrid said.

"Sometimes it takes a fresh set of eyes to see new possibilities." As they neared the Main Street set Vreke took her by the elbow and pulled her into a deserted soundstage. "Though sometimes only eyes that have seen too much are able to spot the truth," he said cryptically, hustling her through the light-lock (a right-angled entryway with an inner door that kept unwanted sunshine out) and onto the floor of the cavernous stage.

"Mr. Vreke, this isn't very proper, I'm afraid," Ingrid said, stepping away from him and onto a vast tape-scarred expanse of black flooring. The walls were padded for sound insulation; the distant ceiling was crisscrossed with rafters and catwalks. She didn't think she'd ever seen such a large interior space before, short of a concert hall.

"You promised to call me Jimmy," Vreke said. "And don't worry. I only want to show you something."

Sure. Even without her memories, Ingrid knew she'd heard that one before.

Still, she waited, instead of fleeing or making a scene. This 'Jimmy' wasn't so intimidating, physically. He was pushing sixty, for one thing— Ingrid was younger, at least as tall, and doubtlessly stronger. If he had anything untoward in mind, she was certain she could set him straight.

Jim wandered over and stood beside a massive camera array set up on a wheeled platform. "Little to the left?" he asked, and Ingrid stepped obligingly onto a masking-tape mark on the stage floor without thinking twice about it, like a seasoned pro.

"The history of images is an interesting thing," Jimmy said as he started the camera rolling. It clicked faintly as it pulled film from a two-reeled magazine. "Some cultures forbid the making of them entirely. In other places, for other people, they become venerated objects of power. We've always known on some level that to represent something is to know it, to own it, and to some degree control it. Sometimes to a very large degree. The making of pictures has always been a magical act."

Jimmy stepped away from the camera apparatus and threw a heavy switch on the wall. A large spotlight came on overhead, showering Ingrid with light and forcing her to squint and shade her eyes in order to see Jim as he stepped back behind his camera and adjusted its focus.

"Cinema is different from painting or drawing, though, isn't it? Different even from still photography, because it so vividly reproduces the animation of life. It generates portraits that become far more vivid in the mind's eye than reality itself, serving in some cases as focal points for the aspirations and desires of thousands of individuals at a time. Such images become imbued with the longings and cravings of all who respond to them. Charged with imaginal potency."

"People sure do like the movies," Ingrid agreed, feeling increasingly nonplussed. She was starting to think this Jimmy character just enjoyed the sound of his own voice.

"Yes they do," he said, continuing to rhapsodize. "Like they've never loved any art form before. The pictures have sound these days and color too. They feel more real with every passing year, despite being more idealized. And that's perhaps their greatest trick—getting so many to believe in them and relate to them, as if life were meant to be as dramatic, as meaningful, or as satisfying as our favorite movies make it seem. Film at its best doesn't so much reproduce reality as *improve* upon it, don't you think?"

Ingrid nodded. Faint purple and blue layers deep within the camera's lens shifted as Jimmy focused it on her, like the iris of a stern glass eye.

"It takes a true artist to arrange such a sequence of images. Tremendous skill is required to achieve that sort of effect. And of course even such an artist is still nothing without an icon, an idol, some worthy vision to point his camera at. A soul to capture with his magic box. Did you know tribesmen in many parts of the world react to the camera with fear and loathing, for that very reason? Not entirely stupid, those people. They still know a thing or two about the worlds the rest of us have forgotten. *Most* of the rest of us. A select few still remember the old truths, as they always have. It reminds one of a golden chain, doesn't it, that continuity of secret knowledge? An aurea catena, as they'd say in Latin?"

"If you insist," Ingrid said. She felt like he was trying to lead her into saying or revealing something, though she had no idea what it might be, and that frustrated him. This Jimmy the Freak was the most baffling of individuals. He certainly lived up to his name.

"I knew a man," he said, still prodding her for something she couldn't even guess at. "Years ago, a man named Boggs, who might've been such an artist, and he'd already discovered a vision to put on film and parade before the hungry eyes of the unfulfilled masses."

"What happened to him?" Ingrid asked, not quite idly. The name sounded familiar, but the incipient memory sank back into the amnesiac murk that churned just below the surface of her consciousness. She was beginning to hate that sensation.

"He wasn't willing to share," Vreke said, in reference to Francis Boggs. "He might be around today if he had."

Ingrid didn't think she liked the sound of that.

"No, Mr. Boggs was not willing to share, not at that time, and my prize escaped me. But fate's a funny thing, isn't it? I wouldn't have believed it in my youth, but I have learned, over time, that if you're patient enough, sometimes a second chance might present itself. Things do have a funny way of coming full circle. And now, today, there's a different artist I might deal with, one possessing even more talent and potential than Boggs. Mr. Hitchcock. A man capable of crafting dreams that all the world will share in common, that will seep into the collective imagination and alter *this* world from the inside out, according to my designs. I don't know how it's possible that you're here, unchanged after all this time, but it doesn't really matter. Now that you're back, you, my dear, are going to be Alfred Hitchcock's subject, and his object... but my possession."

Ingrid still didn't know what this was all about, but when Jimmy removed a tarnished silver watch from the front pocket of his waistcoat and flipped it open to check the time, things became a lot clearer.

The chain on his watch had a large stone attached at the far end as a decorative counterweight.

A fat red garnet, caged in silver wire.

It looked a lot like the stone Ingrid had in her pocket, though it had one subtle, significant difference. The doors to all the locked chambers of her mind swung wide when she saw it, and she had herself back, just like that. She remembered who she was and how she'd gotten here.

Jimmy saw her looking at the stone. He unthreaded the chain from his buttonhole and held it up, watch and all, like a hypnotist starting his shtick. "You *do* remember this, don't you?" he asked. "I wondered what it would take to jog your memory."

"I remember it now," Ingrid said. "And I'm gonna ask you to hand it over, before I plant my foot so far up your ass I'll run the risk of losing a shoe."

Jimmy smiled. "My, but we do have an attitude, don't we?"

"I'm really not fucking around," Ingrid said. "I want my rock."

"Then come and get it."

Jimmy held up the watch, and the stone, tauntingly.

Ingrid started toward him… but found she couldn't start. She couldn't step beyond the column of harsh white light that glared down around her from the ceiling. Faint shadows she hadn't noticed before danced around the edges of the pool of light at her feet—shadows cast by runic shapes marked out in tape on the spotlight's lens.

Jim had bound her into a cleverly disguised circle before she had a chance to see her garnet at the end of his chain.

It was already too late.

"You're not the only one with tricks up your sleeve, Miss Redstone," Jimmy said, tucking the watch back into its pocket on the front of his vest. The garnet, left to hang, flashed and winked like a bloodshot eye, reflecting the blinding beam of blue-white light that held Ingrid prisoner. Both her red stone and Jimmy the Freak's crushable windpipe were a few agonizing feet out of reach. "I've been preparing for the day we'd find the perfect star to put before Hitchcock's lens, and now luck—or synchronicity—has put you in my path again. We're gonna do big things together. So, as a gesture of good faith, why don't you start by finally telling me how to find the Hole in the Sky? I assume the Tree below it is long since gone, but I don't think you'd be here now if the portal wasn't still up there somewhere. Maybe you arranged some new way to mark its location?"

"Fat chance," Ingrid said. "Keep me here until I starve, I won't tell you anything."

"We'll see about that," Jim countered. "Because like I said, when it's done in just the right way, to represent something is to claim power over it. It's a matter of sympathetic resonance. That's the principle that makes a voodoo doll work."

"I know what sympathetic resonance is, you patronizing ass."

"Then you know what it's capable of. Or you might think you do. But I have another trick, Miss Redstone. A new way of exploiting that age-old principle. I spearheaded its development myself, directing the work of the best physicists, chemists, and opticians millions of dollars in research money can buy. My white coats have taken to calling it the 'Pyroptic Anamorph.' From the Greek, you see. 'The Burning Eye That Remakes Shapes,' very roughly translated."

Ingrid shifted her weight to her other hip, considering Jimmy's camera. "So what is it? Some sort of fancy lens?" she said, making an educated guess.

Jim looked like he wanted her to act more impressed.

Tough shit, Ingrid thought.

"Yes, it's a lens," he said testily. "But it's a lens with a memory. It retains a perfect impression of whatever is burned onto it through a device like this one here."

He patted the camera's side, while it quietly chewed its film.

"More than an image, you see. An *impression*. A copy we can reactivate later and view in the round, without need of a screen. The Anamorph condenses the photons it modulates in some way I don't remotely understand, giving its reproduced forms a degree of mass and density. I'm not sure the slide-rule squad understand it either, but it sure does wind them up trying to figure it out. In any case, impressions projected from it are tangible. Touchable. Maybe even fuckable. They're in full color and you hear them when they speak. Can you imagine what a man with my skills might do with a portrait as vivid as that? A portrait, perhaps, of *you?*"

"I suppose I can," Ingrid said. He was threatening her with the perfect voodoo doll. Telling her he could catch her image in his magic glass and use it to control her. He could force her to retreat down into the most private and unbreachable parts of her mind and trap her there, leaving the rest of her catatonic. He might have the skill to move her body around like a marionette or put lines in her mouth for her to speak… but even then he'd never be able to make her give up her guarded secrets.

She didn't believe he could ever do that, no matter how strong a link he had to work with.

The fact that they were still conversing suggested Jimmy didn't believe it either. He wanted information. He wanted to know why she hadn't aged in thirty years, as well as how to find the Hole in the Sky, still hidden from him after all this time. If he forced her to hide away within herself now, he knew he'd never find out.

That was her one bit of leverage.

"Tell me something," Ingrid said. "Is Mr. Hitchcock in on your plan?"

Jimmy hesitated. "Not yet. But I'm sure he'll leap at the deal once he understands what it is that's being laid upon his table."

"Frank Boggs didn't leap."

"Maybe Hitchcock's not an idiot," Jimmy speculated. "My father's scientists had only just discovered the pyroptic glass the Anamorph derives from back in Boggs' day. I couldn't have made the fullest use of either of you then. But now we have another chance, and we'll see how things shake out with Hitch."

"I don't believe we will."

"No? And why not?"

"Because I'll stop you."

"Really?" Jim looked amused. "How? Who on earth do you think you are?"

"I'm Ingrid Redstone, Mr. Freak," Ingrid explained patiently. "And I'll hand you your ass in a hat if that's what I have to do."

Jimmy grinned, pretending to enjoy the banter. "Tell me why you haven't changed since the last time I saw you," he said conversationally. "We can still work something out between us. I'm sure we can."

"Maybe I traveled through time," Ingrid said tartly. "Last time I saw *you* was yesterday, far as I'm concerned, and it hasn't been anywhere near long enough."

Jimmy narrowed his eyes at her, dismissing the truth as a sarcastic dig. "Is it alchemy?" he asked. "The red tincture, the philosopher's stone? Is that where your name came from? Is that how you managed this?"

"My name's my name because it's my father's name," Ingrid said. "And that's all there is to that."

"You're really not gonna tell me anything, are you?"

"What makes you think you'd believe me if I did?" Ingrid came back. "And what would ever make *me* think you'd be true to your word? What kind of a deal can we possibly make?"

"Try me and find out," Jimmy said. "You really have no choice but to trust me."

Ingrid shook her head. "I can tell you to stick it. That's my choice."

Jimmy's affable demeanor slipped, and he went a little berserk. "Do you know what I'm gonna do if you *don't* tell me?" he screamed, stepping right up close to the blinding vertical beam she stood trapped in. "I'm gonna rent out your face and form to any purpose I can benefit from for the rest of your natural life and bind you for an eternity after, and you're gonna march straight into that rather than deal with me this one little fucking *bit?*"

"Guess so," Ingrid said. She hadn't figured a way out of this predicament yet, but it was fun to watch Jimmy go apoplectic.

He looked, in fact, like he could've shot her dead. His mouth was twisted with anger, his eyes bulged, and prominent veins stood out at either side of his forehead. She didn't know what would happen if he had a heart attack. She might be trapped within his circle for some time before anyone found her in here and turned off the hexed-up spotlight.

She was starting to feel a little claustrophobic, truth be told.

"Fine," Jimmy said, once his nostrils stopped flaring and his left eye stopped twitching. "If that's the way you need this to be. But if you're thinking all I can do is bind you back into your own subconscious and parade you around like some big brainless doll—which is all anyone expects from an actress anyway, so believe me, nobody's gonna notice—then you have another thing coming. I don't need anything as esoteric as magic to make you talk. Brute force should do it."

Jimmy pushed the cuff of his jacket back to reveal what looked like a wristwatch, though he raised it to his lips and spoke into it.

"I need you now," Jimmy said, into the device. "Priority One, if you please."

He saw Ingrid looking at the apparatus on his arm and held it out for her inspection.

"Miniature two-way radio on a secure frequency. One of my companies developed it for military intelligence applications. I told you I do have my resources, Miss Redstone."

A door at the far end of the stage slammed open, and a hunched, hulking form filled the doorway, backlit from behind.

"Here's another of my resources," Jimmy said lightly. "An old associate of mine. I believe you made his acquaintance before. In fact, he hasn't said an intelligible word since the day you met. I've kept him on in my employ out of the goodness of my heart, despite his myriad of problems. I'm sure he can persuade you to share the things you know before I set you to my purposes. He was trained in various methods of interrogation before you screwed him up. His work won't even render you unfit for the camera, though if some cosmetic damage does occur, it'll heal. Now that I've got you where I want you, I'm not in any hurry. We can take all the time you need."

Jimmy motioned for the mouthbreather he'd summoned by wrist-radio to approach, and when he did Ingrid recognized the youngest of the Pinkerton detectives Jimmy'd had in his employ back in 1912, the year she'd jumped ahead from. He'd been about her age then but he wasn't young now, or in his right mind. He wore his unfortunate mental condition on his sleeve, exhibiting the vacant stare and obvious hygiene problems of a man with a damaged attention span. He was dressed today in what looked like a rumpled chauffer's livery and not his plain gray suit, but it was clearly the same person.

He recognized Ingrid too. He took one look at her, pointed a tremulous finger, and began to scream: "Witch! *Witch!* *Wiiitch!*" Over and over again. He showed no sign of stopping. Jimmy looked somewhat dumbfounded by his man's reaction. Not what he expected, Ingrid guessed. Not in the least.

"Jesus Christ," Jimmy said. "Thirty years of nothing, and now this. Shut the fuck up, will you?"

But shut the fuck up he would not. The witch-crier persisted with his full-throated, lung-straining chant. "WIIIITCH!" His eyes grew bloodshot and flecks of foam flew from his lips as he continued to point at Ingrid and yell his demented ass off.

Even after decades, the impression she made stayed with a guy.

Jimmy's man was agitated, though, not completely insensate. Even through his bellowing Ingrid could tell he was listening to his boss and preparing to execute his orders. He just meant to shout about witches while he did it. The former Pinkerton's mind was only three-quarters cracked, and he was more than big enough to be dangerous, despite his advancing age.

Especially if he could move freely in and out of this goddamn beam of light while she remained trapped within it.

"Last chance, Miss Redstone," Jimmy said, raising his voice over the ongoing shouts and accusations from his pet madman.

"You can cram that wherever it fits," was Ingrid's reply. "Do your worst, you piece of shit."

"Have at her, then," Jimmy the Freak said to his man, who stepped forward to do as he was told, breathing only to scream. "She can't hurt you now."

NEXT TIME:
Episode Four
SCARRED TIMES

SCARRED TIMES

Chapter One

—December 7ᵗʰ, 1941

INGRID steeled herself. James Vreke, Jimmy the Freak, had her hexed into a space about four feet in diameter, the width of a spotlight beam on the soundstage floor. That didn't mean she couldn't put up a fight.

Her assailant-to-be was big, though—Jim's driver was about her height, as well as fat through the gut and massive in the shoulders. He probably outweighed her by sixty pounds.

This was going to get ugly.

Ingrid knew they'd get her in the end, no matter what she did. She was stuck tight within Jimmy's ring of hexwork and could not break it from the inside. She might get in a few lucky shots with fists or feet or teeth when his man came at her, but all they had to do was bide their time until they exhausted her, and then she'd be at their mercy, like a weary fox treed by a pack of baying dogs.

Such baying as there was continued unabated when Jimmy's driver stepped up in front of her. "*Wiiitch! Wiiiiiitch! WITCH!*"

"Yes, I get it already, I'm a witch," Ingrid said. "You got me there, big fella."

The Yelling Man's only response was to point at her again and deliver another inchoate, slobbering scream. She'd really done a number on that poor bastard, back in the day.

And here she was about to do another one.

"I'm sorry," she said to him, though he showed minimal signs of understanding. "I really am. Things might've been better for you if you'd died in 1912."

The bellowing henchman lunged for her and instead of feinting back Ingrid stepped forward to meet him. (She had the freedom of movement to take exactly one step). She lashed out, snake-strike quick, and clapped Mr. Howl's head between her palms. Hard.

She felt air puff from his ear canals and heard a distinct pop, and now the Yelling Man *really* had something to yell about—though Ingrid doubted he could hear himself doing it anymore.

The hulking middle-aged thug pinwheeled backward, away from her imprisoning beam, now screeching in pain and confusion as well as from madness. He lurched and fell and tried to get up, only to spin and stagger and fall again. His equilibrium was shot, at least temporarily. Ingrid's aim and timing had been flawless, and her would-be torturer's vulnerable eardrums had paid the price.

She and Jimmy both watched him roll around the stage floor, still shouting and trying to get up, only to topple over with each attempt as if the earth were wobbling on some unpredictable new axis beneath his feet.

Jimmy looked quietly aghast.

"Don't go blaming me for that," Ingrid told him. "You didn't leave me with a lot of choice."

"He'll be all right, sooner or later," Jimmy sneered. "And he'll have a helmet on next time. I have this stage leased indefinitely. No one's going to bother us in here—not if this takes us a day, a week, or any number of months. Not as long as the red light over the door stays on. So you're hardly off the hook, Miss Redstone."

"Guess again, smart guy," Ingrid told him, breaking into a grin. She'd become aware of something he had not.

"You think this is funny?" Jimmy said, raising a hand to strike her. "You think this is some kind of joke?"

"Ernest," Dottie Parker said. The tiny writer had snuck into the soundstage after them, unseen even by Ingrid until a moment ago. She pointed at Jimmy the Freak as she stepped out of the shadows near the exit with her little dog at her heels. "*Sic balls!*"

The otherwise personable terrier transformed himself into a whirling dervish with a suddenness Ingrid could scarcely believe. He flew across the stage floor in three swift bounds and launched himself, snarling and snapping, straight at the sorcerer's groin.

Jimmy shrieked toward a soprano register when the little dog latched on and clamped down. He flailed and danced and hopped around like the floor had turned electric beneath his feet.

Ingrid really did have to laugh out loud.

"I hope you don't mind my eavesdropping, dear," Dottie said with her characteristic pout. "But he struck me as suspicious. And his rhetoric was getting stale. This is so much more lively, don't you think?"

"Dottie, kill the light!" Ingrid said. "That's how he's holding me here!"

Dot obligingly dropped the wall switch, and the harsh white beam disappeared like it had never been. Ingrid sprinted to the camera and kicked it over on its side. The lens broke with a crunch and the magazine snapped loose to slide away across the floor, with entrails of curly black film uncoiling behind it. Internal gears gnashed and tiny unmoored motors whirred.

So that was that taken care of. Voodoo lens destroyed, prismatic prison smashed beyond repair.

In the moment of semi-dimness that followed the dousing of the spotlight, Ernest released his grip on Jimmy Vreke's scrotum and bounded back over to his owner, who picked him up.

"Hadn't we better be going now?" Dot suggested, turning to Ingrid.

"I need my stone first. The one on the end of his watch fob. And I need to make sure all that film is exposed. I can't let him keep any pictures of me." The image on his 'Anamorph' had been the dangerous one, the way he told it, but she wasn't taking any chances.

"All right," Dottie said, dropping Ernest and pointing at Jimmy, who was sitting splay-legged on the floor some yards away and frantically prodding at his family jewels, checking for signs of depreciation. "Fetch me something pretty," Dot instructed, and the terrier was off like a shot. He seemed to enjoy this game, clever little guy that he was.

"You're in luck," Dot said to Ingrid. "These are the only two tricks I ever had fun teaching him."

Jimmy yelped and crab-scrambled backward, attempting to flee the vicious lapdog. Ernest leapt up onto the low hill of his belly and unerringly seized the fob chain in his teeth, worrying it loose from its buttonhole in a matter of seconds. Then he was racing back across the floor with a silver watch and a red stone dangling from either side of his toothy terrier grin. He dropped the shiny bit of plunder into Dot's outstretched hand with an obliging wag of his tail, and she handed it over to Ingrid.

"Who says only cats can be burglars?" the screenwriter said, her normally stiff lips twisting up into a rare and surprising smile.

"Not me." Ingrid held up the fob watch, examining the garnet. She brought it close to the polished back of the watch's silver case, and verified that the stone had no reflection. It was hers, all right—her unique and imaginal gift from Mictlantecuhtli. The watch was nice too, with red roman numerals and a thick crystal window on the front that showed the spinning brass gears inside. "I think the field of criminal endeavor should be open to everyone, regardless of gender, creed, or species," she told Ernest, who perked up his ears.

Dottie grinned even wider. "Just who are you, Ingrid Redstone?" she asked. "I heard that man call you a—"

"Witch, Dottie, and that's as good a word as any," Ingrid said, cutting her off before she could fill in the gap with her own preferred vocabulary. "Believe me when I tell you, I'm the best that's ever been."

"I'd say I believe you," Dot said, "but I'm not sure belief enters into this."

"That's fair," Ingrid said. "Before you start worrying about it, we ought—"

The percussive crack of a pistol shot interrupted her. Jimmy the Freak had a gun out of a hidden shoulder-holster and was actually *shooting* at them while he tried to lurch to his feet. Mr. Howl (who'd never stopped making noise) looked to be making a similar recovery. He spotted Ingrid when he got to his knees and brought the volume back up on his booming mantra:

"*Wiiiiiiiiiiiiiiiiiiiiiiiiiiiitch*! *Witch, witch, WITCH!*"

"Run!" Ingrid shouted, seizing Dottie's hand and sprinting for the stage door. Jimmy fired two more shots after them. The rounds went wild, puffing harmlessly into the quilted sound-baffling insulation that lined the studio's walls. Ingrid kicked the film magazine ahead of herself, then scooped it up into her arms before they reached the door, which Dottie threw open.

"Get back here you *bitch*!" Jimmy screamed, attempting to give chase without exacerbating his terrier-inflicted genital injuries. The Yelling Man lurched to his feet and wobbled after them too, he and his boss bellowing about witches and/or bitches as they did their best to pursue the fleeing women.

Chapter Two

THE sight of two panicked ladies and a little dog bursting out a door and racing hell-bent for the lot's front gate inspired more than a few of the studio denizens milling about to emulate them. Tensions were high—nobody really knew what was happening, and running amok seemed as reasonable an option as any. Ingrid heard yelps and shouts behind her and realized as many as a dozen people were following them, men and women both, in costumes and in street clothes. They seemed convinced that she and Dottie had seen, if not the imperial Japanese Army marching down Ventura Boulevard, then at least something worth running away from. And that seemed like good enough intelligence to act on, on this afternoon of madness and uncertainty.

Dot was cackling, her eyes bright with unaccustomed excitement. Ernest bounced along beside them, keeping pace with no obvious effort. Ingrid kept the big double-reeled film magazine cradled in her arms while she and Dottie sprinted, seeking to put as much distance between themselves and Jimmy the Freak's soundstage as they possibly could. The magazine was solid and well-taped, made of hard rubber or Bakelite or something like that, and Ingrid had a devil of a time trying to get it open. She felt like an otter wrestling with a stubborn oyster. She even tried bashing it against the corner of a building as they ran past, but only managed to dent and crack it, without apparent injury to the seal.

She couldn't get the film out to expose it to the sun. The best she could do was to yank it out an arm's length at a time, which she did, though the effort resulted in increasingly long and tangled rat's nests of celluloid trailing along behind her, giving her more chance than she liked of tripping and falling as she fled.

Jimmy the Freak and his defective detective came after them, Jimmy hobbling in a bowlegged, ball-coddling fashion, while Mr. Howl lurched, spun and bounced off the walls as he tried to keep his balance and run in a straight line. He lived up to Ingrid's nicknames for him with every jarring impact, shouting and hollering at the top of his lungs. The gathered flocks of extras and technicians parted to give them plenty of space.

Even running in heels, even with Dottie in perhaps less than stellar physical condition (given her habits and proclivities), the women were able to outpace the men and lose them amidst the maze of narrow passages that made up the studio backlot. Ingrid's last sight of Jimmy had him holding up his wrist-radio (the incredible thing was hardly bigger than a matchbook), no doubt to call in more backup.

They had a bit of a lead. More and more people were following after them, though, convinced by social reinforcement that they must know something the rest did not. The more individuals who joined their flight the more plausible this seemed, and the only problem with it was that their comet's tail of running mates made for a pretty unmistakable indicator of their direction of travel. All a half-bright pursuer had to do was follow along with the crowds.

They had to get off the lot and far away from here. That was the only solution. (Though it was not lost on Ingrid that circumstance had somehow deposited her right back in front of Jimmy the Freak, even after she jumped across decades to avoid him.)

She spotted Alfred, Alma, and Alan up ahead, talking with other people in suits and business attire. Producers and executives.

She, Dottie, and Ernest hurried toward them, elbowing their way through confused crowds.

"Dottie!" Alan said, spotting her as she and Ingrid approached. "There you are, I was wondering—"

"Alan, give me the keys," Dottie burbled. "The keys to the Packard!"

"Dottie, what?" Alan asked, bemused, taking in his little wife's uncharacteristically excitable condition. "You don't drive, you don't even have a license, what—"

"The keys, dear, and don't ask stupid questions," Dot demanded. "This is Ingrid Redstone, and she'll hand you your ass in a hat! *Ha!*"

Dottie continued to giggle like a stoned schoolgirl having the delirious time of her life. Alan looked to Ingrid, but found no answers in her shrug. He fished the keys from his pocket and handed them over. Defying Dottie was not a thing he could do.

"Alfred," Ingrid said. "Mr. Hitchcock—you said something about a murder case William Selig was involved in."

"Yes," Alfred said, looking somewhat taken aback by her and Dottie's sudden reappearance. He winced when Ingrid smashed the film magazine against the ground, still without getting it open. "Yes, I believe he was shot in the arm while trying to defend one of his filmmakers, who was shot dead by a mad employee."

"Do you remember the filmmaker's name? Was it Francis Boggs?"

"Why yes, I believe it may have been," Alfred said. "He's since fallen into obscurity, and most if not all of his films have been lost. That old nitrate stock either burned or decayed so readily. Why do you ask?"

"What year was that?" Ingrid asked further, instead of answering. "Do you remember?"

Alfred shook his head (and his jowls). "Some time in the '10s. Before the Great War. Surely not later than 1915."

"1911," Alma said. "The employee was a Japanese groundskeeper who said a man came and told him Boggs was evil and had to die."

She shrugged, when both Alfred and Ingrid looked at her.

"Movies and murder, our favorite subjects," the little bespectacled woman said by way of explanation. "Put them together and it's the sort of thing I can't help but remember. It's what you keep me around for, isn't it, Alfred?"

Alfred didn't seem to know what to say, though Ingrid did: "Thank you."

Alma nodded, still not entirely convinced about the mysterious Miss Redstone. Ingrid supposed she couldn't blame her. Trouble would seem to follow in her wake, from Miss Reville's point of view.

1911, though. The year she'd skipped. She might've known. Everything went straight to hell when she wasn't around to keep an eye on it. The thought that her Uncle Frank's work had been lost to time already, and his name forgotten beyond its association with his own lurid murder, pained her deeply.

But it was never too late for anything in Mictlantecuhtli's world. That was what Jimmy the Freak didn't understand, and if Ingrid had her way he never would.

The Freak made the scene even as she was thinking about him. Perhaps he'd followed the trail of exposed film. It spun out more than fifty feet behind her by now. Jimmy was in fact standing on it. His Yelling Man wobbled up beside him, pointed at Ingrid, and screamed:

"*Wiiiiiiiiiiiitch!*"

Dozens of heads swiveled in his direction.

"Gun!" somebody shrieked, and Jimmy looked at the remarked-upon object like he had no idea how it had arrived in his hand. Others took up the cry—*Gun! Look out! He has a gun!*—and tried to scatter, in a panic.

Scattering a group of dozens if not hundreds is not easily accomplished between the tightly-packed structures of a studio lot. Ingrid stepped back from the swell of panic that erupted like a fireball between her and the Freak. The danger of someone being trampled or crushed here was suddenly very real.

A powerful arm seized her around the waist and a big hand clapped yet another chloroform-soaked rag over her face. She bucked and struggled and the hand fell away several seconds later. Ingrid wrenched away from this new attacker and sucked in a huge, clean breath. She'd managed not to inhale any of the chemical, but it still burned her eyes.

So she only blearily saw the man who'd grabbed her—one of Jimmy's, no doubt—twisting and screaming as he tried to pull a knitting needle out of his lower back, where it looked to be lodged about kidney-deep.

A second man grabbed at Dottie—who was grinning and triumphantly brandishing her other needle like a miniature rapier—and pulled a gun out from under his jacket.

Alan decked him without hesitation, and twisted the weapon out of his hand as he fell, then kicked the wind out of his lungs for good measure.

"I did attend West Point, you might recall," he said to his wide-eyed wife.

Jimmy and Howl were shoving their way through the crowd, shouting, Jimmy waving his gun. It did more to stir people into a frenzy than disperse them, as there was really nowhere for them to go.

Ingrid yanked on the still-unbroken magazine and Jimmy's feet, tangled in whorls of ripped-out film, went out from under him. He disappeared behind a screen of agitated bodies, taking several others down with him in such close quarters. Ingrid hoped nobody would be hurt who didn't have it coming. She yanked again, and the last inches of film ripped loose from the light-tight case. Ingrid heaved it at Mr. Howl, who still looked uncertain on his feet, and caught him right in the face with it. He flailed over backwards and fell heavily on top of his boss.

Jimmy's gun went off. The bullet pinged off the side of a stage, and people stampeded. Ingrid shoved Dottie and Alma into a recessed doorway behind her. Alan and Alfred squeezed in as well, with some difficulty.

Newly-arriving henchmen of Jimmy's were swept back by the turbulent human wave, which surged past Ingrid and her clump of friends without dragging them along.

The time to flee was now, before Jimmy and his people could rally.

"Dot, where's your car?" Ingrid said. "I've gotta go."

"In lot D, where they exile the writers. You'll never find it yourself. Come on!"

Dottie seized her hand and pulled her into the mass exodus. Ingrid glanced back to see Jimmy and his bleeding, bellowing chauffer shoving each other to their feet, trying to balance though neither of them was feeling particularly stable. Others of his men hurried in to help him up, then Dot pulled her around a corner and he was gone from Ingrid's view.

Chapter Three

DOT and Ingrid made it to Lot D a few long strides ahead of Jimmy and his people. They couldn't get into the car and off the lot fast enough to escape detection, even though Dot trampled quite a bit of landscaping in her haste and smashed right through a red-and-white striped wooden arm that lowered across the exit gate. That she did not drive often was fairly obvious. She flipped Jimmy the Freak the bird and honked the horn when they passed him. Ingrid saw him in the Packard's rearview mirror, gesturing and shouting at his minions while the panicked employees of Universal Studios poured around him like a tidal wave, out the East Gate and onto the streets of Studio City.

Dot and Ingrid didn't get but a couple of blocks before several large rounded cars screeched into view around the last turn they'd taken, along with a longer, sleeker model that sported an elaborate hood ornament—undoubtedly the Freak's personal staff car.

They were being chased.

Dot floored it, and the Packard surged through a red signal just as the bell dinged and the little flag reading STOP dropped into view. Dottie's tires squealed when she left Barham Boulevard and merged onto Forest Lawn Drive, headed east and outpacing their pursuers.

Ingrid thought they were headed in the direction of the old Carretera del Rey, the path back to Mickey, though she couldn't be sure. There'd been nothing but fields and the occasional farmhouse out this way as of 1912. Now, circa 1941, it was all low-roofed cityscape, dotted with planted trees as far as the eye could see. All the way to the snow-capped mountain peaks in the northeastern distance.

Things had changed so much she didn't know how she would ever find her way back to the Silent Tower. There were no Teonanactl mushrooms growing along these paved streets.

The swiftest of their pursuers nudged Dottie's rear bumper with his front one and the Packard spun across the road, barely missing oncoming traffic. Angry horns sounded as Mrs. Parker screamed and fought the steering wheel. Cars swerved out of their way. The auto that hit them shot past as the Packard skidded around in a tight circle, its tires smoking. One of them burst with a muffled pop, and the car listed alarmingly toward its right rear corner.

By the time it settled to a rocking stop on the wrong side of the yellow line, the attackers' car was coming about to have another go at them.

Dottie exchanged one glance with Ingrid and received a nod of approval. She took a quick (but deep) pull of scotch from her silver flask and then, shrieking with insane glee, jammed her foot down on the gas pedal.

Their damaged rear tire tore loose from its rim as the Packard shot forward on a collision course with the carload of henchmen, kicking up a dramatic roostertail of golden sparks.

The car swerved out of their way at the last second and Ingrid could hear the shouts of the men inside, even over Dottie's war-whoop of triumph. A second later they heard a screech and a jarring crash behind them, when the car that had feinted to avoid them plowed head-on into the next pursuing vehicle. Ingrid, craning her neck back, saw the second car's windshield explode outward in a galaxy of glittering glass stars as one of the unrestrained men inside slammed through it and flew out onto the hood.

She couldn't look away fast enough to avoid seeing blood burst into the air along with the glass, but the wreck receded swiftly behind them, and she was able to push the awful imagery out of her mind—though she suspected she might be revisiting it in her dreams for quite some time to come.

The smash-up caused enough of a traffic jam that the remaining pursuers—three more cars that Ingrid could see, including Jimmy's long, low one, sure to be piloted by the Yelling Man—were momentarily held up. Jimmy's car was attempting to nudge past the abstract sculpture in the middle of the road that had been a pair of automobiles less than a minute ago when Ingrid turned back around and sank down into her seat.

"Where to now, lady?" Dottie enquired, cab-driver style. She was still grinning and not at all troubled by the vehicular violence. Their tireless rim made a horrible noise as it ground along the blacktop.

"Back when I came from," Ingrid said, not quite loud enough to be heard over the racket.

"How do we get there?"

"I have no idea. Can you take me back to where you found me this morning?"

"Don't think so, dear," Dottie said. "Maybe Alan could, but I don't remember routes and streets. And besides, I don't think this car is going to make it."

"I need to get back there one way or the other. It's the only way back to... where I started from."

"Which is where?"

"It's not important," Ingrid said, and Dottie looked over at her.

"You owe me better than that. I've risked my life *and* wrecked my car for you, at this point. I'd say that entitles me to some answers, at the very least."

"You wouldn't believe me."

"I'm feeling more receptive than I might on some other afternoon."

Ingrid spotted a dirt access road leading up into the hills behind what signs proclaimed to be the Forest Lawn Memorial Park. "Turn off there," she instructed, and Dottie did so as Ingrid explained: "Those sparks make us awfully conspicuous."

Traveling up the dirt path did curtail both the noise and the fireworks caused by their lost tire, though they weren't getting anywhere fast. If Jimmy and his people guessed they'd taken this road and it wound up leading nowhere, then they might have a significant problem on their hands.

Ingrid hoped their pursuers would continue on east, toward a locale the signs along the side of the highway called Glendale... although she doubted she could be that lucky.

"You called yourself a witch, back there," Dottie said.

"I did," Ingrid said. "And I am. Initiate of the Hermetic Orders of the Golden Dawn in London and the Golden Chain in Los Angeles, now under the patronage of Mictlantecuhtli, the Aztec King of the Dead."

"Holy shit," Dottie said, and Ingrid had to picture Alan cringing. "You're a *fascinating* brand of crazy, aren't you?"

"I'm telling you the truth."

"I know you are. At least I can see you're not lying. For what that's worth."

She didn't go so far as to say she actually believed her.

That was all right with Ingrid. Better for Dot if she *didn't* believe, really.

"So there's organization to it? To your world?" Dottie asked. "You're part of a... a hierarchy, or something, of witches and warlocks and wizards?"

"I'm more of an independent operator these days."

Dot nodded, chewing it over for a moment. "Where is it you mean to go?" she asked.

"1911," Ingrid said.

Dottie stopped the car, calmly, and just looked at her. A group of men stood around on the trail some few dozen yards ahead. Men with horses. They looked like maybe they'd been running sprints down the track here at the rear of the cemetery for a bit of Sunday afternoon diversion, though at the moment they were all huddled around a portable radio, listening to the news from Pearl Harbor in rapt silence.

"What are you talking about?" Dottie asked.

"Mictlan is the realm of the dead, Dottie—the name the Aztec people gave it more than a thousand years ago. My lover is its king. I can travel there by his permission and come back out at any point in human memory. Well, at a lot of points in human memory. I suppose I can't go back before the Nahuatlaca built the Pyramid, can I? That had to come before the Hole in the Sky."

Dottie was openly gawping at her by now. Ingrid realized she was rambling about things the small writer couldn't possibly have a frame of reference for.

"I'm going back in time to save a friend Jimmy the Freak killed thirty years ago," she said. "*That's* who I am, and that's what I can do."

"Holy shit," Dottie repeated. It was becoming her new catchphrase, and wouldn't Mr. Campbell be thrilled about that. "That's why you asked Mrs. Hitchcock about the date of that old murder, isn't it?"

"They're married?" Ingrid asked. "Alma and Alfred?"

"Oh—why, yes," Dot said. "She does use her maiden name, but she *is* Mrs. Reville-Hitchcock, ecclesiastically speaking."

"For fuck's *sake*, Dottie, why'd you parade me around in front of her husband then? And does *anyone* use a married name anymore?"

These film people were worse than the label-phobic sorcerers Ingrid knew, afraid of losing their power by revealing their true identities.

"She hates me because the studio *and* her husband both want me to work on his goddamn picture!" Dottie spat, defensively. "Alma thought the job should've gone to her."

"Well… you need to be nicer to them," Ingrid said. "Don't cock up their marriage. I want you to promise me."

"It's irrelevant," Mrs. Parker said. "Because if you're going back to 1911, I'm damn well coming with you."

"Oh, Dottie…" Ingrid said. "No. You can't do that."

"Pish," Dottie said. "I can't *not*, if what you're telling me is true. We'll bet on every World Series between then and now and become millionaires. Well, maybe not that, as I don't actually give two tugs on a dead dog's cock for sport, so I don't know who won those games, but we'll find *some*thing to bet on, won't we? The outcome of the Great War, maybe. I know who won that."

Now it was Ingrid's turn just to look at her, sadly.

"Well, why *can't* I then?" Dot snarled. She took out a cigarette and lit it with shaking hands. "What makes *you* so fucking special, Miss Witch? Or do you just not want to share?"

"Mickey—*Mictlantecuhtli*—is the King of the Dead, Dot," Ingrid explained. "Crossing into his realm is a one-way trip."

"Then why can you do it? You're pale enough, but you're not a ghost."

"Because I'm… I don't honestly know, for sure," Ingrid said. "I'm different."

"Well, lucky you."

"It has something to do with the things I've learned, and the things I've done, I think," Ingrid said, frowning and considering the question for herself in light of Dottie's having posed it.

"Which things?" Dot asked.

"Yes, witch things," Ingrid said, nodding. "They change you when you learn them, sometimes. They set you outside the normal flow of things and alter your perspectives. They make your actual world into something slightly different from what everybody else calls 'real,' and somehow that lets me cross over. That dual citizenship between the worlds."

"That makes very little sense to me," Dottie said. "It frankly sounds like a steaming pile of horseshit."

"I'm sorry for that. I'd like to show you the things I've seen, I really would. But it is the way it is. I can only travel alone."

Dot nodded, gripping the steering wheel, and her eyes glistened with tears that didn't quite fall. She blinked them back angrily and sucked on her cigarette, blowing out smoke in a hard, brief jet.

"The worst part is I *do* believe you, you- you—"

"Bitch, Dottie. You can say it. I can only imagine how disappointed you must be."

"Can you?" Dot scowled and smashed out her half-smoked cigarette. "You convince me of these miracles, and then you tell me I'm too common to partake?"

Ingrid heard engines in the distance. She poked her head out the window and looked back down the hill in time to see Jimmy's long car and two smaller vehicles pulling off of paved Forest Lawn Drive and onto the dirt access road, behind them.

They'd either spotted Dot's car up here, despite the tree cover, or intuited where they'd gone. Jimmy wasn't going to be outsmarted by a trick as simple as ducking down a side road.

They had perhaps five minutes before Vreke and Company caught up with them.

Ingrid looked over at Dot, who acted so misanthropic and yet had done so much to help her, on such short acquaintance. She was moved by the writer's willingness, even eagerness, to take a ludicrous stand as soon as she found one that needed taking.

Ingrid liked her. That razor tongue defended a damaged yet decent heart. She wished they had more time to talk, and really know each other. But that wasn't to be.

"I think our wheels are on their last legs," Dot said, perhaps seeing the truth of the situation written across Ingrid's face. "So what do we do now, Miss Redstone? Embark on a hike?"

"We part ways, Mrs. Parker," Ingrid said. "The Freak and his people won't bother you once I'm gone."

"You're sure about that?"

Ingrid nodded. "I'll make sure he was never born if he tries."

A time-traveler's threat.

Dottie frowned, and nodded. "Will I see you again?"

"I hope you will. I do have all the time in the world, so... maybe."

Dot lit another cigarette. She wouldn't look at her again. "Why don't you get the fuck out of my car, witch? My husband will be wondering whatever happened to me. I have a feeling I may be wondering that myself. None of this is going to seem very real in the days ahead, I fear."

Ingrid nodded, patted Ernest on the head, and stepped out of the Packard.

She could hear Jimmy the Freak and his people powering up the trail in their big dark cars. She didn't have a moment to waste.

She sprinted over to the nearby men and their dozen or so horses, all of whom seemed to be paying at least as much attention to her at this point as they were to the news on the radio.

A smallish bay-colored stallion seemed to be at the center of the group. A natural charismatic. He whinnied and tossed his mane proudly, and Ingrid zeroed right in on him. She ran up to the older, well-dressed man she guessed to be his owner.

"Bet I know where you got those shoes," she said, pointing at his feet.

When material worked for her, she stuck with it.

The three men who seemed attached to the horse—one of whom Ingrid pegged as a trainer, while the other, a ginger like herself, might've been a tallish jockey—all exchanged startled, even astounded looks.

"Holy fucking shit," the probable owner said. It was a surprisingly popular refrain here in 1941. "Your name's Ingrid Redstone, isn't it?"

"How on earth do you know that?"

"There's a legend about this horse's great-grandsire gettin' won in that very bet you just offered. Won by a redhead named Redstone," the jockey-type told her. "But that can't be you—it woulda been thirty years ago!"

"This horse is Fair Play's descendant?" she asked, looking at him anew. He snorted and almost seemed to wink at her.

"He is indeed, Miss Redstone," the owner said, breaking into a grin. "And he's the fastest horse that ever lived."

"Well, that's convenient," Ingrid said.

"He retired last year," the jockey said. "We been runnin' quarter-mile sprints for the hell of it out here—some race people do, on the weekends, sometimes. The story always went that Fair Play was never sick or lame again when he wandered back after getting won. Like he was still in his racing form till the day he kicked, and I know he sired dozens of colts. Seabiscuit's grandsire was only one. You can't really be you, though. That's just a story, about that bet. You ain't even thirty years old."

"So," Ingrid said. "Can I borrow him, or what?"

"Tom," the owner said, with a gesture toward Ingrid. The trainer, Tom, who hadn't yet said a single word, handed the reins right over.

"Take care of him, okay?" he said now, and Ingrid nodded, just as Jimmy the Freak and his small entourage rolled up into view behind them.

Dottie, bless her blackened little heart, backed her damaged Packard across the trail. Jimmy's big car moved forward to make contact with her bumper. Both engines revved hard and screamed as the Freak's car fought to push Dot's into the ditch.

Several of his henchmen got out of the other two cars, with guns drawn.

Ingrid didn't have even a minute, now. She swung herself up onto the small stallion.

"Jesus, Charles, you're not gonna let her have him, are you?" the jockey said, echoing sentiments another rider had expressed thirty years in the past.

"You pipe down, Red," Charles the owner said. "Of course I'm gonna let her have him. When somebody out of what's practically a fucking fairy tale asks you for a favor, I think the best policy is to grant it. Don't you?"

"Yeah, maybe, but…" Red the jockey started, though he didn't seem to know how to finish. "They were a superstitious lot, these racing people. "Aww, *shit*."

Jimmy the Freak's car managed to force Dottie's into the brush at the side of the trail. Ingrid heard her shout a shrill "Fuck *you*!" at them as she waved her middle finger out the window, with her cigarette holder still clutched in her hand.

It was exactly the way Ingrid wanted to remember Mrs. Parker, if she never managed to see her again.

But now the reiterating race to the Silent Tower was back on. If this horse really was a descendant of the replacement Mickey had made for good old Fair Play, thirty years and a single day ago, then some small part of him must belong to el Rey. He might be able to find his way back to the place where the unusual branch of his lineage began. It was something Ingrid could not do, right now, on her own.

"If you want to throw things at the men in those cars or otherwise harass and assault them, I'd really appreciate it," she said to the horse crowd at large.

"Who are they?" the jockey named Red asked uncertainly, looking back at the cars.

"Spies for the Emperor," Ingrid said. She figured Japan probably still had an emperor. "Show the bastards no quarter, boys!"

Then she waved brightly to Jimmy the Freak as she nudged her heels into her new mount's sides and launched him down the dirt trail at the back of the cemetery with a wild battle cry.

Jimmy and his minions roared right after her in their bulky motorcars, amidst a hail of thrown rocks, dashed beer bottles, and hurled epithets.

Chapter Four

NGRID hadn't quite caught the famous horse's name, even though someone had mentioned it. She thought it sounded like 'Tea Biscuit' or some such nonsense. Racehorses always had the queerest names.

She could easily believe his owner's assertion that this was the fastest horse who ever lived. It had to be true that his great-grandsire was Mickey's flawless reproduction of Fair Play, as no creature of purely natural origin could possibly run like *this*.

He moved like he had a pair of rockets strapped to either side of his ass. His speed felt utterly supernatural. Greenery blurred away into long impressionist brushstrokes on either side of them, and the horse's hooves barely seemed to clip the earth. Riding him felt as much like flying as running.

Ingrid assumed her new friend had been quite the champion in his racing days.

"Find Mictlantecuhtli," she murmured into his velvety triangle of an ear. "Take me back to Mickey now, quick as you can."

The little horse ran like he'd been born to run and not for any other purpose.

Still, the big cars behind her had some powerful motors under their hoods. And the chaparral up here was too thick for Ingrid to leave the path and travel overland. Hooves and fetlocks would've become disastrously tangled in the underbrush, ending the chase too swiftly.

It seemed like a pretty fair match, this horse versus those automobiles, and Ingrid couldn't say how it might shake out. The cars would seem to have the advantage in terms of sheer power, but they were built for paved roads. They couldn't compete with the living creature in terms of agility on this rutted dirt access track through the swath of preserved wilderness that lay between the Valley and the rest of Los Angeles. City drivers had no experience on this sort of terrain, whereas Ingrid had learned to ride from William 'Buffalo Bill' Cody when she was eight years old, with supplementary instruction in stunts and tricks from any number of his famous Congress of Rough Riders of the World, and there wasn't a cowboy dead or alive who had a thing on her when it came to horsemanship.

So the contest was apt to be interesting.

It looked to Ingrid like the path ahead led up and over the low mountains, and then probably down into Hollywood (Home of the Silent Tower; they could put it on a Rotary Club sign at the town limits), if her sense of the geography was correct. Her little horse (and what the *hell* was his name again? Beef Brisket? Wee Misfit?) seemed to know right where he was going, with no more coaxing from her. He climbed easily, swiftly, taking the grade in stride, and Ingrid could hear the motorcars' engines first laboring and then receding behind her. The loudest sound in the worlds seemed to be the drumbeat of galloping hooves.

She enjoyed a moment or two of blessed quiet after she crested the top of the hill and started down the far side, a moment filled only with the tattoo of rapid hooves and the rush of wind in her ears, before the trio of cars topped the ridge behind her and proceeded to hurtle down after her at a jarring, bouncing, half-controlled and fast-increasing rate of speed. Ingrid looked back, though she could probably have heard them coming just fine without the visual confirmation.

It didn't do a lot to comfort her.

"Please," she murmured, leaning down low against the horse's neck, putting her face close to his ear. "Don't let them catch us."

And the horse seemed to hear her. He poured on more velocity in his eagerness to please. Ingrid dug her white-knuckled fingers into his mane when she felt herself slide back in the saddle from the sudden, startling force of his acceleration. She held on tight, as falling off at speeds like these, over brambly and rock-strewn terrain, would spell either painful death or ugly injury.

What she didn't expect to see when she glanced back again was her own Congress of Rough Riders cresting the hill, in pursuit of her pursuers. All of Forest Lawn's horserace enthusiasts came pouring down the mountainside after Jimmy the Freak's three cars—a mounted cavalry at least two dozen men strong. More than a few of them had guns and were firing them into the air like wild west outlaws as they ran down the Freak and his henchmen, whom Ingrid had labeled as enemy spies.

She let loose with her own shriek of glee. Her bay-colored horse responded to her high spirits by feinting right and charging faster still down a hiking trail that was never meant to accommodate vehicles of any kind. He seemed to be having a glorious time demonstrating his talents.

The men in the cars didn't seem bothered by the narrowness of the trail. They took to the new path in a tight single-file line, their tires kicking great billowing clouds of powdery brown dirt up into the air.

The race people from the cemetery came pounding right after them, guns blazing into the sky.

Ingrid grinned. The wind of rapid locomotion whipped her long red hair back from her face. She was finally starting to enjoy her visit to 1941.

When she looked over to her left she saw, to her astonishment, another rider pacing her on a large black stallion. He had the head of a lion and held a fat, twisting green viper in his right hand. Ingrid shouted and jerked back when the snake snapped at her and she slid dangerously over to one side in her saddle. She righted herself promptly and threw her arms around Seed Packet's neck as he rounded a tight bend, hugging the inside of it like the rail at Santa Anita. (She wished she'd caught the poor horse's actual name, as her guesses at it were growing increasingly random.)

The vision was gone when she looked over again, but she knew what it meant—that Jimmy the Freak wasn't content to rely upon firearms and motorcars to bring her down. He had other methods in his repertoire, older and far more dangerous ones.

Ingrid looked to her right and there the lion-headed man was again, on the opposite side of her now, baring his fangs in an obscene, tongue-lolling grin. His black steed's hooves made no noise upon the earth, nor did they kick up any dust.

She knew him, Ingrid did: Lord Vinea, the forty-fifth spirit named in the *Lemegeton Clavicula Salomonis*, the Lesser Key of Solomon the King, also known as the Goetia. The entity was a natural choice for ceremonially-minded Jimmy to evoke in this situation, as Vinea's specific office was to discover '*Thinges hidden, Wytches, and Thinges present past & yet to comme,*' according to the medieval grimoire whose seventy-two entries Ingrid had studied in some detail during her sojourn with the Golden Dawn.

She imagined Deus Es Canis Inversus must have drawn the requisite Circle of the Art right on the floor of his fancy car to effect the conjuration. He *was* good at this stuff. Creative and resourceful, almost like herself. Ingrid had to give him that.

Her ride leapt over a burbling, moss-banked stream that trickled down out of the hills (a stream Ingrid had long ago bathed in with the Queen of California), then suddenly the wilderness gave out and they found themselves running full-tilt down a paved residential street. Lines of cars sat parked along either curb, and rows of posh houses stood situated on green lawns behind them. Signage indicated the street was called North Hobart Boulevard. A character actor named Hobart Bosworth had appeared with her in *Race Tout.* The random memory arced across her thoughts like a shooting star.

The stream was obstacle enough to fox the wheeled vehicles, at least for a minute or two. Their drivers were already backing off from the high bank and angling north toward a bridge Ingrid could see in the near distance, just blocks away. When she looked back over her shoulder she saw that grinning Vinea was riding hard on her heels. He whipped the air with the viper he carried and the wind tore his thick brown mane back from his tawny catface—all in that eerie, dreamlike silence.

The racing enthusiasts were also still in the game. They came sailing and bounding over the stream on their horses to fall in behind Jimmy's cars when the three vehicles rejoined the chase after their all-too-brief detour across that bridge and around the intervening block.

This was not a good day to be suspected of espionage, as Ingrid had counted on. The whole Pearl Harbor thing had tempers running hot.

Ingrid's horse hooked left and sprinted straight down the center of Hollywood Boulevard itself.

Pedestrians on the sidewalks snapped their heads in her direction. Cars with fat rounded fenders veered out of their way with comical haste. Her mount pushed on, running faster than ever and easily outpacing uninvolved motorists who were just trying to use the roads and not win a goddamn horserace. Jimmy and his people chased her through red signals, disrupting opposing traffic and drawing honks, startled shouts, and obscene gestures.

Her horse feinted around a long red trolley as it trundled through an intersection at Western. Tires screeched behind her and hooves clattered. Leering Vinea kept pace on her left, eyeing her while his laboring black horse snorted and tossed his head.

Ingrid's horse dodged away from the demon governor's hissing viper, dropped down two blocks, and hung a right onto Sunset.

So her equine friend *did* know where he was going. That was a relief, though Ingrid had to be the only person on the street currently feeling such an emotion. The sight of the parade she was leading down the middle of the thoroughfare—including a medieval demon, several aggressive motorcars, and a whole posse of whooping men on horseback—was not likely to set the agitated minds of the public at ease.

Someone was apt to get hurt if Jimmy's conjurations caused a widespread panic, and Ingrid didn't want to see that happen. These people had enough to deal with, considering war had broken out in the Pacific.

The Great Earl Vinea continued to pace her in unnerving silence, only now he was snarling too, his bifurcated cat's lips rippling back along his blunt, fang-studded snout. The snake-whip in his hand hissed and spat and tried to strike when Vinea snapped it at her in a rage.

Ingrid ducked aside in the saddle and seized the snake in her fist, just behind its skull, and wrenched it right out of the demonic nobleman's grasp. Lion-headed Vinea yowled, but his big black horse never faltered or slowed its pace.

Ingrid plugged the viper's lashing tail right into the creature's own snapping maw. It clamped onto its own posterior end and began to chow down, swallowing a few inches of its body at a time, tightening into an ever-smaller ring. Its eyes were as mindless as shiny ball bearings.

Ingrid tossed the self-consuming snake casually over Vinea's thick-maned head.

It cinched down around the demon horseman's neck like a collar and tightened before he could get a hand underneath it. He roared in outrage, but the sound died off into a strangled squawk as his snake devoured yet another large gulp of itself, crushing its master's throat in the process. Lord Vinea's sparkling cat's eyes bulged with utterly unanticipated horror.

One moment the demon earl had five chakra points, two less than a standard human being... and then he had only four.

Ingrid looked back to see the creature's popped-off lion head bouncing down the double yellow line behind her like a trophy fallen off the back of a safari caravan. It burst apart into a spray of dust and Vinea's disconnected crown chakra swirled away like so much vapor.

The snake—Ingrid's extemporaneous Ouroboros—finished itself off and disappeared from the road surface with a soft pop she may have imagined more than heard.

Vinea's muscular black stallion continued to run on beside her smaller-but-quicker bay, but without the urgency now, and he looked distinctly confused when the rest of his rider's body fell out of the saddle and shattered on the pavement into the same sort of dust to which his head had also crumbled.

Ingrid lost sight of him when her horse stopped dead in the middle of the street and stood there looking amiably at the chaos surrounding him, like he was at the calm eye of a raging storm.

Jimmy's car swerved to avoid her at the last instant before impact and Ingrid cringed when he shot past, missing her and her unflappable mount by mere inches. His wake blew her hair around her face in a blinding red cloud. Jim's two carloads of henchmen parted from their tight formation and skidded around either side of her. Forest Lawn's Rough Riders came next, a permeable wave of stampeding horseflesh that looked like it would smash her flat but instead engulfed her as the angry race fans bore down on Jimmy.

Her horse wouldn't budge an inch, no matter how desperately Ingrid yanked on his reins. Halfway down the block, the drivers of the Freak's staff car and its two satellites all slammed on their brakes and slid into impromptu U-turns, with their white-sided tires smoking.

Only then did Ingrid look up and realize they were standing in front of the Silent Tower.

That was why her horse wouldn't move—because they'd arrived at her requested destination and she'd been too distracted to notice.

She couldn't go inside, though. Not in plain view of Jimmy the Freak. That would be the same as handing him a key to the front door.

The issue was resolved when a sleek Arabian mare loped past bearing two riders: the quiet horse trainer named Tom and, nestled in front of him, a tiny, prim, middle aged woman holding a lit cigarette in one hand and clutching a large knitting bag to her chest with the other.

Jimmy's long car roared back in Ingrid's direction. An instant before it passed the elegant brown horse, Mrs. Parker removed not her small silver flask but a large green bottle of strong Scotch whisky from her knitting kit. She touched the smoldering tip of her cigarette to a wadded up scarf she'd crammed into the bottle's mouth and dashed the whole affair hard against Jimmy the Freak's windshield.

A bright smear of fire erupted across the glass, and the unsuspecting driver—who Ingrid could still hear yelling from within the cabin—must have jerked the wheel, because the car veered to the right and smashed straight into the nearest streetlamp. Both headlights shattered and the car's front grill caved in around the lamp's concrete post.

Ingrid saw her old nemesis the Yelling Man thrown hard against the steering wheel by the force of the crash. He bounced back against his seat, slumped there, and lay still. The limousine's bashed-in engine faltered and vented steam with a loud hiss.

Jimmy's other two cars screeched to a halt and their occupants piled out. Ingrid braced herself to continue the fight, but the Freak's hired muscle had apparently had enough. All of his men, half a dozen by Ingrid's count, turned tail and ran for it when a sizable crowd of enraged equestrians and interested pedestrians converged on the vehicles. A few folks chased after them, but it looked like they'd get away in all the confusion.

The cars themselves made easier targets for the crowd's ire. People ringed in around them, rocking them back and forth on their springs. Jimmy's grand conveyance received the most attention from the rioters, being the largest and most-ornamented of the three vehicles, despite its being on fire. The cursing mob had it rolled over on its side in very short order. Mr. Freak himself scrambled out through one of the broken rear windows and more or less fell onto the street. He landed hard and the crowd surged in with a collective snarl, but they were driven back when the car's leaking gas tank went up in a fireball, with a hollow bang.

Flaming shrapnel flew and a column of greasy black smoke rolled up into the sky.

Ingrid saw Jimmy throw his hands over his head as he rolled away, extinguishing his coat almost as soon as it caught fire. He found his feet and ran for it. A few observant individuals chased after him, but the spectacle of a blazing, overturned limousine was a compelling sight, and Ingrid guessed that Jim would get away too. He was handy with his sleight-of-mind techniques, and besides, this unruly mob was lashing out half-blindly over an act of war by a foreign aggressor. The Freak and his fleeing rentboys had a ready-made smokescreen of mass confusion they might vanish into if they were half smart, and Ingrid knew Jimmy to be at least that.

He wouldn't find the Silent Tower when he returned to inspect the charred husk of his once-fine automobile. If he hadn't figured out where the old Tree had gone by now, Ingrid was willing to bet he never would. Even his now-dead driver, who'd chased her here in 1912, had never been able to explain it to his employer. Ingrid guessed he'd blotted out the memory in order to function, even to the limited degree he'd been managing before today. It's what people did with experiences they couldn't assimilate.

She doubted she'd seen the last of James Vreke—though she'd seen plenty of him for now.

The Arabian bearing Dottie and Tom trotted up next to Ingrid's bay while the rest of the rioters set about overturning and igniting Jimmy's other two abandoned cars. The acrid smoke from the fires was growing thick.

Dot grinned from ear to ear when Tom helped her down from the back of their horse, setting her on the pavement.

"Do you realize that's Seabiscuit you're sitting on?" She had bright-eyed Ernest zipped into the front of her coat. "*The* Seabiscuit? Who you just rode down Sunset Boulevard?"

Ingrid had to restrain herself from slapping her own forehead. None of her guesses at the horse's name had even come close. "No, I did not know that," she said. The apparently famous animal neighed contentedly. Ingrid swung herself down from his saddle and petted his short-coated cheek, murmuring a quiet thank you. He seemed pleased to have been able to help.

"Where'd you learn that trick with the bottle, Dot?" she asked, turning to Mrs. Parker as trainer Tom took Seabiscuit's reins from her without a word.

"Why, in Spain in '36, dear. Alan and I saw gasoline bombs used against the fascists. It was a criminal thing to do with good whisky, but it was quite a special effect, wasn't it?"

Ingrid nodded her approval of Dottie's effort. Jimmy's car was fully engulfed in flame. They could've toasted marshmallows, though they would've tasted of petroleum and rubber.

Finally Ingrid heard sirens rising in the distance.

It was a good time to be going, then. For all of them.

"Isn't this where we started off this morning?" Dottie asked, sounding surprised as she looked around and took in the neighborhood.

"Yes," Ingrid said.

"Where you needed to go."

"Yes."

"And you're leaving right from here? In your time machine?"

"From there, Dottie," Ingrid said, tipping her chin at the Silent Tower. "I'm going up to the top, and then… well, I'm going."

Dot nodded doubtfully.

"Can I at least watch?"

Ingrid shook her head, sadly. That wouldn't be a good idea.

"And if I follow you up there anyway?" Dot asked. "What would I find, Miss Redstone?"

"Death," Ingrid said. "That's all. Death and nothing more."

"Is that such an insignificant thing?"

Now it was Ingrid's turn for a spot of reflection. "No," she said, honestly. "No, it isn't."

"I wouldn't think so," Dot said. "I envy your intimacy with the reaper, dear, when all I can do is nurture an infatuation."

"Nurture it a while longer, Dot," Ingrid suggested. "There isn't any hurry."

Dottie looked away. "I suppose not," she agreed, though she sounded wistful about it.

The sirens were growing louder.

"And so we part ways once again, before the authorities arrive," Dot said. "Am I right?"

Ingrid didn't need to respond.

"I never imagined anyone like you before, Ingrid Redstone."

"Same here, Mrs. Parker."

Dot smiled, and looked at Seabiscuit. She reached up and patted his suede-soft nose.

"Why don't you ride him home?" Ingrid looked to Tom, the taciturn trainer, still sitting atop his elegant Arabian. "If that's all right?"

She received a nod and helped Dot into the saddle.

The two women looked at each other without knowing what else to say.

Silent Tom cleared his throat. The sirens were uncomfortably loud now. The emergency vehicles attached to them could roll into view at any second.

"Go on," Ingrid said, and they didn't wait. Horses and riders drained away from the scene. Dottie and Seabiscuit vanished up the block, led away by the thoroughbred's trainer.

In a matter of seconds there was only one horse left on the street—the tall black stallion that had borne Vinea the Demon Lord on his hunt.

He was the last lingering remainder of Jimmy's artful conjuration.

She walked over and took his bridle. The big horse didn't seem at all bothered by her. He didn't seem entirely real either, not up close. He was too smooth and too perfect, like a sculpture modeled by an artist with no schooling in anatomy. Mickey's equine simulacra were of far superior quality. Vinea's raven-black hellhorse, quite docile now, would be solid all the way through, and would also return promptly to dust should it happen to be cut apart.

Still, the shadow-stallion had enough substance and mass that Ingrid knew she'd be able to ride him.

She walked him right through the front door of her Silent Tower, unremarked upon by anybody, in the last seconds before the first police cars and fire engines rounded the corner at the far end of the block. She was sure the chaos she'd caused would all be blamed on the news of war—an understandable overflow of tension into violence. There might well be more rioting in the weeks ahead. People seemed pretty high-strung, these days.

Ingrid closed the door behind herself.

Closed it on 1941.

Chapter Five

UPSTAIRS, Mictlantecuhtli stood waiting for her in the doorway between his chambers, with his fleshless arms folded across his ribcage.

"Oh. It's you," he said.

"You were expecting somebody else?"

"I wasn't expecting a *horse* made by somebody else," the shrouded skeleton said. "Especially not a false and poorly crafted one."

"He's all right," Ingrid said. "Fast enough, anyway."

"*He* contains no sub-structures," the King of the Dead criticized, petulantly. "No bones or organs. He lacks nuance."

"I was thinking of calling him Shadow."

The skeleton under the heavy cowl looked at her for a long while. The eyeballs garlanded about his bony shoulders glistened wetly. "Who gave him to you?" he asked.

"I won him, Mickey," Ingrid said. "In a fight. He's mine by right of conquest."

Mictlantecuhtli nodded. This seemed to be an idea he either understood or found appealing. "By right of conquest," he echoed. "Yes."

"Mickey, I need something," Ingrid said.

"Oh?"

"First I need you to put something on." She gestured at his conspicuous lack of surface area. "If you would."

Mictlantecuhtli looked down at himself, miffed, but he did as he was asked and became Mickey. Mickey Hardface, that was, her tall, regal (and fully-fleshed) Aztec king. The strangest and closest relationship of her unusual life.

Ingrid smiled. She always liked to look at him. He was too perfect for her, absolutely custom-made. His shoulders were exactly the breadth necessary to impress her when she wrapped her arms around him. He always knew where, how, and when to touch her, as unerringly as a lover in a dream. It may not have been safe to let him know how thoroughly he affected her, but even looking at him now, with his bared chest and his modesty preserved by nothing more than an abbreviated loincloth, she wanted to press herself against his well-fashioned torso.

Her victory over Jimmy still had her blood pumping.

"You mentioned a desire you would have fulfilled?" her King rumbled in his whiskey-smooth voice.

Ingrid shook her head to clear it. Mickey's hint of a smirk let her know that *he* knew precisely what he was doing to her, what effect he was having, with his nearness and his near-nudity.

Well, she was free to do something about it, if she wanted. She was always freer to do as she pleased with el Rey than she might've been with a human lover. What harm could come from it?

But now was not the time for fun and games. She still had other things on her mind. Maybe she should have left him in his ossified form, but she always achieved her best results with el Rey when she took a firm and decisive lead.

"I need you to find someone for me," she said. "One amongst the dead."

"All right," Mickey said, playing along. "Who?"

"His name is Francis Boggs. Or was, I guess."

The King nodded and closed his eyes. They ticked back and forth beneath his dark lids, like a man deeply dreaming. Ingrid knew he was mentally cataloging his entire realm, which must've contained unfathomable billions of individuals, by her best estimation.

"He is not here," he said, reopening his eyes after less than thirty seconds.

"Are you sure?" Ingrid frowned. She hadn't expected that. "You didn't take very long to check."

"Your Boggs is not here, I assure you."

"Well, what does that mean, then?" He couldn't be in Tlalocan, as he hadn't died by drowning. "Is he still alive, or, or…"

Ingrid couldn't bring herself to voice her worst fear—specifically, that her Uncle Frank might have been eaten by Mickey's creatures, the way his Tzitzimime had once consumed Cynthia Iverson, a dead soldier over whose fate she still carried a heavy measure of guilt. One could still be chewed out of existence and reduced to demonshit post-mortem.

"He may still be bound to the earth," Mickey said. "Either through the exercise of his own will or by the design of a sorcerer." The King shrugged. "It happens."

"He could be a ghost, you mean?"

"Or the enslaved plaything of a skilled magician."

Ingrid didn't have to strain her brain to guess who that might be. Killing Boggs hadn't been enough; Jim had gone and kept him, too.

"Selig, then," she said to Mickey, moving down the list to the next person who might be able to provide her with information. "Colonel Professor William Nicholas Selig, please."

Mickey shook his head. "Your 'Selig' isn't dead from where you stand. Not before '48. It would be easiest if you came over here to speak with him."

Ingrid pushed el Rey aside to lead Shadow, her stallion, into the sacrosanctum, where she stationed him next to the stone altar. Mickey raised his hand and the room vanished around them, becoming in an instant what appeared to be an abandoned, overgrown, and rainswept old zoo.

"He owned a zoo," Ingrid said, less conversing than musing out loud. "Dottie mentioned it."

Mickey pointed down the broad, weed-sprouting midway between two rows of crumbling concrete cells that had been cleverly wrought to look like natural stone caves, except for the rusted iron bars at their mouths. There was almost no light—the interiors of those cells looked so dark they might have gone back for miles, like the geological fissures they'd been made to resemble.

A skeleton dressed in a brown tweed suit and a hat with rainwater dripping from the brim stood down at the far end of the overgrown aisle, with his back to them. Wildly-proliferating palms and tall eucalyptus trees reached toward each other, not quite forming a canopy. Their black foliage danced in the wind and rain.

Ingrid took Shadow's bridle and approached the bones of one of the world's first movie producers. She didn't know why that hadn't earned him a more prominent place in the historical record. She'd been to 1941 and she'd visited Universal Studios, an industrial-scale film factory, so she knew moving pictures were no passing fad, as the nervous stage performers of her day needed to insist, in order to sleep at night for worry over their futures.

"Mr. Selig?" Ingrid said, coming up behind him as he stared forlornly up at a menagerie of life-sized cast-concrete animals that adorned the arched front gates. Rangy lions lounged atop the gatehouses and a monumental ring of elephants stood in the center, up on a huge concrete block, facing out with their trunks triumphantly raised. The sculptures were crumbling, forgotten, their iron frames showing through in some places, but the way they glistened in the rain made them almost seem to shift and move like actual living things. The signage on the pachyderm pedestal changed when Ingrid glanced away and back again. At some moments it read SELIG ZOO; at others, LUNA PARK.

The skeleton in brown tweed turned and looked up at her. His bony face still sported the bushy mustache she remembered from life.

"Ingrid," he said, and seemed almost to smile. "Frank's Ingrid, right? Or should I call you Silence Tower?"

"You can if you like." She didn't bother to correct his near-miss at her stage name.

The dead producer nodded. "What are you doing here?" he asked, looking her up and down. "You look good. Healthy."

"I need to know what happened to Uncle Frank, Colonel," she said. Selig had never been either a colonel or a professor in any capacity, though he'd affected both titles at various times for promotional purposes, and Ingrid had always addressed him by one or the other of them in jest. "I was hoping you could tell me."

"Oh… that was an ugly business," Selig said, looking troubled. He turned his fleshless face back up toward the rain-slicked concrete elephants. "A tragedy. I was shot too, you know, in the arm. I expected to die. But I didn't, not then. Just Frank. He went fast. I hardly think he knew what was happening. He looked so confused by all the blood."

"But what *happened?*" Ingrid asked. Her blouse was sticking to her chest and shoulders, and she was beginning to shiver in the cold.

Mickey, ever attuned to her physical needs (even the non-sexual ones), first manifested a new suit for himself then removed the jacket and placed it around her shoulders. It smelled good, like her lover's skin, and kept her as warm as an embrace.

"Who did it?" she continued to prod. "And why? And when? Specifically."

Selig's skeleton seemed somewhat at a loss. "Well… as to *why*, exactly, besides madness, I don't suppose there's any way to know. It was Frank Minematsu that did it, our caretaker. A man we both considered a friend. He got the gun he used out of our own property room. I got it away from him after he shot Boggs, but not before it went off again. That empty look in his eyes when he turned it on me was the most shocking sight I ever saw. It was like he wasn't even himself at the time."

No, he wasn't, Ingrid silently agreed. He would have been nothing but an empty shell driven by the will and rituals of Jimmy the Freak.

"*When* was it, professor?" she asked. "That's the important part."

"1911," Selig's skeleton said. "Some months after you'd gone back to Europe."

Ingrid nodded. That was the lie she'd told to cover up her extended stays here in Mictlan. "More specifically?" she pressed.

"In October, the end of October," the dead man said. "The 27th. Minematsu said later that a man came to him the day before, gave him a gold watch—which never turned up during the investigation—and told him that your Uncle Frank had to die when that watch's hands lined up at the top of the dial the next afternoon. He said he was promised a rain of gold from the skies if he succeeded, I remember."

More like getting pissed on by Jimmy Vreke. Still, that was good. All the information she needed, really. But she couldn't turn her back and walk away from the lonely corpse standing in the middle of his ruined dream of a zoo.

"Colonel," she said gently. "There's no need to stay here like this. You can choose to visit a happier time."

"Like back when I knew you?" He seemed to smile, as well as a skeleton can. "Do you remember the wrap party we threw at the Angelus after Frank completed his photography for *Race Tout?*"

"It was in my suite," Ingrid said.

"That irritable manager threatened to call the police. I had to buy him off. I can't remember the man's name, but was he ever livid."

"Kittering," Ingrid murmured. "Herman Kittering."

"Yes, that was it. Poor man. We caused him any number of headaches, didn't we?"

And worse, Ingrid thought, nodding. "Still, that *was* a good time, wasn't it?" she said, taking the dead moviemaker's frail hand in both of hers. "Here, close your eyes," she said, (even though he had no eyelids to speak of), "and remember it with me."

She'd been quite pleasantly drunk, she recalled, and had enjoyed a kiss with more than one handsome man over the course of a boisterous, music-filled evening. Later, when she'd been too tired and woozy to move from the main room's sofa, she laughed over deep and philosophical subjects she couldn't now remember with this man, Professor Selig, and her dear Uncle Frank. She fell asleep sometime before the sun came up, safe and warm under a blanket one of them tucked around her shoulders.

Ingrid realized she no longer felt Selig's thin phalanges against her palm.

She opened her eyes. The dead producer had disappeared. Off to re-attend that party, she hoped, back when his world had held such promise.

She was alone with Mickey and Shadow now, amidst the gloomy ruins of the zoo. The rain made the King's copper skin gleam and the stallion's coat shine. Neither of them were at all affected by the cold. Neither was she, really. She'd only been shivering from force of habit.

"We could build a fire in one of these caves, if you like," el Rey mused, squinting down the midway through the rain, "and keep warm while we wait out the rest of the night."

Ingrid shook her head. "Not yet, Mickey. I still have something I need to finish. I need 1911, okay? October 26th should do."

He eyed her coolly for a long moment before raising his hand and restoring them to the inner chamber at the top of his Pyramid. Once it was done, he held out the same hand, palm up, and waited.

"What are you doing?"

"Is it not customary in the realworld to 'tip' one's servants?"

"Oh, Mickey… don't be a shit," Ingrid said, and had to think of Dottie Parker. It was hard not to latch on to her vocabulary.

"Fine," the King said, still in a snit. His wet linen shirt still clung to his body, though the rain that had drenched it was long gone.

"It's important to me to see this through," Ingrid explained. "I'll come back to you as soon as I'm done, but for right now, please help me. Please."

Mickey nodded. "As you would have it, my love."

He never ignored her direct appeals. It was at such moments that she thought he really *did* love her, in his way… and that she felt just the same.

"The day you require awaits," he told her. "Shall I send my Tzitzimime to assist in your endeavors?"

"Oh, hell no," Ingrid said, too quickly. "I mean, no thank you. What I need to do won't be difficult, now that I have some information. They won't see me coming. Besides, your buggers are pretty nocturnal, aren't they?"

"This is true," Mickey said. "And you do have your mount."

"Yes." The King's opinion of Shadow had gone up since learning she'd claimed the half-real horse as plunder. "I could use fresh clothes, though."

Mickey made it happen. Ingrid clutched the silver watch she'd taken from Jimmy the Freak as her ruined clothing dusted away then spun back into clean fabric that swaddled her and swiftly became a new skirt, shirtwaist, low heels, and a broad-brimmed, feather-plumed hat—all appropriate to the early '10s. The outfit would do (though she was looking forward to the fashion of the future, after having glimpsed the 1940s).

She looked at the watch in her hand. The one with her garnet on the end of the fob.

"How about a silver necklace too?" she asked, pulling the wire-wrapped stone from the end of the fob chain. "A thin one."

It appeared. Ingrid strung the garnet on it, then the King clipped it safely around her neck. At last. He even sealed the chain; she'd find later that there was no clasp or obvious point where the ends had been joined together. She pocketed the watch the stone had been attached to, as she wasn't done with *it*, either. She thanked Mickey for his trouble with a kiss, then took her imaginal animal's bridle and led him out through the doorway, across the barrier, and into a year she'd skipped the first time around.

She looked back and raised a hand to Mickey as she led the tall stallion into the hallway and from there into the elevator, which was approximately the size of a stall in a stable. (The Tower was still under construction back in this era, but finishing its lifts had been a top priority.)

Downstairs, outside, the weather was nice. Autumnal and cool, with mounds of white cloud coasting slowly along overhead. No workmen lurked—October 26th was close enough to Mickey's favorite holiday that he didn't want any humans hanging around, and had given them all the week off. The Silent Tower was again the only building for miles in any direction, fronting on a street that was only paved for a few hundred yards. Today, as of 1911, it was only three-quarters complete, and the twentieth century hadn't yet filled in around it.

Ingrid took the by-now creased and torn phone directory page with the Edendale address of the Selig Polyscope Company on it and re-read it. 'Edendale,' as she'd learned in '41, lay to the east of the San Fernando Valley—northeast of where she was right now.

She mounted up and rode hard in that direction, not wanting to waste a minute.

Timing was going to be everything, if she meant to outfox the Freak.

Chapter Six

—*October 26th, 1911*

THE Edendale studios of Selig Polyscope were modest, to say the least, when compared with the monumental filmmaking machine that was Universal Studios circa 1941, but as of 1911 the facility was state-of-the-art, and Ingrid was rather impressed with it.

The Spanish-style façade, modeled after the old Mission San Gabriel and constructed using real adobe, faced onto Allessandro Street. The whitewashed walls looked thick and rough-surfaced, and the orange roof tiles blazed cheerily in the mid-morning sun.

Ingrid tied Shadow up out front (though not *right* out front), to one of several new western-style hitching posts that had probably been installed for the sake of shooting cowboy movies. She adjusted the brim of her hat to hide as much of her face as was reasonably possible, and then snuck onto the studio lot.

Actually she strode onto the studio lot, while projecting imaginal banishing pentagrams out from her heart center. This was no more dangerous to living creatures than a withering glare, and it had the effect of making her hard to notice. It took a lot of effort and concentration, but as long as she didn't draw attention to herself or make direct eye contact she could walk right past people she knew and they'd find themselves too distracted by something in their thoughts to notice.

She was glad she knew the trick because she'd already spotted her Uncle Frank (almost as portly as Alfred Hitchcock, these days, though far less dour and jowly in his expressions) talking with, of all people, Mr. Colonel Professor William Selig. They stood at an intersection between studio buildings. Both men looked so vital and real that it made Ingrid's heart ache. They looked that way because they *were* vital and real, with no inkling of the early deaths and ruined zoos that lay in their futures along the current timeline.

If Ingrid had her way, all that would change. Uncle Frank would make his films and Mr. Selig would sell them, for decades yet to come, and by the time they died their natural deaths many years from now the legacies they deserved would be secure, and their names would be remembered for as long as memory lasted.

That was her intention. It was the hardest thing in the world not to look at her well-loved friends as she passed by them, catching a snatch of their animated discussion over a second story they might shoot with leftover Roman Empire sets and costumes.

She wanted to hug them both, but they believed her to be touring Europe in the employ of a magician billed as Mumford the Maleficent, and the less disruption she could cause here, the better. She wanted to see to her task and get the hell out, then pop forward to the 1912 she'd expected the first time around. A 1912 in which Francis Boggs would be alive and well and glad to see her.

This had to be a surgical-style intervention. Minimally invasive. She didn't know how much leeway she had to make changes in the course of events, or what sort of consequences might follow, so she put Boggs and Selig behind herself without so much as a glance in their direction.

The man she was looking for was Japanese. Minematsu. According to what Mr. Selig's future dead self had told her, Minematsu had been given a gold watch by a stranger just this morning, and Ingrid was familiar enough with Jimmy the Freak's operating procedures to recognize his fingerprints all over that story.

The gold watch had to be hexed with a mesmeric trigger. Ingrid couldn't figure it any other way, based on Colonel Selig's account of the shooting. Jimmy would've contrived a pretense for laying the tainted timepiece on Minematsu, something like pretending to step in front of a speeding cart so that the mark could pull him back, save his life, and accept a gratefully-given reward. There wouldn't have been any nonsense about her Uncle Frank needing to die; that story would appear in Minematsu's head only later, after the deed was done, for the benefit of judges, juries, and possibly executioners.

Uncle Frank, meanwhile, would have been given a deadline for accepting Jimmy's terms. Part of agreeing to them would be to give *her* up as well—to make of her an image that Jimmy might exploit, as well as to finally learn the secret of the Hole in the Sky. If the Freak received a phone call with a yes answer before the deadline, he'd break his own spell and call off his pre-programmed assassin remotely. If the answer was no (or no answer at all by the appointed hour), then one of Boggs' trusted associates would go berserk and murder him, out of the blue, as if by magic, right after checking his new fob watch for the time.

Such a seemingly random crime could never be traced back to Jimmy, who was jealous enough of his secret technology to insure it with murder. If Boggs refused to work with him (as he had and would), then Jim wanted to be certain the director would never tell anyone else in

Hollywood about the unique properties of the Pyroptic Anamorph he'd seen.

Ingrid could easily lift a watch from a man's pocket, but that wouldn't solve the problem, as Jimmy surely had a fail-safe built into his spell. (Ingrid knew because she would have.) If Minematsu were to 'lose' his watch, either by accident or design, she assumed the homicidal suggestion would activate as soon as he noticed the loss and he would kill Boggs the very next time he saw him. There'd be no waiting even for tomorrow's deadline, if the watch were to mysteriously disappear.

The obvious solution would seem to be for her to kill Minematsu first.

But Ingrid had no taste for cold-blooded murder. She really didn't know if she could do it. Fortunately, she did have one other option. She had *another* watch, one also owned by Jimmy the Freak. The silver one with a thick crystal embedded in the case that showed the brass gears inside. He'd kept it attached to her stolen garnet until Mrs. Parker's dog stole it back.

She'd prepared counter-orders on the long ride out here and attached them to the silver watch. They'd seem to come from the original source, Jimmy Vreke. When Minematsu opened the silver chronometer, the Freak's spell would be cancelled and his plan to commit remote murder if Boggs declined to join him would be defused.

And all Ingrid had to do was switch out the watches.

She spotted a trim black-haired man in khaki work clothes crouched near the corner of a glass-roofed stage. He was mending a bicycle he'd flipped upside down to rest on its seat and handlebars. When he stood up, job done, and righted the bike, Ingrid casually bumped into him.

She touched the caretaker's arm as if for balance while slipping the gold watch from his pocket with her other hand and replacing it with the hexed-up timepiece from thirty years in the future.

Exchange made. Her own wards would keep him from noticing that the object itself had apparently changed from gold to silver.

"Oh! Excuse me," Ingrid said, feigning surprise. "How careless. My head is right in the clouds today. Are you all right, Mr. Minematsu?"

"Hai," the small man said, nodding and confirming his identity while looking at her nervously, like he was the one who'd committed a blunder. "Yes."

"Good," she said. "My apologies."

She walked away from him, raising her hand in a wave without looking back.

She exited the studio grounds by the rear gate, then hurried around to the front of the property to reclaim her half-real horse.

Only then did she pause to examine the watch she'd lifted from Minematsu.

It was a nice one, if plain. Its smooth case was fashioned from high-carat yellow gold, and lacked the crystal window looking in on its spinning works that the silver one sported. There seemed to be nothing remarkable about it in any way (until she looked deeper, with her specially-trained eyes, and glimpsed the skeins of pulsing, still-active spellwork Jimmy had swaddled it in).

She wasn't going to open that watch—no more than she'd open a corked vial of plague-infected blood.

She slipped it back into her pocket, mounted up, and rode away.

That was it, then. The deed was done. It seemed like such a small thing, stealing a watch, that lives should turn on it, but she supposed lives often turned on less.

There was no hurry in crossing the mountainous acreage that would remain wild as part of a vast urban park at least through the middle of the century, according to her memories of the future. She let herself relax and enjoy the ride. It was a fine day to be outdoors and on horseback, with crisp cooling breezes and warm clear sunlight balancing each other out. Shadow knew where he was going, which was nice. It left Ingrid free to think. Imagining the conniptions Jimmy the Freak was likely to throw when all his carefully-laid plots came to nothing made her smile.

It astonished her that an act as insignificant as swapping one watch for another could have repercussions as profound as the saving of a life. She had to wonder what else might be accomplished, with a little foreknowledge and a lot of careful planning.

Archimedes once said that given a long enough lever and a place to stand, he could move the world. Ingrid was coming to realize that Mictlan could be that place to stand, and that her own will might supply the necessary leverage.

She began to dream of other improvements she might make to the ongoing course of human events. She'd never felt more powerful, or more quietly confident in her own skills and cleverness.

It was mid-afternoon by the time Shadow delivered her back to the Silent Tower.

Mickey was upstairs, waiting for her in the sacrificial chamber, as usual. He'd put on his skin and dressed in the sort of elegant modern suit she liked, just to please her.

"My love," she said to him, dropping her horse's bridle to step into his arms and kiss him, without reservation or restraint. Mickey was only too happy to respond.

When they came up for air and separated, he said: "I take it you were successful in your endeavor?"

"I think so, Mickey." She pulled out the gold watch Jimmy the Freak had given to Minematsu earlier in the day. "Here—I thought you might want this."

The King took it and held it up by its chain to examine it. "Yours by right of victory?" he asked with a wry smile.

Ingrid nodded. "Something like that," she said. "I'd like you to keep it here."

"It will be my honor." He slipped the gold watch into the pocket of his well-fitted trousers, which Ingrid figured was the safest place for it. It wasn't apt to hurt anyone living as long as it stayed amongst the dead, atop the ever-growing pile of Mickey's collected trinkets.

"What now?" Mickey asked.

Ingrid grinned. She was exhausted. She'd skipped across thirty years in the last three days, and not slept or eaten well between them. She could've consumed a whole roast pig then passed out for a week—not to mention bathing until she sloughed off an entire epidermal layer—but at the moment there were other things she wanted to do far more. She was grateful to Mickey, more pleased and proud to know him than she had ever been. They were going to change the world together.

To a small degree, for Francis Boggs, they already had.

"Can we go back to Luna Park, just the two of us?" she asked, and they were there before she finished the question. Alone with the dark and the lashing rain, in the middle of William Selig's dream of his abandoned zoo. The precipitation felt blissfully cold on her face, the cleansing drops pricking her skin like tiny frozen needles. The skies in Mictlan never got lighter than one might expect on an overcast day, but they could get a lot darker, and more turbulent.

Ingrid took el Rey by the hand and led him into the nearest of the old animal cages that had been stage-dressed as caverns. The iron bars at the mouth had long since rusted through and fallen away, and the deep interior of the space was dry and empty, black with shadows. The rush and echoing drip of the rain outside were the only sounds, other than her own quickening breath.

Mickey made a gesture and a crackling campfire sprang up from the stone floor (even though there was no wood to speak of). Reflected flames glittered in his intense black eyes and flowed like syrup over his skin. He'd switched from his European suit to his Aztec ornaments while her back was turned.

Ingrid stepped up close and let her fingers join the firelight in tracing out his solid chest and thickly-muscled arm. The golden cuff around his bicep looked like melting butterscotch. She realized her own clothing had disappeared as well. She didn't miss it. The skin-tightening heat the fire radiated against her back made a soothing and welcome counterpoint to the warmth of Mickey's embrace when they came together, their bodies communicating without a word spoken between them.

They kissed, gently for a moment, then with increasing roughness. Ingrid wasn't in the mood for tenderness now, not at all. Her nerves crackled like the fire behind her. She felt inflamed and excited by what she'd done in 1911—specifically that she'd rewritten history, not by cheating Death but by making an ally of him. For the first time she truly felt worthy of being the lover of a god, a magnificent figure of myth and legend in her own right. While she'd never been unnecessarily modest, neither was it like her to wholeheartedly believe her own press. Yet her sense of excitement was only growing.

She was Ingrid Redstone, doer of things no one else could do, seer of things no one else had seen, and she felt immensely proud of herself.

If there was any dark spot at all, any rain on her one-woman parade, it was that she had no peer or friend to share it all with, back in the realworld. Someone who understood the significance.

Mickey lifted her off her feet to lay her down across a bed of fresh sweet hay overlaid with silk carpets that he'd made appear at the back of the cave, without her even noticing.

She locked her arms around his neck and her legs around his hips, pulling him down on top of her. His breath in her ear made her tingle all the way down to her toes.

All she wanted now was the satisfying obliteration of her loneliness only timeless Mickey could make her feel, and then to sleep deeply within the protective circle of his arms, feeling wrung out and pleasantly sore after being sated on all the athletic diversion her body could handle.

Was that so much to ask?

Not for *la Reina de las Brujas*.

Ingrid grinned against Mickey's massive shoulder when he pressed into her, generating seismic waves from her secret epicenter that made her entire spinal column quake.

By the time el Rey reached the culmination of his own pleasure she was barely conscious enough to know it. Even half-asleep, she kept the core of herself screened away behind constantly-repeated banishing mantras. Mickey divined his best insights into her wants and needs at these moments when her guard was as close to down as she ever let it get, but she knew better than to allow her King to penetrate any deeper into her head.

That was why she would never, ever let herself cry in front of him.

Chapter Seven

INGRID awoke to the sound of an explosion that rocked the ground beneath her and sent dust sifting down from new cracks in the concrete ceiling. Her first thought was that she was back in 1941, and under heavy bombardment.

She sat up, pulling a silk sheet around her bare shoulders. She felt stale and sticky and in need of a bath, not nearly as rested as she would've liked. Their campfire had long since gone out, and Mictlan's flat gray light poured in from the mouth of the artificial cave, bright enough at the moment to make her squint.

The otherworld shook around her again. The cage floor rippled like liquid.

Mickey was nowhere to be seen.

Ingrid stood and wrapped the sheet about herself, holding it closed at the front. She stepped out of the cave-shaped cage, shielding her eyes to look around for her King.

He was standing not far away, in the center of the old zoo's midway, clad in the heavy red robes of his office and looking up into a gray sky that appeared to have been violently torn open.

Flat, empty, and somehow mindless white 'light' showed through the seam. Light didn't seem to be the right word, as the whiteness beyond the sky felt more like blankness than illumination, though it was as hard to look at as the sun.

For her anyway. Mickey didn't seem to have any problem. He turned to her briefly, his eyes ablaze, and said: "Get back inside."

Ingrid ducked back under the cover of the false cave, though she stayed right at its mouth, watching her King.

He turned his attention away from the shattered sky, and that was when Ingrid noticed the Others.

There were many of them. Many thousands, in forms varied enough to fill a dictionary of myth. Some Ingrid recognized, like the capering Shiva Nataraja, ringed in fire; a clutch of wrathful Buddhist demons with blue, green, and red complexions; and the beast-headed pantheon of ancient Egypt. Many others she could not identify.

Many others.

They stood arrayed on terraced plateaus that had sprung up around the zoo in the night, like an audience or an enormous jury. The latter was probably the better comparison. Most of the faces Ingrid could make out had sententious expressions stamped upon them, and nobody looked eager to applaud.

The populations of distant mythologies all looked down upon Mictlantecuhtli, accusing him. Ingrid saw Anansi the Spider, Thor with his hammer and his long blond hair, and the raucous Gede—cemetery gods from west Africa who were venerated in boneyards throughout the Caribbean. All of them and countless others had murder burning in their eyes as they regarded her Mickey, who let his illusory flesh dissolve away to stand before them in his truest and most intimidating skeletal form, with his robes blowing in the noiseless wind around him.

Ingrid had no idea what was going on, but the ground shook again beneath her, and the broken sky cracked further. Chunks of it fell and shattered in the invisible distance, and more flat white emptiness showed through behind.

One particular dark-haired goddess dressed in flowing Greek linen seemed to have been elected to address Mickey. She hung in the air before him, vaguely illuminated around her edges.

"You will issue no ultimatums," Mickey told her, continuing a debate Ingrid hadn't heard the start of. "You are in no position, Lady Eris, by your own accounting."

"Do not be a fool, Mictlantecuhtli," the entity called Eris said. Her hair tended to change with every glance, both in color and style. Now it was short and spiky and red as blood; now a shaved-down purple fuzz; now a garden of tumbling green curls. Eris' eyes were not the same color, nor were either of them ever the same color twice.

She, like the fractured sky, was not the easiest thing to look at.

"Your mindless defiance helps no one," she said to Mictlantecuhtli, who snarled audibly in response. "Least of all you."

"That is my concern," he said.

"No more," Eris contradicted him. "Your carelessness results in the demise of the real, and that is *our* concern."

Ingrid felt a sinking feeling in her gut. 'Demise of the real' did not sound positive. She wondered what could have happened, and how it could possibly be Mickey's fault.

"Discord is your purview, Lady Eris," Mictlantecuhtli said to the confusing Greek. "I would think you would appreciate this unprecedented occurrence more."

"What occurs is not discord," the goddess corrected him. "Your witch has turned the realworld's skies to fire! This is beyond destruction, for there remains no hope of cyclical rebirth. It is annihilation, obliteration, the end of all that is. The end of *your* world as well as every other, Lord Death. This cannot be denied. The progression of decay is advanced already, and must be apparent even through your deliberate obtuseness."

Mictlantecuhtli folded his armbones across his ribs. "And what would you have me do about it, Lady Eris?"

"Bring forth your witch. Let her explain her actions. Let us learn if they might yet be undone."

Ingrid cringed.

"This I will not do," Mictlantecuhtli said. "The Red Witch is under my protection, and answerable to none but me."

Mars stepped forward to take his place at inconsistent Eris' side. He was armored and scarred, anointed with blood, laden with blades, bows, and guns. "Then we will storm your realm," he said, "and take her, and force her to repair the damage she has done."

"You're welcome to try," Mictlantecuhtli said. "But you will not have her."

He raised a hand and ranks of the dead sprang up from the earth to stand between them and the disgruntled denizens of the imaginal worlds. The point was clear—el Rey's armies were vast, and a fight with him would not be easy to win.

"For the love of dogs!" Eris shouted. "Even you cannot be this stupid! We will not allow you to kill all the worlds in the name of stubbornness, Mictlantecuhtli. You cannot hope to win against us all, if war must be declared."

"You threaten me with oblivion when oblivion awaits?" Mictlantecuhtli cackled. "That is not the strongest position from which to make demands."

Ingrid realized she was trembling. They believed she'd set the sky on fire? She didn't know if Mickey could defend her against all these gods and monsters, or where they'd gotten the idea that had sparked their wrath.

Although that wasn't entirely true, was it?

She had done *one* thing recently that was dramatic and unprecedented enough that it must somehow be the source of all this otherworldly enmity. She couldn't begin to imagine how it could have gone wrong, at least not on such a massive scale that all these pantheons had rallied together to defend their imaginal territories.

They seemed to understand that Mickey held all the cards, though, and that had to be good news for her.

Frustrated Eris put her hands on her hips and seemed about to say something more, but Mictlantecuhtli spoke before she was able:

"If this injury to the system of worlds springs from my realm or the doings of my guests, then it will be repaired by me," he said. "You need not concern yourselves."

Another sizeable section of curved gray sky fell from its moorings and shattered against the slope of a mountain on the far horizon. Tiny distant figures scrambled to get out of its way. Otherworldly heads by the score swiveled toward the noise, then turned back again to glare at Mictlantecuhtli.

"We *are* concerned," Eris said, "and your skull must be as empty as it looks if you find this response excessive."

"As I have said, I will repair it," Mictlantecuhtli repeated. "Now go from my realm and trouble me no further, or the next words we exchange will be harsher by far than these."

The hooded skeleton that was the King of the Dead turned on his heelbone, putting his back to Eris, Mars, and so many other self-aware embodiments of humanity's needs and truths. He strode away from them, flayed flesh-cloak billowing out around him, and into the shadows of Ingrid's cave. Thousands of years worth of stalagmites and stalactites deposited themselves at its mouth half an instant later, sealing it shut behind him by gnashing together like enormous pointed teeth.

They were alone—for a moment at least. Ingrid didn't know if an attack would be forthcoming. There was no light, but she could see Mickey anyway as he grew his flesh back over his bones for her. He retained his cowl and his necklace of eyes.

"What have you done?" he asked once his loincloth had knitted itself back on.

"I don't know," Ingrid said.

"Now is the time for neither games nor lies."

"I... I changed something," Ingrid admitted. "Just a small something. I don't see how it could've led to the problems those... those *others* were talking about."

"Tell me what you did."

"I saved someone. I altered the circumstances and timing of his death."

Mickey nodded beneath his hood. "The one you call 'Boggs.'"

"Yes, my Uncle Frank. He's my friend. He was murdered because of me. It wasn't right, it wasn't fair, and so I fixed it."

She knew she sounded defensive. She clenched her jaw and stopped explaining.

Mickey snapped his fingers and Francis Boggs' bones appeared, as visible to Ingrid as the King was in the unrelieved blackness of the cave. Whatever else might have happened, her revisions *had* kept Jimmy the Freak from anchoring Boggs to the earth after his death.

The new skeleton of her old friend spotted her, and seemed almost to smile. "Silent Tower, as I live and breathe," he said, and then winced, looking down at his desiccated body. "That was an inapt turn of phrase, wasn't it?"

"Uncle Frank," she said, taking both his bony hands in hers. "When did you die? And how? I know it's rude but I have to ask. It's important."

Boggs' skeleton cocked its skull at a quizzical angle.

"Why, the same day as everyone else in the world," he said. "December 21st, 1916."

Chapter Eight

MICKEY raised his hand and the three of them were back inside his sacrificial chamber. The first thing Ingrid noticed was a clear, black, star-flecked night sky out beyond the realworld side of the door. The office Oscar San Martín built had vanished. The view was much as she remembered it from the old Tree-Below-the-Hole days.

Much as she remembered, but not exactly the same, as Ingrid saw when she edged nearer to it, peering past Mictlantecuhtli to get a look.

There was no outer chamber on the other side of that door, now. The original pyramid's sanctum had been burnt away, along with every structure and sign of life on the ground below. There was no Silent Tower anymore, nor a Hollywood for it to stand in. All of it had boiled away. Ingrid moved her hand close to the barrier, afraid of it as she'd never been before, and the blistering cold she felt against her palm before she yanked it back inclined her to believe there was no more atmosphere out there either.

She might've been the last living creature in existence, for all she knew.

"When?" was all she could croak, turning to look at Mickey with wide and horrified eyes. "When *is* this?"

"The one-thousandth, nine-hundred and sixteenth 'year,' by your counting method. At the time of it when the earth has strayed as far as it is able from the great god Sol."

Ingrid took that to mean it was the winter solstice out there, when the planet's orbit carried it as far from the sun as it ever got, resulting in the shortest days and longest nights of the year.

Not that seasons would seem to have much bearing on the burnt-out husk of a world she saw below her. She couldn't imagine the surface of the moon would look much more barren.

1916, and the realworld was dead. That meant the otherworld, the one she was lucky enough to be standing in, had to be on the verge of dying. The two fed each other like Siamese twins sharing a vital organ, and neither could exist except as part of a symbiotic set.

She'd known the realities had an 'immune system' of sorts since it robbed her of her memories that first time she went out traveling, and now she saw why: because the nested structure of worlds was fragile enough to collapse catastrophically under the strain of too much careless alteration.

Ingrid didn't know what to say or how to feel, much less what to do about any of this. The scale of the devastation humbled her. An entire world, *her* world, burnt black. It was too much to contemplate.

"We didn't mean for it to happen," her Uncle Frank's bones said softly, from behind her. "We didn't know it could. We never imagined anything like this."

Ingrid turned away from the door and the airless void beyond it.

"It was that watch of Minematsu's," her friend's bones said, and Ingrid felt her heart sink. "That weird crystal in its case."

So it was her fault. Beyond a shadow of a doubt.

"But *how?*" Ingrid said. "How could a watch—*any* watch—cause this?"

Boggs' corpse shook its head. "Not the watch, per se, so much as that crystal, the one that looked in on the gears. Odd thing, that was. Strange optical properties. Tommy Persons, our cameraman, was the first one to notice. You remember Tommy? He saw something I never did understand about the way light passed through it one day when Frankie Minematsu happened to check the time out in the bright sun. It reminded me of a prototype of a new trinket a would-be producer named Vreke once showed me. We tried to buy that watch off Minnie, but he said he got it as a gift from a man whose life he saved and he wouldn't part with it, not at any price. He was always willing to let us *play* with it, though. To experiment with it. To see what we could do with those strange optical properties unique to that little lens."

That little lens. What had Jimmy the Freak called it? Ingrid bit her lip as she made an effort to recall.

The 'Anamorph.'

Yes, that was it. The Pyroptic Anamorph.

She'd assumed she'd broken the special lens when she overturned Vreke's camera back in that 1941 soundstage. She'd never guessed (though she probably should have) that he'd hidden one of his special Anamorphs away by having it embedded in the case of his silver pocket watch.

She would never have swapped it for the gold one he'd planted on Minematsu had she known it contained a piece of occult technology that would still be dangerously advanced thirty years in the future.

"What did you do with it?" Ingrid asked of the remains of Francis Boggs, Los Angeles' first full-time filmmaker, in a low, pained voice. "What did you make happen, Uncle Frank?"

The skeleton looked as distressed as Ingrid sounded.

"You have to understand we didn't know what would happen," he insisted. "We suspected it would be destructive, I suppose—that was the whole point, after all. That's why we took it all the way out to Nevada to test. Away from populations and buildings. Miles away. We tried. But we had no idea. You have to believe me, we had no idea."

"I believe you, but I need to know what the hell you're talking about," Ingrid said. "Just tell me what *happened.*"

"It was that lens, you see," Boggs' troubled skeleton repeated. "That lens. It wasn't just a thing to focus light—it somehow changed its structure in response to the wavelengths that passed through it. The information it captured could be fixed in place and played back later by reversing the process Tommy came up with. I never did understand, but Tom always had a head for that sort of thing. He adapted a standard camera to burn pictures into Minnie's magic watch crystal, and a high-intensity projector to play them back. To bring them back to life. And believe me, they were more lifelike than any images you ever saw. Better than photographs by far. They had dimension and color and even sound, clear like no phonograph ever was. You could feel it if they touched you. Because that lens somehow 'condensed light to a slow vibration,' as Tommy put it. He came to believe that's what matter is, the substance of everything—just slowed-down light. Working with that thing changed his whole picture of reality."

"None of this is really explaining why the world's a cinder, Uncle Frank."

"Well... you have to remember the war," the dead director hedged. "What the news of the war was like. The numbers of the dead they printed in the papers after Ypres, and the Somme... They looked like misprints. We thought they had to be. Too many zeros. We couldn't imagine carnage on such a scale. Nothing comparable had ever happened in all the history of the world."

Ingrid felt sick. Was the history of the 20th century one of constant world-wide warfare? She knew hostilities would break out between Japan and America by 1941, but this earlier great war her Uncle Frank spoke of was news to her.

"After the sabotage of the munitions dump on Black Tom Island in New York Harbor, when it became obvious that America would be entering the war... we had an idea we thought might head it off. It was just an idea. We wanted to try it out before we took it to the government.

If it worked the way we believed it would, we thought it might make a weapon intimidating enough to put an end to the Great War, and to every war. We wanted to end violence and suffering. That was our goal. We thought we were doing good."

"Just tell me what you did. Please."

"We took a picture of the sun. Burned its impression into Minematsu's watch crystal."

Ingrid let the implications sink all the way in. "Holy shit," she whispered.

"We thought it would be destructive," Boggs repeated, "but on a limited scale. Or else we would never have tried. I still don't know if Minnie's magic lens reproduced the sun actual size or if it just ignited the atmosphere, but that piece of weird glass started to burn white-hot the instant Tommy's projector beam hit it, and it wouldn't stop. I didn't have time to turn away, much less run for cover. Like there could've been any cover. All I really remember was a blast of heat so hot it felt cold and a light brighter than any I ever imagined… and then here I was. Just here, with everybody else from the world."

Ingrid was too stunned to know what to say.

"*All?*" she whispered, turning to Mickey. "Really all?"

The King gestured toward the door that exited onto what was left of Mictlan. Ingrid went over to look, dreading what she knew she would see.

Down on the plain, there were a lot of skeletons. So many that Ingrid's capacities for metaphor deserted her. They covered the ground from horizon to horizon and barely seemed to have any room to move about, they were so tightly packed.

Ingrid believed it could be everyone down there—everyone in the most absolute sense. The endless carpet of smooth gray craniums all crammed together looked like goosebumps across the surface of the world.

"Is this occurrence the result of your machinations?" Mickey asked her, his voice a low rumble.

Ingrid nodded.

"It has brought about the cessation of all that is," the King explained. "My realm endures while others perish because it is glutted on the thanatonic energy of multiple genocides, but it will not endure for long."

"Are you telling me to undo it?"

Mickey shrugged. "I am not insisting."

Ingrid looked up at him, surprised. "What about the other pantheons? They'll attack before they fade away."

"They may. But they cannot force my hand. All they could hope to do would be to feed upon my reserves, which will be depleted soon in any case, with no fresh lives to replenish them."

"And that?" she asked, tipping her chin toward the surplus of corpses filling up the ground below. "Does that bother you? The cessation of all that is?"

"If it be your wish, my love, then all that is will cease," said the King. "Fuck it. I won't be told what to do."

Ingrid looked to Francis Boggs, then back to Mickey.

"It might be easier if you made me," she murmured. "Forced me."

"I will ask you," Mickey said. "I would *prefer* not to meet oblivion, if it may yet be avoided."

"But you will do it? For me, if I ask?"

"For you I will."

Ingrid nodded. She couldn't hope for more devotion than that.

She couldn't ask him to go through with it, though. Not really.

"But if I steal the silver watch back from Minematsu, he'll kill you," she said, turning to Boggs and blurting out the complicated facts. "It's not his fault, it's something he's being made to do, by someone with power over minds and thoughts. But I can't change it. The best I could do was switch out the gold watch for that silver one, which I stole from the man who's using your groundskeeper. But if the silver watch goes missing or I give him back the gold one, the command activates."

"And what exactly does that mean?" Boggs asked.

"That Frank Minematsu shoots you dead in 1911," Ingrid told him. "That your films are lost, and your legacy forgotten, too."

"Oh," the remains of the filmmaker said. He swallowed hard, despite his lack of an esophagus. "So it's me or the rest of the world?"

"No," Ingrid said. "It's *Minematsu* or the rest of the world. I can still go back and kill him first, before he kills you. To hell with these damn watches."

Boggs' skull seemed to frown. "But you said it's not Minnie's fault. Something he's being made to do, didn't you tell me?"

"Yes, but… it's him or the *world*, Uncle Frank."

"No, Ingrid," Francis Boggs said, taking her hands in his bony fingers. "And don't you dare think that way. Don't you even *consider* doing what you just said, not for a second. Don't say it out loud again. I won't have you making a choice like that, one you'll live with for the rest of your days and beyond, like killing an innocent man. I won't see you become a murderer on my behalf."

He squeezed Ingrid's hand.

"It *is* me or the world. And given that choice… it has to be me." The skeleton looked resolved, and then he said what he'd always said as a director when he made up his mind: "It's my decision to make, and that's what I decide."

Ingrid nodded, fighting tears. *Not in front of Mickey*, she reminded herself, breathing deep. Never in front of Mickey.

At the moment, not breaking down was more difficult than any challenge she'd ever faced on stage. But she was equal to it.

"Go on and give Minnie his gold watch back," Francis Boggs said, and Ingrid embraced him, fiercely, her chest aching like some powerful fist was squeezing her heart. Her Uncle Frank was as frail and small in her arms as a skeleton should be, but he hugged her back hard.

Chapter Nine

THERE wasn't much more to it than that, in the end. Mickey dialed back the days, back past the firestorm that erupted from the Nevada desert on the winter solstice of 1916, and all the way back to the afternoon of October 26th, 1911. Ingrid rode Shadow back out to Edendale and picked Frank 'Minnie' Minematsu's pocket for the second time that day. The diminutive gardener smiled when the same clumsy skyscraper of a redhead from that morning bumped into him again, and he never noticed Ingrid repeating her deft trade.

As she was sneaking back off the grounds of the Selig Polyscope Studio she passed by an open office window and again overheard the voice of her Uncle Frank Boggs.

She paused to listen.

"Well, his equipment is interesting, but I don't like his attitude," he was saying (and sealing his fate as he made his decision). "I think I'm going to tell Mr. Jimmy Vreke to go and vuck himself. With a 'v.' Get it?"

"Sorta joke that only works on paper, Frank," a second voice said. Ingrid recognized the laconic drawl as belonging to Thomas Persons, Uncle Frank's right-hand man when it came to the technicalities of film production. "And not very well even there."

"Thing of it is, I'm happy here, working for the Colonel, and there's something about that Freak I just don't trust. The predatory interest he showed in Ingrid Redstone after *Race Tout* premiered is only part of it. I'm glad she's off in Europe somewhere, and far away from him."

"I know what you mean."

Ingrid glanced back. Minematsu was perhaps a hundred yards away, standing in the late-day sun and paying her no mind as he checked the time on his gold watch.

She couldn't save her Uncle Frank's life. Not now, not after the hash she'd made of her first attempt. But she might yet save his afterlife.

This time around she'd removed the fob chain from the gold watch, before giving it back to Minematsu. That was a risk, altering the physical base of Jimmy's complex hex, but it was one she was willing to take, as only the binding portion of his spell appeared to be attached to the golden chain.

She drew it from her pocket now, wrapped its ends around the first two fingers of either hand, and pulled with all her might until one of the high-carat links yawned open. Ingrid thought she felt a little extra snap when the chain gave way, like a tiny electric jolt, and took it as confirmation that the scrap of hexwork attached to it had also broken. She threw the pieces of chain aside in disgust, like they were two twitching halves of a viper she'd torn apart before it could bite. Her bruised fingers throbbed in time with her pulse.

Death would now be the release it was meant to be for Boggs. He'd move on to Mickey's world, at least. Vreke would not be able to bind his soul into post-mortem subservience.

It was better than nothing, though not by much.

Ingrid looked back again and Minematsu was gone now, off to some other job on some other corner of the lot.

She hurried away. Back to Shadow, and back to the Silent Tower.

She wondered if that name, Silent Tower, would always be a torment to her now, as she let the hellhorse stroll home at his own pace. She hardly noticed the scenery they cantered through, not even as the westering sun poured sideways through the foliage, lighting the leaves and casting long shadows.

She wanted to run back to the studio to warn her Uncle Frank, to tell him to get out of town tonight, to get him on board a ship and bound for Europe or Alaska or anyplace else, but she knew it wouldn't do any good. Minematsu would come gunning for Boggs as soon as the Freak's deadline expired, and he'd be able to find him anywhere in the world he went. Jimmy had of course included in his foolproof spell a link between the men that entangled them on a fundamental level across all of time and space. Ingrid had seen it when she examined the ethereal algorithms he'd wrapped around the watch. Jim knew what he was doing, all too well. And if she interfered with Minematsu in some way, prevented him from being there to accept the watch in the first place, Jimmy would simply find himself a different post-hypnotic patsy.

Ideas like jumping back another twenty years to murder young master Vreke in his nursery did occur to her, but she had no stomach for assassination (even assuming she could break through the concentric protections he'd inherited to do it, the personal wards built up over generations like growth rings in a tree trunk. Jim's forbearers had hexed him up against malign intentions before he was ever born).

The Freak had played her to a checkmate in this game of life and death, though it tore at her to admit it. Any action she might take now would only postpone the inevitable, at best, and could obliterate her world, at worst. She'd seen it burnt to charcoal once already.

Boggs wouldn't suffer if she let events play out as they were currently destined to do. She couldn't say nobody else would get hurt, as William Selig would be shot in the arm, but he wouldn't be killed. He'd live to start a zoo at some point in the years to come, and then live to see it ruined.

While her Uncle Frank would die in 1911, and time would wash away his memory, like he'd never been. It was the fate he'd chosen, rather than see her lose her soul to save him.

Ingrid was lost in her thoughts, too hollowed out to know how to feel. She was vaguely surprised when Shadow stopped in the middle of the short stretch of paved road in front of the Silent Tower. She hadn't noticed when they rounded the last ridge before it came into view.

The sky was bruised with purple twilight and black storm clouds that moved in off the ocean in the west. It would rain before morning rolled round again. Unless Ingrid chose to roll it somewhere else.

But she didn't want to do that, not quite yet, though she didn't want to see Mickey either. She didn't trust herself around him at the moment. She felt too volatile. And she thought she owed it to her Uncle Frank to stay in 1911 until noon tomorrow, when the hands on Minematsu's gold watch would line up at the top of the dial.

She led Shadow inside the building Mictlantecuhtli had made for her and stabled him in the lobby. He didn't need to eat or drink and he wouldn't soil the carpets, so she just left him there.

Ingrid went upstairs, but not all the way up. Between the ground floor and the top floor very little of the Silent Tower was decorated or finished off. Many of the details required to make a space useful for work or habitation had yet to be installed. The only walls on most floors were bearing walls, those needed to hold the place up. Beyond that, the middle stories of the building were as wide open as industrial lofts, and just as echoingly empty.

Ingrid found an abandoned dropcloth on the third floor, stiff with senseless spatters of paint. She wrapped it around her shoulders like a shroud and huddled in a corner near a large window to wait out the night. Mickey would've made her a feather bed to sleep in if she wanted to head up to his chambers, but she preferred hard uncarpeted floors and coarse canvas to comfort and luxury, right now.

She rested her forehead against the cold pane and fell asleep that way, soothed by the sound of the rain, with her warm breath blooming rhythmically into clouds of condensation on the dark window glass.

Chapter Ten

INGRID woke the next morning stretched out on her side, with a clear, bright sunbeam warming her face and blazing through the hair that fell across her eyes.

She sat up and checked Jimmy the Freak's silver watch, the one she'd brought back from the future, with a Pyroptic Anamorph embedded in its case. It was ten-thirty a.m., local time. She would have enjoyed either breakfast or a bath, but she had nothing to eat or wash with, so she sat instead. Crosslegged on the floor, listening to the sound of her own breath, which seemed magnified in the general silence. She drew chthonic currents up through her chakras for a while, then reinforced her vision of banishing stars after evoking the Guardians of the Four Quarters anew. It was magical maintenance she'd neglected for longer than was wise, and it felt good to stretch her imaginal muscles.

When the hands on her silver fob watch aligned at the top of the dial, she closed the case, took a breath, and went upstairs to welcome Francis Boggs to the afterlife.

SHE arrived a moment before Mictlantecuhtli pulled the freshly killed director's bones out of his skin all of a piece and stood them up next to the stone altar that dominated the sacrificial chamber.

"Ingrid!" Boggs said, spotting her at the first chamber's door and hurrying to block the portal to the second. "Get out of here, what are you doing? Run, it isn't safe!"

"It's all right, Uncle Frank," Ingrid said. "The King and I are old friends."

She eased past the frightened skeleton in the doorway and stood next to Mictlantecuhtli, who put a bony, companionable arm around her. His cowl stirred in a wind no one else could feel.

Poor Boggs didn't know what to do, or what to think. Ingrid had to remind herself that this was a different dead Boggs than the one she'd spoken to last night. This one had died five years younger, and without destroying the world in the process, which had to be a humbling experience. That first one had bravely accepted his fate in the name of the greater good, but this new one might be expected to feel different about the circumstances of his unanticipated demise.

"But... Minnie ran mad or something. Shot me, I think," Boggs said, his skull seeming to frown. "Colonel Bill was fighting him, last thing I saw before... before..."

"Before you were here."

"Yeah," Boggs said uncertainly. "We... we have to help him. Don't we? The Colonel?"

"He's all right, Uncle Frank," Ingrid said, aware that her old friend was confused and distressed by her lack of urgency. "Well..." she almost filled in the detail about Selig being shot in the arm, but decided against it. "Yeah, he's all right."

"But Minnie shot me. I know he did. Why would he do that? I don't understand what happened!"

Ingrid tried to take his hands, but the dead director was having none of it. He threw them up and backed away from her.

"And you!" he barked. "What are you doing *here*? I thought you were in Europe, not, not... wherever we are!"

"It's called Mictlan," Ingrid explained. "It's the realm of the dead, Uncle Frank. That's why you're here."

"So what's that make you? Saint Peter?"

"It's true, and it's real," Ingrid said. "I'm sorry."

But Boggs' bones seemed only to find this funny. "I know a dream when I'm having one," he said conspiratorially, snickering as he patted her on the arm. Ingrid found the mood swing disconcerting. It wasn't like the affable, steady man she'd known in life.

"He doesn't believe it after what you just did to him?" she murmured to Mictlantecuhtli. Boggs' empty flesh, laid out across the altar stone, was still being nibbled on by insects that could be called upon to clump into Tzitzimime.

"Your presence here has confused him, I think," the lord of death growled in response. "Reminded him of realworld concerns he no longer shares."

"Is that why you skin them?" Ingrid asked. "To help them let go?"

"It is not altruistic," Mictlantecuhtli said. "It is the way things are. The dead relinquish their hold on life and so move on from it, while the denizens of my realm are sustained. Both the living and the dead are tormented when the dead remain unquiet, and my minions go hungry without flesh, so all benefit from the arrangement."

Boggs had started idly pawing through the collection of trinkets and baubles Ingrid had given to Mickey. He held up a high-crowned hat garnished with a peacock feather and a single velveteen shoe. "What is this, the prop department?" he said rhetorically, ignored by Ingrid and her King.

"What happens when they can't… move on?" she asked.

"They fragment," Mictlantecuhtli said. "They dissolve and disappear, and fertilize the existence of this place. Sometimes they stop functioning and sit still, or else they wander aimlessly, in either case until they are found and then consumed. At that point even the realworld's memory of them dies."

Boggs dropped the artifacts from Mickey's collection and stared off into nowhere, like he was trying hard to remember something.

"And I did this to him?" Ingrid murmured. "By being here?"

"Not necessarily. Those whose deaths are sudden or violent, whose heads are filled with the concerns of the living world, are often unable to come to terms."

"I can help him, though, right? Or you can," Ingrid suggested. "The way you helped Walt Whitman, that one time. Remember? He doesn't have to get consumed."

The King hedged, and hesitated.

Ingrid didn't wait for him to answer. "Uncle Frank?" she said, stepping up and placing a hand on the new skeleton's shoulder.

"Ingrid," he said amiably, as though surprised and pleased to see her. "I was just dreaming about you. When did you get back from Europe? I want to put you on film again, as soon as possible."

"Uncle Frank, do you remember where you are?"

Ingrid gestured toward Mictlantecuhtli, still done up in his full death drag. Denuded bones, necklace of eyes, blowing cowl and bloody obsidian blade in hand.

He raised his other hand in a little wave.

"Oh, yeah," Francis Boggs said, and then began to scream, much the way Jimmy the Freak's old hireling had (or would, in Ingrid's personal past and the rest of the world's chronological future).

"No, no!" she said, panicking a little herself. "Uncle Frank, it's okay, I mean, it's—"

Ingrid stepped closer to the terrified dead man, meaning to comfort and soothe if she could, holding out her arms, but he only panicked. He moaned and gibbered and dodged around her, shrieking and shrinking back when confronted by Mictlantecuhtli.

"Uncle Frank! Please!"

But the dead man was no longer listening—not to her, and not to reason. He slammed into the wall with a degree of force that made Ingrid wince, but Boggs barely seemed to feel it, being so wrapped up in his need to escape the nightmare he'd found himself in.

"Uncle Frank! Francis Boggs! Stop this!"

Ingrid again tried to corral the frightened corpse, but he dodged and evaded her.

"Mickey?" she barked. "Make him stop!"

Mictlantecuhtli raised a hand and Boggs' feet adhered to the floor. He was stuck fast, and looked dismayed by the development.

"Ingrid..." he said, looking at her with large pleading sockets. "Don't do this. Let me go. Please, I'm not ready to be here. Let me wake up! *Please!*"

"I can't," Ingrid whispered, barely able to speak. "You're not asleep."

"*No!*" Boggs shouted. "I don't accept it! I *won't!* I don't want you here to meet me—that has to mean that you're dead too, and I can't... I just can't... no... please, no..."

The bones of her oldest friend sat down on the floor and began to sob, wrenchingly, in utter despair and desolation. Ingrid realized she was backing away. She was shaking too, just watching him. She'd never seen him cry before in life, and it upset her more than she would've imagined.

"Will he ever stop?" she said, looking up at Mictlantecuhtli, who shrugged, very slightly.

"Only to begin again," the King said. "This is the pattern he follows now."

"Can't you at least make him know I'm not dead? Can't you help me comfort him at *all? Please*, Mickey! Please!"

The King seemed at a loss, and Ingrid thought he would say there was nothing he could do. Then: "My Tzitzimime can be quick, if you would see his torment end."

The words hit her like a punch, and she was very nearly sick over the image they conjured up.

"Oh, Mickey..." she moaned, unconsciously putting a hand over her mouth. Her eyes felt as large as baseballs. "Isn't there any other way?"

Mictlantecuhtli cocked his head, considering her query for a long and serious moment.

"No," he said, and Ingrid felt like something deep within her chest was caving in. "He is too far gone."

"I can't watch it," she said, when she was able to speak. "I can't be here!"

Hysteria was already rising in her voice. She couldn't handle this, bearing witness to a friend's agony when there was nothing she could do to ease it. She simply could not.

"Then go, my love," Mictlantecuhtli said, "and leave him to our ministrations. He will suffer no further, I promise you."

Ingrid threw herself against her King, who manifested flesh in a flash in order to embrace her.

"Thank you, Mickey," she gasped, then pulled away and fled, out the door, out of the office suite and back into the real, as her eyes blurred with tears she wouldn't dare let fall until she was safely far away from Mictlantecuhtli and his Silent Tower.

Chapter Eleven

—*August 15ᵗʰ, 1939*

GRAUMAN'S Chinese Theater turned out to be an Oriental fever dream rendered in neon and concrete, with a forecourt that opened onto Hollywood Boulevard.

Searchlights crisscrossed the black night sky above the gaudy movie palace. Throngs of people crowded the street in front of it, straining for a glimpse of one of the stars arriving by limousine for a gala premiere. Messrs. Lahr and Bolger and Morgan were there, according to the grapevine, though Miss Garland apparently was not. The young actress was in New York City, rehearsing for a play. The names meant little to Ingrid, who was somewhat divorced from the popular culture of the day.

She guessed the gathered crowd to be many hundreds strong. They filled the sidewalks and the street, making both impassable. Ingrid looked over the sea of heads and smiling faces, toward the distant box office and the forecourt that crackled with startling camera flashes.

She was the only person on horseback, other than the mounted police who were there to keep the peace.

She steered Shadow into an alley behind the imposing stone block of a Masonic temple across the street from the theater and dismounted. She guided the pseudohorse into the actual shadows of a recessed rear doorway, with which he seemed to blend. No casual passerby would see him there.

Ingrid walked down the alley and emerged back onto Hollywood Boulevard. From there she edged through the crowd, smiling and apologizing to those she jostled. At the perimeter around the organized premiere she slipped past security and strode right down the red carpet, just like she belonged there. Her dress, a shockingly slinky silk gown Mickey had made for her, matched the walkway, as did her glossy scarlet shoes. She smiled for the cameras and waved, and felt the fans' attention on her as palpably as a lingering touch, even though none of them had any reason to recognize her.

She looked around the theater's forecourt, with its collection of celebrity footprints pressed into concrete. A temporary Munchkin Village had been installed for this occasion, and photographers were busily snapping away at its small, colorful residents.

Nobody recognized her, yet neither did they seem to think she looked out of place.

Ingrid again easily bypassed the ushers at the door, despite her lack of a ticket or invitation. Unseen imaginal stars projected from her heart center deflected their attention onto other things.

Inside, the Chinese proved no less garish, or enchanted. It managed both qualities at once. Red and gold columns stood along the lobby's walls, framing murals that depicted everyday life in an exotic and obviously imaginary rendition of the Far East. A massive, intricate chandelier hung overhead, and the carpet felt thick underfoot.

Ingrid acquired a bag of popcorn, then slipped unnoticed up a staircase that was not quite concealed in the lobby's far corner.

Large opera boxes filled out the upstairs floor, four of them, instead of a proper balcony. Two were already in use, occupied by people Ingrid assumed to be the premiering film's producers and their families. They paid her no mind, beyond a few polite nods and smiles. They didn't know her, but neither did they know who she might be with.

She claimed the box on the furthest left for herself and closed its door behind her.

The sudden sense of being swaddled in luxurious privacy made her shiver. She might as well have been all alone in the vast auditorium.

It wasn't long before the lights went down and the film began.

The story of Dorothy Gale from Kansas was a familiar one to Ingrid. *The Wonderful Wizard of Oz* was published in 1900, and her Uncle Frank had given her a copy for her birthday that year. At seventeen she thought perhaps she was too old for the fantastical children's story, but had quickly fallen under its spell. Eight years later Frank Boggs had been instrumental in the production of *The Fairylogue and Radio-Plays*, a touring presentation of the Oz story that combined elements of stagecraft with new moving picture technologies. The show had featured as the narrator Mr. L. Frank Baum himself, author of the original novel, and it had used filmed segments directed by Boggs as well as animated magic lantern slides designed by artist Michel Radio of Paris to tell the tale. Live actors also came into play at certain points in the narrative, seeming to the audience to step right down off the flickering screen and into their reality, separated from them only by the apron of the stage. People had fainted upon seeing the effect in 1908. At least one or two at every performance of the expensive production's short-lived run, to hear her Uncle Frank tell it.

Ingrid had even appeared in one of the very last performances of the show, understudying the role of Glinda the Good for Evelyn Judson, who'd come down with the flu. It had been mid-December in New York City, and bitterly cold. She and other members of the troupe would attend a party given by Mr. Nikola Tesla later that night, a man as far ahead of their time as Ingrid was herself, with whom she would greatly enjoy talking, and the next evening she would board a train bound for the west coast, where she'd been offered a role in her Uncle Frank's next venture, a movie from an original script he'd written, titled *The Heart of a Race Tout.*

But it was that night in New York she was thinking of now. When she'd risen up from the hidden trap in the stage floor, resplendent in her white gown, rising into and blending with the projected image of Glinda on the screen behind her for just a moment before the powerful theatrical spot blotted out the movie footage, making her real. She heard gasps from the packed house and felt their wonder rising toward her, clouding her head like some sweet, intoxicating smoke.

Basking in the artificial glory generated by her Uncle Frank's clever special effect had been one of her favorite moments on stage, as well as one of her favorite memories, period. It'd been simply magical, and she'd known even then she would never forget it.

And so it was that Francis Boggs haunted her thoughts as the first reel of the new *Wizard of Oz*—the 1939 version she'd heard (or would hear) Alma Reville-Hitchcock speak of in 1941—rolled by in black and white.

The movie's headlining cast was far too small to include all the characters that populated her Uncle Frank's crowded screens. Nick Chopper the Tin Woodsman, His Majesty the Scarecrow, and the Cowardly Lion all seemed to feature in this one, based on the lobby cards and posters on display out front, and she wondered which of her other favorite characters from *Fairylogue* would make the cut. Tik-Tok the Machine Man, or Jack Pumpkinhead, Whose Brains Were Seeds? The Hungry Tiger, or Mombi the Witch? Perhaps the Rubber Bear?

The Dorothy they'd cast seemed old for the role (when compared to eight-year-old Romola Remus who'd played the character in *Fairylogue*, anyway), but she was quite lovely and very sweetly earnest. Ingrid was charmed by her and her little dog; they reminded her now of another brave Dorothy she'd known. The twister that carried their house away was an impressive effect, but it wasn't until they arrived in Oz and the movie exploded into a glorious sensory overload of saturated color that she started to cry. First to weep and then to sob, wounded down to the floor of her soul to think that her dear Uncle Frank, who'd loved both this story and the movies themselves so well, had never had a chance to experience the twin miracles of color and sound alive on a screen for himself. The *Wizard of Oz* was like nothing Ingrid had ever seen, and she could only imagine how excited Francis Boggs would've been over it.

She pledged to remember him always, because Mickey had assured her the rest of the world would quickly forget.

She cried for all the stories they would never tell together, cried like she hadn't since she was an awkward and miserable girl, cried hard enough that she was sure the people in the next box over must have heard her, which she found mortifying, though the embarrassment did nothing at all to help her stop.

She wasn't able to do that until long after the credits had rolled, the lights had come up, and the people in the audience had all gone home.

NEXT TIME:
Episode Five
INGRID'S ACID TEST

EPISODE FIVE

~BONUS SHORT SUBJECT~

INGRID'S ACID TEST

—*February 6ᵗʰ, 1966*

INGRID closed the front door of the Silent Tower behind herself and hurried to a taxicab that idled at the curb. Vapor curled into the crisp evening air from the yellow car's exhaust pipe. It was winter, and the short-skirted fashions the dead wore into Mictlan from around the middle 60s had not been conceived with cold weather in mind. Ingrid loved the little outfit her King had made for her, though—a vivid crimson dress, simple as an A-shaped smock, that barely reached the middle of her thighs. She wore elegant gloves and cute, low-heeled shoes that matched. Silver chandelier earrings dangled from her lobes and a pile of upswept hair sat atop her head. Her black velvet handbag was no larger than an envelope. All it contained was a clutch of dried mushrooms, wrapped in a square of waxed paper.

The only other object she carried was an antique silver fob watch, which she kept buttoned into a pocket of her short-waisted, black woolen coat. No money, keys, or identification. Even the kohl around her eyes and the rouge on her lips had been painted on in the otherworld, by a skeleton the King's butler Winston had introduced as Maksmyllian Faktorowicz. He'd asked in a Russian accent to be called Max, and was apparently an authority on twentieth-century trends in cosmetics. The make-up would remain as he applied it until just before dawn, when it would vanish entirely, like it had never been there at all.

Too bad Max couldn't have bottled products with that nifty property while he was alive, Ingrid mused, nestling into the back seat of the taxi Winston had called for her. He would've made himself a fortune.

She toyed with the fat red garnet she wore on a silver chain around her neck and named her destination, then looked out the window. She had to peer through the pale ghost of her own reflection in the glass. It was not yet seven o'clock, but the sky above was as dark as blue ink, soon to be black and dusted with cold stars. The neighborhood's office buildings looked largely empty, with only a smattering of random windows lit in their facades. The sidewalks were dark and deserted. Few restaurants or retails stores called this neighborhood home. It wasn't an area into which strangers or tourists tended to wander.

Ingrid's breath fogged the window when she leaned close. Faint auras of condensation rose around her fingertips where she touched the glass. Her driver steered them westbound onto Sunset, a street that was better lighted and more populated than the blocks immediately surrounding her building.

The ancient hexwork around the site of the Silent Tower still subtly inclined people away. As perceptually slick as the building tended to be, however, an unanticipated visitor had recently wandered all the way up to the King's Chambers. He'd gotten into 'Miguel Caradura's' office suite and carelessly crossed between the rooms.

Ingrid didn't know if 'recently' was an appropriate term. 1966 was a full eighty years past the date of her birth, though she didn't look or feel like an octogenarian. An exact accounting of her age was no longer possible, given all the time she'd spent in timeless Mictlan, but nobody would've guessed her older than thirty.

So it was recently according to her perceptions that Mickey brought the unfortunate seeker from '66 to her attention, thinking she might appreciate him as a curiosity. He was the first living person to cross the barrier between worlds since Winston Watt was thrown across during a fight in 1910. (Ingrid never had learned all the details of that story, but she didn't think the perpetually exasperated manservant would be amenable to her asking questions.)

She'd been the last person to cross prior to Winston, and the first ever to return. The bony butler remained bitter about that. Winston may have been an initiated man in life, a privileged member of both the Order of the Golden Chain and the far more exclusive Cult of Mictlantecuhtli, but none of his mystical insight had kept his flesh on his bones.

Ingrid still didn't know where her own free pass came from, and Mickey hadn't figured it out either. It wasn't merely that she was female—Winston once confessed that he'd pushed several women across before he died, trying to puzzle out her secret. A prostitute with no magical pretentions, a spiritualist medium of dubious authenticity, and even a sister member of the Golden Chain. All were skeletons now, bound to the realm of Mictlan. Ingrid's suspicion was that her affinity with the element of earth acted as a sort of inoculation for her, a rough equivalent of having returned to it partway already. Some deeper level of initiation into the great mysteries than Winston's victims had attained must have made the difference, in any case. But she had no way of knowing what it was for certain, or when in her experience it might have occurred.

She had no idea what might prepare someone else to cross.

The scruffy, wide-eyed kid from '66 who stepped across the barrier with an uncomprehending grin plastered on his face hadn't been so lucky.

He didn't even seem to realize his flesh had dusted away—not until Mictlantecuhtli stepped in behind him, and the King's thin hand dropped onto his shoulder.

He turned around to see a tall skeleton in a black cloak, and Ingrid standing with him—a dramatic redhead nearly as tall as the figure of Death.

"Whoa," had been the extent of his commentary. His lips were gone, but Ingrid had the feeling he was grinning in his own mind. He'd been so thin in life that the fit of his t-shirt and jeans barely changed in death. "I thought Halloween was, like, three months ago, man."

"I think you're gonna find it's Halloween all the time now," Ingrid said, casting an eye up and down the length of him.

That was when he looked at his hands and realized what had happened. He hadn't *understood* it, surely, but he got that something catastrophic and irrevocable had occurred while he wasn't paying attention.

He stared at those fleshless fingers for a good long while before looking back up at Ingrid and her King and reiterating: "Whoa."

"Did you come here on purpose?" Ingrid asked him. "Did you come looking for this place?"

"Naw, just wandered in. The door wasn't locked, no lights—I thought I might find a place to crash."

"If you have not sought me and have abandoned your foolish flesh by accident, then begone," Mictlantecuhtli told him, and that was what he did. He slunk out of the sacrificial chamber and into the realm of Mictlan, with one distrustful glance back at the skeletal cat in the cloak and his tall redheaded girlfriend.

Ingrid spotted a folded-up slip of blue paper sticking out of his back pocket and she snatched it as he left, thinking he wouldn't need it anymore, whatever it might turn out to be.

She unfolded the flyer again now, in the back of a cigarette-scented taxi that carried her northwest up what was called the 101 freeway these days (though less than a century before it had been the old Spanish Royal Road, *el Camino Real*—otherwise known as the King's Highway).

Ingrid considered the handbill.

She hardly knew what to make of it. Its bulbous lettering was drawn in such a way that the words seemed to throb and writhe. They'd been poorly printed in dark purple ink on light blue paper. The page bore the address of a church in the San Fernando Valley, of all things, as well as a legend that made very little sense to Ingrid, though the sound of it was intriguing:

Can <u>YOU</u> Pass The Acid Test?

It was a question she did not feel prepared to answer.

But if the people who could were finding their way up to the top of the Silent Tower circa 1966, then she thought she ought to pay them a visit, if only to see what they were all about.

THE 'church' on Haskell Avenue was unlike any other house of worship Ingrid had ever seen, looking like nothing so much as a monumental wooden sculpture of a fat Bermuda onion. Her taxicab dropped her off some yards away from the unusual building and then pulled around in the gravel parking lot, rather quickly, and was gone without a trace.

Ingrid turned back to the big onion. Spicy eucalyptus trees stood tall around it, silhouetted in black against a starry night sky. Strange, loud music emanated from within.

There were people about, perhaps a dozen or so that she could see around the grounds, smoking and talking in pairs or small groups. More than a few seemed to notice Ingrid. Cigarettes dangled forgotten from slack fingers, and conversations seemed to trail off. An ethereal girl with long straight hair danced up to her, took both of her hands and looked up into her eyes for a long and apparently emotional moment, then twirled away again without a word. A pair of longhaired young men with coils of thick cable looped over their shoulders paused to watch the exchange. They'd been lugging some sort of lighting equipment around the back of the building, and they resumed their efforts like professionals as soon as Ingrid swiveled her head in their direction.

The amount of electronic equipment in evidence surprised her, when she made her way across the grounds and peered into the big onion itself. A round church, like the Hagia Sophia or an ancient pagan temple. She found that interesting. Only it was dark inside, more like a theater than a shrine, and wildly aswirl with multicolored lights. The music was deafening and disorganized, almost as if the performers were making it up as they went along. Projected film clips and abstract, pulsating imagery climbed up the onion's curvaceous inner walls, up toward their narrow apex. Some people, mostly the younger ones, were dancing in the center of the space, while some of the older and more churchgoing types hugged close to the walls. Individuals representing both camps bore expressions of either rapturous wonder or uncertain horror as they absorbed the scene around them.

What in *hell* was going on here?

The sight confronting her inside the big wooden onion reminded her of nothing so much as one of those demon-teeming hellscapes painted by Hieronymus Bosch.

A large, strong hand clamped onto her shoulder, making her start.

"You comin' in or not, little lady?"

Ingrid turned and looked up into the eyes of the owner of that hand. He stood an inch or two taller than her, making the 'little lady' label relatively applicable, if no less patronizing. His short hair was crisply parted on the left. He was whipcord thin, clad in a t-shirt and jeans, and his bright eyes glittered with manic energy.

"I'm Neal," he said, grinning at her. "Neal Cassady."

"Hugh Romney," a shorter companion of his said, stepping around Cassady to interject. Hugh had a shock of dark, wavy hair, a tweed jacket over a pink and blue t-shirt, and a stuffed trout on a leash. The 'leash' was actually an invisible-dog toy of a sort that Ingrid was familiar with from carnivals and state fairs—a leather collar attached to a long curve of wire that would bob along companionably like an unseen pet when carried by an imaginative child. Hugh's stuffed fish, buckled into the collar, seemed to swim through the air ahead of him. "Just call me Hugh, like all my friends do."

"Ingrid," Ingrid said, offering her hand. Cassady took it and kissed it as though he found the gesture amusingly archaic. "Can you tell me what this is? Hugh? Mr. Cassady?"

"*Mr.* Cassady!" he repeated, rolling his eyes. "Yes, I can tell you what this is—it's a pagan rite."

"It's an exercise in consciousness-raising on a mass scale," Hugh contributed.

"It's a party," Cassady said. "It's a dance."

"It's a service."

"It's a show."

"It's a sacrifice."

"It's *your* personal life at *this* moment in time, and it's every other moment experiencing itself through you, and through me, and through us, and through everyone, right here, right now, in this instant, in this place, tonight!" Cassady crowed.

"I see," Ingrid said, though she wasn't at all sure she did.

Hugh took her hand and led her inside, behind his levitating fish, with Cassady sticking close at her elbow and talking a mile a minute. Ingrid couldn't hear a lot of it over the amplified music, but she was already getting a feel for the gist of this animated beanpole's rap.

"They're called the Dead," he shouted into her ear, upon seeing her give the bearded musicians the once-over. "The Grateful Dead! Ain't they a trip?"

"It says the Warlocks on the bass drum," Ingrid observed.

"Yeah, they changed last month," Cassady said. "I drove 'em down from Frisco on the big magic bus. Gonna bring some of that up-north scene down here to all you Lost Angels. Can you dig it?"

Ingrid knew most of the words he used, though the manner in which he strung them together struck her as somewhat arcane.

Hugh took her other hand and led her toward the center of the floor, where two large punchbowls were set up. "You're here for the Test, right?" he said. "The Acid Test?"

"Here to receive the sacrament of the electronic shamans?" Cassady echoed. He ladled some punch from one of the bowls and drank it down before filling a second paper cup and offering it to Ingrid.

"I'd like to know what it is," Ingrid said. "Someone gave me a flyer, and I was curious."

"Well," Hugh said, pointing to one of the punchbowls and then the other: "this bowl's for the cats, and this one's for the kittens, dig? Which sorta feline are you?"

"Miss Ingrid looks like a tiger to me," Cassady said, grinning.

"Tyger, Tyger, burning bright," Hugh said.

"In an onion, watching lights," Cassady extemporized. Ingrid took the paper cup he offered.

"That's the *electric* kool-aid," Hugh warned. "The other's the unleaded. Just so you know."

Ingrid nodded and gulped down the shockingly sweet beverage, doled out from the container identified as the cats' bowl. She had no idea what the man with a fish on a leash was talking about, though it seemed meaningful enough to him.

It was only then that she realized, with no small amount of panic, that she'd left the tiny purse containing the mushrooms she needed to find the Silent Tower in the back seat of that damn taxicab.

THREE hours later she'd almost forgotten again, though she periodically remembered in a vague sort of way that there was still a problem that needed addressing. It was hard to focus on. People were undergoing religious revelations all around her. Either that or making out. Some may have been doing both simultaneously, which didn't strike Ingrid as incongruous or improper at all. Even the music had improved, or at least seemed to make more sense to her now. She felt entrained to the band's rhythms, riding the same groove they were. That everyone here was. A lot of the slang that these people in their tight, short, and multicolored clothes employed was starting to come clear to her as well.

Her mind felt like it was gradually expanding, and would soon encompass the entire world.

Hugh seemed to have backed off to let Cassady take the lead in the flirtation game (though he did at one point poke his trout-on-a-wire up the back of her skirt, startling her). Ingrid couldn't tell if he was leaving off pursuit rather than compete with the force of nature that was Cassady or acting out of loyalty to someone else, but the result was that she found Hugh easier to talk with. She still didn't know who these people were, though she'd learned they called themselves the 'pranksters.' She'd learned their 'sacrament' was something to be reckoned with, too. She was starting to see how one of their number might have accidentally found his way into the Silent Tower—the first time that had ever happened, as far as she knew, in the building's history. The place had always been too well protected, until now.

The idea that she might find her way home via the same loophole the unlucky hipster had fallen through was beginning to take shape in her head when she saw a familiar face in the crowd.

He looked a quarter-century older than he had the last time she'd seen him, and he hadn't looked so young then. He was dancing with abandon nevertheless, accompanied by three girls whose combined ages probably didn't equal his when added together. The expression on his face was predictably joyous.

It was Jimmy the Freak. Still alive and kicking, more than fifty years after their first meeting. Ingrid could hardly believe it. She still had the man's old silver fob watch in her pocket.

Would she never be rid of him? It was starting to seem like their fates were connected by more than chance. She knew it was him beyond a shadow of a doubt when he spotted her and waved cheerily, looking no less amazed to see her.

It was time to get the hell out of here.

Ingrid faded back into the crowd even as the wizened revenant that was the Freak started toward her, across the dance floor.

The Pranksters' 'acid' would be more than sufficient to rend asunder the concealing veils around her Tower. Its sensory effects felt like distilled versions of the visions inspired by her old fungal friend Teonanactl. All she really needed was a ride back to Hollywood.

"Hugh!" she said, spotting a newly-familiar face in the strobe-lit crowd. The flashing light made all the dancing bodies look like they were projected at eight frames per second.

"Ingrid!" the bushy-haired Prankster said.

"Do you have a car?" she shouted, over the pounding music. "I have to go!"

"I don't have a car," Hugh said, "but I do know one hell of a driver."

INGRID couldn't tell if the bus really looked the way she was seeing it, or if Prankster punch was playing practical jokes on her perception. All of the whirling lights and projected images from inside the onion might have been playing across the wheeled leviathan's surface when it rumbled out from the darkness at the rear of the church grounds and crunched around the gravel driveway, nosing toward the street.

The paint job consisted of wild whorls of red, blue, and yellow. The destination placard above the windscreen bore a single, evocative word:

FURTHER

"Cowboy Neal!" Hugh said, when Cassady (now sporting a slick-looking western hat that he wore cocked far back on the crown of his head) opened the bus's accordion door with a pneumatic control. Neal looked down at them from his perch on the seething mechanical monster's tape-mended driver's seat.

"Clamber aboard, Tiger Lady," he said, and Ingrid did, followed by Hugh and his pet fake fish. More than a few of the heads assembled for the acid test applauded the appearance of the mythic dreambus.

Ingrid, looking back out the still-open door, saw old Jimmy at the rear of the crowd, just then exiting the gently respiring wooden onion. She didn't think he saw her, and she ducked quickly back from the door, which Cassady closed before anyone else could climb on.

"Now would be a good time to go," Ingrid suggested, and Cassady stomped the pedal. The big bus lurched forward and almost seemed like it would tip over when Cassady hung a hard left out onto Haskell, then they roared away south.

Ingrid didn't think Jimmy the Freak was any the wiser.

FURTHER featured an open-air observation deck on its roof, and Hugh escorted Ingrid up there for a smoke while Cassady piloted them over the hills along winding, picturesque Coldwater Canyon. The air was as cold and clear as glass, while the galaxies overhead turned like the gears in a great cosmic watch. The grass her escort rolled up into a joint was a new strain he'd bred himself, he said, on his Hog Farm up in a northeast corner of the Valley. Illegally, under prohibition conditions, as simple hemp had apparently been outlawed since 1939. That rather 'blew Ingrid's mind,' as the Prankster's peers might have said. There were virtually no restrictions at all on which plants and chemicals people could trade in, back in the era with which she was most familiar. Jimmy Vreke's family had made their fortune dealing in such things. Hugh's homegrown hempflowers tasted earthy, fruity, and resinous on Ingrid's tongue, and the smoke induced a soothing silliness that colored their conversation in shades as oddly unexpected as the paintjob on the bus that carried them.

She told Hugh about fleeing from Jimmy the Freak. Overcome by a fit of candor, she went on to tell him that she was both a time-traveler and a witch. The young poet listened with rapt attention, never expressing a word of disbelief. All he said, thoughtfully and earnestly, when she had finished, was:

"Nobody should have that kind of power."

"Maybe not," Ingrid conceded. "Nobody keeps all their promises, too. Maybe Nobody should run for President."

That notion seemed to delight Hugh. He giggled. "Yeah, maybe Nobody should," he agreed, handing the carrot-shaped cigarette they were sharing back over to her. They'd stretched out on the floor of the deck, on the roof of the bus, out of the wind, and they stared up at the churning stars (as the black canopy of branches overhead allowed). "I'll name this after you," he offered. "The strain, I mean. If you like. Let it be known as 'Ingrid' forevermore."

Ingrid nodded, grinning in appreciation of the proposed herbal tribute.

Foliage above gave way to powerlines, streetlights that left trails across the retinas, and tall office towers that stretched away toward perspective-points in the sky. Ingrid had given Cassady the best directions she could, and she and Hugh went back down into the main fuselage of the cosmic conveyance as soon as she thought they were getting close to the Silent Tower's neighborhood.

She instructed him to turn off of Sunset, and then there it was, as plain as anything. Her familiar old building seemed to shudder and shimmy when she looked up at it, while directing Cassady to park in the lot across the street.

The Prankster's acid dissolved the site's ancient ring of barriers so thoroughly it was like they'd never been there at all.

That would have to be seen to. Straightaway.

"Thank you, guys," Ingrid said. "It was great of you to give me a ride like this."

"There's nothing here," Hugh said uncertainly, peering out the window. "This whole block's, like, deadsville. Y'know?"

He didn't know the half of it.

"We can't leave you off *here*," Cassady said, clearly sharing Hugh's dim assessment of the neighborhood. "Chivalry may be dead, but it ain't buried, Tiger Lady. There ain't nobody around for a mile."

"Then where's the danger?"

"Well, nobody we can *see*," Cassady amended. "There could be lurkers."

Ingrid smiled. "I appreciate the concern, boys, but I'm pretty sure I can take care of myself." She unsheathed a six-inch knife from its mooring on her left thigh, under her skirt, and flipped it up to spin and flash in the air before catching it and re-sheathing it, just that quick. The blade was visible for barely a second, and in that span Hugh and Cassady each sucked in a sharp, surprised breath.

"Guess you do have claws, then, Tiger Lady," Cassady said, though uncertainty was still evident in his dilated eyes.

Hugh was staring up at the Silent Tower.

"What is that place?" he asked. "That's where you're going, isn't it? Up there?"

Ingrid nodded.

"It's not... it's not an *ordinary* place, is it?"

"No, I suppose it's not. But it's a place you'd do well to forget."

She touched the pneumatic control at Cassady's elbow, and the accordion door folded open with a hiss. She stepped down into the street, then turned and looked back up at the pair of Pranksters framed in the narrow door, staring after her.

"Go on," Ingrid said. "Further's one thing, boys, but this is much too far."

Cassady closed the door, and Hugh raised a hand as the bus rumbled away. Its rear bumper, she noted, bore a sticker that read 'WEIRD LOAD.'

Ingrid waited till its taillights disappeared around the corner at the end of the block before she strode into the Silent Tower.

She stepped into the elevator and rode it all the way to the top floor. There, she clicked down the hall, straight toward Miguel Caradura's closed office door.

Her King was waiting for her when she opened it, in his skeletal Mictlantecuhtli aspect, framed as usual in the doorway to the second chamber. Ingrid could see the bloody altar stone behind him. Shadow, her black, semi-substantial spirit stallion, stood calmly in the first room, where she stabled him these days. Being mostly dust bound together by will he required no particular maintenance, and so she saw no need to make other arrangements for him. He could always find his way back here, too, without vegetal assistance. Ingrid thought she might be better off riding him out into the realworld on future excursions, no matter how modern and urbanized the city got. He blended seamlessly with any shadows he passed through, and tended to be forgotten by those who saw him in the light. Ingrid wondered if a cloak borrowed from Mictlantecuhtli might let her partake of that useful brand of virtual invisibility as well.

"My love," the King said, tipping his hooded skull while Ingrid ruminated. "Who are your new friends?"

Ingrid frowned, and even as she was about to ask him what he was talking about she heard the elevator bell ding behind her. She turned around to see Hugh and Cassady stepping out of the car to the left of center.

Their jaws went slack in comic synchrony when they looked past Ingrid's shoulder.

"You shouldn't be here," she told them, sadly. "You really should not."

They came right toward her anyway.

Ingrid wasn't sure how to handle this. If they wanted to cross the barrier after her, should she let them? It was a horrible thought, but she certainly didn't want them bringing a busload of their weird confederates back here.

They entered the first chamber, their eyes as wide with wonder and fear as any sacrificial victim's had ever been.

"You should go," she murmured, "and forget this place."

"I will," Cassady said, "If I can ask one question first."

Ingrid nodded, and Cassady turned to address Mictlantecuhtli.

"When?" he asked.

"Two years and one day from your now," was the King's prompt answer. "You will drink a wedding toast, and it will be your last."

"Two years..." Cassady breathed, looking humbled.

"Two years and one day," Mictlantecuhtli said.

"And me?" Hugh asked. His voice cracked when he did.

"Many years," was the King's dismissive response. Hugh stepped back, reprieved and chastened.

"Can I change it?" Cassady asked, still contemplating his forecasted fate.

"Do you want to?" the King asked, and this question Cassady was not so quick to answer.

"Please go," Ingrid said. Her voice was low and pleading.

Hugh nodded and tugged on the sleeve of Cassady's t-shirt. It seemed to break the taller man's reverie, and they did go, together, without another look back.

Mickey stepped aside and Ingrid crossed the barrier, into his inner sanctum.

"Will you have Winston call a locksmith?" she asked, and mentally dialed the hours forward to approximately eight a.m. the next morning. El Rey nodded. His manservant had been organizing the King's realworld business even before telephone service became available in this neighborhood, but nowadays he could call out from the otherworld. Mickey had even sent him out physically, once, clad in borrowed flesh on the day after Halloween of 1875, with several bills Ingrid gave him to invest with the Farmers & Merchants bank, downtown. With the benefit of otherworldly foreknowledge the King's realworld fortune had been conflated into something rather vast by the middle of the twentieth century, and he enjoyed wielding the influence that came with it.

If Ingrid wanted something done, in this world or the next, all she had to do was ask.

"I'll be right back," she said to Mickey, then went downstairs into a cold morning in 1966 to watch the locksmith she'd requested install a heavy deadbolt on the front door of the Silent Tower, as well as to collect the new lock's key.

In an era when mass exploration of the mysteries had become a cultural phenomenon—if not a party game or a weekend diversion—it would never be safe to leave that door unguarded again. The ancient wards around the Silent Tower had been rendered null and void to the eyes of an ever-increasing number of people. Eventually the protections might break down altogether.

The only solution she could come up with—to lock the damn door—was a simple one, but then simple solutions were often the most effective.

She stood back in the clear morning sunshine and watched her locksmith ply his trade.

AND NOW, OUR FEATURE PRESENTATION
~EPISODE SIX~
THE FLOWER WAR

~EPISODE SIX~

THE FLOWER WAR

Chapter One

THE King did his best to keep her entertained.

He made a Spanish-style *rancho* for her, of the sort that monopolized the southern California landscape throughout the 1800s. Ingrid, who'd first arrived in Los Angeles in 1908, had never known the ranchero way of life, though she'd heard some of the local oldtimers reminisce about it fondly, and she supposed she could see why. Her King's otherworldly simulacrum of that era included a sprawling main house with a flower-shaped fountain burbling away in its central courtyard. All of the rancho's single-story buildings had red-tiled roofs and thick adobe walls that kept the interiors cool even in the worst of the stifling summer heat. It was definitely summer, although the skies above never brightened beyond a flat silver, no matter how the weather might feel.

He fashioned acres of orchards and vineyards with picturesque arbors, as well as miles of rolling hills over which Ingrid might ride her favorite horse, Shadow, for hours on end, until she was weary enough to sleep without dreaming. On the hottest and stillest afternoons she hiked alone into the foothills, where she might bathe in slow-moving streams or else climb to lonely hilltops to watch clouded-over, artificial sunsets, tinged red and orange by the smoke from distant wildfires.

Mostly she just let the days drift by, unremarkable in their similarity, reminding her of the endless lazy summers of her childhood, when she hadn't bothered to know what day of the week it was for days and days on end.

The world el Rey de Los Muertos made for her felt real in every detail, but all she had to do to see any aspect of it change or disappear was to ask. Mostly she didn't bother. She was content enough with Mickey's choices. He'd come to know her tastes quite well, even though they communicated but minimally, anymore.

In the evenings there were balls and fancy parties to attend, held on the neighboring ranchos or as far away as the Pueblo de Los Angeles, which would grow into downtown by what Ingrid thought of as 'her day,' in the early 1910s. Wagonloads of women in bell-like skirts stepped down from their carriages in front of fashionable townhomes by warm torch and lantern light, while straight-spined *vaqueros* chatted to one another from atop their prancing horses.

They were all dead, these subjects of el Rey, though they seemed not to know it. Their masks of false flesh might slip for a little while if they thought Ingrid wasn't around, revealing bones beneath, but otherwise they stayed committed to the illusion they'd been conscripted into by their King, whose will they had no power to oppose. They all put on a show of behaving like the privileged relations of 19th century cattle barons they remembered being. Men drank and smoked and sometimes brawled, while ladies twirled across dancefloors or gossiped in small knots. Their dark eyes glittered and their bared shoulders glowed under the candle chandeliers, in warm tones of caramel and honey. Everyone deferred to Lord Mictlantecuhtli, her Mickey, whom they knew as Señor Miguel Caradura—one of the pillars of their small, spread-out community.

Nobody seemed to guess that he was the lynchpin of their entire illusory existence.

Ingrid loved to dance with Mickey at these events, shaking her ass and shimmying her hips in ways that would've been far too shocking back in the real 19th century. She continued to pick up 20th century moves on her occasional and random jaunts back into the realworld. (Places where people gathered to dance and drink were always easy to visit briefly, to capture the feel and flavor of an era without incurring unnecessary complications.) She didn't care that the dance styles she toyed with at Mickey's soirees were incongruous with the re-created times and wouldn't reach the real LA for decades yet to come. These were *her* parties, arranged for her pleasure, and she'd damn well dance how she wanted.

She took her King to bed only rarely anymore, even though they tangoed almost every night, and he bore this with surprising equanimity. She expected more complaints, or at least some complaints, but Mickey delivered none, and Ingrid suspected he might be playing some sort of game. Or maybe he thought she was playing games and was biding his time to see what sort of move she might make. It could be hard to gauge the thoughts of an otherworldly paranoiac.

The last time he brought her to a climax was right after she thought she'd saved the life of her Uncle Frank. She supposed it wasn't Mickey's fault, the way that turned out, but things hadn't been the same between them since. Something in her had changed, and she didn't know how to bridge that distance anymore.

Admitting it made her wistful. Her own private, actual world had diverged significantly enough from the 'real' that the two would never totally align again, and yet she found herself aching for the company of the friends she'd left behind. She felt an increasingly desperate need to reach out to those few touchstones she still had in the land of the living— that bare handful of individuals who'd ever even come close to understanding her. She realized with sad dismay that she could literally count them on a single hand.

After all she'd done and seen, she still had no one to share it with. No understanding ear. Mickey had never been that, as voracious as he could be for details he might use to make himself feel more real. Her relationship with her King was an intricate dance of intrigue and second-guessing, seasoned with the self-satisfaction that came along with being a new thing, a unique creature, a surprise even to the gods. She'd never guessed how tiring that might become. Mickey could make almost anything she might desire, but all she wanted anymore was the simple comfort of companionship, and that was one boon he couldn't seem to grant.

Most of a season passed in this fashion. There was discontent; but there was also luxury and freedom from any obligation. Ingrid found the balance comfortable enough to live with, and she might never have challenged the status quo on her own. How could she leave, when there were sumptuous feasts from which she never gained an ounce, as well as wines and liqueurs that set her mind reeling yet never caused a hangover? When she might invite any historical personage she'd ever wished to meet to come dine with her? Anything she desired could be had or done, here in Mictlan. The entertainments were more lavish than any the realworld might provide, the possibilities truly endless.

So why, Ingrid had to wonder, did it all feel so empty? Like a pleasant but pointless dream—one from which she increasingly wished to wake. That was a truth she had trouble acknowledging, except during the darkest nights of her soul. What normal life could she go back to now, after having known Mickey and his world? Things may have reached a point of stagnation between them, but she couldn't imagine leaving.

The problem was, she no longer knew how to carry forward anymore, either. All she could see her way clear to do was let the imaginal days roll by or to timehop recreationally, as it amused her. Contravening the laws of time and space according her whims had become an idle pleasure. Everything of consequence she'd tried to do with that ability, all of her good intentions and clever plans, had come to nothing, so she'd set her grand ambitions aside.

She couldn't even rouse herself to take revenge on Jimmy the Freak. Ennui seemed to have settled into her bones.

All she was doing now was keeping herself distracted while she waited for something to change.

Chapter Two

WHEN Ingrid went upstairs to the King's Chambers at the top of the Silent Tower one afternoon not long after her weekend jaunt to 1966, she found Winston, Mictlantecuhtli's majordomo, waiting for her with as sour a look pasted on as his fleshless face could manage.

"He would have you join him at your earliest convenience, Lady Redstone," the bitter servant said, with a barely-concealed sneer.

"Thank you, Winston," Ingrid said, ignoring his conspicuous resentment. Winston may have been a capable sorcerer in life, though in death he was chiefly valued for his ability to sign for the King's deliveries at the door between worlds. He'd been as instrumental in the building's construction as its architect, Oscar San Martín, who had long since dissolved into oblivion, while stubborn Winston remained.

It was strange that Mickey hadn't met her at the door himself. He'd never left the help to greet her before.

It didn't feel right, not at all.

Ingrid smiled.

"Shall we?" she said, and marched purposefully across the sacrificial chamber and out the far door to emerge onto the top of Mickey's Pyramid—the imaginal one on his side of the barrier that he loved so well he'd never bothered to take it down, despite the original, realworld version having been nothing but rubble for almost a thousand years.

The sight that greeted her on the plain far below was not the one she expected.

Arrayed on the ground and stretching from horizon to horizon were vast armies of the dead. They stood arranged in ranks and files—an ocean of corpses drafted into service and lined up for inspection. Ingrid could only make out details of the costume and equipage of the very nearest platoons, but even these bristled with an incredible variety of weapons. She saw blades, bows, rifles, spears, cannon, rockets, and any number of other infernal-looking devices she could not name. Many of the skeletal soldiers showed clear evidence of the tools of their trade having once been used on them. They stretched away in neat blocks, all the way past the gently curved edges of the visible world.

"Winston?" Ingrid said, unable to keep the dismay out of her voice. "What is this?"

"These are the assembled armies of the dead, my love," Mickey said, from where he stood on the top of the Pyramid, behind her. "What does it look like?"

Ingrid almost shot back with something sarcastic, then figured this was probably not the time for it. Mickey had on his most elaborate ornaments and his tallest fan of feathers. He held a staff made of several spines' worth of strung-together vertebrae, topped with a grape-cluster of skulls.

"It's a little unexpected, is all," Ingrid said. "What are you doing here?"

"Having my revenge," he told her.

"For?"

"Really?" he said. "Are you insensate? Do you not remember the *assault* mounted upon my realm by its neighbors?"

"You mean after I almost broke the universe?" She'd been under the impression he'd put all of that unpleasantness behind them. "That was really sort of a diplomatic response on their part, all things considered. Don't you think?"

"I do not. And their temerity will be paid for."

"Oh, Mickey…" Ingrid said. "I don't think this is a good idea."

"It is not an idea," said the King, banging his staff on the roof of the pyramid he stood atop, like a figure on a weird wedding cake. "It is a certainty."

Ingrid shook her head. She didn't think he could be dissuaded. When Mickey set his mind on something…

"So, what?" she asked, indulging a bit of genuine curiosity. She'd always figured the great Imagination was a large enough place for all the various and disparate faces people gave to their eternal truths to find a home, but the politics of how they all coexisted was still a mystery. She hadn't traveled much beyond the defining boundaries of Mictlan, though every other realm that had ever been imagined should theoretically be out there somewhere. "You're gonna storm Olympus and Parnassus and Arcadia? Then on to Asgard and the Pure Land and the Six Lokas too?"

"Olympus seems as good a place to start as any," Mickey said, and raised his arms up to the unchanging gray sky. "And we are expected. My emissaries have offered terms."

The skeletal armies assembled on the plain below stood at attention and saluted their King. Billions of them, all at once. The sound of that many bony fingertips simultaneously tapping that many fleshless foreheads was vast and oceanic. The echo of it rolled across the land like a wave.

"What now?" Ingrid said, looking up at Mickey. "You march?"

"We have marched, and arrived, as I have willed it."

Ingrid turned around along with all the dead soldiers down on the plain, and saw that a new mountain peak had appeared on the far horizon. A ring of white columns stood at the cloud-shrouded top of it. She thought she could see small figures draped in white gathered at the center of the ring, peering anxiously in their direction.

One of them lifted effortlessly off the ground and floated swiftly across the landscape, above the armies of the dead. He was rather good looking, sporting nothing less than the body of an actual Greek god. He settled near Ingrid at the top of the Pyramid, right below Mictlantecuhtli's feet. Small, downy wings grew from the sides of his sandals, and he wore little more than those insubstantial shoes.

"Greetings, Hermes," el Rey said from his exalted position on the roof of his inner sanctum. "Is Olympus prepared to surrender?"

Hermes bowed his shaggy head. "We are, Mictlantecuhtli."

"Why?" Ingrid asked, and Mickey glared down at her. "Well?" she continued, glaring right back. "I'm just curious."

Hermes glanced up at Mickey for permission—which he received in the form of a nod—before answering.

"Our influence is much diminished from what it was, Lady," the Olympian spokesman explained. "We occupy but a corner of the Imagination, now, where once we dominated, and our territory shrinks at a steady rate as we fade from living memory. Our mobility and even our consciousness desert us in our decline, as we calcify into mere literary preservation. Mictlantecuhtli owns all of those who honored our names in life."

"Surrender is their only option," Mickey said. He raised his gold-cuffed arms again, and the ranks of the dead all raised whatever weapons they carried with a united shout of victory.

"Olympus is mine," the King of the Dead announced, and his voice boomed out across the otherworld.

He looked down at Ingrid.

"Who's next?" he asked.

She wasn't in the mood for this. She felt unusually drained. Almost ill, she realized, as she broke out in an all-over sweat. The fabric of her dress stuck unpleasantly between her shoulderblades.

"What about... what you normally do?" she asked, drawing in a shaky breath. Her acute discomfort was already passing, though she suspected it was the sort of thing that might recur in successive waves. "Processing the dead, and such," she continued, distracted. Her head hurt more than a little bit. She hadn't been feeling right for a while now. "Who's taking care of that while you do this?"

"Such work continues unabated," Mickey said with a shrug. He didn't seem very interested in the question. "I have many aspects. Why, do you wish to see someone?"

Ingrid nodded. It hadn't really been on her mind, but she supposed there was someone she wanted to see again. She'd once promised to try, anyway. And it might be a way to distract martially-minded Mickey from this dangerous new conquest business, which was going to be a problem if left unchecked. She knew her King too well by now to think it wouldn't.

Mickey leapt nimbly down from the roof of his chambers and took her hand. His grin was broad and earnest. He was having fun, and he wanted her to share in it.

She supposed that was nice.

"Who can I bring you?" he asked, as he escorted her to the sacrificial chamber.

Chapter Three

O H, shit," Mrs. Parker said upon finding herself in the first of the King's Chambers and seeing Ingrid waiting in the second, through the doorway. "Does this mean what I think it means?"

Ingrid nodded. "Hi, Dot," she said. Mictlantecuhtli stood next to her, skeletal and imposing in his robes and eyeballs. The sight of him was hard to misinterpret.

"I don't know if this counts as seeing you again or not," the wizened woman said, studiously ignoring the tall memento mori at Ingrid's side.

"Me either."

"Well, I feel better, anyway," Dot said, looking down at her own frail arms. She bent them at the elbows and flapped them up and down like scrawny featherless wings, seeming surprised at the newfound mobility. "My God, but it's awful to get old, Ingrid. It was never my intention."

"Has it all been that bad?"

"Alan died four years ago. Suicide, that son of a bitch. And then my poodle Cliché went too. Not to mention everyone else I ever cared about. Mr. Benchley, Mr. Fitzgerald… every one of them. Last year I fell and broke my shoulder and I've hardly been able to raise my arms to type since. I was about to have a Broadway play produced, next season, after all these years, and I've watched myself shrivel into something one might expect to find beneath a brickpile outside of Cairo. So yes, it's all been rather horrible."

Ingrid looked down, disappointed and chastened. *Sorry I encouraged you to live,* she thought but didn't say. Dot may or may not have accepted the apology.

"This is the room at the top of that damn building, isn't it?" Dot asked, realizing. "I was never able to find my way back here, and believe me I tried. Alan drove me around for hours. I *would* have come up here with you back in '41, if I'd had any idea. That was the day we entered the War, wasn't it, the day I met you? 'World War II,' they call it now, like it's a fucking sequel. I wouldn't have minded expiring before having to see how *that* horrorshow finally panned out."

"How did it pan out?"

What had gone on in the world she'd saved?

"Don't you know?" Dottie asked. Then: "No, you plainly don't. Well, we won, my dear. We stopped the march of Fascism across the world, and only a few million people had to be murdered before we took the threat seriously. Then all we had to do to win the day was obliterate two Japanese cities with atomic bombs, and a jolly time was had by all. I'm being facetious, there, you see. It was genuinely a fucking nightmare."

"Dottie, is that true? Is that what happened? Whole cities?"

"Hiroshima and Nagasaki," Mrs. Parker said. "Full of women and children and possibly even a man or two who didn't entirely deserve it, gone in a literal flash. That's the threat we've lived with and the world we've lived in, ever since."

Ingrid swallowed hard, feeling a shade of her earlier nausea return. "Mickey?" she murmured, hoping for a denial of Dot's report.

"There is no other feast to equal it," he said, disappointing her. "Nor one prepared so *fast*. Would you like to see?"

Ingrid closed her eyes. "Thank you, no," she said, and her voice sounded tight.

"I don't like this death, either," Dot complained. "It doesn't suit me. Where's my rainswept night? There's nothing romantic about keeling over on an eighty-degree afternoon in a tiny apartment that smells of dogshit."

"If you would have selected the circumstances of your demise," Mickey said, "you should have beaten me to it."

"Well, I didn't wait seventy years for *this*! Who's going to feed my dog now?"

"Cross over," the King instructed.

"And if I refuse?"

"Dot…" Ingrid warned. "Don't."

"Oh, and why *not*?" the dead woman demanded, putting her hands on her hips. "Like *you* play by the rules. Look at you, you haven't changed in twenty-five years!"

"It hasn't been that long for me," Ingrid said. A few months, half a year at the most.

"You only prove my point," Dot said. "Did asking permission get you where you are? Did doing as you're told get you what you wanted, or put you where you wanted to be? Ever?"

"I may not be where you think I am," Ingrid said.

"I know you're someplace practically beyond my imagination. I know you've had experiences no other human being has ever had."

"So come and join me," Ingrid said. "I know how things work over here. I have an in with the management. If you want rain, we'll have rain. It can be any way you like."

"Tell me, though," Dot said, shaking her head as though she already knew the answer, "is there anything I might do over there that matters? Anything that makes a difference in the world, that would give me purpose? Because that's what I've always wanted, you know. Purpose. To do something that *counts*."

"Purpose is no longer your purpose," Mickey said. "It is too late for that. Now cross over."

"Please, Dot," Ingrid said. "Just do it."

But the tiny old woman only smiled. "You can't make me, can you?" she said to the King, echoing one of the first things Ingrid had ever said to him. "You can't cross that barrier yourself."

"*I* can, though," Ingrid said, stepping across to seize Dottie by the shoulder and pull her over before she mouthed off to the point where she angered Mickey and spoiled her own afterlife.

But her hand went right through the little woman's arm.

"It tickles!" Dottie said, cackling at Ingrid's dismay. "Oh, that's delightful!"

"Mickey?" Ingrid said, looking back over her shoulder at him, framed there in the doorway.

"She is merely an idea of herself," the King grumbled. "Insubstantial, over there."

"I was hardly ever more than an idea of myself anyway," Dottie said, "so that suits me fine. I don't suppose there's any reason to go on looking quite so prehistoric, either, is there?"

Long-gone elasticity returned to Dottie's skin. Her hair darkened back from gray to brown, and her rumpled housedress became a sleek beaded gown. She looked down at herself, grinning, apparently quite pleased with the transformation.

"You don't know what you're saying, Dot," Ingrid said to her. "You really don't."

"I rather like the idea of haunting something," Mrs. Parker continued, as though Ingrid hadn't said anything at all. "That has a certain gothic appeal."

"Dottie, *please* go over!" Ingrid shouted. "Please! Don't make me responsible for this!"

Dot looked surprised by the outburst. She looked up at Ingrid with large dark eyes and waited a moment until her tall friend was calmer.

"I think not," she said, and Ingrid could see her quietly deciding, once and for all. "I believe I still retain a chance of doing something worthwhile in the world if I stay over here. A slim one, maybe, but this is *my* adventure, Ingrid Redstone, and I'm strictly past tense as soon as I step through that doorway. Now isn't that true?"

Ingrid nodded. She had to admit it was.

"Then I'm staying," Dot said. "For a while, at least. I've got acquaintances I'd like to bedevil from beyond the grave. I want to hear the poisonous things I know they say about me."

"Go if you would go," Mictlantecuhtli said from the doorway between his chambers. He vanished even as Ingrid turned to look at him, and reappeared behind Dottie. "Before you miss your chance!"

Dot shrieked as Mictlantecuhtli's bony arm looped around her throat. *He* could grab her well enough, where Ingrid couldn't. He looked like he was grinning.

"Mickey, *no!*" she shouted. "Please, don't!"

The King of the Dead looked up at her from under his cowl… and let go of Dottie in the instant before his realm reclaimed him. He flickered back into existence in the next room, next to his altar, empty-handed.

An instant on the realworld side of the reality-lock was the best he could manage, and even that cost him a superhuman effort. He could extend his will a little more successfully (to turn on the lights or occasionally operate the lift), but he bounced back to the sacrificial chamber every time he tried to leave it. Ingrid had seen him make the experiment on any number of occasions.

"Take it as a kindness when I warn you never to return," he said, turning to address Mrs. Parker, whom he'd left in the first room with Ingrid. Whether or not Dot heard him was another matter, as she was already in flight, darting out the door marked 'Miguel Caradura' to escape into the realworld as a ghost.

It was down to Ingrid and her King, once again.

"You could have pulled her in with you." It wasn't a question. She knew the answer before el Rey nodded.

"You spared her for me?"

Again, Mickey tipped his head in the affirmative. "I did, my love."

"I- I appreciate that."

"You should," Mickey said darkly, putting his hands on his hips. That gesture usually looked petulant to the point of funny, but Ingrid didn't feel like laughing now, not even inwardly.

"I thought you said my being here didn't necessarily have to… you know, wreck them."

"It does not," Mickey said. "Your acquaintances would seem to be troubled individuals to begin with, and from this arises difficulty."

Now there was an assertion Ingrid could in no way deny.

She decided she should probably stop trying to attend the deaths of friends, at least from the post-mortem side. She'd have to find some other way to occupy her mind.

THE FLOWER WAR

Chapter Four

—June 12ᵗʰ, 1981

THE nearest movie theater to Ingrid's Silent Tower was a thing called the Cinerama Dome. The imaginative structure resembled a giant golf ball sunk halfway into the earth at the side of Sunset Boulevard, with an acre of shiny cars parked out behind it. The Dome was twenty years old by now, ill-maintained and frayed around the edges, but it still struck Ingrid as wonderfully futuristic. It was another round ritual space—reminiscent, at least to her, of the onion-shaped church in the San Fernando Valley where she'd passed the Merry Pranksters' acid test.

Back in 1966, that had been, when that bulbous temple and this hemispheric movie house had both been brand new.

Ingrid approached the theater from the rear, sticking to the darker and more sparsely populated streets south of Sunset. She rode Shadow, her demon-stallion, who blended into any phenomenon that shared his name. That was a useful trait, as a horse on the streets of Hollywood this late in the 20ᵗʰ century would otherwise have been a conspicuous sight. Ingrid might have been almost as eye-catching herself, except she was draped in a cowl borrowed from Mictlantecuhtli, and had pulled the hood up over her fox-red hair. The heavy robe made her as hard to see as her horse.

She dismounted and left Shadow in an alley off De Longpre Avenue, with the King's cowl rolled up and stuffed in a saddlebag. When she looked back from halfway across the parking lot she could only spot him by squinting hard at the spot where he should be.

Nobody would trouble him, not this late at night, and he'd be waiting to take her home later, after the credits rolled on the ten p.m. screening.

Ingrid had no particular need of a ticket. She bypassed the box office and sashayed past the bewildered teenaged ticket taker, who looked like he wanted to say something but didn't quite dare. She didn't need any special trick—the combination of looking glamorous and behaving like she belonged exactly where she was carried enough influence.

She slipped into the big auditorium before drawing any more attention from the staff and took a seat near the back of the house. The hexagonal concrete blocks that made up the theater's domed roof made her feel like she was sitting inside a giant tortoise shell. Young ushers in matching shirts were still picking up popcorn boxes and soda cups left over from the 7:30 show. None of them did more than glance at her, perhaps feeling they lacked the authority to say anything, even though the doors hadn't officially opened.

Ingrid folded her arms across the back of the chair in front of her and rested her chin on top of them, and watched the rest of the crowd settle into their chosen seats over the next twenty minutes.

They were an excitable bunch, receptive and ready to laugh or applaud. Had she been waiting in the wings of a different sort of theater and about to go on stage, she would've been heartened by the electricity she perceived.

By the time the lights went down and the previews for upcoming releases started to roll, Ingrid realized someone was watching her.

He seemed familiar, but she couldn't get a good look in the flickering dimness, with the house lights down. He was on the far side of the auditorium, nearer to the screen, and he kept looking back in her direction.

It made her uncomfortable. Maybe she should've held onto Mickey's cloak rather than leaving it in her saddlebag, but she hadn't expected to need it indoors.

Still, she was used to being looked at, and the film was compelling, one she'd come specially to see. A paperback guide to the 20th century's best movies she'd picked up on a brief, tentative jaunt into the year 1995 singled it out as both a popular and a critical favorite. On previous evenings she'd visited 1962 to see *Lawrence of Arabia* and 1977 to see *Star Wars*. Tonight it was 1981, and the fare was *Raiders of the Lost Ark*.

The picture opened with a handsome man in a leather jacket and a fedora hat leading others through a lush jungle. He carried a bullwhip that he used as a weapon and a tool. He seemed to be a treasure-hunter, penetrating an ancient temple containing a golden idol that was protected by a series of ingenious traps.

When Ingrid saw that idol her heart seemed to stop in her chest.

It reminded her uncannily of another she'd seen, a thousand years ago. Califia's totem had been carved from green stone while the movie prop looked like it was worked in gold, but the figure was the same.

Identical.

Unmistakable.

Ingrid was so startled she lost the thread of the movie. This was more than coincidence—it was synchronicity. And synchronicities tended to occur in clusters. She might expect more improbable events in the immediate future. It was one effect of cutting sideways across the flow of time: recurring patterns got drawn along in her wake.

The creep on the far side of the auditorium was still staring.

She glared at him, trying to put him in context. He looked *so* familiar. It hit her suddenly—the man resembled James Vreke, Jimmy the Freak, though it couldn't possibly be him. This guy looked the way the Freak had in 1941: gray-haired, perhaps in his mid-fifties, yet still hale and attractive.

But that was forty years ago. Well, it hadn't been that long for Ingrid, but it should have been for Jimmy. And the last time she'd laid eyes on him, in '66, he'd been ancient.

That was why she hadn't been able to place him sooner.

Maybe this guy was Jimmy's son, or even his grandson.

The moviegoer who looked so much like her old nemesis caught her staring back and smiled. He even raised his hand in a wave. He pointed at himself, raising his eyebrows, and the intended message communicated clearly:

Hey! It's me! Remember?

It *was* Jimmy the Freak. It really was. Running into him was a second uncanny coincidence in as many minutes. She had no idea how he could be here, but then she didn't really know how *she* could be here, so she wasn't going to split hairs over it.

She was simply going to split. Same as last time. If he followed her, she'd handle him. Jim's fate may have been tied to hers by synchronicity, but that didn't make this a homecoming dance.

Ingrid stood and hurried up the aisle, making an effort not to run, feeling chased out of the theater by Jimmy Vreke's eyes even as Indiana Jones was chased out of the golden idol's temple by a rolling boulder up on the screen behind her.

THE lobby was deserted when Ingrid emerged from the sloped corridor that connected it to the auditorium. Popcorn jockeys slumped behind the snack bar, looking bored. She barely spared them a glance before hurrying out one of the Dome's side exits and into the warm summer night.

Once outside, she didn't bother with not running. It was easy, as she was dressed comfortably, in jeans like she hadn't worn in seventy years. The dead reported that women wore dungarees as commonly and casually as men by now, and she saw many individuals amidst the crowd gathering for the midnight screening who confirmed it.

She pushed through them and sprinted for the back of the parking lot.

She looked back toward the big half-sphere when she was on the far side of dark De Longpre and saw a figure she thought might be Jimmy standing near a rear exit, the door of which swung closed behind him as he turned his head in either direction, scanning.

Scanning for her, and spotting her, too. Ingrid saw the distant man start to weave his way through the sea of parked cars, coming after her. Her damn hair made her pretty distinct, even at a distance. It was a fine thing on stage, but not so much right now.

The Freak was *waving* at her again, calling her name like they were old friends as he hurried across the lot. Had he forgotten shooting at her, with a goddamn gun, back in 1941? Acting like they were old chums struck Ingrid as so rude that it entered into the territory of egregious offense.

She ducked into the alley where she'd left her horse and whipped Mictlantecuhtli's cowl out of her saddlebag. She slung the cloak around her shoulders and pulled the hood low over her eyes.

Then she stood back against the wall and waited another fifteen seconds or so for Jimmy to step into the dark alley after her. This was no good, bumping into him every couple of decades, especially if he wasn't going to be the right age when it happened. He had to be dealt with. And he deserved it, too.

"Ingrid?" middle-aged Jim said, tentatively, before she stepped out from the shadows behind him and kicked him in the back of the knee. He fell hard, banging his head on the asphalt, and Ingrid was on him in a flash, driving the air out of him with a kneecap planted in his solar plexus. She drew her favorite knife from an inner pocket of her denim jacket and pressed the long blade against his throat, hard enough to hurt.

He wanted to gasp, but didn't quite dare. He relaxed, opening his hands and staring up at her with wide eyes from his prone position on the pavement.

"Hiya, Jimmy," Ingrid said. "Long time no see."

SHE patted his pockets for weapons but didn't find any. He did have a wallet, with a driver's license and credit cards in the name of James Vreke.

It really was him. Not a son or other relative, and not the broken-down wreck he should have been at nearly a century old. She couldn't explain it.

"You murdered Francis Boggs. And ruined Frank Minematsu's life to do it," she said. Any other concerns could be addressed—or not—after this particular grievance.

"Yes," Jimmy said, without evasion.

"Then you won't be surprised by what happens next." Ingrid pressed harder with her blade, dimpling the shaved skin of his neck as deeply as she could without quite breaking it. Swallowing hard would have caused him an involuntary tracheotomy.

Jimmy squeezed his eyes closed. His fear was in no way feigned.

"I am sorry for it," he managed to say. "If my life is what you need to make it right, you can take it. Or ask me to, and I will. I accept your condemnation."

Ingrid hadn't expected that. She thought about taking him up on the offer. All she had to do was press her blade down and draw it across his throat. It would be no different than slicing through a hard loaf of bread.

It could be done in a second… but not by her.

Not like this.

Her flare of anger faded away. She reluctantly removed the blade from Jim's throat and sat back on the pavement, in the middle of the alley. After a few moments of limp, breathless relief, Jimmy the Freak sat up too.

"Don't thank me," Ingrid said. "You sucked the satisfaction out of it, is all. Smart, really."

Jimmy nodded. "Like I said—all you have to do is ask."

"Shut up," Ingrid said, shaking her head and sighing. "Why aren't you ancient?"

"Alchemy!" Jimmy said brightly. "Remember I asked you about that once? It's been on my mind for a long time, and I thought maybe you were onto something, Miss Red Stone."

"*You* made the Philosopher's Stone?" She made no effort to hide her incredulity, even though the evidence before her eyes was quite convincing. The Freak's youthful appearance was as shocking to her now as hers must have been to him, back in '41.

"Yeah," he said, and he couldn't help but grin. Then an idea seemed to strike him. "Hey. You wanna get a drink or something?"

T HE first quiet place they came to, walking west down Sunset, was the tatty-looking Moon Ling Chinese Restaurant. It was tucked away into a charming Spanish-style courtyard that made up for the smell of old grease, and it did have a full bar. They took a table in a palm-shrouded corner of the patio, maximizing their privacy even though they were the only customers in the place. Ingrid felt like one of a pair of adulterers meeting for an illicit cocktail when a smiling waitress with a perky ponytail took their orders and then flitted away, leaving them to their presumed tryst.

Jimmy was amiable, affable—a perfectly pleasant companion. Ingrid almost had to remind herself to stay mad at him. She'd been wary enough not to get in a car, but she was having trouble kindling her hottest fury. Something had changed in her since the loss of Uncle Frank. Something had darkened. And she *did* believe the Freak would kill himself to atone, if she required it. Samurai-style. His contrition was that real, at least.

She figured she could hear what he had to say before she decided what to do with him.

And she was curious. He looked better than he had in 1941, now that she could examine him up close.

She'd never had a drink with an alchemist before. Not a competent one, anyway.

"You gonna explain this to me, or what?" She felt no further need to elaborate. He knew what she was interested in.

"It was my father, Jacobus Vreke, who started the Work," Jimmy said. "A long time ago. Back in the nineteenth century. He pursued it assiduously all his life. That's why it was waiting around for me to finish."

"Which *you* somehow did, when dad never could?"

Jim tipped his head modestly. "Stroke of luck, really," he said. "Hardly my doing at all."

The smiling waitress reappeared with their drinks and then was gone again. Ingrid sipped her red wine. Jimmy rattled the ice cubes in his tumbler of Scotch, making her think again of her caustic and besotted friend, Mrs. Parker. She'd hoped to know the churlish little idealist better in the wonderland that Mickey's realm could be, but even though she'd befriended Death himself, there were other ways to lose someone.

"I met a man, you see. A Santero, a Santería priest. In Cuba, this was, back in the 1950s, before Castro and all that. When I was old. And he did something to me."

Ingrid sipped her wine and waited. It was rich and tart on her tongue. 'Castro' was a district in San Francisco, as far as she knew.

"I think he meant it as a curse," Jimmy said. "Meant it to drive me insane, to punish me for a life wasted in wickedness. And it did change me—just not in the ways I think he expected. Or maybe I'm underestimating him, and he intended everything that's happened since. I don't suppose I'll ever know."

"Never say never," Ingrid said. She didn't know if she meant it to sound like a threat or a reassurance. "So what did he do? And what's it have to do with anything?"

"He put music into my head."

"I don't know what that means."

"Music," Jimmy repeated. "Something that had never been any particular part of my life for more than eighty years. He… woke it up in me. Gave me an understanding of it that had never been there before. All of a sudden I couldn't stop hearing it in my thoughts, and understanding it on a different level when I heard it with my ears. The mathematics behind things like harmony, resonance, and rhythm came clear to me, like flashes of insight, and I felt a new connection to the psychology behind it. The semiotics, if you will. The secret language that lets arrangements of notes and chords resound within human hearts and minds. And *those* insights, well… they led to other flashes. Suddenly I understood things about reiteration and reverberation that allowed me to bring about the apotheosis of the Great Work in less than a year, after two lifetimes spent trying. Mine and my father's, that is."

"So you're aging backwards now? Is that what you're telling me?"

Jimmy nodded. "Just about year-for-year, so long as I keep swallowing the Red Tincture on a regular basis. I figure I'll try to level it off when I'm back to the equivalent of thirty-five or so. Youth is one commodity it's possible to have too much of."

"So you've got yourself another lifetime," Ingrid said. "Good for you."

It felt strange to be reminded that others were out there walking left-hand paths of their own, and that some of them might be almost as convoluted as hers.

"I understand how you might feel I'm undeserving," Jimmy said. "Turning an intended curse into a blessing and living far beyond my years. Turning it into a gift, even"

"What about the lead into gold part?"

Jimmy waved a hand dismissively. "That's mostly a metaphor. But I had plenty of money already. After a certain point money snowballs into more money, you know? Why, you need gold?"

She thought about it. Money was nice, but Mickey had plenty. If Ingrid wanted some, all she had to do was arrange it through Winston, and there was never a qualm or a question when she asked. Her needs these days were minimal, especially since she'd been spending most of her time in the otherworld. She wasn't certain she aged while in Mictlan. During her last couple months over there she hadn't even menstruated. Nothing grew or changed except in Time.

"My bills are covered," she said in answer to Jimmy's query about her financial situation. Her burgundy was down to the last few sips. She felt suddenly like going, and checked her watch for the time.

"Hey," Jim said, smiling. "I remember that."

He meant the silver fob watch. She'd taken it from him in 1941. Before that he'd worn her precious imaginal garnet on the end of the fob chain, since stealing the stone from *her* all the way back in 1912.

"Do you know what it is? Did you ever figure it out?"

"What do you mean?" Ingrid said, exaggerating her level of ignorance. She knew the watch was much more than a time machine that only ran one way.

"Here, let me see," Jimmy said, holding out his hand, but Ingrid held back the watch, suddenly on her guard.

Jim only smiled. "That's all right," he said. "Wouldn't be smart to trust me completely. If you would open the case, though?"

Ingrid pressed the winding stem and the case-cover with the lens embedded in it popped obligingly open. The brass gears spun inside. She looked up at Jimmy, who removed something that looked like a pen from inside his jacket.

"You remember I told you about my Pyroptic Anamorph, back in '41?"

Ingrid nodded.

"Well, that's the original, that window right there in your watch case. The very first prototype, ground from glass harvested out of the Great Sand Sea in western Egypt. The Pharaohs considered that place to be the Land of the Dead, you know. Desert glass was sacred to them. It was fused solid from raw silica by a meteor strike twenty-eight million years ago. It was ancient when the old people were young, and it has properties unlike any other glass on earth."

He aimed his pen at the lens in the watch's up-flipped lid and pressed a button on the side of its barrel. The end of it winked a startling red, and a slim scarlet beam stabbed out to penetrate the Anamorph Ingrid held in her hand. She winced at the flash of brilliant crimson light that burst out of the watch, and nearly dropped it.

But the lens had never contained an image of the sun, not in this timeline, and the glare resolved itself into a figure. A life-sized, three-dimensional portrait of a man, rendered all in red.

It was Francis Boggs. Her Uncle Frank.

Ingrid gasped.

"No other glass *remembers*," Jimmy said.

The ruby figure of Frank Boggs leaned in, smiling, as if to examine the watch she held. She'd carried it around all this time with no idea. The projection's dimensionality was astonishing. Uncle Frank looked exactly as he had in life (or would have looked while standing next to a red neon sign).

"So this is how you mean to change the world, is it?" the picture said, looking up and raising an eyebrow. Ingrid could imagine him holding the lens in his hand circa 1911, when Jimmy must have burned this image onto it in order to entice Boggs with the new technology and its possibilities.

Now it appeared as though Boggs and Ingrid were facing each other and holding the watch on overlapping palms. Ingrid touched his forearm, and felt it. The image wasn't solid, exactly, but it was tangible. Mostly there. Real enough to generate sound.

The picture broke up, vanished, and started again, repeating its one line on a loop. "So this is how you mean to change the world, is it?"

Jimmy switched off the penlight, and Francis the Red disappeared.

"I suppose they'd call that a 'hologram' today," he said. "The Anamorph is a fractal storage medium, you see, with information distributed holistically throughout the entire crystalline structure."

"And that?" Ingrid asked, tipping her chin at his pen.

"Hmm? Oh—laser pointer. Newfangled thing. Made in China. I was thinking of buying a company that imports them. You think kids would want to play with this?"

He twirled the pointer's red dot absently across the courtyard's walls and floor.

"Maybe cats," Ingrid said, shrugging.

Jimmy nodded and handed the device to her. "Keep it," he said, nodding at the silver watch as she closed the case. "So you can always look at what's on the lens."

Ingrid nodded. She was grateful, but couldn't bring herself to thank him.

"You must think I can't possibly deserve this second chance I lucked into," he said. "But I want you to know the thing that santero did to me back in Havana changed me. I don't consider these gifts mine to keep. I don't plan on holding onto my extra life any longer than it takes to feel like I've made up for some of the careless, stupid, selfish damage I did on my first go'round. Like killing your friend. Not that I can ever hope to atone for a thing like that."

"You can't. And I can't forgive you," Ingrid said, gazing at the watch in her hand. The second hand swept around the face, magnified by the window of special pyroptic glass. "But keep trying. I guess it counts for something."

Jimmy nodded, looking down at the ice cubes melting in his tumbler.

Ingrid stood. So did Jimmy. He held out his hand. To shake, was Ingrid's first thought, but no, he was offering her a card. She took it.

The Topless Tower, it read. It was small and rectangular, printed in fancy script on thick off-white stock, like the calling-cards people used to announce themselves with, back in the day.

"What's that?" she asked, considering the name. "Like a burlesque club?"

"Not exactly," Jimmy said, with a wry smile. "Drive down Santa Monica and you can't miss it, as long as you have that card. Otherwise you'd pass right by and never see it."

Ingrid nodded. It was astounding that he'd never figured out the secret of *her* tower. Maybe it was his closeness to the question that blinded him to the simple answer.

"If you ever need... well, whatever, contact me," he said. "I'd like to see you again, if possible."

"Thank you." Ingrid tucked the calling-card away. "It does count for something."

She even hugged him before they parted ways, prompted to a fit of sentimentality by having been shown the hidden picture her watch contained. She felt immediately weird about it. Things were far from square between her and Jimmy.

The walk back to De Longpre and Ivar was quiet, and just long enough to clear her head. She held the fob watch in her hand all the way back to the alley where she'd stashed Shadow, and then held it all the way back to the Silent Tower. The ghosthorse found the building without her having to pay any attention.

She spent that night in the spartan corner of the third floor where she bedded down now and then when she needed a night alone. She'd bought blankets and a pillow and left them there for use whenever she might need them. Sometimes they were stiff, ancient, and dusty; other times soft and new, depending on how far from their purchase date in 1925 she happened to wash up. By '81 they were little more than tattered rags, but she didn't care. The night was balmy. She slept well and contentedly for the first time in a long time, until late the next morning, with Jimmy the Freak's old watch lying near enough that she could listen to its constant, comforting tick.

Chapter Five

—*October 1ˢᵗ, 950?*

INGRID clicked her fingers, pointed, and Shadow leapt obligingly out through the Hole in the Sky.

She leaned out to watch him fall. It was a long way to the ground, but his powerful leap gave him more than enough range to clear the tender oak sapling that had sprouted up directly below her.

Shadow hit the earth hard and his legs folded at wrong angles under the force of the impact. Ingrid winced as he was driven face-first into the dirt, and lay still.

For a moment.

Then the black stallion twitched, stirred, and stood up again, on legs that straightened out in the instant before they were called upon to bear weight. Within seconds he looked all right, exactly as if he hadn't just dropped the equivalent of thirteen stories onto the unyielding ground below.

As long as the spirit-stallion's simplified chakra string wasn't disrupted, he should be able to recover from just about anything. As long as he wasn't chopped in two.

She threw a backpack and a set of saddlebags loaded with supplies down after her trusty mount, then tossed out a long coil of rope. It unfurled as it fell, its far end disappearing into the tree's small canopy of autumnal foliage. The rope had a fat knot in it every foot or so. Ingrid intended it for use as a rudimentary ladder. She secured the end around an iron railroad spike that she drove into the stone floor of the King's chamber with a mallet, then began to climb down, using the knots she'd tied as precarious hand- and footholds. Her arms and shoulders were screaming by the time she set her soles back down on solid ground. Untangling herself from the young Tree that grew below the Hole— which her rope ladder deposited her in—proved to be the most difficult part. She was scratched and sticky, with orange, russet, and gold leaves tangled in her witchy hair, by the time she set her feet on solid ground.

She missed the convenience of the demolished Pyramid, though the growing oak was surely a safer thing to have on this site.

Safer for all the worlds involved.

Ingrid took a deep breath. The air this far back in time was pristine, unpolluted, clear as a polished lens. She could see for miles. No buildings intruded on the view, no structures of any kind, not anywhere from horizon to horizon. Birds trilled in distant trees. The meditative stillness of untrammeled nature struck her as deeply primordial.

A thousand years back, this time around. Almost. She hadn't yet dared to look as far ahead into the future. She dreaded finding another era in which her native reality was blackened, ruined, and devoid of life because of her mistakes. Visiting the past wasn't safe either (as she was gambling the future she knew as her present every time she did so), but it was what she wanted.

She looped the straps of her nylon backpack over her strained shoulders and mounted up. Shadow felt as structurally sound beneath her as he'd ever been, despite his crunching suicide leap. She didn't know how she'd ever get him back up there, but that was a concern for another day.

She looked up and considered the point high above her head where her knotted rope seemed to disappear into empty air. Into the Hole in the Sky.

Ingrid pulled on the reins to turn her stallion south, and they set off down the ancient trading track that wouldn't even be the Camino Real (much less the 101 Freeway) for a number of centuries yet to come. They cantered along at a moderate pace, enjoying the temperate weather as well as the unspoiled countryside. Ingrid felt no need to race. She had the time she needed. She'd planned carefully.

THE journey south took five and a half days. Shadow required neither sleep nor sustenance; Ingrid therefore slept in the saddle for several hours each night before making camp, clutching at her horse's mane while he continued to walk steadily. She met her own nutritional needs with salted beef jerky and dried fruits from zipper-topped foil pouches that she'd acquired late in the 20th century. The only times she stopped were to relieve herself or think the occasional long thought over some beautiful bit of scenery, or to refill her two unbreakable plastic canteens from handy streams or springs.

By dawn of her third day on the road, Ingrid knew she'd be expected when she arrived at her destination. Word of her approach was traveling south faster than her half-real horse, and the evidence of it gradually became apparent.

People came out to line the sides of the trail. Only a few knots at first, grinning pairs or trios who would bow their black-haired heads as she neared them, then point and mutter excitedly amongst themselves as soon as she rode by. There were no living horses in the Americas at this time, or redheads either, so Ingrid knew she presented quite an unprecedented sight to the locals she encountered.

The number of sightseers increased with every additional mile she traveled. Old folks and small children turned out. Ingrid might have expected more of a carnival atmosphere to pertain, but the crowds became more solemn as they grew larger.

There seemed to be a sense amongst them that they were gathered to witness something special. When Ingrid said the name of the person she sought they knew it and nodded with reverence, then pointed her further south.

By the time she reached the village that would one day seed the great city of Tenochtitlan, dozens upon dozens of individuals had prostrated themselves at either side of the trail. More dark eyes peered at her from the safety of chaparral cover or from the entrances to simple shelters. The silence as she passed through this impromptu honor guard was absolute, but not intimidating. No one meant her any harm. Ingrid felt certain she was marching toward exaltation rather than execution. These people seemed pleased to see her. Whether that was because they recognized her from their tribe's tales and legends, or due to the novelty of her dramatic appearance and bizarre mode of transport, she could not remotely have said.

The tribespeople got better dressed as she neared the village center. They wore gold, polished stones, bits of shell. They'd painted their faces and bodies, and wore tall, wavering feathers with their brightest fabrics. These urbanites, clustered here near the settlement's core, had enjoyed plenty of time to prepare themselves before Ingrid's rumored arrival, and they'd spared neither effort nor expense.

She felt like a visiting dignitary, if not a deity arriving to oversee a festival convened in her honor.

When she neared the heart of the village (the *calpulli*, as she remembered such a hamlet being called), she found an entire royal court waiting to receive her at the entrance to the marketplace. (The *tiyanquiztli*, that was.) She remembered at least the rudiments of the Nahuatl language she'd been exposed to on her previous visit to these people, which had occurred some four decades ago, by their reckoning, in a different village. A smaller one that had lain many miles to the north, and had a mud-brick pyramid dedicated to Mictlantecuhtli just outside it.

Ingrid saw the assembled potentates and prominent citizens gasp in a breath at the sight of Shadow, with her atop him, but none of them fled or displayed discourtesy.

They parted for her. Guards with shaved heads stepped aside to reveal a gnarled, dark-skinned old woman cradled in the muscular arms of a strapping Shorn One. Her hair was white and wiry, her eyes bright with quick thoughts and sharp humor.

It was Califia, the Queen of California. Old now and physically weak, at the end of her life and her reign.

The elderly monarch grinned enormously when she saw Ingrid for the first time in so many years. Her teeth were still as white and even as piano keys, despite the ravages of time evident in the bend of her spine. She swatted at her bearer's shoulder when Ingrid dismounted from Shadow, snapping a few irritated words at him, and the strong young man assigned to lug his sovereign around set her down on her feet and all but leapt back away from her, looking comically chastened.

It wasn't easy for the frail queen to walk out to greet her guest, yet it was plain she meant to do so. She squinted up at Ingrid when she was still a few feet away, looking her up and down and then right in the eye, with a questioning eyebrow cocked.

"Otztli?" she asked softly, and Ingrid had to shake her head in bemusement. It wasn't a word she'd heard before.

Califia shook her head as well, smiling in pleased disbelief. She reached out and took both of Ingrid's hands. "Mictlancihuatl," she said, and Ingrid's head swam at the sound of a wrong name. She had her garnet on its chain, though, and steadied herself by reaching up to touch it.

"Ingrid," she said, patting her breastbone to indicate that the paired syllables designated her.

"In-Grid," Califia repeated, nodding, rolling the word around in her mouth. "Ingrid." She poked herself in the sternum with her own thumb. "Cal-Lee-Fee-Ya," she said, over-pronouncing and searching Ingrid's face for signs of comprehension.

"Yes," Ingrid said. "You're Califia. Niltze, Califia."

Niltze meant 'hello,' or something like it. It was a greeting, anyway. Califia nodded, and her warm brown eyes suddenly welled with tears.

"Ingrid," she said again, hobbling into Ingrid's embrace. Ingrid squeezed her as hard as she dared, stroking the old queen's white hair and feeling a bit choked up herself.

This was better than waiting around on the wrong side of Mickey's door for her friends to arrive. The rest of the world, the rest of the tribe, faded into temporary irrelevance all around them. She and Califia comprised the whole of the universe, for the moment.

"Notztli ce," the queen murmured, and kept repeating it in a whisper as she stroked Ingrid's back and hair and nuzzled her tear-damp face in against Ingrid's neck, and the women held each other. The phrase must have been a description rather than a proper name, because Ingrid could hear it with no challenge to her equanimity or her memories.

"Notztli ce..." the Queen of California said again, wonderingly, while Ingrid hugged her close.

S HE'D timed her visit carefully. She knew the old queen was due to arrive in Mictlan tomorrow morning, and intended to be *there* for her as well. It would take another week to ride home to what would one day be the Los Angeles region and the Hole in the Sky above it, but she'd be able to return to the same moment, through the auspices of Mickey, and attend Califia's death from the otherworld side. Hopefully she could ease her into a happy afterlife with more grace and success than she'd managed with Finn, Mrs. Parker, or Francis Boggs.

Califia seemed to understand that Ingrid's presence was a harbinger. That her return portended death. But she showed no fear, and seemed to understand that her personal goddess had come back to escort her on, which was a wholly unprecedented event in the experience of mortal people, and an obvious boost to the grinning crone's already dilated ego.

If her tribe respected her before, they now regarded her with a sort of sanctified awe, and Califia was enjoying her last gasp of celebrity. Everyone wanted to touch her, or at least see her, to take a mental snapshot of their matriarch in the intimate company of the pearl-skinned, flame-haired goddess who hadn't aged or changed in any way during the lifetime that had passed since her last appearance. The elderly amongst the old people confirmed it for the young.

The people partied that night, as they had on the occasion of Califia's coronation. By nightfall most everyone was drunk and dancing, while laughing, shouting children took full advantage of the lapse in supervision.

When the sky deepened to indigo and bonfires began to blaze, Califia took Ingrid to her private *xahcalli*, or thatch-roofed house. They closed out the rest of her entourage and left a contingent of Shorn Ones outside the door, with their backs to it, to guard the women's privacy.

Califia had made her way as an itinerant midwife before graduating to queen forty years ago, and her xahcalli was consequently loaded with mementos ranging from the sublime to the arcane to the outright obscene.

But only one item on display amidst the bones and feathers and brightly-painted talismans caught Ingrid's eye.

It was a small stone carving, not quite a foot high. It depicted a native person with broad, flat features and small, almond-shaped eyes. The subject's long hair was tucked behind tiny ears, and its lips were drawn back in a strange, pained rictus. That grimacing face dominated the piece. The head alone was larger than the rest of the figure's body.

It was made of ordinary greenstone with inclusions of garnet instead of solid gold, but otherwise it looked exactly like the idol stolen by Indiana Jones at the start of a movie she'd never gotten to finish, thanks to Jimmy the Freak.

"Tlazolteotl," Califia said, naming the figure and nodding in a meaningful way when Ingrid picked up the carving from the tree-stump pedestal it stood on, to examine it more closely. Ingrid repeated the name, which her tongue had some difficulty with.

"Tlazolteotl Ixcuiname, Tlaelquanai," Califia reiterated. She hobbled over to close both of Ingrid's hands around the carving and push it against her breast. Take it, it's yours, the gesture said. It's a gift.

"Tetlautili," was the word Califia used, scanning Ingrid's face for understanding. Gift.

"I couldn't, really," Ingrid protested, and tried to hand to stone idol back, but the queen was having none of it.

"*Tetlautili*," she insisted, and wouldn't let it go until Ingrid zipped the carving away inside her nylon backpack.

Then Califia stood back again and looked up at her, reading the weariness, the loneliness, and the recent pain on Ingrid's face. Ingrid felt like she was being looked through rather than at.

"Notztli ce," Califia said again, shaking her head and smiling, and the deep and true affection Ingrid saw reflected in the tiny crone's warm eyes made her want to weep.

Califia knew it. Her brows knitted together in tender sympathy. She took Ingrid's hand and led her to the corner containing a queenly collection of furs, skins, and finely-woven reed mats, where they lay nestled together throughout the night.

INGRID told the queen everything—about the Hole in the Sky and Jimmy the Freak and her Uncle Frank, about Dottie Parker and Phineas Pagán, the whole lurid tale—even though she knew Califia couldn't understand it. Confessing felt like lancing an infected wound, and Ingrid was drained by the end of it.

Califia listened attentively for many hours, though she really couldn't have followed. Still, the important things were clear between them. Califia kissed her forehead, her cheeks, her closed eyelids, and soothed her, even rubbing her belly gently, which Ingrid found intimate and calming. She accepted Califia's gift of solace gratefully, needing it more than she'd known she had, even though it was she who'd come all this way intending to offer comfort to her oldest friend during *her* time of need, and not the other way around.

THE Queen of California went quietly, just before dawn, while Ingrid cradled her. She knew the timing beforehand, from Mictlantecuhtli; she also knew she couldn't have faced this if she'd arrived any sooner, or spent more time amongst the Nahuatlaca people. It was wrenching and almost unbearable to watch the light of consciousness fade from her friend's eyes, yet being at her side when it happened was the greatest honor of her life by far, and she would not have chosen to be anywhere else at that particular moment.

"Have no fear," she whispered, in a voice that sounded thick with emotion, and Califia nodded, understanding and appreciating the sentiment, if not the words themselves. "I'll be waiting for you on the other side, I swear."

INGRID went quietly herself not long after, mounting up and riding out from the Nahuatlaca village as preparations for Queen Califia's elaborate funeral feast moved into full swing.

She hid her improbable hair under Mickey's cloak, so none of the people realized she'd gone until she was many miles away, and that was just how she wanted it.

She stopped to bathe in a clear pool and eat a light lunch culled from her diminishing stock of plastic-wrapped supplies. The weather was still summery-warm this far south into what would be considered Mexico, by Ingrid's day.

She took her time about her ablutions, enjoying the cool water and the feeling of being washed clean after so many days of hard travel. Relaxing in the ferny shadows, she ran her hands over her own belly the way Califia had, remembering the queen's touch and realizing she'd put on a bit of weight, even though she hadn't been eating or feeling especially well. Yet she was discernibly rounder through the midsection than she had been the last time she stopped to evaluate such things.

Before she set off again, she unwrapped and examined the stone sculpture of Tlazolteotl Califia had gifted her with. The figure depicted was clearly the same one from the opening of *Raiders of the Lost Ark*. She wouldn't be surprised if the gray-green example in her hand had been (or would be) the model for the movie prop, they were so similar in design and execution.

Synchronicities like that meant factors beyond random chance were in play. The recurrence of this image in such disparate times and places was bound to have a special meaning for her.

Ingrid realized for the first time that the carving depicted a young woman, not a long-haired boy. Her disproportionately small body had nubby breasts, and she was crouched down, straining and in pain as the face and hands of a second tiny figure emerged from between her legs.

The statue was pregnant, giving birth, and Ingrid had never noticed.

'*Otztli?*' Califia had asked. The very first thing, as if her sharp old woman's eyes had divined some subtle sign.

Pregnant?

Ingrid dropped the figurine and her hands fell to her newly-round belly. The firm curve Califia had caressed in the night while sweetly murmuring '*notztli ce*,' a description Ingrid now realized could mean nothing other than '*my pregnant one*.'

SHE re-mounted Shadow, telling herself it couldn't be, that it *couldn't possibly be*, and another horrible thought struck her—Seabiscuit had been a descendant of Fair Play. A descendant! When Fair Play had been nothing more than a copy of the original made by Mictlantecuhtli by the time he was put out to stud. Seabiscuit's handlers would never have known Ingrid's name if not for the stories handed down along with his bloodline as minor legends.

She remembered thinking, once, that if Mickey barely understood circulation, then it would be a very long time before he evolved a grasp on the internal mechanics of reproduction. But if he was now capable of fashioning fake horses that sired subsequent generations of champions, then maybe that time was up.

Ingrid was carrying Mictlantecuhtli's child.

She'd never believed screwing a figment of the imagination could result in pregnancy, even though there were any number of mythological precedents. Stories of half-divine parentage had been repeated down the generations, all around the world. Scripture and folklore were rife with them.

The small meal she'd eaten burned like acid in her expanding gut. Ingrid imagined she could feel it happening, her deepest innards inflating cell by cell, and she did not find the sensation pleasant at all.

Her hands shook when she grabbed the reins and spurred Shadow to his fastest gallop. Both her canteens were full and she could eat her packaged food in the saddle, so they barely slowed until they came pounding back over the southern hills and into sight of the Sapling Below the Hole in the Sky.

Chapter Six

THERE was no getting Shadow back up to the Hole so she left him, turned him loose, forgetting Mictlantecuhtli's cowl was still in his saddlebag. That was careless, but she had good reason to be distracted.

The weighty stone sculpture of Tlazolteotl in her bag thumped her in the back repeatedly as she climbed her knotted rope, leaving the base of her spine sore and bruised by the time she hauled herself through the Hole in the Sky.

"Have you enjoyed your travels, my love?" Mictlantecuhtli asked. She'd hoped he might not be here. Since he'd started his campaign to dominate his otherworldly neighbors, he was often busy with conquest and revenge.

Ingrid nodded. In his skeletal aspect, her King looked a million miles away from being able to father a child. He didn't even have the proper equipment. He'd have to put his flesh back on before he'd look capable of it.

He cocked the skull beneath his cowl, as if considering or noticing something new about her. "Are you all right?" he asked.

"Sure."

He knew something was up. It occurred to Ingrid that he must have worked hard to improve his physicality, and might be waiting to see if his efforts had borne fruit. The proof of which would be to see *her* bearing fruit.

How like him to spring it on her, with no discussion or consent.

That *bastard*. Ingrid had never been so angry, with him or with anyone. She felt violated. But this was not the time to level accusations. Not before she knew how she wanted to play her hand.

She yawned and stretched instead of shouting, feeling no need to fake it. She really was exhausted. "Just tired," she explained. "It was a harder trip than I imagined, even with the superhorse. Or pseudohorse. I had to leave him down there, by the way, and I forgot your cowl. It's still in his saddlebag. Would you like me to get it?"

Mictlantecuhtli made a dismissive gesture. "It matters not. Would you now see your Queen, as we discussed?"

Ingrid nodded, trying not to look reluctant. If she changed her plan now, Mickey would want to know why. Maybe she should never have come back here at all, but there was no other return to the modern world.

"As you would have it."

Mictlantecuhtli raised his fleshless hand and Califia appeared next to her, right there in the first chamber. The royal crone looked momentarily surprised, but then she saw Ingrid and smiled.

"Notzl—" she began, about to address her as *notztli ce*, 'my pregnant one,' before Ingrid cut her off.

"Niltze, Califia!" she said brightly, turning to the ghost of the old queen and pleading with her eyes for her not to give the secret they shared away. Trying to hide it from the King may have been a wasted effort, but if he was going to experience any blind spots within the memories of his subjects they would probably be related to the mysteries of birth, which were not naturally any of his affair.

Califia was no less perceptive than Mictlantecuhtli. She paused, head cocked, then darted her eyes toward the robed skeleton in the doorway for the barest fraction of a second before nodding and holding out her arms to attempt an embrace.

"Niltze, In-grid," she said, and looked surprised when her limbs passed through Ingrid's body without stirring so much as a hair. They weren't on the same plane of being anymore (though in this place the planes overlapped a bit).

Califia realized she was standing unassisted and moving around without any sort of pain. She grinned so hugely she could have pulled a facial muscle and did a few steps of one of the ecstatic whirling dances Ingrid had seen the Nahuatlaca perform. The queen concentrated and made herself young, same as Mrs. Parker had. New cables of thick, dark hair coiled down to her shoulders and pushed the gray right out of existence. Her womanly curves re-inflated, and within moments she looked as majestic and imposing as Ingrid remembered from the fire-lit night of her coronation.

She seemed to like her afterlife so far. Ingrid didn't want to rob her of it. This had become an overriding concern.

"Cross over," Mictlantecuhtli said, and Ingrid thought she heard a Nahuatl echo of the words in her head, like a dubbed-over movie. She wondered if Califia caught a similar ghost of English while hearing her native tongue.

"You will be held responsible if this one does not join us," the King said, glancing at Ingrid.

The Queen of California also looked to Ingrid, who nodded.

"Go on," she said, tipping her head at the doorway that framed Mictlantecuhtli. "Your world can be whatever you want it to be, over there."

Califia still looked reluctant to go. Unwilling to leave her.

"It's all right," Ingrid said.

Califia took one last long look at her, then turned to Mictlantecuhtli. He stepped aside to admit her to the second chamber with a flourish, which he sarcastically exaggerated for Ingrid's benefit.

He didn't even bother laying Califia out on the sacrificial slab. As soon as she entered Mictlan he merely sliced his small obsidian blade downward in one swift, hard stroke, bisecting the tall lady from forehead to crotch (same as he once had with Finn). Her flesh fell slowly away from the bones beneath in two symmetrical halves.

Califia just stood there, staring down at the two rumpled mounds of skin lying at her feet. When she looked up Mictlantecuhtli plucked her eyes from their sockets with the first two phalanges of his right hand and deftly added them to his double-looped necklace.

Ingrid stepped across the barrier and took the bereft skeleton in her arms. Califia felt so small now, lighter and more frail than she had been even as she lay dying—more like a bundle of twigs than the lovely woman she'd been moments before.

"That's all now," Ingrid whispered, trying her best to soothe and ameliorate the shock, though it wasn't easy as Califia no longer possessed any soft parts that invited a caress. "The worst is over," she reassured. "You'll be all right now, I promise."

Mictlantecuhtli stood back, watching them without comment, while his robes blew and billowed silently around him.

Califia's memories were his now. Her entire being had been absorbed into the vastness of his realm.

Ingrid saw him smile when he learned what that old midwife had divined of her condition.

He didn't know if Ingrid had figured it out for herself yet. Califia hadn't been certain. But he did know his experiment had worked, and he looked as smug as a well-fed cat over it.

"Escort her, if you will," he said magnanimously, tipping his head toward the second door. The one beyond the altar slab, that let out onto the realm of the dead.

Ingrid nodded a thank you and took Califia by her cold, fragile hand. The queen should be safe enough now, free to make of Mictlan what she would. That was the important thing. Together they stepped outside, onto the top level of a massive step Pyramid, exactly as they once had back in the realworld, in a year the calendar labeled 910A.D.

The structure lurched beneath them, like it might in an earthquake. Ingrid had to steady herself against the doorjamb. When she peered out and looked down, the sight that greeted her was stunning enough that she almost forgot her anger at Mickey, for a moment or two.

THE Pyramid of Mictlantecuhtli was moving beneath them, traveling, its leading corner peeling back imaginal ground the way the prow of an ocean liner carves through water. Skeletons by the score dragged it with ropes and cables they'd looped around the base, incredible numbers of them, so many that they could run flat out like sled dogs and still pull the artificial mountain behind them. Mictlantecuhtli changed aspects and became the Aztec king who had so fired Ingrid's imaginings, then swung himself athletically up onto the roof of his inner sanctum, the very top of his now-mobile pyramid. More corpses gathered in its wake, helping to push. The wind generated by the structure's pace swirled Ingrid's hair around in a crimson cloud. Califia looked staggered, though that may have been because her empty eye sockets were so round.

Mickey planted his spine-staff on the roof at his feet and leaned into the breeze, grinning as the moving air blew both his hair and his long-feathered headdress back from his forehead.

"Mickey?" Ingrid called up at him. "You wanna tell me what the fuck is going on?"

"We are riding into battle, my love. You and your guest shall have front-row seats, as they say."

"No, thank you, Mickey," Ingrid said. "I don't want to do that."

"It is already done," said the King. "And you will bear witness to my triumph. Now stand and watch, witch."

Several more pyramids rolled into view over the distant, gray horizon. These were smooth-sided and sandy in color, and there were three of them, huddled behind a large stone sphinx.

The Sphinx, in fact, or at least an imaginal analog thereof (like Mickey's pyramid). It looked newer, more detailed, and more animated than in any image of the realworld version Ingrid had ever seen.

It stood, snarling, raising its hackles and puffing its tawny mane before Mickey's mobile mountain ground to a stop at a strategic distance. Chips of limestone flew and pattered into the surrounding dunes when it shook its massive head and roared.

Ingrid could see a clear line in the sand where the gray influence of Mickey's world crowded up against the bleached beige of the ancient realm the Sphinx was poised to guard.

She also spotted figures amidst the dunes, some cowering behind the pyramids. Many of them had animal heads on human bodies. Some didn't look quite Egyptian. She thought there might be a Japanese dragon shifting around, trying to hide beneath the sands. Maybe more than one.

"Surrender now," Mickey called out to them, and his voice resounded. "My victory is assured. You would be wise not to anger me before it is achieved."

Ingrid recognized ibis-headed Thoth and hawk-headed Horus, standing their ground. The goddess Nuit arched her dark, star-flecked body above them, and Ra burned in the form of a winged solar disk that rode a distant corner of the sky.

"What's going on here, Mickey?" she asked. "They're not all Egyptian."

"No," Mickey said. "The gods of the Nile Valley have foolishly cast their lot with others less strong and well-remembered. The pantheons of Babylon and Sumer have sought sanctuary with them, as have the dragons of both east and west. Look—Marduk is there, with the curly beard and the serpent on a leash. And behind the second pyramid are the eyes of the sky, Amaterasu and Tsukuyomi, the sun and the moon, as well as the weather-*oni* Raijin."

Ingrid nodded as her King pointed them out, each in turn.

"They cower here in despair, in contemplation of my reach and influence," he observed, breaking into a self-satisfied smile.

Ingrid could hardly blame them. Mickey's skeletal armies were so vast they boggled the mind. "What do you do now?" she asked. "Attack? With your army?"

"It is not necessary," the King said. "But they don't know that."

"None of this is necessary," Ingrid observed.

"That is not so," Mickey said. "Never again will my realm be threatened the way it was. I will not allow it."

"But where does it *stop*?" Ingrid had hoped he might be done with this crap, after claiming Olympus and a number of other mythologies. How much 'vengeance' did one god need? "You can't conquer everything."

Mickey stared down at her, looking genuinely surprised by the idea. "I don't see why not," he said. "It may take time, but time is something I have."

"An illusion of time."

The King sneered, irritated that she wouldn't share his enthusiasms. "When did you stop being fun?"

Ingrid was about to make some weary protest, but he cut her off.

"You are correct, my time is illusory," he said, "though my commitment to it makes it as nearly real as anything else experienced here. But we can dispense with it if it frustrates you. Consider the Shinto-Egyptian coalition and the refugees it harbors conquered."

"How?" Ingrid said.

"Like this." Mickey grinned and snapped his fingers. His teeth sharpened and his face elongated into a snout. His skin sprouted a short coat of dark fur. His ears shifted to the top of his head and stretched into long triangles.

He became Anubis, the jackal-headed Egyptian funerary god. He held a set of scales in one hand and a dripping human heart in the other. He retained his Aztec loincloth, golden ornaments, and feathered headdress.

The imaginal stage dressing around them also changed. They found themselves standing amidst the three smooth-sided pyramids, while Egyptian, Babylonian, and pre-Buddhist gods scattered in a panic. Skeletons rose out of the sands to subdue them, while Anubis threw his head back and bayed laughter at the skies.

Mickey had learned to become any death god he wanted, Ingrid realized. Any figure he syncretized with, anyone whose aspects and functions he shared.

"I didn't know you could do that," she said, trying to sound unimpressed.

Aztec-styled Anubis turned back into Mickey, her tall and handsome King. "Nor did I," he said, grinning. "Until I tried."

The fight was already over. Mickey's infiltration of this new territory had happened too fast for any of the imaginal refugees to mount a meaningful defense.

"But can't they do the same? Can't one of them become *you* and undo what you did? Hades or someone, another death god?"

"Perhaps they could have, had they maintained a united front after you repaired the damage to the worlds you caused, but they did not. They let old enmities divide them, foolishly affording me a chance to dominate them one by one, and failed to ride to one another's aid. Now it is too late for unity. My territory grows larger with each conquest, as does my strength, so that few remain who may yet stand against me."

"Which few?" Ingrid asked, trying not to sound like she was fishing for information.

Mickey shrugged, and the studied nonchalance behind the gesture belied a touch of frustration. "Those who are believed in still resist me," he said. "Those with large, living cults devoted to their names. That fat monk, for one, and the Man Jesus too. But even this problem may yet be solved."

Ingrid was afraid to know how.

"I am reminded of the sexual act," Mickey said philosophically, squinting off toward the horizon as he walked amongst his new captives, leaving Ingrid and the bones of Califia to follow him. The deities of Phoenicia and Ur were here, and the diminutive Fair Folk of Tir-Na-Nog, as well as the Egyptians and Shinto Kami who seemed to form the backbone of this resistance. All had been or were now being wrestled to the dirt by overwhelming scads of corpse soldiers. "The interplay of dominance and submission and the union of contrary elements that it forges," the King continued. "Conquest is like that. What I take is mine by right of victory. New traits and aspects and influences. I gain much from such contacts. I am enlarged."

Ingrid wanted to protest that sexual relationships weren't meant to be about acquiring qualities one party wanted from another, but she didn't think she'd be able to sell it. Not to Mickey.

He stopped and turned and looked at Califia. She took Ingrid's hand, but didn't shrink back from his attention in any way.

"Your people, the old people, understood this," he said to the fresh skeleton. "They planned wars for this very reason, the exchange of populations and the integration of cultures. '*Xochitl Yaoyotl*,' yes? 'Flower War?' Pollination by violence?"

Again Ingrid heard Nahuatl in her ears when Mickey spoke it, but English in her mind.

"Xochitl Yaoyotl," Califia repeated, nodding. She looked around herself and then back to Ingrid, seeming all too vividly to understand what was going on. She must have been getting her own spontaneous translation. She saw as clearly as Ingrid did that Mickey meant to use this new trick to harvest whatever he wanted from the rest of the worlds.

"In 'time,'" Mickey said, smirking over the irony of it, "I will penetrate and pollinate your realworld as well, my love."

"What do you mean?" Ingrid snapped.

Mickey suppressed a grin, pleased to note her reaction. "You'll see," he said, his small eyes glinting. "One day."

This was maddening. She couldn't tell how much he knew.

"You look tired," he said, looking her up and down, perhaps reading her weariness as a positive sign. He seemed to be gauging her reactions, testing to see what she knew about his plans. "Would you rest?"

"I *am* tired, Mickey," she said. "All this jumping around, it upsets my equilibrium. I think I'll go back and sleep a few more nights under a sky with a sun that rises and sets. The living need their cycles, you know."

Mickey narrowed his eyes, but he let the inner sanctum of his Pyramid reappear around them. The mythic captives from beyond Mictlan and the King's legions were whisked out of sight in an instant.

Was he really going to let her leave? She couldn't understand why, when he had solid evidence that she was carrying his child.

When she thought about how easily he'd subverted mythological boundaries to become Anubis and attack the Egyptian pantheon with their own death deity, another possibility occurred to her.

What if Mickey had a body, an avatar, flesh of his flesh, living out in the real?

Would he be able to occupy *it* the way he had the figure of Anubis? From the inside out?

"Do you really think you might be able to do that?" she asked, hoping to goad him into better explaining his cryptic threats. Prodding him the same way he'd prodded her. "Find a way to leave Mictlan?"

Her King shrugged. "It would require a sacrifice," he said. "A space in the real would have to be made for me to fill. A body prepared. I would have to steal across the barrier between our worlds at the moment such an offering crossed from your side, slipping out through the door as they open it, essentially, and seating myself in my new form before I'm pulled back here. The timing would have to be flawless."

"You've thought about this."

"I have," Mickey said.

Thought about it a lot, or so it seemed to Ingrid. That was why he'd bothered making himself complex enough to father a child. And that was why he was letting her leave.

So he could grow an escape pod in her womb.

Califia's bones were staring at her stomach. She looked up, into Ingrid's eyes, and Ingrid knew the former queen was putting two and two together as well.

Had Mickey seen their furtive glances? He could be all too observant.

"What era would you like, my love?" he asked, gesturing toward the door that led out to the real. "One near to your native timespan?"

Ingrid nodded dumbly, too shocked by the implications of what Mickey was planning to concentrate on what he was asking.

"You will find 1915 outside," he said.

"That's perfect. I can work with that. Maybe I'll go visit my parents."

She made herself give Mickey a hug and a peck on the cheek, like nothing was wrong. All his suspicions would have been confirmed by the sort of hurried exit her instincts told her to make.

She embraced Califia's skeleton again, and looked her in the eye sockets for a meaningful moment, silently hoping she'd be all right. Mickey wouldn't destroy her, not before he had a chance to pore over the details of her memory. Right?

Ingrid stepped across the barrier, back into the realworld, not too far along from where her personal chronology had taken the first of its bizarre hairpin turns.

The last thing she saw, as she made her getaway out the far door of the King's Chambers, was Califia raising her bony hand in a goodbye wave, with Mictlantecuhtli looming portentously behind her.

Chapter Seven

—*May 01, 1915*

DOWNSTAIRS, outside, early in the spring of 1915, signs of human habitation were finally cropping up on the horizons around the Silent Tower. Another building some miles to the north seemed almost to equal it in height. There were houses, too, many more houses, and Ingrid knew still more were on the way. Even the street right out in front, the one that was only paved for a few hundred yards, looked to be in more general use. The dirt road it turned into was now graded and smooth, free of daisy-sprouting wheelruts. Cars came past here, at least occasionally. Either Hollywood or Sunset boulevards might be paved all the way to downtown, by now, or else the blacktop might stretch all the way to the coast.

Francis Boggs had been dead to this world for four years. Queen Califia for a thousand. Dottie Parker was a fledgling writer somewhere, just now sharpening her tongue.

Ingrid whistled for Shadow, just for the hell of it, even though she'd abandoned him a full millennium in the past.

So she was startled, to say the least, when he emerged from a copse of trees perhaps a quarter-mile from the Tower and came trotting toward her. She supposed there was no reason he should have degraded over time. He'd never been real enough to suffer maladies like aging.

Mictlantecuhtli's cowl, the one she'd borrowed for her trip to the distant past, was still wadded up in the saddlebag. When Ingrid shook it out she found that it was stiff and crusty, stained with something that came away on her hands in ancient rusty flakes.

Blood.

There'd been a lot of it, too. Ingrid had to wonder what had happened, who might have found and ridden her shadow-stallion during the centuries he'd been left to wander the hills of southern California like a ghostly apparition. She didn't suppose she'd ever know. She might have asked Mickey, but she was going to need to keep her distance from him for a while. Six months at least, she estimated… unless some other arrangement could be made.

A final, decisive, medical one.

That was a black thought, and she admonished herself for even having it.

There was an undeniable practicality to the idea, though. Doctors could be paid to do the sort of thing she had in mind. Not legally, or safely, and yet such things were done. If not by physicians then by medical students, veterinarians, or midwives. Ingrid knew of herbal remedies herself, like pennyroyal tea, or various concoctions of black hellebore, tansy, and worm-fern root. She'd studied all the things a good witch should—though not closely enough to be certain she could avoid poisoning herself if she tried them.

Besides which, Mickey was sure to know if and when she did it, and she couldn't imagine what tortures he might devise for the killer of his child, his anchor to her world.

So abortion was out, and that was all right. These considerations terrified her. Growing up around performers she'd seen any number of girls get into the sort of trouble she now faced. (Well, relatively speaking. Her trouble had extra dimensions added on.) But some of those girls had died seeking to nip their problems in the bud. More were injured in ways that could never be set right.

Ingrid had always taken a high degree of care to prevent such complications from blindsiding her… except when it came to Mickey.

If only she'd made the connection about the horses sooner, before the last few times they'd gone to bed. If Mickey could render Fair Play capable of siring the line that led to Seabiscuit, of course he could do the same for himself. But she hadn't thought about it. The same way she'd never noticed that the Tlazolteotl sculpture nestled in her backpack (so like the one she'd once seen on screen at the Cinerama Dome) actually depicted a woman in the throes of childbirth.

Ingrid took the icon out now, Califia's gift to her, given while she was still alive. The queen had noticed her condition right away. Hence the significance of the present. Ingrid turned the stone figure over in her hands and considered the tiny face between its legs that was frozen in the act of looking out onto the world for the very first time.

She couldn't let it become Mickey's face. Not only because she shuddered to think of what he might do to this world, what memories and abilities he might retain from his imaginal state, but because it was reserved for someone else.

Her child. Possibly.

Ingrid's personal ambitions had never run toward motherhood. She'd always imagined it was a question that would work itself out, in time. But now, when faced with the reality, imagining who her child might turn out to be overwhelmed her with a wave of sentiment and terror that almost drove her to her knees.

She set Califia's Tlazolteotl down, then threw her arms around Shadow's neck and buried her face in his wind-scented mane, needing to hug someone, *something*, for what comfort there was in it. Nobody else was available. The prodigal demon horse snorted and whinnied, content to oblige her, and Ingrid held onto him for dear life.

She'd never felt more lost or lonely in all her strange existence.

SHE really had no time to linger. Mickey would want to keep tabs on her. His servant Winston's reach wasn't as long as it would become in later decades, but Miguel Caradura's growing network of living employees, informants, and spies was already formidable.

That made getting far away from here her first priority.

She bundled up the Tlazolteotl icon and shoved it into her nylon backpack. Her clothes were hideously inappropriate to 1915. She was still wearing hiking gear she'd acquired in the 1990s, in preparation for her trip to pre-Columbian Mexico. Cotton 'cargo pants' with multiple pockets; light, rubber-soled sneakers; and a man's work shirt. She shook out Mictlantecuhtli's old robe and threw it around her shoulders, grimacing at the metallic smell of dried blood that was permanently embedded in the fibers. It would help her hide in plain sight. The cowl was as imaginal as the garnet around her neck.

Ingrid reached up and touched the stone.

She could take it off, and throw it away. She'd forget her name and the rest of her life if she did, but she could have her baby and bring it up believing she was nothing more than some ordinary girl who'd gotten herself in trouble. She'd be impossible for Mickey to find without a name.

Only that might not work, as she hadn't strayed all that far from her native time. This era might be too familiar to challenge her sense of belonging, and that may have been why Mickey offered it as a destination. The amnesia provoked by losing her garnet hadn't been complete in 1941, and hadn't affected her at all when jumping from 1910 to 1912. It might be quite minimal now.

Further complicating matters was the fact that the chain Mickey had given her to wear the imaginal rock on had no clasp. It was too short to take off over her head, and too strong for her to break by pulling on it. She could decapitate herself before any of the delicate-looking links gave way. She suspected it would prove equally resistant to the clippers, pliers, blowtorches, or hacksaws a professional jeweler might apply to the task of cutting it off.

There was no practical way to remove it, and that too was likely a part of Mickey's plan. He wouldn't have let her go without some assurance he'd be able to find her later, by one method or another.

So she was stuck with herself.

She swung herself up onto Shadow and headed east, taking to the fields and stands of trees rather than sticking directly to the road. She saw several cars headed back in the other direction before she reached downtown. Any one of them could have contained henchmen summoned by Winston and charged with tailing her. She didn't think anyone in them could have seen her, though.

She really didn't know what to do next. She wanted to go home to her parents in San Francisco, but that wouldn't be safe for them. It struck her that she would also have to avoid hospitals, despite her condition, because people died in them. It wouldn't do to be seen by anyone set to expire in the near future, as Mickey could triangulate her location in the realworld through reports delivered by the recently deceased. He'd done it before and would do it again.

Hiding out from el Rey was going to take all her skill.

FINALLY she went back to the Hotel Angelus, for lack of any better option. The secret delivery door down the block was still there, and she got it open without much trouble. The labyrinthine basement of the grand hotel still offered services such as tailoring, a hairdresser, a florist, and entertainments that included a bowling alley and a small theater. The next level down housed kitchens and the laundry, while the third and lowest floor was a catacomb of disused hotel fixtures and other supplies. Disappearing down there was easy. Warding off the entrances to keep Mickey's creatures out wasn't much harder.

Ingrid found a large, forgotten closet in which to stash Shadow, and managed to move around undetected with the help of Mickey's cloak. There were mattresses to sleep on and she had ready access to clean linens. She was able to filch the food she needed. After a few weeks the ghost stories her pilfering inspired got some of the more superstitious cooks to start leaving small offerings of fresh fruit, candy, or sandwiches in a corner far away from their workspace. Before Ingrid finally left the Angelus, months later, the practice escalated to the point where whole prepared meals were being left out for her at regular intervals. No search of the basement ever turned up a squatter, and yet the food continued to disappear, so the kitchen staff decided the wisest course was to continue propitiating the hungry interloper who haunted their shadowy corridors.

The days passed slowly, and Ingrid's midsection grew like a waxing moon. She was tough, physically hardy, and the pregnancy wasn't difficult so much as uncomfortable and unnerving. She distracted herself with books from the lending library two levels up, which she surreptitiously borrowed in the night. She ran through a lot of Dickens and Twain, long novels she could immerse herself in.

She tried not to think about what labor and delivery would be like, yet found herself worrying about it at almost every minute of the day. If not actively, right up at the front of her mind, then on some subliminal, viscera-tightening level. The fear never let her be.

IN the end she was too frightened to go it alone, in a dark hotel basement with no medical supervision. It seemed like a bad idea on more levels than Ingrid could list.

The solution she found was a doctor named Sarah Vasen, who lived and worked out of a small rooming house on Pico, not far from the Angelus. She handled only maternity cases, so no random hospital patients should be dying in her vicinity. Ingrid had recently overheard an older maid whispering to a distraught young colleague that the doctor was known to quietly provide services for free, in cases of genuine need.

Ingrid had never felt more in need in her entire life, by the time her water broke and her contractions finally began, a long half-year after she first sought sanctuary in the bowels of the Angelus.

She brought Shadow out of mothballs. He seemed none the worse for wear after having spent six months in a storage closet.

Getting her spirit steed out through the hidden access tunnel Herman Kittering had told her about in 1912 was no trouble. Three years ago, that had been, by the calendar. It seemed like so much less to Ingrid, and so much more.

OUTSIDE it was evening, and almost November. A dangerous time of year for her, close to the days when the dead could walk alongside the living. She hadn't thought about that. The hotel's massive boiler room ensured that its entire subterranean realm held steady at about seventy-five degrees, no matter what the weather was like upstairs and outdoors.

Tonight it was nippy, but she did have Mickey's cowl to keep her warm. The telephone directory put Dr. Vasen's office at 1110 West Pico, barely six blocks from the Angelus. It still took Ingrid more than half an hour to get there, as she had to pause in the shadows between a pair of streetlamps to ride out a bad contraction, digging her white-knuckled fingers into her horse's mane to keep from falling right off his back and breaking herself on the cold sidewalk.

The house Dr. Vasen rented a wing of was small, but also charming and quietly luxurious, with large, leaded glass windows and tendrils of ivy snaking up its red brick walls. The shingle out front read: 'Dr. Sarah Vasen-Frank,' and, beneath that, in flowing script: *practice devoted to maternity cases only.*

So far, so good.

A middle-aged man opened the front door even as Ingrid was working out the mechanics of dismounting from Shadow without killing herself. He stopped dead.

"Excuse me," Ingrid said. "I need Doctor Vasen."

The gray-haired man looked up at her, and his jovial face ran pale.

"Not yet," he croaked, in a tiny voice. "Please."

Ingrid had no idea what he was on about until he added: "We've only been married three years, after waiting our whole lives to find each other. It's just too soon. Please."

She understood. On her shimmering, half-there horse, under the King's cowl, the poor man had mistaken her for the Grim Reaper himself.

Ingrid pushed back her hood, revealing her human face and vivid hair rather than a staring skull, which she hoped would come as a relief. "Don't worry," she said. "I'm not who you think."

Though she had made his acquaintance. All too intimately.

"Oh," the gentleman said, and then he noticed the pronounced bulge of Ingrid's belly. "Oh, my god, of course you're not. I'm sorry, I don't know what came over me."

He hurried over to help her down from Shadow.

"I'm Saul Frank. Have you seen my Sarah before? Are you already a patient?"

Ingrid shook her head and gritted her teeth against a fresh wave of pain that washed over her, obliterating all other sensation until it passed. Mr. Frank took her hand and she squeezed it hard, feeling weak with gratitude.

"Let's get you inside," the kind man said.

D R. Sarah Vasen-Frank turned out to be as gentle and generous toward a stranger as her recently-acquired husband Saul. Ingrid loved them both desperately within ten minutes of making their acquaintance.

She'd never been treated by (or even met) a female physician before, and Dr. Sarah was the first ever to practice in the city of Los Angeles, she learned from the reassuring chatter relentlessly delivered by the lady's rightfully-prideful spouse.

They got her out of the era-appropriate clothes she'd liberated from the hotel laundry and into a soft, clean bed. There were no other patients. Ingrid had come just in time—Sarah was giving up her practice next week, and the Franks were retiring to Edendale together.

People named Frank in Edendale. Ingrid marveled at the fresh synchronicity. Frank Boggs, Frank Minematsu, and now Saul and Sarah. That cluster of reiterated symbols made her feel like she'd come to the right place. She wanted to ask these newest Franks in her life to say hi to Colonel Selig when they got to Edendale, but another, harder contraction drove the notion right out of her brain.

She took care of her own anesthesia, ultimately, by giving a false name that was *almost* a description—Regina de Tumbas. Saying it aloud when Dr. Sarah asked sucked the consciousness right out of her, like water drained from a tub. She surfaced now and again, briefly, when pain spiked through her and Dr. Sarah encouraged her to push, but then she sank right back under again.

She didn't know whether or not she'd remember herself when she woke, and almost hoped she wouldn't.

S HE did remember, it turned out, with little more confusion than she experienced after an especially vivid dream. Her hand flew up to grab hold of her imaginal garnet before she opened her eyes.

The baby was gone. Out of her. She could tell, because she'd never felt more empty.

The room was silent, filled with soft white light. Ingrid guessed it was mid-morning.

When she turned her head, she saw sweet, bespectacled Dr. Sarah sitting in a chair near the window, lit by a shaft of drowsy sun. She was rocking a swaddled child. She smiled when she saw that Ingrid was awake.

"Would you like to hold your baby, Regina?" she asked.

Ingrid started to cry.

She *never* cried, except when she did, and on those occasions she was completely captive to the need for it. This time she couldn't begin to stop. Weeping so hard caused her middle to throb, but it was nothing next to the emotional pain that left her feeling like she'd had her chest cut open and salt poured directly into a lacerated heart.

Saul came and took the baby away, back to a quiet bassinet in a separate nursery. Dr. Sarah drew off a dose of sedative with a steel needle and shot it into a prominent blue vein just below Ingrid's elbow, then sat with her and stroked her red hair back from her white forehead until black narcotic sleep stole her away from her sorrows once again… if only for a little while.

T HE next time she awoke it was dark, and she was alone in the largish room that served as the practice's maternity ward. She could hear cozy sounds of tranquil domesticity coming from the far corner of the house. Clinking tableware, and easy conversation.

Ingrid longed terribly to join them, her new heroes, the Franks.

But she couldn't. She might not have another chance to make such a clean getaway.

She retrieved her 1915 garb from the closet where it had all been folded up and stashed away, and dressed gingerly. She didn't know how easy she needed to go on her poor overtaxed body. She didn't really care. The worst of her pain lay in a deeper place than her now-vacant womb, and she didn't know if that injury could ever be healed.

She snuck into the nursery before she left.

Her baby was sleeping peaceably, wrapped in white cotton, with a small stuffed lamb placed near its head. Ingrid felt like she would crumple in on herself at the sight of it.

She didn't even know if the child was a boy or a girl. She didn't want to. She couldn't, not right now. She had the name she'd given Dr. Sarah, as well as a date and location of birth. Whether the Franks chose to use the false name or translate it to something more 'American sounding' for the birth certificate, records would be kept. She'd use them later, to figure out who the child was. She'd hire a detective if she had to. She wished she could move the kid to a different era right now, so that it might not have to grow up under the shadow of the world wars she knew to be looming on a near horizon. Her baby might have no more difficulty with the barrier between life and death than she did, so that trick might yet be possible. She resolved to try, when she could.

It meant she'd have to square things up with Mickey, and that wouldn't to be easy. Not unless she was willing to hand over a living infant for him to use, and a cold day in California was apt to come first.

Ingrid kissed the tips of her first two fingers and touched them to the sleeping child's forehead. That was as much as she could do without breaking down and giving herself away. Being run through with a sword would have to feel something like this.

But her child would have a chance. A chance at a life of his or her own. And leaving was the only way to ensure it.

I'll be back for you, she swore, locking the vow away in her heart. *When I can.*

The final thing she did before stealing away was to leave behind the one object of any value she still possessed: the stone Tlazolteotl statuette Queen Califia had given her, what seemed like a very long time ago. She stationed it on one of the Franks' many bookshelves, amidst other *objet d'art*, and put a light hex on it to keep it from being noticed until after their move to Edendale, or ever connected in their minds to her baby. That wouldn't be safe for the child, and the gift of an image of a protector of midwives was meant for Sarah and Saul, even if they never understood the significance.

It seemed like far too little after their incredible kindness. There was nothing Ingrid could ever do to repay them, but she promised to always remember them, if nothing else, along with Califia and Dottie Parker and her Uncle Frank. The names she honored most.

OUTSIDE again, wrapped up in Mictlantecuhtli's robe, she whistled for her horse and he seemed to pull himself together from the nearest shadows to come trotting toward her, tossing his head and shaking out his raven mane.

She mounted up and rode hard for the Silent Tower, though travel on horseback was surely medically contraindicated for a woman who'd given birth less than two days ago. She gritted her teeth and dealt with the pain.

Her child was safe behind her, and that was all that mattered to her anymore. She meant to make sure things stayed that way.

"L ADY Redstone," Winston said, as Ingrid opened the door to Miguel Caradura's office and stepped into the first of the King's Chambers at the top of the Silent Tower, leading Shadow behind her.

"Where is he?" she said, crossing the room and shoving past the stuffy skeleton.

"Fighting his battles," Winston said wearily. "He would see you directly."

"Then he can haul his ass up here."

Winston would've raised his eyebrows, if he'd had any. "I will inform him of your wishes," the skeletal butler said, and vanished.

Ingrid couldn't believe it. This was far too good to be true. She'd come steeled for a fight, to have things out with the King once and for all, but if Mickey was this committed to his stupid illusion of time then she was happy enough to skip the theatrics.

If she could travel, she might have other options.

She turned and mentally dialed the years forward wildly, aiming for some time after 1981. She overshot the mark, but couldn't tell by how much. Nothing she could do about it anyway, with bare instants to get out undetected.

She jumped across the barrier and ran for the door, grabbing Shadow's bridle as she went.

"Lady Redstone!"

Dammit!

Ingrid looked back as she hurried out the exit. Winston already had a telephone in his hand, a tiny futuristic flip-open type with no wires, so she guessed she'd pushed the century pretty far forward.

She had no idea what she might find outside the Silent Tower now.

"Wait!" Winston shouted after her. "The King arrives!"

But Ingrid didn't wait around to see him.

Chapter Eight

—December 31ˢᵗ, 1999

WHEN Ingrid and Shadow burst out the front door of the Silent Tower, it was just after dawn. The neighborhood looked run-down and disused—though bulky, shiny, enclosed trucks lined either curb. Cars large enough for a race of giants. A nameplate on the nearest called it a Lincoln Navigator.

Ingrid swung her leg over Shadow's back and dug her heel into his side, spurring him to run before anything Mickey might send or anyone Winston might summon could arrive on the scene.

Too late. A long-nosed Japanese *Tengu* demon stepped out from behind one of the large vehicles and cleaved Shadow's head right off his neck with a curved blade at the end of a staff. The rest of the black stallion burst into a cloud of charcoal dust beneath Ingrid, dumping her unceremoniously to the pavement. She cried out when she scraped her hands, attempting to break her fall.

She rolled over, scissoring the Tengu between her legs and slamming it face-first to the ground. Her innards screamed and the edges of her vision swam with black spots, but she got Mickey's new servant (his by right of conquest, she had no doubt) over onto its back, her knee into its diaphragm, and her knife out of its sheath at more or less the same time.

The demon's head came off with one deep and satisfying stroke. Its four chakras unspooled and blew away, while its physical body withered to something that could easily have been a clump of old rags and twigs rotting on a backstreet sidewalk.

Ingrid stood up woozily, pulled Mictlantecuhtli's heavy black cloak out of the saddlebag that was almost all that remained of her useful old ghost-horse, and threw it around her shoulders. It should help hide her from the eyes of Mickey's conquered demons, and she should have put it on sooner. By now she was blackly angry. She was going to miss Shadow, and she chided herself for losing him so needlessly.

She spotted a lone horseshoe lying in the dust—probably the physical foundation Jimmy the Freak had built the creature around in the first place. She picked it up.

She was going to have to be more careful if she meant to stay a step ahead of Mickey and his forces. His Tzitzimime had always been strictly nocturnal, and his dead subjects could only walk on certain days per year, but that Tengu was clear evidence that not every beast he now controlled would be subject to similar limitations.

As if cued by the thought, three large black automobiles roared around the corner at the end of the block, traveling at what Ingrid assumed were greater than legal speeds.

Humans, called by Winston. They'd been hired, as far as they knew, as muscle for a secretive underworld figure called Mickey Hardface. They would have been given her description and been charged with the task of dragging her back upstairs to the rooms at the top of the Silent Tower. The magic cloak wouldn't hide her from them in broad daylight. It would help her blend with shadows and incline attention away, but it did have its limitations.

She feinted back around the side of her building, into what was by now a dark and narrow alley. That was decent camouflage—one of the realworld's natural blind spots. A place you didn't want to meet anything. If she stayed very still and projected her banishing stars as hard as she could, she might get the hirelings' eyes to slide by her.

She stepped back behind a large blue trashbin to collect her focus.

She almost stepped on a very old, very dirty man lying under a grimy blanket.

The derelict looked up when she crouched down, and put her finger to her lips. The old man nodded.

Ingrid looked around the edge of their sheltering bin and saw that one of the three black cars had stopped near the mouth of the alley. Its three occupants were out of the vehicle and looking around. For her.

One of them started down the alley. Ingrid held her breath and he hurried by, sparing a glance for the homeless man but failing to spot her. Mickey's black cowl probably helped her to blend with the surrounding sacks of garbage.

The footsoldier was starting back toward his car when Ingrid heard a cellular telephone ring in his pocket.

She looked back at the old man sleeping in the shelter of the trashbin, and saw that his eyes were fixed and staring. Glazed over. He'd died in just the past few moments.

And already Winston was on the goddamn phone.

The henchman stopped, unfolded his flip-phone to answer the call, and turned around frowning.

Ingrid had already ducked back behind the bin.

Mickey's man approached, pocketing his phone, not seeing how he could possibly have missed her, even though he'd been in a hurry. Ingrid cringed, waiting for him to correct his mistake. She had no idea how to get out of this.

It was just a stroke of luck that the hired footsoldier thought to lift the trash bin's lid to check inside before looking around the back of the thing. Ingrid leapt up in a flash and slammed that lid down on the back of the man's head, using both hands to do it. He grunted once and slumped away, to lay still on the pavement next to the freshly deceased beggar.

The lid was heavy. Ingrid wondered if she'd killed the guy even as she went running for his car at the mouth of the alley. Her curiosity was satisfied when she heard two more cellular phones ring in the distance, bearing reports of the third man's demise and location.

They had moronically left their car's doors open, and its motor running too.

Ingrid slid in behind the wheel and tore away down the street while the other two henchmen were still figuring out what had happened to their confederate back in the alley. She'd never driven an automobile before, but the modern versions were actually less intimidating than those available in her own time. No clutch, no crank, no gearshift—just two foot pedals and a wheel for steering, and she could deal with that. She mashed her foot down on the right-side pedal, the accelerator, and was rewarded with a satisfying burst of forward motion even as the car's rightful occupants shouted and ran after her. It was too late for them. She was gone, with enough of a lead to avoid the other two cars full of hired muscle that were cruising the neighborhood. Their occupants were on the lookout for a redheaded witch on a big black horse, and not a girl in a stolen car, so she evaded them with ease.

THE Topless Tower appeared exactly as described: towering (of course), but also intimidating, empty-looking, and unfinished at its uppermost levels. Girders and rebar bristled from its crown like a topknot of wiry hair. Ingrid held the calling card Jimmy Vreke had given her circa 1981 as she cruised through the Santa Monica neighborhood the Freak's hideaway threw into shade. The place seemed so obvious and unmistakable, dominating its otherwise-desolate block off the 405 freeway, that Ingrid had to wonder if the card wasn't some odd sort of joke.

She set it on the seat next to her and parked her vehicle, badly, squealing its tires against the curb. She winced, though she was doing pretty well for her first time driving a motorcar of any kind.

Then she sat there for a moment with the engine ticking as it cooled, staring out the windshield and trying to remember why she'd come here.

She glanced over at the little square of cardstock lying on the leather passenger seat, the one that read *The Topless Tower* in flowing script, and when she picked it up all of her intentions came rushing back to her.

So that card was a genuine security measure and not some weird Edwardian affectation on the part of Jimmy the Freak.

She got out of the car and hurried to a side door of Jimmy's building, reflecting that a tower of one's own was starting to seem like a *de rigueur* accessory for a powerful Los Angeles sorcerer. She wondered if she'd started that trend, or if credit had to go to the Aurea Catena, who'd technically gotten there first when they erected their downtown Temple in 1885.

Ingrid hadn't seen or spoken with Jimmy himself since the drink they'd shared after her interrupted attempt to catch the premiere of that Indiana Jones movie (to which two sequels had by now been made, while she hadn't managed to watch the first one all the way through).

She was still ambivalent about Jimmy, to say the least. But he had offered his hospitality and his aid, she believed in good faith, and she didn't have any other resources to draw upon at the moment.

The Freak was a known travel junkie, often on the move. She hoped she'd find him *in absentia* today, as she never wanted to have to thank him for anything in person.

WHAT'S the password?" Ingrid was asked, by a gruff female voice issued through a sliding panel in the door, like a 20s-era speakeasy.

"I forgot," she said, and the door was promptly opened for her.

Now that had to be a joke and not a real ticket to admission. Didn't it?

The owner of the gruff voice turned out to be another ginger like herself, and not so gruff at all, really. The intimidating bark of a voice was just a put-on. She was nearly as tall as Ingrid but bone thin and liberally freckled. Her unruly orange hair sprang off in unpredictable directions, like a frozen explosion.

She introduced herself as Phyllis. Phyllis Stein.

"Is Jimmy here?" Ingrid asked, after shaking hands with the door's guardian and introducing herself as an old acquaintance of Jim's, whom he might remember as the Red Witch.

A description was the best she could manage. She wasn't about to give these people her true name. Even the bad joke she'd taken as a Latin motto upon her initiation to the Aurea Catena might be too much to trust them with.

Phyllis shook her head, then left Ingrid alone momentarily while she went to make a phone call. When she came back she looked considerably more impressed with the stranger who'd arrived on her doorstep, if not outright humbled.

"Jim was planning on chasing New Year's celebrations around the world in his new jet," she said, "but he's started back now he knows you're here. Shouldn't be but a couple of hours. In the meantime I have standing instructions to provide you with absolutely anything you can think of to ask for, Miss, ah… Witch? I oversee a lot of the practicalities around this place, like making sure the utility bills and the property taxes get paid so nobody official ever takes notice of us. Not even Jimmy can hex away the IRS!"

Phyllis snorted when she laughed at her own joke. Ingrid liked her.

"But anyway," the Freak's female factotum said, "everything we have is yours to use. Jimmy seemed especially concerned that you be well taken care of."

"I need a place to work, mostly," Ingrid said. "Maybe something to eat."

"Not a problem," Phyllis Stein said, gesturing for Ingrid to follow as she headed down a long hallway toward a bank of elevators. The two redheads got into a car together, and Phyllis pressed a button that started them rising, up toward what top there was to Jimmy the Freak's tall tower.

INGRID needed advice, and there was only one source she could think to ask. She'd need to perform a rite of evocation to contact the necessary entity, and that was why she'd come to visit Jimmy's enclave—because his freaks would have handy everything she might need to conduct her operation.

Phyllis showed her to a large room in a quiet corner two levels down from the dance floor. The room had been designed for conferences and business presentations, then retrofitted by Jimmy's crowd for the viewing of movies. The back wall boasted a vast library of films, all stored on brick-sized black 'cassettes,' or large silver platters called 'laser-discs.'

The first thing Ingrid asked Phyllis to fetch for her was a copy of *Raiders of the Lost Ark*.

Next she requested candles, chalk, a copy of the *Lemegeton Clavicula Salomonis*, and lunch.

As soon as she had the book she set herself to copying out the details of the traditional Circle of the Art onto the floor of the conference-room-turned-cinema, down near the end of the space that featured a large projection screen. She placed the candles around her circle, at each of the four points of the compass.

By the time she was done making her chalk marks on the stiff, durable carpeting, Phyllis had returned with a dish Ingrid had never heard of before, which she called something like 'pepperoni pisa'—perhaps named after the famous leaning tower in Italy. It was round but cut into triangular wedges, packaged in a flat cardboard box, and it did have an

Italian flavor to it. Ingrid was hooked from her first bite, and ended up eating four slices before she finally felt full.

Then she lit her candles, rolled a chair into her chalk circle, and started the movie playing on the room's big screen, to the quiet surprise of a baffled Phyllis. Jimmy's capable assistant had opted to hang around without being specifically invited, Ingrid noticed, though she didn't really mind. It was nice to have a little company.

She performed banishings as Indiana Jones hacked his way through South American rainforest at the opening of the film. The circle on the floor was mostly a formality, an exercise meant to get her in the proper frame of mind. Phyllis was not included inside her workspace, but she should be safe enough, being well within the concentric rings of hexwork that protected Jimmy's Topless Tower.

When Dr. Jones made it past the traps that felled previous fortune hunters and found his way into the chamber containing the golden fertility idol, Ingrid paused the image on the screen.

"Is that significant?" Phyllis asked, seeing the way Ingrid stared at it, not quite frowning.

"It's Tlazolteotl," she murmured. She needed to concentrate.

"Testicle Oatmeal?" Phyllis repeated doubtfully.

"It's Aztec. Tlazolteotl Ixcuiname Tlaelquanai," Ingrid said, trying not to sound short with the helpful girl. "Shh, now, please."

Phyllis obediently sat down and kept quiet, somewhere in the room behind her. Ingrid forgot about her.

She turned her attention back to the golden face frozen up on the screen. Califia's goddess. Light poured down onto it in a white shaft. Its thin lips were raked back from gleaming teeth. Its eyes were blank. You could see the idol was meant to be giving birth if you really looked, but you weren't apt to notice otherwise.

The rest of the room seemed to drop away into darkness as she contemplated the movie icon. A prop in a film that had long since claimed a place in popular mythology, and therefore staked out territory within the great imagination.

Ingrid hoped that would be enough to make this work.

"You made a gift of my image," Phyllis said, from behind her, and Ingrid whirled. "To the ones who gave you aid. You do me honor, witch, and yet you have erred."

Phyllis Stein wasn't the only entity sharing the room with her anymore. Nor was it the same room. It had instead become a perfect copy of the ruined jungle temple millions of moviegoers had seen Indiana Jones enter in his quest for fortune and glory since 1981. Ferns cascaded down from niches in ancient stone walls. What little light seeped in from above had a green chlorophyll tinge to it. When Ingrid whipped her head back she saw that the large screen on the wall had become an altar, and on it stood a golden Tlazolteotl idol, looking weighty, cold, and very solid. It was exactly like the one from the film, only in three dimensions. Really there, as far as she could tell.

Phyllis had been altered as well, by a thin perceptual screen (though Ingrid could see it was still the same woman underneath the glamour). Her thick cables of autumnal hair were bound back with cotton bands. She had dark paint around her mouth and a stripe of it down her chin, and she wore golden cuffs around her upper arms, rather like the ones Mickey favored.

She was still sitting in an office chair, and she had a computer-machine on her lap. A portable one that folded up. It looked to Ingrid like the offspring of a briefcase and a typewriter. Phyllis turned it around so that Ingrid could see the images on the screen.

"Look. This child I ride divined these pictures in her scrying glass. Pictures of a gift you passed on to others."

'Phyllis' stood and approached, stopping just outside the chalk circle on the carpet. Ingrid stayed where she was.

The computer's screen showed what she believed was called a 'web page.' It displayed pictures from the collection of a private museum and research facility in Washington DC called the Dumbarton Oaks. Several of the photographs unmistakably depicted the greenstone statuette with garnet inclusions Queen Califia had given her a thousand years ago, in commemoration of her pregnancy. The same statuette she'd left behind as a tribute to Dr. Sarah Vasen-Frank and her husband Saul, in turn.

"That's it," Ingrid said, scanning the article about the piece that accompanied the pictures. She gathered that the museum had acquired the artifact in 1947, which led her to guess the Franks' heirs had sold it off after their deaths. The idol in the famous movie had indeed been modeled after this piece. There also seemed to be some controversy over the question of its authenticity, with a number of experts avowing that it didn't look as worn as it should for an object claiming to be so many centuries old.

Ingrid could have offered an explanation, though not one that would satisfy scholars. Readers of fantastical novels, maybe, but not hard-nosed academics.

"It was made in my honor by the hand of Cihuatlatoani Califia," the possessing spirit explained, using the borrowed voice of Phyllis Stein, who probably hadn't counted on serving as a makeshift medium for an Aztec sex goddess when she woke up that morning. Ingrid hadn't expected it either, though maybe she should have. Phyllis was handy, and energies always flowed along the path of least resistance.

"Califia was pledged to me long before Mictlantecuhtli," the Phyllis-goddess said. "My Califia, deliverer of souls, destroyer of pyramids, wanderer from distant lands. I hold this name in my highest regard."

"Me too," Ingrid said.

"She presided over birth and death on behalf of her people. I am the patroness of midwives, a protector of mothers and the children they cherish. Knowledge of the moon and its cycles is mine to grant or withhold. Mistakes are mine to punish or forgive. It was beloved Califia's final wish that you should come under my protection as well, Red Witch."

"But?" Ingrid could guess what was coming next.

"You gave my face away," the goddess inside Phyllis said sadly, meaning the stone idol. Her eyes looked truly pained. "My Califia intended that you should keep it, that you might one day invoke me in your hour of greatest need."

"I had nothing else to give," Ingrid said. "They took me in, and my child."

Tlazolteotl nodded Phyllis's head. "That is unfortunate," they worked together to say.

"Does that mean there's nothing you can do?"

"I cannot enter Mictlantecuhtli's realm, unless you bring my physical aspect across the border. Then I might subvert that barrier, and the will of Mictlantecuhtli might also be subverted, if not defeated."

Ingrid nodded. She took that as a no on the help. Not without the statue.

It had been in her hands hours ago. Mere hours, and now it felt so out of reach. Without Mictlantecuhtli's cooperation she couldn't pop back and snatch it out from under the Dumbarton Oaks' buyer at auction in 1947. Califia's last gift was locked away from her by unmerciful time, which she was no longer used to being on the business end of.

"Well, that's all right," Ingrid said, trying to sound brave about it. "The couple I gave it to saved my baby. I wouldn't take that gift back if I could. Not ever."

Tlazolteotl nodded the head she was using. "This pleases me," she said. "I would aid you if I could."

"I'd let you," Ingrid said. "If I could."

After that, there wasn't anything more to say. The evoked goddess couldn't leave Phyllis Stein's body until Ingrid let her go—granted her License to Depart, in the parlance of the Art—which she did by pointing the electronic wand that controlled the televisor at the golden idol on the altar and pressing the button that restarted the movie. Ingrid's vision swam as the screen reappeared in the place of the altar and the crumbling temple evaporated, like a vivid daydream dispelled by a shake of her head.

She was in Jimmy the Freak's conference room again, near the pinnacle of his Topless Tower. Indiana Jones was running away with his golden idol—but only up on the wall-mounted screen.

"Here's your Classical Yodel," Phyllis (who was still wrestling with the pronunciation of *Tlazolteotl*) said from behind her. Ingrid turned, and the girl showed her the laptop computer with images of her lost goddess on the screen. The greenstone idol that now resided in the collection of the Dumbarton Oaks museum, a continent away. Pictures she'd called up before Tlazolteotl took over.

Phyllis wasn't aware that anything had happened.

She didn't remember being the goddess at all.

"A friend gave that to me a long time ago," Ingrid said, tilting her head toward the picture displayed on the computer screen. "But I gave it to someone else. Wish I had the time to get it back now."

"You know, I've seen that movie a dozen times," Phyllis said, frowning as she scrutinized the internet images of the original stone statue, "and I never noticed that thing's in the middle of giving birth before."

Join the club, Ingrid thought. She took Jimmy the Freak's old silver fob watch from her pocket to check the time, before remembering a watch that had jumped across a century wouldn't be set to the correct local hour. "What time is it?" she asked.

"Not quite two p.m.," Phyllis said. "Jim expects to arrive by nightfall, he said."

Ingrid nodded. She'd be out of here by then.

"You're welcome to stay for the party," Phyllis told her. "I can find you a quiet room to nap in before then, if you like."

Ingrid nodded absently, still considering her watch. "Maybe some painkillers too," she said, wincing at the bruised ache and the unpleasant pulling sensations she still felt deep inside her belly when she moved around. The aftermath of giving birth. She wondered why nature insisted on doing things the hard way.

"Check," Phyllis said. "I'll put you a few floors down. Club level's filling up already. It's gonna be a hell of a night."

"Why?" Ingrid asked. She hadn't looked at a newspaper to see when she'd landed. "What day is this? And what year?"

"New Year's Eve," Phyllis said, looking bemused but asking no questions. "1999."

Last night of the long millennium. It seemed fitting to Ingrid that she should be here to see the end of her century.

She looked down again at Jimmy's watch, there in her hand, with its special pyroptic crystal lens embedded in the case.

"Hey," she said, looking up suddenly at Phyllis. "Are you any good at this sort of thing? Ceremonial evocation?" She swept an arm over her arrangement of candles around the chalk circle she'd drawn on the floor.

"Pretty good," Phyllis said. "And there's others around here a lot better. A few trained by Jim himself."

Ingrid nodded. She had the beginning of a desperate Plan B in mind.

She picked up the copy of the *Lemegeton Clavicula Salomonis* Phyllis had dug up for her earlier. The book was a newly-printed hardcover edition, which astonished her. Copies of this text had been rare things for privileged eyes when she learned the system, even amongst the membership of London's Golden Dawn, at the turn of the 20th century. Three hundred years before that, being caught with one by church authorities would have merited an immediate death sentence across most of Europe.

Now the old operating manual was an object of historical curiosity, likely reprinted for the titillation of subversive scholars and maladjusted teens.

Time sure could flit. (*Oh, shit*, her mental Dottie Parker tacked on.)

Ingrid flipped to the entry for Vinea, the lion-headed horseman Jimmy the Freak had sicced on her back in 1941. The page featured a drawing of the sigil needed to connect with the spirit, like a semiotic phone-exchange number. She scanned a few lines of the attached description to confirm what she remembered reading about Vinea's office and powers:

'He, at ye Command of ye Exorcist, may Build Up mightie Towers, or else may Throw Down their great Stone Walls.'

Skills like that might solve some of her problems.

Not the worst of them... but some.

She sketched the demon's sigil onto a nearby pad of yellow paper, then tossed the book to frowsy Phyllis.

"Take that," she said. "Entry forty-five. Governor Vinea. I need you to call him up and have him make something for me, okay?"

The sort of full-scale evocation she was talking about would take more time than her off-the-cuff attempt to speak with Tlazolteotl, but Jimmy's people seemed more than capable of laying the groundwork.

Phyllis Stein went away with a few more instructions and small requests—for Teonanactl mushrooms or something like them, as well as any weapons they might have handy—leaving Ingrid alone in the quiet screening room. Faint noises of excited party preparation reached her from far corners of the building. By midnight more people in this city would be focused on one event, one moment in time, than there had been since the priests of the old people tore open a hole in the sky by sending tens of thousands of individuals on to their next lives from the top of their pyramid.

She wound her watch and synchronized it to a clock display she discovered on the front of a movie cassette player.

Tonight, at the stroke of midnight, when all the city of Los Angeles was focused on the mystery of time itself, Ingrid meant to channel every drop of that gathered attention into the lens embedded in her watch's case. Jimmy's Pyroptic Anamorph, the glass that remembered. And then she'd see what she could do with it—with a little help from lion-headed Vinea. If she timed it right she might have a chance to seal off the Hole in the Sky. Barring that, her chosen ally might be able to bring down the Silent Tower itself.

Maybe.

She sat down and started *Raiders* over from the beginning, figuring she might as well watch the damn thing while she worked. She'd only been trying for twenty years. And she liked Indiana Jones. She was partial to a man who looked good in a fedora.

Ingrid unsheathed her knife from its concealment on her left thigh and set about scratching the Sigil of Vinea into the smooth surface of her watch's crystal lens.

TWILIGHT was on by the time Phyllis Stein woke her. The sky beyond the parted curtains had turned a rich, deep blue, and was awash in ribbons of gold-edged cloud.

She'd fallen asleep in her high-backed office chair. 'Pisa' slices may have been delicious beyond compare, but four of them at once had left her in need of a nap.

The logo of a laser-disc manufacturer was bouncing silently around on the big wall screen. Ingrid had seen the melting faces and the big warehouse at the end of *Raiders*, however, before passing out. It wasn't a long flick, though it was truly epic in scope when compared with the silent, black-&-white one-reelers that had been the state of the art when she made *Race Tout* with Francis Boggs.

She'd finished vandalizing her watch crystal, too. She held it up and examined her handiwork as the timepiece spun around at the end of its long fob chain, the gears inside whirling and gleaming. The sigil on the glass was clear and unmistakable.

"Jimmy's jet's about to land at Van Nuys," Phyllis told her. "He'll be here in less than an hour."

Ingrid nodded. She still felt bleary-eyed, but she was glad for the notice.

"I scrounged some clothes I think will fit you, and there's a bathroom with everything just down the hall if you want to shower and change or whatever. Got some of the other stuff you asked for too."

She handed Ingrid a large plastic bag filled with folded garments and a much smaller one containing several pills, squares of paper, and some dried plant stalks. Ingrid looked at that one first. The old deflective wards around the Silent Tower had been pretty ragged since the 60s, but she wasn't taking any chances.

"Something for pain, like you asked," Phyllis said. "And Psilocybin mushrooms, and a thousand micrograms of pure lysergic acid diethylamide on the paper tabs. Plus I put in some Ecstasy, I don't know if that's useful, but I thought I'd give you options."

Ingrid nodded. She'd never heard of Ecstasy before, but she might be willing to try something new under these unusual circumstances. She'd never heard of 'acid' either, until she met the Merry Pranksters.

She went and 'showered,' which was a rare experience for a girl who hailed from an era of bathtubs filled with hand-drawn water. She next used a big cartoon gun to blast hot air onto her hair while brushing it out, drying and smoothing it at the same time. Amazing!

She dressed in the clothes Phyllis had been kind enough to find for her, which included black jodhpur pants that fit like she'd been dipped in ink, a snug black turtleneck, and glossy black leather boots that all but made Ingrid drool. She threw Mictlantecuhtli's flowing cloak around her shoulders to complete the ensemble.

She washed down two each of the pain pills and the Ecstasy tablets with water from the sink, then went downstairs, on the lookout for familiar Phyllis.

The halls of the Topless Tower were more crowded than they had been that morning. People were gearing up to party. Ingrid turned some heads, but many of the individuals here were more eye-catching than her. She saw more tattoos than she'd expect at a circus sideshow. Even the boys wore multiple earrings, if not studs through noses, eyebrows, and tongues. Other kids had hair pomaded up into lethal-looking quills, and many wore what looked like tubes of neon light around their wrists or necks.

Ingrid found them all a little overwhelming.

'99 looked like '66 turned upside down in more ways than one.

Everyone she asked knew Phyllis, and Ingrid wandered in the directions she was pointed until she found her concierge.

S HE was all the way downstairs, deep in the cavernous concrete parking garages. Ingrid discovered her presiding over a ring of meditators, half a dozen of them. Each was utterly quiescent and arranged around a Circle far more elaborate than Ingrid's chalk rendering had been. An excellent artist had permanently painted it in multiple colors on the gray concrete floor.

The operators had affixed a triangular black mirror to the wall before the circle. It was eight feet in height at least. Its uppermost point touched the garage's ceiling. In the dark glass Ingrid could see the lion-headed figure of Lord Vinea, dressed for a fox hunt in a top hat and tailcoat, standing right where Phyllis's reflection should have been.

These people were ready to operate. Ingrid was deeply impressed. The Golden Dawn had never gone to so much trouble.

"We have your demon for you," Phyllis said, "and we've got him fired up enough to manifest things all the way solid, as long as he's got a physical base to start with."

Ingrid held up the lone horseshoe she'd scavenged from the ash pile of her Shadow's remains. "Ask him if he remembers this."

"You can talk at him from there," Phyllis said. "He'll talk back to you through me."

Ingrid nodded. "Vinea," she said, projecting her voice as if she were on stage: "Remember me?"

"Red Witch," he mouthed, his velvet muzzle rippling back as he bared his teeth in a grin. The voices Ingrid heard—two of them, distinctly—both issued from Phyllis's throat. One was her own, a smooth contralto; while the second was lower, male, and insinuating. "You bested me quite cleverly, and then you tamed my steed."

"That was me," Ingrid agreed.

Vinea bowed graciously. "All that I am is yours to use," he and Phyllis said. "Or else these people will never stop tormenting me."

That's the way the game was played. "I could use a replacement," Ingrid said, and tossed him the horseshoe, over Phyllis's head.

Instead of shattering the mirror, the iron shoe became a tall black horse as it passed through the reflection, causing the glass to ripple. Vinea stepped aside for it.

The new horse (Shadow II, already christened in her head) turned around and stepped back out of the black mirror. He pranced around within the tight perimeter of Phyllis's Circle of the Art.

"Break the circle to let him out," Phyllis said, in her own voice. Vinea's was gone.

Ingrid stepped across the painted ring to catch the new ghosthorse's bridle. He already had a saddle, as well as quite a number of twisting green snakes coiled over his reins.

Riding crops, of the sort Vinea wielded. They'd come in handy.

"You asked for weapons," Phyllis said, and tossed a short, sheathed sword over to her. "Jimmy gave me permission to offer you this."

Ingrid drew the blade from its lacquered scabbard. It was curved, single-edged, beautifully crafted. She guessed it was Japanese in origin. "Is it special?"

"Jim called it the Dancing Sword of Kuro Yamabushi. It's very old, supposedly made by a swordsmith-alchemist way back when in old-time Japan. He said it fights for you. All you gotta do is hold it and project your intentions."

Ingrid swung the thing tentatively. She could fence; it was a basic stage skill. This felt like an ordinary blade, if especially well-wrought and balanced.

"I guess we'll see about that," she said, re-sheathing the sword and sliding the scabbard through her wide leather belt. Its curve hugged her hip comfortably. She strung a few of Vinea's snake whips alongside it for ease of access. "Thank you for it."

Phyllis nodded. Ingrid noticed she was wearing the Sigil of Vinea as a lamen—a metal breastplate, in this case gold, with his symbol etched into its gleaming surface.

"Is there any way you can shine that into the sky?" she asked, pointing to the symbol on the lamen. "Right at midnight? When everybody who's thinking about the new year can look up and see it?"

"You mean like the Bat Signal?" Phyllis said, considering. "I don't see why not. There's a laser projector in the big room, for shows and shit. Should work, as long as there's some cloud cover. I'll get some people to move the equipment up to the roof."

"Yes, please," Ingrid said. She liked lasers, like the little pen Jimmy had given her in '81. She used it often to look at the 'hologram' of her Uncle Frank that the watch crystal contained. "Right at midnight," she repeated. Here..."

She unsheathed her knife (which she'd strapped on over her tight jodhpurs), looped a lock of hair around her fingers, and neatly chopped it off. She tied the twist of red hair into a knot and tossed it across the circle to Phyllis. Phyllis got the point immediately and returned the gesture, slicing off one of her own copper coils and flipping it across the protective rings to Ingrid.

They each pocketed their physical link to the other, through which a torrent of aetheric energy could and would be transmitted between them, later that night, if all went according to plan.

"I'm gonna take off now," Ingrid said. "Thank you for everything, Phyllis."

"What?" Jimmy's assistant sounded distressed. "But—Jim'll be here in twenty minutes! He said he's been waiting twenty years to see you again."

"Miles to go before I sleep," Ingrid said. "He'll understand."

She *could* have stayed—she had more than six hours remaining before midnight—but she didn't want to see Jimmy the Freak. Accepting his help was hard enough, knowing he'd murdered her Uncle Frank so long ago, no matter how contrite and changed he might be today. She still couldn't bear the thought of having to thank him face-to-face, and she would have to, if she lingered any longer. She wasn't going to risk having it be one of the last things she ever did. "Tell him I may be back," she said to an incredulous Phyllis. "After."

It was dimly possible that she might need a place to sleep tomorrow night. Not likely, but possible. She took Shadow II's bridle and began to lead her replacement horse away, toward the elevators.

"Wait!" Phyllis said, and Ingrid turned.

"Did you..." Phyllis began, uncertainly and uncomfortably. "Are you... I mean, Jimmy said you came from the past. Not *his* past, you know, but *the* past. That statue you said you used to own has been in that museum since 1947. And the clothes you came in, it's like you... traveled in time. O- or something."

"I was born in 1885," Ingrid said. "I came here from 1915."

"Holy shit," Phyllis said.

Ingrid wondered if she'd read Dottie Parker. "Give Jim my thanks," she said. "I *am* grateful, I just... I've gotta go. We have a complicated history, me and Jimmy."

"I understand," Phyllis said, though there was no way she could. Unless she had a complex relationship with Jim herself. Ingrid appreciated the sentiment, either way.

"Sigil in the sky at midnight, big and bright as you can make it," Ingrid reminded. "Please don't forget."

"We've got big lasers," Phyllis promised. "Scrounged secondhand from a planetarium. Plus some old things that went missing from Cal Tech. They'll see your symbol from downtown to Venice, I promise."

"Perfect." Ingrid led Shadow II into a freight elevator and started them rising. She raised her hand in a wave, and Phyllis returned the gesture. Ingrid had faith in her. She'd see that everything was in place at the appointed moment.

That left Ingrid with a few hours to kill, and that was precisely what she meant to do with them.

B Y the time she led Shadow II outside, into the unwelcoming cul-de-sac near the freeway that the Topless Tower dominated, Phyllis's pain pills had almost erased her abdominal aches, and her Ecstasy tablets were beginning to live up to their name. Ingrid had an improbably positive feeling about her prospects. Her thoughts popped and sparked in an excitable fashion. Her body wanted to move, to run, to dance, to screw, and she realized she was grinding her teeth. Her limbs felt flooded with an excess of energy that cried out for athletic dissipation. Finding the Silent Tower later wouldn't be a problem.

As soon as she stepped beyond Jimmy the Freak's wards three *Alu* demons congealed out of the darkness to greet her. They were black-furred, yellow-eyed, vaguely canine in form, though larger and more hulking than even the best-fed wolves would ever be. They were of Babylonian derivation, but Ingrid had no doubt these were recent conquests of Mictlantecuhtli's, sent into the realworld to herd her home like a pack of monstrous sheepdogs.

Half a dozen more Alu stepped out of the shadows behind the initial three.

Ingrid made a ritual gesture and their simplified chakra strings sprang into vivid relief. The subtle energies permeating all things were more apparent than ever before. She thought the effect would tend to linger, amplified as it was by Phyllis Stein's ecstatic brand of chemistry.

She strode out to meet Mickey's creatures, pulling the magic sword she'd been given from her belt, scabbard and all, and slamming it down onto the nearest dog-demon's head, bludgeoning it to the pavement. Shards of broken fangs sprayed across the asphalt. She drew the sword and it pulled in her hands like a gyroscope, like a thing with a life and a will of its own. She loosed her anger down her arms and out through the blade as she spun with it, dicing the next two Alu into several pieces.

They tumbled aside in chunks that had leapt toward her as whole creatures, then exploded into clouds of noxious-smelling dust.

So maybe she'd send Jimmy a thank-you note later.

She swung herself up onto the back of Shadow II, holding the Dancing Sword of Kuro Yamabushi at the ready. The rest of her ex-lover's wolfpack fled with their tails between their legs as Ingrid took to the streets of Los Angeles on the final night of 1999.

S HE found plenty of other creatures to fight as she rode across the city, taking a rambling route east toward the Silent Tower.

Mickey's hired human forces didn't trouble her much. As long as she stayed on the move and kept clear of the recently dead, they had no way of tracking her. Few of the new demons Mickey had at his disposal were smart enough to give a coherent description of her location.

It didn't stop Mickey from trying. He sent Indian *Asuras* after her as well as Japanese *Oni*. African *Kishi* that looked like handsome young men ran at her out of alleyways and Ingrid could hardly tell they weren't human until they turned around and parted their long hair, revealing the leering, slavering second faces in the backs of their heads, which she promptly removed for them by tossing Lord Vinea's self-consuming snakes around their necks.

People saw her. Regular people, New Years' celebrants out on the streets, wandering from bar to bar or smoking in clusters on streetcorners. They stood and gaped while they watched her fight, or else tried to take pictures with tiny cameras, though Ingrid couldn't imagine those would turn out. Light found beings from the otherworld permeable and slippery, and didn't bounce off them in quite the same way it did off things that were strictly real.

She didn't give a damn one way or the other. Let them watch. Nobody'd ever believe a word, with or without photographic evidence, so what did it matter?

The nocturnal Tzitzimime came out in force after dark. They dove out of the sky as points of light that resembled stars but became insects when they buzzed near. They would clump together into tall, chitinous, feminoid forms to grasp at her. Ingrid responded by slashing off their limbs and puncturing their shells, cutting their heads loose and mowing them down from horseback as fast as they wanted to reform.

Mickey no longer cared if she lived or died—that much was clear. Dead might even be his preference. Once she was his subject he'd be able to override her personal will at any time he chose. He'd learn where and when she'd hidden their baby. He could even send her out to fetch it, quite against her will, as long as he could dredge up enough patience to wait until the day after Halloween. More likely el Rey would send Tzitzimime after his prize straightaway, and the thought of those awful bugbitches putting their feelers all over her child only redoubled the satisfaction Ingrid took in killing them, over and over again.

She was never going to let Mickey get hold of that infant. She'd decided. She'd close off the door between worlds and make of herself an earthbound revenant the way Dottie Parker had, so that he could never force her to reveal the baby's location. She meant to ensure its continued safety and anonymity if it was the last goddamn thing she did with her wildly improbable life.

And so she burned her way through the last hours of the 20th century, by venting her fury on anything that came at her out of Mickey's sphere. Mictlantecuhtli and the creatures of his realm had come between her and her child, and she was raging. Like a wildfire. She periodically checked the time on Jimmy the Freak's old watch during her rampage, as she fought and hacked and slashed and slaughtered, not even coming close to slaking her thirst for violence but still taking a certain grim satisfaction in what she did manage to dole out. When it got to be 11:40—when the palpable excitement of a millennium's end was beginning to crackle in the cold, clear winter's air, in neighborhood after neighborhood all across the city—she pulled on Shadow II's reins to turn him in the right direction and rode hard for the Silent Tower.

Several hells' worth of monsters came after her, but the time for fun and games had regrettably passed. She pulled up her hood and gave them the slip.

All she had left to do now was redraw the ancient demarcation between life and death, and underline it for good measure.

Chapter Nine

W HAT have you done with my son?" Mictlantecuhtli demanded as soon as she walked through the office door. She took the time to station Shadow II in a corner. Winston stood beside the King, holding a cellular telephone to the side of his bony head, where his ear would have been in life.

"What makes you think it's a boy?"

"My daughter, then," Mictlantecuhtli said, sounding at first surprised, then looking thoughtful. "I have never before considered becoming a woman," he mused. "What's it like?"

Ingrid put a hand on her hip. "I've got nothing to compare it with."

"I am in no mood for games," the King of the Dead said in his echoing voice. He stayed in his most terrifying aspect—that of a flayed skeleton with a necklace of eyes, shrouded in a cloak made from human skin. "You have stolen from me."

"That's an interesting interpretation. I notice 'my love' has gone right out the window, too."

"Your treachery threatens to kill my affection for you, yes."

"You wanna maybe put on some skin? It's pointless trying to look you in the eye when you don't have any."

The skeleton became Mickey, her King, ornamented with feathers and gold. He looked more stern and angry than she had ever seen him. He kept his garland of leaking, gristly eyeballs on through the transformation.

"Tell me where you have hidden my child."

"I won't. Forget about it."

"You forget to whom you speak. I ask as a courtesy. I have other ways of learning what I would know."

"I'm sure you do," Ingrid said.

Mickey snapped his fingers and Califia appeared, dressed in flesh and looking just the way Ingrid remembered her from life. Mickey pushed her into the doorway and asked, "Shall I have my creatures chew the marrow from her bones?"

"*Leave her alone!*" Ingrid barked.

"Obey me and she's forgotten," Mickey said.

Califia looked right at Ingrid, pleading with her eyes. Pleading with her not to surrender to the King.

Ingrid gritted her teeth, and stood her ground.

"Winston, call the humans." Mickey shoved Califia aside in disgust. "Instruct them to throw Lady Redstone through this doorway as soon as they arrive."

The skeletal butler nodded and pressed a button on his telephone as he stepped aside, and the King stood back to bellow up at the ceiling as loudly as he could:

"*Tzitzimime!*"

Insects came boiling out of the walls and up from the cracks in the floor. Shadow II reared back as cables of tiny ants coiled up his legs. Wasps went for his eyes, and green mantises shredded his dust-based flesh apart with their scissoring jaws. He was gone in seconds.

Ingrid was less upset about it this time. If she survived, she could have another made.

She drew her sword. It slid from its scabbard with an ominous metallic *sliiisssh*, and light seemed to drip down the exposed blade.

The bugwomen held back, hovering on the verge of full solidity. They kept their colonies loose, squirming and swarming, permeable to her blade. They could try to engulf her, but she'd cleave their chakra strings apart if they got that close, and maybe puncture a vital whorl if she got lucky. If they went for Califia, she'd take them apart.

She and the insect demons were at a stalemate.

The living henchmen would be here any minute, though, and they'd have guns. Mictlantecuhtli would catch her as she died if someone shot her, the way he'd almost done with Dorothy Parker, on the occasion of her disappointing demise.

A moment after crossing Ingrid's mind, Dottie appeared.

"What the fuck are *you* doing here?"

"Finding purpose, dear," Mrs. Parker said. "And that's a fine greeting, by the way."

Further discussion of the point was curtailed by the arrival of Mickey Hardface's hired goons—ordinary humans who believed they were footsoldiers in a crimelord's employ.

Mickey traded in his loincloth and feathers for a modern-day suit, to better meet the expectations of his living minions. It didn't take him as long as the blink of an eye.

They crowded into the doorway to the first chamber with their guns drawn, but they pulled back on the threshold when they saw the sea of churning bugs that milled around the perimeter of the room.

"I am Miguel Caradura, known unto you as 'Mickey Hardface,'" the King told them in his most commanding voice. He pointed to Ingrid.

"And I order you to throw that woman through this doorway. Or else shoot her in the head."

"I think not," Dottie Parker said.

"Your opinion does not count, ghost. There is nothing one such as you can do to stand against the living."

"Except frighten them. Like this." Mrs. Parker raised both her arms and shouted, almost gleefully: "Everyone—*sic balls*!"

The dogs came together from the dusty remains of Shadow II almost too fast for Ingrid to see. There were well more than a dozen—small, snapping, snarling, and yapping. All were lapdogs, a lifetime's worth of miniature breeds like terriers, dachshunds, and poodles, and each was black as pitch in color. Ingrid even recognized a raven-coated, spectral version of little Ernest amongst them.

The pack of tiny dervishes flew at the henchmen's genitals, and they reacted as men would. They screeched and shouted, swearing at the dogs as they tried to swat them away. Some dropped guns, and all were driven back from the door, out into the hallway.

"Clever trick," Mickey said, addressing Dot. "But your freedom is not as secure as you imagine. Your physical remains were destroyed by fire. 'Cremated.' You have nothing left to anchor you in the real. So I will let my consorts gnaw you out of all existence."

Dottie smiled.

"Tzitzimime," Mickey said. "Consume her."

The bugwomen fell upon Mrs. Parker in swarms that focused into a confusing tangle of snapping mandibles and rending limbs. They couldn't tear her apart, however, or even catch hold of her.

Dottie's ghost stood fast, smirking in that wicked way she had.

"How is this accomplished?" the King demanded.

Dottie's revenant removed a blue-and-white paperback book from her illusion of a handbag and held it up. The picture on the cover was of her. The title was *The Portable Dorothy Parker*.

"It's called *living* memory, you shortsighted piece of shit," the ghostly author said, breaking into a rare grin. "Clearly, sir, you are not a reader."

Ingrid laughed. It didn't please Mickey.

"*Winston!*" he shouted. "More men! Summon more men than she has dogs!"

Winston retreated to a corner, frantically dialing his cellular phone.

Ingrid checked her watch. It was nearly midnight. She'd almost missed the appointed hour. All of Los Angeles was poised to ring in the next millennium, everyone longing toward a better tomorrow. In seconds the Sigil of Vinea would be projected onto the night sky for half the city to see, from the pinnacle of Jimmy the Freak's Topless Tower. The symbol would act like a net for all of that concentrated energy as it distracted and refocused the attention of everyone who looked up and saw it.

All she needed were a few vital moments.

The second hand on her watch swept around toward midnight. She popped open the case, pointing the Anamorphic crystal toward the doorway between the worlds. She took out the laser pen Jimmy had given her so long ago and trained its beam through the scratched-up lens.

A reproduction of the sigil she'd etched there bloomed large and ruby red. The blazing symbol pushed both the King and Queen Califia back from the portal, helplessly.

The image of Francis Boggs Jimmy had recorded onto the glass all the way back in 1911 stood in the doorway and seemed to address Ingrid as it delivered its one line:

"So this is how you mean to change the world, is it?"

"It is," Ingrid murmured. She stepped forward and set the watch down on the threshold between the worlds, taking care to keep her pen's red beam pointed into the lens when she stood back, sweeping her sword around to fend off any encroaching Tzitzimime.

Mickey screamed with rage when the picture of Ingrid's Uncle Frank changed into one of lion-headed Lord Vinea, still rendered in blazing scarlet. The Governor laughed when Mickey struggled to reach through the aetheric fence his sigil had become. He turned and bowed, doffing his top hat in the King's direction.

"Lord Vinea," Ingrid said to him, "seal up that door. For good."

Vinea raised his hand as if in benediction, and the crystal embedded in the watch case began to grow. The piece of polished glass fused by a meteorite that once hit the Egyptian desert broke out of its metal frame, building upon itself layer by layer. The rapid expansion was fueled by energies funneled across the city to Ingrid by Phyllis, through the aetheric link made by their exchanged locks of hair. Ingrid in turn poured the current into the glass, which responded. Spiky new accretions of crystal blossomed across the doorway between the King's Chambers, filling it from the floor up.

By the first minute of the next millennium, the Hole in the Sky would be scarred over for good, and the Silent Tower would, for the first time in its weird history, be only what it appeared to be—a perfectly ordinary office building.

And Ingrid would be stranded in the year 2000. Separated from her child by an ocean of time, for good. From her parents, too. They'd be long dead by now, and she'd never seen them again, or said goodbye.

Her throat tightened into a knot. At least her baby would be safe, and free to live a life.

One that she would never be any part of.

Lucinda Swire had warned her she might face a choice like this one day. Warned or threatened—she'd never known which.

Mickey was still bellowing threats of his own. The crystal wall Vinea was generating out of a city's hopes for its own tomorrow was nearly a third of the way complete. Ingrid couldn't see the demon's sigil burning across the sky, but Phyllis must have come through. None of this would be working, otherwise.

And then the pencil-thin beam projected from the end of the laser pointer faltered, for just an instant.

It was the damn battery. Ingrid used the pen to see the image of her Uncle Frank when her thoughts were troubled, and her thoughts had been troubled a lot these last few months.

Mickey used the momentary stutter and disappearance of the sigil the laser's beam had been projecting into his realm to dart forward like an athlete and boot Jimmy the Freak's old fob watch away from the threshold. The partial crystal wall that had sprung up around it shattered into fragments, and the watch flew past Ingrid's head to break audibly when it impacted against the wall.

Her heart sank.

It was the 21st century now. Her moment had passed. Midnight had come and gone, and the Silent Tower was still open for business.

"Now, witch," Mickey said as he stepped into the doorway and glared at Ingrid, "your tortures begin."

He clapped his hands.

"Tzitzimime! Bring her before me, by any means necessary."

The swarms of insects siphoned off into three distinct clumps that hovered on the verge of solidifying.

Ingrid readied her sword. Escape was her mission now. Her child's only chance. Plan A may have failed, but if she died tonight, she'd have no more secrets from Mickey.

"Uh, excuse me?" an unfamiliar male voice said from behind her, causing Ingrid to whip her head around.

Even the wary Tzitzimime paused, waiting to see what this new development might portend.

A strange young man stood in the first chamber's door. Strange in the unfamiliar sense, but weird as well. The blazer he wore over a t-shirt looked rumpled, and he seemed to regard everything he looked at with a high degree of childlike wonder.

He had a small package cradled under his arm. "I've got a delivery for Ingrid Redstone."

"That's me. Who the hell are you?"

He laughed. "Well, I was a graduate student this morning. Back in the 20th century. In the 21st I'm an art thief, a millionaire, and an international man of mystery."

"We're kind of in the middle of something," Ingrid said.

"Oh!" The erstwhile grad student's pupils looked enormous. Ingrid could smell the alcohol on his breath from across the room. "Right, of course, sure you are. I can see that. Awkward. You know, I think there might've been something in those drinks I had on the plane. I'm seeing trails."

He waggled a hand in front of his face and giggled at it. This guy's third eye looked peeled all the way open. Ingrid figured he must have taken (or been dosed with) something psychedelic. She could feel Mickey's patience with the intrusion evaporating, though his creatures hadn't yet made a move toward her.

"Shit, that's a lotta bugs," the wayward scholar observed. "You know some guys just went running out of here, yelling and swatting at their nuts?"

"To the point, please," Ingrid said.

"Right, okay, anyway, you won't believe this." The kid made a visible effort to get his train of thought back on track. "But I get this phone call, okay, about seven hours ago. Voice on the other end of the line tells me to name a price for bringing this"—he held up the package he'd brought with him—"here, to you, by midnight. Guess I'm like a minute late, I hope that's all right."

Ingrid nodded. She was starting to think it might be just fine.

"So I say, 'twenty million,' thinking it's all a joke, that it's gotta be a buddy of mine, but the voice on the phone tells me to go and check my bank account online, and I watched the zeros roll in. No negotiation, just, there it was. Cab picked me up and took me to Dulles International ten minutes later. Private jet flew me out here. All I really had to do was get the piece out of its case and bring it with me. It was nothing, there's not even security, just a locked door, and I had the key. So here—this is for you. Somebody really wanted you to have it."

The priciest delivery boy in history handed Ingrid his twenty-million-dollar parcel.

"Dude faxed me this address, and a note for you." He took a folded sheet of paper from inside his coat and handed it over. "Doesn't make a whole lot of sense."

He seemed utterly unselfconscious about having read it.

Ingrid unfolded the page and had a look for herself.

> *Ingrid—*
> *So sorry I missed you! I saw the disc you left in my player (go, Indy!), and I had a look at your internet history too. Plus Phyllis mentioned you have a midnight deadline on your special operation.*
> *I know you once said there's nothing I can do to make amends, but I hope this token lets you know I'm still trying. Maybe it'll come in handy if you find yourself needing a 'plan B.'*
> *Here's to days to come as well as days gone by,*
> *—Deus (Ex Machina!) Es Canis Inversus*

"What on earth is it?" Dottie Parker's ghost asked, looking as puzzled as everyone else.

Better to show than tell. Ingrid tore the newspaper wrapping from the greenstone carving of Tlazolteotl that Califia had given her a thousand years ago. Califia herself crowed with delight. Jimmy the Freak had paid an astonishing fortune to have it liberated from its niche in a distant museum and returned to her possession. He'd also dosed the courier with some kind of mind-expander, to make sure he'd find his destination despite the weakened hexwork around it. Ingrid dimly realized this meant Jim must have figured out the secret of her Silent Tower's location some time ago, but elected not to approach it. His interests really had turned from death to life. She supposed she was proud of him.

The idol seemed to throb in her hand. It grew warm, then hot, but didn't burn her. The power coursing through it was nothing less than the fire of life itself, distilled and undiluted.

She turned to face Mictlantecuhtli, her former love and her greatest adventure, for what she hoped was the last time.

"We are Tlazolteotl," she said, raising the idol above her head, in a voice that was not her own. Or not *just* her own, as hers was certainly one amongst the chorus that issued from her throat, resoundingly enough to shake the walls of the King's Chambers. Skeins of plaster dust sifted down from the ceiling. She had no idea what she was going to say until words came out of her mouth:

"We are Ixcuiname, She of Two Faces. We are Tlaelquanai, the Redeemer of Corruption."

The stone statue glowed in her upraised hand, blazing more brightly than the golden copy in the movie. Ingrid's entire field of vision turned vaguely blue, as if someone were shining powerful azure lights right outside the range of her peripheral vision. She liked to think her eyes might be glowing. That would've been a striking special effect.

"We forgive or punish transgressions upon our sphere as we see fit, and in this our authority exceeds even yours, Mictlantecuhtli."

The King winced at the volume and power of the goddess's voice. He shielded his eyes, standing in the doorway and looking bleached out by the ever-brightening light that issued from the idol squatting on Ingrid's upraised palm.

"*Tzitzimime!*" Mickey screamed, and the bugwomen snapped to attention, their swarms liquefying and melding into their familiar avatars of an Ant, a Mantis, and a Wasp.

The grad student who'd brought the statue pressed into a corner, where he pointed at the bugwomen and began to hyperventilate while he attempted to scream.

"Tzitzimime," Ingrid said, as a new understanding of the bugwomen bloomed within her mind. Her thoughts were vast and ancient around the edges now, yet still somehow her own at the core. "Remember your origins. You each were stitched together from the remnants of brave warriors fallen in the fight to prolong the tale of your kind. Before Mictlantecuhtli claimed your remains and made of you his servants you were our *Cihuateteo*: women lost in the struggle to wrest life from death, who never knew the children they delivered to the worlds. Those too shattered to find their peace in the House of the Rising Sun. This is the source of your torment, Tzitzimime—your hunger that can never be sated. Now the same anguish is shared by this our child, who has brought honor to the name of Tlazolteotl. This Red Witch is one of you. Look upon yourselves, by our authority, and *remember what you were!*"

"Don't listen to her!" Mickey screamed. The desperation in his voice was unmistakable. Even the bugwomen heard it. They cocked their heads and continued listening to the goddess inside of Ingrid instead of following their King's orders.

She'd never seen that happen before.

"The witch we ride this night fights the war in which you fell. She struggles for the life of her child, so that the memory of her kind may know another day. In this she is not your enemy. In this, she is your sister. In the name of our Califia we therefore intercede. We stand in defiance of King Mictlantecuhtli, and we annul his will. Tonight, my fallen warriors, my tortured ones, *you fight for Lady Red Stone!*"

The bugwomen turned to face Mictlantecuhtli. Mantis stepped forward to defend their redeemer, Tlazolteotl, interposing her green carapace between Ingrid and the King.

Mictlantecuhtli may have replaced their lost minds with spare traits he borrowed from the creatures of his realm, but Tlazolteotl owned their fierce and broken hearts.

This couldn't last, though, and Ingrid knew it. There was only so much chthonic force she could channel up from the earth and into the idol to be projected as fiery will before her own mind was burnt away like a sheet of tissue paper tossed over a blazing flame.

Mickey snarled. Hordes of his conquered demons materialized behind him—some varieties she'd tangled with already, others she couldn't even name. Tlazolteotl's word held no power over them.

"They're coming," Dot's ghost murmured, cocking her head as if to listen. "More gunmen. More than I have dogs for."

"Tzitzimime," Tlazolteotl said calmly, through Ingrid's lips. "See to them."

The bugwomen broke, shattering into swarms that rose to meet the threats pouring into the chamber from either door. The by-now-regretful graduate student who'd been commissioned by Jimmy the Freak to deliver the statue screamed as the wave of insects rolled over him, leaving him unharmed (except perhaps psychologically).

Clouds of bugs met monsters at one door and mobsters at the other. Both groups were driven back. The hired goons never had a chance to bring their guns into play. The host of demons in Mickey's thrall were likewise chased off by insects, back into the otherworld.

"And you as well, Califia," Ingrid+Tlazolteotl said. "Our will prevails in your case, too. Have at him, if you would."

Califia grinned, manifesting one of those big clubs her warriors fought with, a *macuahuitl*, like a cricket bat studded around the edges with broken glass. She laid into Mickey with it, grunting in satisfaction when its shards bit into his side. Of course the injury wasn't 'real' in the strictest sense and began to knit back up immediately, as soon as Califia levered the macuahuitl free of his ribs, but Mickey was committed enough to his illusions of physicality and time by now that the queen was able to deal him several more vicious strikes before he could regain himself and flee his own Chambers. Califia cried out in Nahuatl for her personal guard, her Shorn Ones, and their bones rose from the floor of the inner sanctum to chase after their bewildered King.

He'd be back, though—as soon as Tlazolteotl's will stopped powering Califia's loyal soldiers. Which would have to be soon. Ingrid's arms and shoulders were beginning to shake. She didn't have a lot of strength left, but this was almost over.

"Califia!" Tlazolteotl said, before the Queen of California could leave the second chamber in pursuit of Mictlantecuhtli. "Hurry now, and cross over. You may use this stone as an anchor in the living world. You will invite the wrath of the King if you stay in his realm. Is this solution acceptable unto you?"

"Tla," Califia agreed, with no fuss or discussion. She stepped across the barrier between life and death and embraced Ingrid.

The light died out of the idol and it became plain gray-green stone again. Ingrid moved to return Califia's embrace… but there was no one to put her arms around.

Only a small stone statue in her hand.

She turned to the student who'd delivered it on behalf of Jimmy the Freak, helped him up, and pressed the Tlazolteotl idol back into his hands. "Take this back where you got it, and keep it safe forever, okay?"

"O-okay," he said. He was shellshocked from his encounter with the bugs, and all the other horrors he'd unwittingly witnessed. Ingrid knew the look of someone who wanted badly to go home.

"Don't remember this," she suggested, hexing him a little to ensure it would happen. "But if you find a lot of extra money in your bank account tomorrow, you have to do something good with it. That's your responsibility, and the price of walking out of here with your mind in one piece. Tell yourself you won it with a lottery ticket. Understood?"

"Yes," he croaked, nodding and bowing as he backed out of the room. Ingrid heard him break into a run as he hurried down the hall. Back to his life, and an unexpected new chapter of it.

Tlazolteotl had gone. Ingrid was only herself again. Mickey would be back very soon now. The Tzitzimime wouldn't remember their brief change of heart, either. They were Mictlantecuhtli's creatures, ultimately. They'd be returning with him in force, tormented and mad once again, now that their goddess was gone.

Ingrid didn't want to waste this chance.

She turned to look down at the ghost of Mrs. Parker.

"I must say I am exhausted, dear," Dot said. "Remaining coherent for this long is a tiring business. I could sleep through an age."

"I know how you feel," Ingrid said. "I didn't expect you to come, Dottie. You saved me."

Dot smiled, a touch sadly, looking down at the paperback edition of her own collected works that had let her stand for a moment against the implacable will of Death, and Ingrid couldn't imagine any writer ever feeling she'd pulled a better trick.

Mrs. Parker still managed to look ambivalent about it. "Did I matter after all, then, Ingrid Redstone? In the end?"

"I can't speak for anybody else, but you sure as hell did for me."

She tried to embrace Dot too, but again it didn't happen. She was left clutching Dot's book to her chest. She knew she'd read it over and over again, the way she'd once looked at the now-lost Anamorphic image of her Uncle Frank, whenever she needed solace.

It was time to travel.

1915 wasn't safe to return to—not for her or her child. Mickey would have Winston and every demon he could rouse out looking for her. What she had to do now was hide, regroup, and formulate another plan.

Some other plan.

The thought exhausted her. She felt like a recursive figure caught up in rippling cycles of myth, running one more time from her Silent Tower, the place where all her tales began and ended. She'd left her King on rather bad terms this time out and was parted from her only child, but she wasn't done yet.

Only the dead had no hope, and Ingrid was very much alive.

Though perhaps not for long, if she didn't hurry.

She stepped through the door between worlds, into the sacrificial chamber, and dialed the years back carelessly, spinning time like a roulette wheel. Maybe it would keep spinning behind her, and throw Mickey off her trail. She could hear him returning, enraged and shouting, his sandals slapping the stairs as he took them at a full run.

Ingrid took a deep breath and stepped out the door. She thought she might be leaping into 1949, or possibly 1950. Not long after the world's second big war. She wasn't sure, but had no more time to linger. She realized—too late—that she must have dropped Jimmy's magic sword when the goddess possessed her. There was no going back for it now. The Aztec altar chamber had already disappeared behind her, replaced by the illusion of a mid-century office. An empty one, furnished with a desk, two filing cabinets, and an oak coat rack.

It seemed like she'd done it—escaped into time. But this was not an idea she wanted to wait around to test.

Catch me if you can, she thought as she hurried out the far door, putting Mictlantecuhtli and his suite at the top of the Silent Tower behind her, without looking back.

S O she never saw the King's Englishman, Winston Watt, flicker into being beside the office's blond-wood desk.

He picked up the handset of a rotary phone and dialed the number of Big Juan San Martín, son of Oscar San Martín—a living man who served el Rey in this era as his father had served before him, back when a Tree still grew below the Hole in the Sky.

THE END

Ingrid returns in GRAVES' END: A Magical Thriller
seanpatricktraver.com

This book is dedicated to my good friend and comrade, My Wife
—*L. Frank Baum's dedication from the* Wonderful Wizard of Oz, *1900*

Acknowledgements

There are more than a dozen real historical figures (and a couple horses) mentioned in this book. Some of their names are still famous; others, less so. They've all been incorporated here with liberal artistic license and sincere respect.

I'd also like to thank: Catherine P Langwagen at CassiopeiaArt.com for a cover I'm happy to have you judge this book by; the amazing Jay Holben for his multifaceted expertise; Amy Vox for providing editorial clarity; Brett Hargrave for posing patiently with a plastic skeleton; and Kent Hargrave for beers by the pool.

My family has been supportive well beyond the limits of reason. Tam, my lamb, provided patience and insight over the course of many (many) drafts.

The LA chapter of the Horror Writers' Association has been a great source of camaraderie and information, and the Iliad Bookshop has been the best day job/research library I could ask for.

About the Author

Sean Patrick Traver is a man of few words. (Except for the ones in this book, I guess.) He also appreciates irony.

seanpatricktraver.com